About the author

John Goddard taught English for over forty years at university level and at various schools in Australia and, briefly, in England. His love of literature is what inspired his teaching over all that time. He is retired and lives in the Blue Mountains west of Sydney, writing and keeping track of children and grandchildren spread all over the world.

SMOKE GETS IN YOUR EYES

John Goddard

SMOKE GETS IN YOUR EYES

Vanguard Press

VANGUARD PAPERBACK

© Copyright 2021
John Goddard

The right of John Goddard to be identified as author of
this work has been asserted by him in accordance with the
Copyright, Designs and Patents Act 1988.

All Rights Reserved

No reproduction, copy or transmission of this publication
may be made without written permission.
No paragraph of this publication may be reproduced,
copied or transmitted save with the written permission of the publisher, or in
accordance with the provisions
of the Copyright Act 1956 (as amended).

Any person who commits any unauthorised act in relation to
this publication may be liable to criminal
prosecution and civil claims for damages.

This is a work of fiction. Names, characters, businesses, places, events and incidents are
either the products of the author's imagination or used in a fictitious manner. Any
resemblance to actual persons, living or dead, or actual events is purely coincidental.

A CIP catalogue record for this title is
available from the British Library.

ISBN 978-1-80016-037-8

Vanguard Press is an imprint of
Pegasus Elliot MacKenzie Publishers Ltd.
www.pegasuspublishers.com

First Published in 2021

Vanguard Press
Sheraton House Castle Park
Cambridge England
Printed & Bound in Great Britain

Dedication

For Roslyn, Anthea, Megan and Andrew

CHAPTER ONE

Penelope half tottered, half stumbled across the Green. She was fifteen months old, with strong little legs and, with nearly two months of independent uprightness behind her, she was safe enough if still a little precarious, not always able to maintain balance. Doug watched her carefully; he was pleased to have her walk a short distance away from him and then come back, as delighted as she was herself at her great exploit. But his mind was only half on his daughter. As he waited for Libby to pick her up and amuse her for an hour or two and for Jenny to be ready (he checked: there was still plenty of time) he thought mostly of the service to come, thought of it with dread. He could manage the reading well enough, he knew, and felt some weird pride at being asked. But the rest of it? Well, he would have Jenny to hang on to.

The child marched earnestly towards him, hips swaying with determination, and held out her arms to him. This was his future, he thought, and the idea that it could be snatched away – after one year or eighteen made no difference – was more, much more, than he could bring himself to consider. He lifted her high, pretended to release her and watched the joyful shout break her face wide open. Just then a friendly voice came from behind him.

"She knows you won't drop her. Isn't she doing wonderfully?"

"Thanks for coming, Libby. Yes, she's superb," and both Doug and daughter beamed, for different reasons it may be supposed. Libby laughed too at the sight of them. "And you're sure this is OK?"

"Of course it is. I'm one of the general patrol for around the grounds and I'll be happy to have Penny with me. She's always a good conversation starter – or stopper, sometimes."

Libby was quite right, Doug reflected. She was a vibrant yet sensible and always helpful person and, as they stood together, the child reached towards her quite comfortably. Libby was a great help to their little family – it saved her from unwanted time on her hands, she said – and

Doug was grateful. He did wonder, though, if she was really making herself unavailable. Poor Blaize.

Doug glanced at his watch again – quarter to two. He was observed.

"I told you I'd be ready in time," said Jenny, coming from their little house which looked onto the Green. It was not said waspishly – no, almost with a loving awareness of her husband's addiction to details. "Hello, Libby. This is very good of you."

"As I said to Doug, it will be fine, no trouble at all." She began to distract the child with a toy lion she took from her bag. "Now go along. I can't say enjoy yourselves. I'm sure it will be done," she hesitated, "well enough. The College knows how to manage an occasion, even one as grim as this." She began to walk away, encouraging the child to join her in roaring like a lion. Yes, they would manage fine.

"We'd better be at the chapel, then," he said and took Jenny's hand. She was only sorry when, after a few paces, he removed it, perhaps thinking it unseemly to arrive hand in hand at a funeral. And no ordinary funeral, either: but that's not fair, Doug thought, because there's no such thing as an ordinary funeral. He did not look forward to meeting the mother once again. And he was desperately glad to have Jenny with him.

"We'll both be gritting our teeth," she said to him, as though following his thoughts. "Just trying not to let it show."

Robert Fitzpatrick had come through a tumultuous time – father dying, mother's cancer, mother remarrying, school time missed and re-adjustments necessary – but he had come through it amazingly well. By the end of Year 11 he had been flourishing again, mainly because there was openness and trust at home but partly because school was secure, predictable and, truly, helpful. The boy had found in Doug Anderson what he knew he would find – a willing, non-judgemental ear and patient common sense; what he was delighted to find in addition was the cheerful warmth of Mrs Anderson, an optimistic resilience that did him a lot of good. He visited them more than was strictly necessary for mentoring purposes, even in Year 12, when his need of the willing ear had waned. He said that the visits kept his spirits up, kept him focused and buoyant. He would often drop in for fifteen minutes before the evening meal in the dining hall and would play companionably with Penelope, waving a rattle at her and just enjoying, as he saw it, the simple ordinariness of their life. Such moments did not get in the way of his studies – he claimed that they enhanced his ability to use his time profitably.

He must have studied very profitably, because he earned the highest marks across all his courses and gained a place to study law at university. Why law? He could not really say, and his mother hoped it was for his own sake, not born of some futile desire to please his late father, or of an even more futile desire to keep up with his much older brother Barrington, whose email of congratulations from London was all too brief. Robert was convinced that he would find it stimulating and he clearly had a mind that needed stimulation. Whether this was the right way for him to get it, time would tell.

A week before the university term was to start, at the end of February, he went to a weekend party on a country property. His friend had invited around a dozen of them and it was to be a final holiday bash before the rigours of study swept them all up again. That was the official line, anyway – two or three were not going on to study, now or ever, if they could help it; and some others were convinced that first year university would be a breeze. Nevertheless, they made a lively weekend of it and, at about five in the afternoon, Robert set off for the two-hour drive back home. He was alone in the car, having arrived later than the others, but two other young men left just after him, for much the same journey, at least at first.

What happened next? The boys in the car behind saw some of it, really only the end, the climax, you might say. Robert was on a good secondary road, with the highway only a very few kilometres away, coming around a long, steady curve. He was aware of some large hawthorn hedges on his right, good windbreaks, but nasty, dark, prickly things. On his left was an irrigation channel which allowed little room off the bitumen on that side. About two hundred metres ahead, a small break in the hawthorn signified a side road and out of it came a truck piled high with hay. It turned left, in his direction and there should have been no difficulty in making the turn onto its own side of the road. But… the truck swung wide, into the path of the young man who made to swerve left but then, as he saw the truck come even further onto his side of the road and remembered how close the irrigation channel was, aimed, too late, to swerve far right and avoid a collision that way. The truck, too, tried to correct its course and the crash happened in the centre of the strip. The other boys saw the catastrophe, seemed to feel the impact from a couple of hundred metres away, but, because of the curve, they had not seen the full sequence of events, the truck's initial misjudgement and Robert's attempt to avoid it. They called 000 immediately, but they had seen the crash and the utterly mangled state of Robert's little white hatch. They knew there was no hope.

A family service and cremation had been held and now, a week later, a memorial service was to be held at the College, on the Friday afternoon that would have been the end of Robert's O-week at university. It was important for the school to have such a service and Mrs Fitzpatrick had willingly agreed to it, perhaps because of some vague notion that to keep the process going was to put off life without her son. But could it be for the good, wondered Doug, as he took his place near the front of the chapel? Would it really help to calm that toxic mixture of grief and outrage that was felt not only by the immediate family? Could they confront the horror and the waste and stare those things down, knowing that explanations were impossible? And yet, Doug kept on telling himself, no matter how brief the life had been, it was well worth celebrating.

They sat in their designated places and Doug felt in his jacket pocket for the sheet of paper, the reading printed out in larger than normal font, so that he should have no trouble looking up and down. He had tried to prepare well, but he knew that he would feel anxious, dry in the mouth. Charles Herbert came in and sat just behind him in a row reserved for council members. Doug was sure that elsewhere in the chapel there would be familiar faces. Well, he would say hello to them later – it felt rather crass to look about in welcome beforehand. He fell to going over the details of a stained-glass window to his left, not a large window but delicately done, depicting Jesus welcoming little children. A couple of onlookers were depicted, gazing vaguely into the distance, apparently cut off from the main scene, and he wondered whether the students in the chapel belonged to the group around Jesus or to the disengaged ones. All of the House, Robert's school home for his years in the College, would be there, and all of Year 12, and several past students, friends from Robert's own Year 12. The whole school could not possibly be accommodated, not with so many visitors – hence Libby and some other staff on patrol. On the whole, Doug was glad he was not one of them.

He felt Jenny squeeze his hand. He looked, and saw that Parslow, the headmaster, was ushering Mrs Fitzpatrick and her husband, Austin Phillips, into the chapel. All the way up the aisle they came, trying to look neither to right nor to left. They eased themselves into their row in the front and Doug noticed that Parslow gave a very slight nod to the chaplain, a nod of "Let's get under way." Too much waiting was not good for anyone.

The chaplain gave a subdued welcome and expressed the hope that the service, filled with sadness as it must be, would nevertheless prove that celebration could come out of grief. Mrs Fitzpatrick, he said, had requested the hymn 'Abide with me', and so he asked them all to stand and sing.

The singing surprised Doug. Of course, this congregation was used to singing, was expected to sing, and perhaps they did so automatically. But when he came to 'Swift to its close ebbs out life's little day', and glanced at Mrs Fitzpatrick barely able to hold the service sheet, he marvelled that anyone could sing in the face of such a brutally shortened little day. Then his thoughts flew to Penelope; and though he read 'I am the way, the truth and the life' well enough, he was aware of almost nothing more until the service ended, because he was with Penelope tottering triumphantly on the Green, or with the children in the stained-glass window. And he was wondering how he could possibly put all the pieces together, cause them to make sense. There were just too many gaps.

After the service, guests, former students and current Year 12s were invited to refreshments in a large marquee erected near the chapel, on the edge of one of the ovals. Parslow would have preferred a more solid and impressive location, but what was he to do? His own home and garden? Not quite handy enough, and too festive. The dining hall? But it meant a day's work to clear it and put it back together again. A classroom block opened up? Tacky, utterly unimpressive, and you could never tell what might be lurking on the walls. The marquee, at any rate, was large enough for maybe two hundred, with space to serve and for some chairs. After all, people didn't have to stay all that long. He didn't want them to, because he needed a meeting with Professor Donald before the afternoon was out, to tick off aspects of the building programme. To the marquee, therefore, they went.

It wasn't crowded after all. The Year 12 students dashed in, got themselves some food and stood in groups outside where they felt more comfortable. The ex-students barely made it in at all, because they were torn by a need to be respectful and an even stronger wish simply to catch up and to exchange news. So the others, various adults, were taken in or ambled in in twos and threes, making commonplace comments about the service, how suitable and how fitting it was, how well Mr Phillips had spoken. Phillips stayed resolutely with Mrs Fitzpatrick (they had married some time ago but she was firm that for today she was Mrs Fitzpatrick) and helped her through the several conversations that had to occur, even if nobody much wanted them. Jenny Anderson had gone to find Penelope but Doug stayed and spoke to Mrs Fitzpatrick. All his interactions with her son had been so positive that, although she smiled at him in a desperate sort of way and wanted to thank him, he only felt the thanks stick in his throat. He had rather hoped to meet the elusive Barrington but things in London were too pressing for him to attend. Doug moved on, feeling a sense of relief that he was now at leisure to speak more naturally to others.

Sam Baker was there, chatting easily, it seemed, with Matron South. He had retired from the College more than a year ago, having been both Doug's head of English and housemaster of the House, the oldest boarding house in the College. He told his former matron of his last fifteen months, of his writing (it hadn't got all that far), of his walking and of a trip to Europe he would like to make. It was the very home of clocks, he told her. It was as though he wanted her to see that life ticked on merrily enough for him, especially as his parting from the College had been something less than jovial. But then Doug came across to them and it quickly became apparent that the death of Robert Fitzpatrick had hit him hard.

"You think that the boys will go on for ever," he said. "Perhaps we think so because it allows us to think that we will too. Nonsense, of course, but we all deceive ourselves. And we move on, all too quickly."

Matron South came in at that. "I fear," she said quietly, "that it will be a very long time before Mrs Fitzpatrick can move on. She doesn't know what to feel, except for all sorts of things at once, and that is overwhelming."

It was a long speech for Matron and Sam was inclined to brush it off, in the cause of his own moving on. But Doug, who still worked with her and respected her, thought he could see her point.

"Yes, Matron, there are far too many conflicting things to cope with, aren't there. One son suddenly dead and the other absent; confusion as to whether Robert was on the wrong side of the road; a wish to attack the truck driver for killing her boy and a stronger wish to forget the man completely. It must be all so confusing, quite bewildering for her. Today's service may not have given much relief."

Sam stared at him but Matron realised that the service had not given Doug much relief either.

"I'll see you in the House when you're on next," she said. "The kettle will be boiling." She moved off to where Barney Custance, current master of the House, was trying to be cheerful with some council members. He seemed not to be making a very good job of it.

"So, how was your year, young man?" said Sam, happy to change the flow of the conversation. "I hope it was a good one. Your little girl, as I understand it, is perfection itself."

Doug could only agree to that and both men relaxed. He said that he had enjoyed the English teaching, his students had gained excellent grades in Year 12 and altogether life was going well for him and Jenny.

"And your new English chief? Mrs Madigan, if I remember rightly."

"She had a good year too." He knew the answer Sam wanted to hear but it would not have been a true one. "She knows her stuff and she gives us our head, sometimes. And she takes a pragmatic approach to the assessment programme."

Sam grinned at that and asked if she were in the gathering. He clearly wanted to put a face to his replacement.

"Well, no, that's the strange thing. Late last year her elderly father died, way up in far north Queensland, and then in January her mother too. Poor Felicity has gone to wind things up – she was in a terrible state herself – and it looks as though she'll miss all this term, maybe more."

Baker raised a questioning eyebrow. "And so...?" Surely, thought

Doug, he couldn't be imagining a way back in.

"You may not have met Ben Fraser, the new deputy…"

"… was introduced to him on the way in…"

"… but that's him with Ralph over there. Well, Parslow said that since the absence of Felicity Madigan was of such uncertain length, he would ask Fraser, who teaches one English class, to act as supervisor of the department in the interim. It's an odd arrangement."

"So not Flem? Not you? The headmaster does nothing predictably."

Doug flushed and Baker registered the distress.

"I'm sorry, Doug. You ought at least to have been considered for the position when I left."

Doug had no real idea how much Sam knew. Himself, he had remained reticent about the events of, what, nearly a year and a half ago now. He ventured, "I suppose you knew he wanted me to come into the House. When I knocked him back, he acted as though I were a traitor or something. If I want to get any further, it won't be here."

Sam nodded and was about to say something about 'carpe diem', but he saw that Doug was not with him. In fact, as so often these days, Doug's last comment had caused his mind to jump to Penny and then to his wife, for whom her work in the gallery was hugely satisfying. It wouldn't be easy to leave the College without uprooting the whole family.

Sam saw this and, with an odd feeling that, as when he worked in the College, he had somehow contributed to the young man's distress, said only that he wished Doug a very good year.

"And now," he said, "I really must catch Ralph before he slides away. You'd think I could do it up in town, but he's such an elusive one."

"And I've had about enough here," said Doug and then realised that he had not meant the remark to apply to Sam. "I mean with all this," and he gestured around the marquee. "I've said what I can, but it is all so sad, such a horrible waste. I'll slip away – best wishes, Sam."

There was a brief handshake. Sam reflected that, with so much of promise, of a joyful future to plunge into with wife and child, Doug did not have any reason to stay among the grief stricken, or amongst the nostalgic, like himself. He wondered how the younger man's career would develop: he knew that it would not be like his own. Those times existed no longer. He was about to accuse himself once again of excessive nostalgia when he felt a clap on his shoulder. He swung his gaze away from the retreating Doug.

"I say, Sam, you don't actually wish you were still here, working with this lot, do you? I don't – I've got over that. Don't be anxious over Anderson; he'll survive."

Sam thought that there was much more going on in Doug's life than Ralph supposed. But all he said was, "I've got over it too, Ralph," trying very hard to clear his mind of the thoughts thus interrupted. It was clear that Langton did not really believe him. "And hello to you, too," he said as he tried to take up a new conversation. "It's good to see you. It really is."

Langton was the former College deputy. He had retired at the same time as Baker did, though in his case it was because of chronic heart problems. He had heard in the past and had had to re-interpret so much gruff irony in Sam that he thought he could always read his former colleague. Now, for once, he wasn't sure.

"Yes, I know I haven't communicated as I should have," he said. "I was afraid I wouldn't be able to tear myself away unless the break was absolute. But today has surprised me – nothing to do with the occasion, of course – because I'm happy to be back and more than happy that it doesn't touch me any more. I can meet them *all*," he underlined the last word, "without flinching."

There was no need for either man's gaze to seek out Parslow. They both knew what was meant. Sam gave a sigh and said, "I had expected my memoirs to be a way of writing it all out of my system. But I've found I can't really take the job seriously."

"I'm sorry to hear that." Sam gave him an odd look. "I would enjoy reading vintage Baker. But you're right – perhaps that's not how memories are erased."

"Oh, I wasn't trying to erase them! No, I wanted to organise them, control them, pigeonhole them as we used to do to so many other matters."

"There's no way of pigeonholing someone like Allan Parslow. Or like young Anderson with whom you were so deep in conversation. Better, in fact, to let it all go. Come, let's get another tea – I feel a chat coming on."

"I'd rather something stronger."

"So would I, but it's not being served. Look, I'm glad to see you and I don't want it to be a signing off. Let's baffle the prefects serving tea as they used to do to us in the dining hall."

"Or tried to do," muttered Sam and he chuckled and let himself be led to the long tables. Langton indicated firmly that he wanted both the sausage roll and the chocolate cake, but he grinned at the prefect as he did so.

"Today, sir, anything is permissible."

Hamish Fanning, who remembered well Langton's bewildering array of rules for the dining hall, rules never quite mastered by his successor, returned the grin. Sam looked at the boy with delight and said, "Well done, lad. You mustn't let old codgers like us put anything over you. It is good to see you, Hamish. I hope all is well with you."

"As well as I could wish, Mr Baker." But the boy was already serving someone else.

"Come on then, Sam. I saw a few tables outside." The two former staff members took their tea and food and left the marquee.

Stopped once or twice by former students, Doug Anderson was greatly relieved when he was at last out of sight of the marquee. It is wearing to be congratulated – or thanked – for doing something which, all knew, one would have given anything not to do. Of what consolation was it, to him or anybody else, that he had read well? He had not often been of one mind with Sam Baker in the past, but he was now: get on with a life that was still developing, don't look back. If he could not feel entirely confident about how it was developing, he could nonetheless enjoy the sense of vast and enticing possibilities. And one of them was only fifteen months old.

He cut back past the chapel and around the Green. The gums beyond the Green, a long line of them between the open space and his own house, were stringybarks mostly and there was a large pile of their detritus beneath them, a haven for tiny creatures good and bad. He must remember to keep Penelope away from that area. The younger boys from the House enjoyed the shade to be found there and attempted to make constructions out of even the feeblest pieces of bark. They could look after themselves.

He found Jenny still with Libby Caraton, chatting over teacups and biscuits while Penelope amused herself with blocks and cars. Was that a bit absurd, too advanced for such a little child, Doug wondered. Did it matter, anyway?

"I'm glad you're here," said Jenny. "For you, I mean – it can't have been much fun in the marquee."

"It was pretty ghastly, yes. I had a few brief hellos with old boys but I didn't have much enthusiasm for it. Anyway, they had each other and that is what they wanted. Sam Baker wanted a chat, though."

Jenny raised an immediately critical eyebrow. She had seen Sam, Doug's supervisor in both the House and the English department, as self-serving and not to be trusted. "I wouldn't expect you to waste much time on him," she said.

"He knew a lot of what was going on back then, more than I realised. He was sympathetic today."

"A bit late for that," was all the reply he got. Libby, meanwhile, had stayed politely silent, helping Penny to build and then gleefully destroy a small tower of blocks. But she came in with:

"There were worse heads of department, you know. I lived with Helen Meiklejohn," as though the mere mention of the name, of a science teacher filling in for a term and treated with disdain by one who could not face doubts or questioning in any form, trumped any other claim to have been treated poorly. Doug was only too ready to shift the direction of the conversation.

"Do you keep in touch, Libby? Where is Helen now?"

"She went to Western Australia. A girls' school. It wasn't to get away from here – she found home too constraining. Did you know that Parslow encouraged her to come back?"

"Really? Well, good for him, I suppose."

"Or was he just blind to what was going on? He runs his own race, and we keep up as best we can."

So do we all, Doug thought, one way or another. Libby would not stay at the College all that long and Jenny would miss her. So would Doug's colleague in English, Blaize Rascham. But that relationship was going nowhere. Doug supposed that Libby had made that clear and that

Blaize understood. Once, they had seemed to be good friends and Blaize now looked somewhat lost. Certainly he didn't drop in on the Andersons as he once might have done: others' familial bliss was not what he needed shoved before him at the moment.

A sudden smell arrested them and Libby made a face as she picked up Penelope.

"Let me deal with this," she said. And then, "Look at that fixed determination on her face. Now where does she get that from?"

Left alone, Doug and Jenny relaxed, no longer on show. Libby was a good friend but there were things not aired in front of her.

"You did your bit well, Doug." She saw his frown and followed with, "I know others will have said that, and you wish they wouldn't, but it wasn't easy, was it? Let's get back to some normality tonight. Do you feel you could go out for pizza, perhaps for Libby too? They don't like delivering on campus, always get it wrong."

Doug was aware of all sorts of odd connections, or non-connections, in what she had said, and he thought that normality would be better achieved without Libby. He nevertheless agreed, sensing an agenda so far hidden from him.

"That will be fine. I love hearing her read to Penelope. Everything becomes a grand drama, even Spot."

They both smiled, comfortably and companionably, and when Libby came back in he suggested Supreme as an all-round good choice.

"But no anchovies, please no anchovies," exclaimed Libby.

"Too strong? Too likely to swamp everything else?"

"Exactly," said Jenny. "Stick to the basics, do them well, don't be overwhelmed by supposed strength. That's life at the College, isn't it?"

Doug stared. Now he was sure there was some other agenda. He removed his tie, found the car keys and went out.

For some time, after the departure of the grieving family and other guests, the campus remained quiet. Eerily so, given that it was a Friday afternoon, normally a relaxed interval between the classroom week and the vibrancy of weekend sports. The students had been cautioned and, unaware of when the caution might be lifted, they slunk around the grounds or stayed in the boarding houses. Even there, behaviour was restrained – strained, in fact, since the boys were either overawed by the occasion, those older ones who had been part of it, or wholly unsure how to respond and thus reckoning it best to lie low. As for the House, it was only when they saw Mr Custance step back across the Green and into his study that things loosened up. Tension was released and the routine of a Friday afternoon was warmly embraced. The boys did not in any case wish to dwell on the fate of Robert Fitzpatrick. If they had, they would have been led to acknowledge that, well, there but for the grace of God…

In a rather different way, headmaster Allan Parslow needed to put the events of the afternoon swiftly behind him. He was pleased with the way in which his school had presented and conducted itself. He felt that he had played his own part appropriately; he was content that the visits of his former colleagues, Langton and Baker, had been brief and reasonably inconspicuous; and he needed now to get back to business with his chair of council, Professor Gregory Donald. As soon as he felt free to do so, therefore, he led Donald briskly around the oval and into his business office in the main administration block He guessed that they might not have long together – Donald was often pressed for time, and not always by his work but by the force of his wife Irene – and some discussion was imperative. It began as they walked.

"You all did well, Allan. An awful occasion, but worthily carried off."

"Yes indeed." Parslow made the briefest pause in their walk and gestured across the oval. "Just imagine, Greg, when that side of the oval is the new boarding house. Splendid but not ostentatious; long and low, nestling in just before that rise. We are just about ready to begin."

"As you told council at our last meeting." They marched energetically on. "Nothing holding you up in any way?"

"Not in the least. I want to show you the final specifications and all the permits. We need also to discuss the state of the building fund and how much we can divert in from other sources."

"It will have to be a short chat. I need to be up in town…"

"We need fifteen or twenty minutes only," said Parslow as they entered his office. "I have everything laid out along the window bench here."

It took more than twenty minutes, more like forty, but, as it was the kind of discussion both men thoroughly enjoyed, neither complained. Irene would have to wait. Their dinner engagement would go ahead, but Donald readily convinced himself that there was no point in being early. Together they looked with approval at all the designs and saw how all the latest technology was to be incorporated. They discussed how the shortfall from the building fund, only another seven million dollars or so, was to be made up and they considered how best to use the Old Boys network to support the project. It was around five thirty when Parslow ushered his chairman out to his car and saw him safely on the road. When he had done so, he stood and looked across the oval once more. Some building projects, he reflected, could interrupt the daily life of a school quite badly. This one would not, and, if ten or eleven months would suffice, then by the start of the next year his greatest work so far would stand in confirmation of a man who possessed energy and vision. He rubbed his hands joyfully in anticipation of that day.

Also in his office by the end of the afternoon, checking rosters and other arrangements necessary for the running of a busy sporting Saturday – cricket, rowing, swimming, basketball: the College would be bursting – was Mr Ben Fraser, the deputy headmaster. A man in his late forties, Fraser had come to the College a little more than a year previously, on the retirement of the long-serving Ralph Langton, whose ill health, as we have noted, had precipitated an early finish to a distinguished career. Langton had known the school in its every detail, essentially because he had constructed most of its systems himself, and Fraser had quickly realised that it was pointless, impossible, to try to be another Mr Langton. The man had obviously been a labyrinth of rules! Still, he had had to tread carefully, showing that in some matters he would do things in his own way and yet not disrespecting anything his predecessor had done. It was a fine balancing act and, when he and his wife Sarah discussed it, they decided that, with the first year behind them, they felt solidly established in the College, both of them in charge of their roles. So now? Work hard at the essentials, support Parslow, publicly at least, and wait to see what opportunities might arise.

Fraser had quickly – and in some ways accurately – summed up his energetic headmaster. He saw him as one who confided deeply in no one, so that it was better not to confide in him. He saw him as one who wanted to keep the College, especially the teaching staff, guessing as to his next move and so Fraser spent a good deal of time analysing what was being done and predicting what would follow. He saw that Parslow felt a great need to be in total control and so he played the role of fervent supporter, eager to help with any problem that might arise. In fact, he was just beginning to anticipate issues. Thus it was that he had suggested to Parslow that he might take the most able class of Year 11 English students, so as to keep his headmaster better informed on prospective student leaders and likely student successes. In the same way he had put himself forward as a short-term replacement for Felicity Madigan, so that the head did not have to raise unrealistic expectations in the minds of any of the regular English teachers. It had been a good suggestion and it amused Fraser that Parslow very quickly came to see it as his own. He did not see himself as manipulative – simply as a good manager and a loyal deputy who tried to release his head from day to day affairs so that he could devote himself to higher things. Given the huge building project about to commence, Fraser reckoned that Parslow would need plenty of release time. In this we can see that Fraser did not grasp the full strength of his head.

Part of Fraser's strategy – he had announced at the outset that he would do this – was to get to know his staff. At morning tea, or at any other occasion, he almost never sat, or stood, in the same place twice in a row. Instead, he would sit next to a teacher he hardly knew, to say hello, to discover what that colleague was like, what his or her interests might be. He certainly built up a picture of the mighty College chessboard, how each department, or house, or sporting activity was structured and operated. He needed to see all this if he was to be an effective administrator and supporter/advisor to his head. Staff would take bets on who would find Mr Fraser sitting next to them today, or which department he would begin to work through next week. Having announced his strategy, Fraser could hardly be surprised at this gossipy reaction. In fact he encouraged it, reckoning that it made the whole activity seem light-hearted. In truth, it was nothing of the sort.

He checked his arrangements, took with him his To Do list for the next morning and walked home. He and Sarah Fraser, whose two children, twin girls, had now left school and flatted together near the university, had only occupied Ralph Langton's apartment for an introductory period and now were more spaciously housed at a short distance from the centre of the College. It was a private location, well hedged and quite commodious enough to cater for their girls during vacations and for visitors at other times. They enjoyed the new house and became regular hosts of small gatherings – only six or eight at a time – on weekends. Sarah loved being the gracious hostess. It all added to their feeling of being well entrenched and increasingly in control.

With Mr Custance back in the House – Barney, though the boys would not call him that to his face – energy, Friday evening spirits, began to return. The noise level rose, the rough 'n' tumble sprang up here and there, any pretence at study ceased and preparations for the weekend began. It might be sport or possibly time away with family or friends, though not much of that, as it was still rather early in the year; but there was always a list, to be confirmed by a prefect and handed back to Mr Custance by eight on Friday evening.

It was Hamish Fanning who had that responsibility on this particular Friday. Giving up on his economic theories assignment (he had spent an hour on it since the marquee closed and he was bored with the topic already) he took up the list, saw only six names on it and began a search through the House. Hamish was a more than capable student and his subjects were mostly of the mathematics and commerce variety, with modern history thrown in to leaven the dough. His father had insisted on economics in particular. But then, Charlie Fanning had a wildly inflated opinion of his own business acumen, so it is no wonder that he was also wide of the mark in his understanding of his son. Hamish had no intention of being like his father; his interests, at the age of seventeen, lay in the wider world, in international relations and he reckoned on scoring highly enough in almost any subjects to gain the necessary place. If economics was involved, Father would not object; but it was what he planned to do further down the track that would not, Hamish knew, meet with his erratic and selfish father's approval. If Father thought that law would be a prestigious career for his son, he had another think coming!

He took the list and loped along the corridor to the House common room, always a useful starting point. He checked off two names there, for whom arrangements were exactly as on the list. He checked off two more in the Year 8 dormitory, easily the most comfortable of the open dormitories because of the substantial refurbishment in the wake of a huge storm and 'water event' two years previously. And then at Matron's door, coming out, he came across Ben Ford of Year 10. Ben looked very pale – he was a fragile boy at best, tentative and nervous in his dealings with any kind of authority, one whom Matron South had needed to watch very closely since the boy had come through a bout of glandular fever in Year 9. He started a little when Hamish Fanning approached him.

"Ah, Ben, just the man. I'm doing the weekend list. Nothing changed? Still on the train in the morning?"

Ben was very agitated and seemed to gasp out his response.

"I'm hoping to change it to tonight. I'm not too good – ask Matron" (he clearly needed her reinforcement, as though his own evidence would not stand up to much) "and Mum can drive down tonight but not tomorrow morning." He paused and seemed to lose confidence in himself even more, if that were possible. "Matron thinks it would be better than the train," he mumbled.

Fanning wanted to be brisk about this, but not unkind.

"Yes, well, you know, a change to Friday night needs Mr C's approval. Have you been to see him?"

"Not yet. But since you're here, you could change the list. Mr C leaves it all up to you prefects, we all know that." The boy, fifteen years old, thin but nearly six feet tall, looked pleadingly at the prefect.

"For some things, Ben, not for this." Hamish felt some urge to defend his housemaster; he could hardly have said why. What Ben Ford had implied was more or less true. The prefects were given a largely free hand in the running of the House on a daily basis and Barney Custance seemed content if they kept him briefed. This should have suited the prefects admirably, but it was such a departure from the regime of the retired Mr Baker that they felt uneasy with it, as though they were being asked to participate in something dubious. Hamish Fanning, for his part, regarded Mr Custance as pliable and slack and so did not respect him; but he was not sure about making a decision like this, not if it could come back to bite him unexpectedly. It was not the same as organising a clean-up, or liaising with Matron about supper, or giving a detention – not the same thing at all.

"I saw Mr C come back a short while ago. Go and get his OK first, Ben, that's the way it should be done. I'll find" (he consulted his list) "Phillips of Year 9, he's my last one, and then I'll see you at his study. Won't be long."

"I suppose so," muttered an utterly unconvinced Ben Ford.

"Just tell him it's on Matron's advice and he'll agree." Ford brightened a little at that and shuffled off. It took Hamish only a couple of minutes before he ran Phillips to ground in the laundry, hunting for rowing gear for the next morning. His name was duly ticked off – next stop, housemaster's study. Custance was at his door, talking to Ford, and he saw Hamish approach.

"It's all sorted, Hamish. Mrs Ford will come this evening, so please amend your list. All right, Ben?"

Ben Ford gave one or two coughs confirmatory of his poor state, thanked his housemaster and departed.

"You know, Hamish," said this senior member of staff, "I think you could have made this call and told me later. I really want you Year 12 boys to use your initiative – I know you have plenty."

"It seemed such an unusual departure, sir," said the boy, calmly and confidently. "But I'll know now for next time. Is there anything particular for tonight, sir?"

"Supervise the supper for me tonight, Hamish, you and the other prefects. Give me the list later, or now if it's all complete."

"It's done, sir, if you alter the Ford entry." He handed it over. "I'll see Matron. She might be in possession of leftovers from the marquee – I noticed that the guests weren't hungry."

"Go to it then," said Mr Custance, who had lost interest. He went back into his study and closed the door. Hamish stared at it for a moment. All of a sudden he wanted to mutter something about doing the man's job for him but he repressed the impulse, as essentially unworthy, and went in search of Matron. After all, what could even a prefect know about all that went on behind the scenes. He gave Mr Custance the benefit of the doubt, just.

He found Matron, as he suspected, preparing supper from a box of bits and pieces she had procured from the refreshments provided at the marquee. He smiled at her and thanked her for her forethought, then checked that nine o'clock would do as usual.

"Yes," she said, "unless Mr Custance wants it earlier."

"I think it's just us prefects on duty tonight, Matron."

She could not help raising more than half an eyebrow. To Matron South's mind, it was 'us prefects' far too often. But she busied herself with the plates of food and said that nine would suit her perfectly.

"Do you happen to know how Ben Ford's weekend leave was sorted?" she asked.

"Mrs Ford is coming tonight – your recommendation, I believe. Anyway, Mr Custance was happy with that – happy to have left it up to me, I think."

He had risked that comment and was not disappointed with the result.

"Indeed...? Well, I.. Mr Baker... I'm glad it's all arranged."

The seeming incoherence of this reply told Hamish all he needed to know. It would not have happened like that in Mr Baker's time; and though Matron would not criticise the new housemaster and though she and Mr Baker, so rumour had it, had had a falling out of some kind, nevertheless Matron clearly preferred a stricter regime and a tougher conception of the housemaster's role. It wasn't just the boys, then, who thought that things were all a bit loose.

"Thanks for everything, Matron. See you at supper."

"Yes, Hamish. Send some up at ten to nine to fetch and carry." She turned away, back, as she would see it, to her area of responsibility. She hoped she had not betrayed any genuine doubts about Mr Custance's area of responsibility – not to a student. Then again, the boys could see it for themselves. She sighed, and then was annoyed with herself because an image of Mr Baker at House supper had flashed into her head. She tried to stamp the image out and decided that a visit to the laundry room would do it. As in so many things, she was right.

Penelope was unsettled. Maybe the day had been too exciting, too stimulating for her, thought Jenny as she sat with the little girl and tried to stroke her into sleep. Slowly, slowly her action took effect and, as the little body relaxed, Jenny did too and gazed comfortably around the child's bedroom. It was bright and cheerful, even in the fading light of an early autumn evening. It contained all that a fifteen-month-old could need ('O reason not the need' she imagined Doug saying to her and she smiled) with soft toys and blocks and books – already a long shelf of books – and Duplo and mobiles and friezes and trucks and cars on a city streetscape mat. But how much of all that did an adored and indulged child really need? They made life enjoyable and they certainly made for a warm, secure, reassuring little space. Surely that, and lots of love, was what any child needed.

She looked back and saw her child soundly asleep. It was now her turn to relax and she was grateful that she could. For the first twelve months of Penelope's life, her sleeps had been only another cause of anxiety, but at fifteen months surely the parents were safe. And it was that feeling of safety, Jenny realised, that allowed them both to get on with their individual professional lives and also, as it happened, to enjoy their daughter more. Yes, Doug, she would say, safety is what we need – it's the foundation stone.

As she got up and moved out to the living room, where Doug would be getting his things together for a weekend in the House, she reflected on their discussion earlier with Libby Caraton. Safety? Was Libby's, in a totally unexpected way, threatened? Perhaps that was putting it too strongly, verging on the hysterical. But you had to take these things seriously, and then take action, maybe preventing a problem rather than solving one. It was all confusing and she wanted to go over it quietly with Doug, now that the domestic day was done. He was just putting papers in a briefcase as she entered the room, marking, she supposed, though he never seemed to get any done during a House weekend. He was too busy attending to matters that arose, or just simply chatting to the boys. He glanced up at her, his expression clearly a question about Penelope.

"It took a while, but she's fine. Coming down from a day of highs takes time, doesn't it?"

"I wish Libby wouldn't be quite so energetic with her so close to bedtime. It winds her up until she can't cope with any more."

"We couldn't have done without Libby today. She is a real friend. Can we talk about what she was saying? Or are you done for tonight?"

"There's nothing," said Doug, "that can't wait until the morning. I'll go across at seven. And then I'll try to look in from time to time and see how you two are going. I know it makes a long weekend for you."

He put aside the briefcase and drew her across to the couch. Even – or especially – in their tiny house, it was important to section off areas, to make spaces that could be thought of as separate from school. He must, he thought, be nearly due for a bigger house, though that would not alter the need for delineated spaces.

"I'll get us some tea in a second. What should we do about Libby, do you think?"

Jenny was often one who came to swift conclusions and wanted immediate action. On this occasion, however, she was unusually tentative.

"We've done the first necessary thing, I suppose," she said. "We've listened and tried to be supportive. Libby would have appreciated even that much."

"And she really thinks there is no one else to confide in?"

"It looks like it." Jenny paused and ran her hands through her hair, a gesture common enough if she was puzzled, more or less at a loss. "We hinted at Blaize, but a knight in shining armour, a guy she thinks of as frankly a bit dim, is the last thing she needs now."

"I can see that. Blaize would mean well; but he'd be even less subtle than me." Jenny blinked at him and laughed. He went on, very seriously: "I don't want *you* taking this all on yourself, as a problem you have to solve. You've listened. You've given a couple of obvious strategies. And I can keep an eye out in some situations; and so we wait. It's all so nebulous."

Jenny burst out at him. "But that feels like waiting for something awful. I can't do that. What, just wait until Fraser does something predatory?"

Her colour flamed up high, because she wanted to protect her friend, the only woman on campus she could call her friend, and because she hadn't a clue how to do it. Doug, as usual, tried to steady the ship.

"But Jenny, what have we got? Fraser doesn't register personal space, he sits too close to her in the common room. We can prevent that. Then he calls in to her flat, once with Mrs Fraser as they are out on a walk and once by himself saying that Mrs F was too tired to walk today and did she want to join him? She didn't and said so – and that was last

Sunday, with nothing since. Has he got the message? I don't know, but I can't see what else we can do but watch and wait."

"It's too like doing nothing." Jenny looked at him pleadingly but she saw in his face that he could not take any further steps yet.

"It won't be nothing, because both of us will keep in close touch with her. We can keep her from being alone – we both know how she adores Penny; and we can keep our eyes open and hope that there is no sequel, nothing at all."

"She will still be uneasy, Doug, and now she won't stay very long and I will miss her." It had come out in a rush, but Doug responded carefully:

"You know, I'm surprised she has stayed as long as she has. She is a very fine teacher but she is not really suited to this sort of place." He gave his wife a comforting look: "You won't have her here for very long, Fraser or no Fraser."

"He's a sleaze!" she exclaimed, not wanting to consider Doug's assessment of the situation and longing to burst out in vexation, somehow, anyhow. He pulled her closely to him and felt her, after a moment or two, relax against him.

"Penny's well asleep. Let's tidy the kitchen together and have an early night – together." He was only too aware how often her early nights were not his.

"Yes," she murmured, "that would be good for both of us." They wandered to the kitchen and she muttered, half to herself, "Penny is fifteen months old now. Maybe…"

"This is the first I've heard of it," he said. "We do need an early night."

The Saturday morning, like many in March, dawned fine, a little fresh, with the promise of a warm day to follow. But well before sunrise, which, with daylight saving still in effect, was not until almost seven o'clock, Doug was busy. He wanted to leave things as well arranged as he could, not because of guilt, he told himself, but because it would simply be helpful. Penelope had stirred at around half past five, demanding attention. There was no way, at that hour, that she would sleep again, so it was into bed with him and Jenny, who would have slept on but for all the tickling and horse riding that developed on the other side of the bed. So he left Jenny telling stories to Penny, had his shower and organised their breakfast. He came back in, shortly before seven, saying that he would look in on them during his patrol, later in the morning.

"What on earth is your patrol?" asked Jenny in surprise. "You're in the House."

"Ben Fraser left me a brief note. He wants staff to go walkabout, leave the House to Matron when almost everyone's on sport or away. I think he may be suspicious of the outlying areas and wants a spot check. He thinks the House can look after itself for a bit."

"Another one who thinks that, eh?" She hoisted herself higher on the pillows and sat Penny on her tummy. Doug solemnly shook hands with his little girl, who was obviously used to such a formality, and then gave them both a mighty hug.

"I'll call in; have a good morning," and he was gone. Jenny lapsed back into thought but Penny was having none of that and so the day had to begin. There was always plenty to do. Maybe, she thought, I'll get time for the puzzle. She had discovered a shop that sold jigsaws for all ages, including some with large, wooden knobbed pieces that were unpainted. She had in mind a colourful seaside scene. They had had plenty of good beach days over the summer and Penny had responded well to both sand and waves. Could she decorate the pieces while Penny played around her? Probably not.

Nine o'clock, just after, and the House quiet. Doug sat back in his cubbyhole of an office. Everything was in order and all the boys had gone about their business. Doug had to do a shift – nine thirty until eleven – of marshalling at the pool, an easy enough job; though, if it was all fifty metre events, seeing the start of every race but never the finish was a bore. When that was over, he would call in at home and then 'patrol' until lunch in the dining hall. He looked at the papers poking out of his briefcase: maybe in the afternoon? Year Ten had completed a pretty traditional unit on war poetry but had then gone on to a study of *Fly Away Peter*. Malouf's style, he thought, seemed to be challenging for many of them. Their responses would have to wait. He grabbed hat and water bottle and went out of the House. As he left, he glanced at Custance's study door. It was firmly shut, no sign of the man this morning, and the notice of the tutor on duty pointed to Mr Anderson. Doug sighed, and supposed that even housemasters needed a morning to themselves now and again. He marched briskly off in the direction of the pool.

At five to eleven, prompt as always, Blaize Rascham turned up to relieve Doug of his marshal's clipboard and supervise the second half of the swimming competition. He quickly saw where they were on the programme, said he could take over straight away and wished Doug a peaceful Saturday afternoon.

"Not much of that," said Doug. "I've a weekend in the House and now Ben has me doing one of his patrols. With everyone occupied, I don't know what he thinks I'll find."

"He thinks the quiet times are the most dangerous. That's when the boys suppose that nobody's looking."

"Well, it will keep me occupied, if nothing else." Doug tried not to be too cynical, especially with Blaize but, with all that had been said of Fraser yesterday with Libby, and then again later with Jenny, he was not too well disposed to any of the deputy's ideas or arrangements. "And you, Blaize? After the swimming?"

Blaize sparked up a little.

"I've suggested to Libby that we have an afternoon down at the beach. I just feel that getting off campus would be good for her." His face clouded. "She'll say there is too much marking to do. And there always is – but time away is good, too."

"I agree. Tell her that Jenny and I think that an afternoon at the beach would be an excellent tonic."

He smiled broadly at Blaize, indicated that the butterfly swimmers had been called (not many of them, given that hilariously exhausting stroke) and set off on patrol. Suddenly he changed his mind. He would go home first and touch base with Jenny about the conversation he had just had. He doubted whether Blaize could share his feeling of being generally comfortable with his lot, but there was not much he could do to help him. He had supported Blaize in his plan for the afternoon, purely to have Libby out of the school, safe from an unwanted caller. He winced at the thought that he might have raised expectations.

They were not at home! But there was a note pinned to the door announcing Playtime at the Playground. He could take them in on his way to the basketball courts. And there they were – stroller parked under a tree, mother holding a delighted Penny as she slid down all two metres of the baby slide. Given the squealing, it might as well have been from the top of Everest.

"It's lovely and fresh out still. Some exercise and then she'll have a good afternoon sleep."

"Good idea. And you...? the puzzle?"

Jenny was peeved at being seen through so easily but she smiled and nodded. Penny pointed to the swing and he strapped her in and began gently to push.

"I saw Blaize at the pool. He said he wanted to get Libby off campus for a break this afternoon and I said we would both support such a good idea." He looked a little dubious. "Would you have supported it?"

"Well, obviously I know why you said it. They can sort out the details themselves. It can't do any harm, I guess."

"No, unless Blaize starts to think of himself as the protector. Getting her out of harm's way like that – do you think he knows something?"

Penny yelled energetically because the pushing had stopped. "Sorry, little one," he said, and then, to his wife, "Another case of watch and wait, eh? I'll call in later at home, so long as I won't be attacked with a paintbrush."

He understood her pretty well and she was glad of it. He gave his little daughter a friendly pat and continued on his way. He would go via the copse – he supposed that that was what Fraser meant by an outlying part – and then past the basketball courts back to the House. A deserted house was, after all, as much a temptation as a patch of scrub if one wanted to be up to mischief.

The copse was, in truth, not much more than a patch of scrub. Covering about an acre, it was a little notch of, mainly, silver birch trees on the edge of the campus. That part of the College grounds was the closest to some local light industries and the copse must have been conceived as a screen of some sort, to keep the real world at bay. The trees were pleasant and the grasses and small shrubs growing in the area lent it a woodland appearance, so very different from Australian bush or from the cypresses that fringed other parts of the grounds, acting as windbreaks between sections and preventing any other growth beneath them.

There was a path through the copse, a narrow dirt track, used often by joggers as part of a five-kilometre loop through the grounds. It was cool on the path, which wound daintily through the trees, so that one saw it for only a few metres ahead. A jogger or a patroller could therefore come on a miscreant rather suddenly, a smoker, perhaps, though they were much rarer than in the bad old days, or, not a miscreant at all, someone lonely or wanting a respite from the constant observation that was a boarding student's life. Doug walked briskly along the path, not expecting to find anything out of the ordinary and least of all what he did find. In the middle of the copse, at a sharp turn of the path, lay a cat, obviously dead, its little black and white body stretched stiff, awkward, limbs oddly splayed out. Doug drew a sharp breath. All was quiet. He could not bring himself to move the creature and his thoughts jumped immediately to Fred Jones, the chief groundsman, who dealt with all estate matters. Jones was immensely capable, a straightforward and helpful man who lived in a welter of arrangements and assorted bits of information and equipment. Jones would see to it and, with a shudder, Doug walked on.

The copse gave way suddenly to a nondescript grassy area beyond which was a small pavilion and store, created originally to serve a couple of asphalt basketball courts, little used now. For on the far side of the courts stood a grand gymnasium, housing two indoor courts with all the modern paraphernalia of electronic scoring and with a reception area for refreshments and fraternisation after the games. Three boys were practising shots on one of the outside courts which were otherwise empty. Doug nodded briefly to them and went into the building. The noise was sudden and he stopped just inside the entry, having no real business there. Both courts were in action, apparently on a common time, because Doug had barely entered when a bell rang and both games stopped. He glanced up at the electronic board – only the end of the first quarter. He was about to retreat when a "Morning, Doug" and a hand on his shoulder made him look sharply around.

"Oh, Ben, good morning. Busy here, isn't it? Not out on patrol, though – I've seen nothing."

He realised suddenly that he had indeed seen something, though not the sort of thing Fraser was worried about, or affected to be worried about.

"I don't suppose you've seen Fred Jones this morning?"

"Not lately. Why? Is there a tree down? What do you want him for?"

Fraser's tone was unexpectedly terse, impatient. He was sweeping the courts with his eyes, obviously in search of someone. He was not concentrating on Doug.

"I'll tell Fred you're after him," he said and plunged further into the gym, to the spectators' area on the far side. Doug shrugged and made a second attempt to move out. He was for a second time prevented.

"Why, Doug, old man, what brings you here? I thought you were a swimmer. You'll have to grow another six inches at least for this Brobdingnagian sport."

Flem Harry, undoubtedly the most eccentric of his English teaching colleagues, smiled broadly at him.

"You're hardly a giant yourself, Flem. No, I'm just out on one of Fraser's patrols. Only looking in."

"Better not to," said Flem and with a wide gesture, much too dramatic, indicated the racket that echoed through the building. "You're not masochistic, like some of us. You don't belong in this chaos. My team's on in forty minutes or so, so we've got to get 'in the zone', as the boys tell me. See you!"

Everything had to be larger than life with Flem, whether it was his teaching or the parties he held at his little house on the edge of the campus or just his ordinary conversation. And yet he seemed determined to conform, to play an acceptable part, even if he had to play it grandiosely. Doug recalled that, a couple of years ago, Flem had overstepped the mark, conniving at some irregular tactics in a debating team he supervised. Parslow, so the story went, had cut him down to size and a devil-may-care Flem had tried to re-invent himself as a pillar of society, albeit as an absurdly flamboyant one, a pillar so highly decorated it made you want to laugh; but it was a pillar just the same, supporting the school structures of which it had chosen to be a part. Doug had no idea whether to trust this new Flem or not. He and Jenny now hardly went near the parties – well, Penelope was a fine excuse, but Flem's mixture of too carefully calculated witticisms and fear of being caught out made for an uneasy atmosphere. They had been enjoyable once – now better avoided. From the doorway, he took a last glance back and saw Flem now in animated conversation with Ben Fraser, the latter looming over him as he gesticulated. He would have been much too close if Doug had been standing in Flem's shoes – worse, he suddenly reflected, if it had been Libby standing there. Vexed by what he saw, though uncertain why he should be, he continued his patrol and met Fred Jones putting the heavy roller away. He mentioned the cat.

"I got rid of one only two weeks ago," said the groundsman. "In about the same spot. There must be a feral war going on, I reckon. We'll deal with it."

And that was all. Back in the House, with still half an hour until lunch, he walked through the dormitories and studies but no one was about. He would not have time before lunch to make a proper start on his marking and so he went and sat in the pleasing sunshine on a low brick wall outside the main entrance to the House. He heard isolated sounds – a cricket match must be under way on the oval – but he saw nobody. How was that possible, he wondered, on a busy Saturday in a bustling school? But it was not bustling where he sat and he decided to enjoy ten minutes of it, if he could, ten minutes of just sinking into an inner quietness, free of the absurdities of Flem or the futility of the patrol – or of dead cats.

CHAPTER TWO

For Jenny Anderson, it was hard, it was impossible, to decide whether the last fifteen months had dragged, inching forward day by clumsy day, or had whooshed by, making it difficult to keep pace, to feel that she was even remotely in charge. She liked to feel in control of matters; and so she adored her work at the gallery, selecting, arranging, documenting. She could put forward an idea to Sylvia Marriette, the gallery director, receive encouragement to explore and come back a month later with a detailed plan, a comprehensive design for an exhibition that might take place twelve months into the future. It was exhilarating work, full of possibilities, and she held all the threads in her own hand. At the gallery, Jenny felt, there were no loose ends.

As mother of a tiny baby, how different it was! There had been seven months of maternity leave, at home nearly all the time, wondering each day whether anything at all had been achieved. Managing Penelope, she supposed, was an achievement of sorts, feeding her, tending to her every need. But in her mind, domestic chores didn't count. Once the baby's room had been filled and decorated, what more was there to do? The College afforded pleasant walks, but there was no company for the long, empty days, sometimes empty weekends, in an almost completely male school environment. There was Libby, of course, but she was busy with her teaching, as Doug was Such staff wives as there were on campus were older and tended to be utterly immersed in the College and its ways. They complained right enough, but that was mostly for form. They had no interests beyond the College and their attendance at school events, let alone those in the wider world, betrayed a patronising vacuity of thought. No, there was nothing for Jenny there.

When Penelope was six months old, or a little more, she had gone back to the gallery two days a week and experienced both relief and release such as she had never known. The day care arrangement was fine, as it allowed for some flexibility of hours; and the refreshing plunge back into the world of ideas and textures and forms and relationships kept her spirits buoyant. Another six months on and she was back to her normal appointment, twenty-four hours per week spread over three or four days as she and Sylvia should decide. Doug had called her 0.67FTE: whatever it was, she said, it suited her very well. It provided plenty of stimulation, the time to do a thorough job – and enough time for Penelope.

She found that she could not dote on her daughter in quite the way Doug did. She decided that this was not a concern: rather, it was a manifestation of her worry. She was constantly anxious that something would go wrong with the child. It was an anxiety of a kind that never afflicted her professional work, or her own artmaking, with which their house was filled. No, it was a feeling that, though so much of herself had gone into the making of the child, her little one was still very vulnerable, vulnerable to life in a way that an exhibition never could be. Be rational, she told herself – this is a child, not a collection of artworks, and you want her to develop in all the wonderful ways that a child can. Yes! But that involved risk, and risk was hard to deal with.

So why take the risk again? For surely that was what she was contemplating when she wondered aloud whether fifteen months plus nine months was a sufficient gap. Was it a feeling that just Penelope, delightful as she was, would not be enough? But enough for whom? For herself, she supposed, thinking back over the strange sense of fulfilment that had come over her now and again, in spasms as it were. The feeling fascinated her, at least partly because – was this to go against her own grain? – she did not really understand it. There was a lot to discuss with Doug here; they worked as a team and did not believe in unilateral decision-making. She knew that he loved his teaching and, mostly, his other duties, sporting and pastoral. But then, he could love those things just about anywhere. What if it became best for him to make a move, to seek promotion or just a new position elsewhere? Would she have to give up the gallery if it was a move to distant parts? And how would she keep her work going anyway if there was to be another baby? It was too hard – the threads were not all conveniently in her hand. Well, it was week seven and an end of term holiday had to be planned. That she could do, with confidence, and they would enjoy discussing the possibilities in the evening.

She was right about Doug – he could get very wrapped up in his teaching, absorbed in both the content and the efforts of the boys, sometimes barely fumbling but often successful, to come to grips with the subject matter. He wanted his students to develop in their skills but he was more interested in how they might develop in their understanding of complex ideas and register their development in writing or in speech. He could take a poem about a guy playing a trombone in a public telephone box at one o'clock in the morning and cause students to speculate, as Andrew Taylor's poem does, about potential relationships, how fragile they might be, and how important it is to capture a moment, especially one that seems so unlikely, perhaps bizarre. For Doug, literature connected with life to a degree that surprised even his English colleagues, who needed it to connect, most of all, with the syllabus. They never laughed at him, but they felt that he took the poems, plays and novels a bit too much to heart.

It happened often enough at the College that texts tried and true continued to appear on the lists for study. Felicity Madigan had obviously wanted to modernise but one year could only achieve so much. Then she had been absent and there was no strong impetus for change elsewhere in the department. They all had their reasons – a variety of reasons, of course – for maintaining syllabus favourites; favourites which, Doug felt, could always be given fresh life because for the students they often were new and fresh. Thus it was that *To Kill A Mockingbird* was still on the Year 9 course – a novel, along with the Gregory Peck film, that lent itself to thorough study and gave considerable enjoyment. Doug was convinced that it would have been a better novel without Dill; but authors cannot always be expected to know what works and what doesn't. The *Mockingbird* it was to be, then, and there was clearly enough racism in Australia to give the study bite.

What he had not expected was the students' concern to focus on poverty and to wonder why the novel said so little about it. Whereas classes in previous years had felt, reasonably enough, that the injustice dealt out to Tom Robinson was at the heart of the novel, an injustice to be met with courage, not with ignorant brutality, this class wanted to do something different. They wanted to support the Cunninghams; they cheered when the pastor locked the church doors until a sufficient collection was raised; and they felt an unusual sympathy for Mayella Ewell, for the barren, miserable existence from which she saw no escape. They became animated:

"Atticus is a sensible man. Why doesn't he do something about the horrible conditions he sees around him every day?"

"He helps as he can. He does a lot of work for nothing – Atkins, look up the phrase 'pro bono' for us."

"Is that enough, sir? He's well off – he should do more."

"Is he well off? He tells Scout that they are very poor; they do live a very simple life."

"He has a full-time servant. Even we can't have that, and we are considered well off."

Suddenly it was all about themselves. They were obviously the children of affluence, with no personal experience of poverty at all. Nevertheless they were eager: if there were people living in destitution, homeless, virtually beggars, what right had they to live in luxury? This was heady stuff, Doug thought, not what he had planned, and he did not want the study of Harper Lee's famous novel to turn into an attack on worldly wealth by youngsters who had not even the glimmer of an idea of what it would be like to give up all they had and took for granted. They were not hypocrites but they had little life experience. He looked at one, a boy from the House, who had, two nights ago, complained about the inadequacy of supper. He said:

"Don't try to make a book say what you think it should – not before you've looked really hard at what it does say."

A clever boy, Sam Quick, not the supper complainer, came in: "People are disadvantaged in lots of ways, sir. It can be money, or racism, or just plain snobbery. Why shouldn't we take a stand when we can?"

He had too many ideas going on in his head for him to sort them out clearly; yet he meant well.

"Take a stand, Sam, as strongly as you think justified. And there may be times," he gulped, "when we have to, even if we don't want to. Atticus has to shoot the rabid dog, and he has to take on the Robinson case, though he is very aware of the dangers. I'm not encouraging anyone here to shirk an issue. Take a stand – responsibly, mind you."

As he spoke, he wondered how good he was himself at taking a stand. Had he ever stood up to Sam Baker when he felt put down? He had refused the headmaster, once, and look where that had got him. Would he take a stand, or would he prefer to lose himself in his books? Or, even more, in his wife and child? He feared that there were limits to his stand-taking.

"Now, for Monday I want you to…" but the bell rang. He managed to say, "Go back to the night scene at the Robinson house, where Bob Ewell comes along, and ask yourself why this scene has to happen at night, why it has to be a scene of darkness. There will be an essay set on this for the following week. Please stand."

They did, with the expected groan at the mention of an essay, though Doug knew that they would manage it well. He sent them on their way, made a quick note in his journal of what he had asked them to do, wondered how the class had got to where it had, and then promptly moved on. There was plenty to get through in the day and he couldn't afford to be swamped by Year 9. He smiled – after all, they were Year 9s and they would forget about the class and move on too.

Late in the previous year, an unwelcome notice – not unexpected but unwelcome all the same – had come to the College from the State Educational Authority. This body, supposedly independent but funded by the government and obliged to follow the dictates, or whims, of the Minister for Education, had notified the College that its seven-year accreditation cycle had come to the moment of renewal and that an inspection of the College's curriculum, down to the finest detail, would occur in Term one of the new year. There followed an extensive list of pieces of documentation to be prepared and a date, towards the middle of March, for the inspection itself – a day, two at the most, when the critical eyes of a team of six would assure the world that the College was carrying out its role in an approved manner.

The staff had been informed and the student-free days at the end of the year had been used to check curriculum documentation. During the current term, work samples had been collected, mostly samples derived from Parslow's assessment system, which pleased him immensely. He had assured the council, through Greg Donald its chairman, that all was well and that the school would pass its inspection *summa cum laude*.

After all, he knew the chief inspector quite well and felt confident that such a sensible man would register the excellence of the big picture and would not fuss unduly over any little irregularities. There shouldn't be any, of course, but it was good to know the man in charge. It was with some annoyance, therefore, that Parslow received a reminder a week before the inspection was to take place with a note to the effect that the chief inspector was recovering after a recent operation and that the team would be led by the science expert, one Mrs Di Klaussen. It shouldn't matter, Parslow felt, and yet he hated even a minor disturbance to carefully made arrangements. He phoned Mrs Klaussen to assure her of a very warm welcome to the College and was pleased to find in her a sensible woman, committed, she said, to helping schools perform at their best. It was a polite conversation, even to the extent that each assured the other how much they were looking forward to the meeting.

Parslow had divided responsibility for collecting and checking the required information between Ben Fraser and himself. He had compiled a substantial dossier on the College in facts and figures, tracing the development of facilities and results over the seven years since the last inspection. (What a perfunctory exercise that had been, he remembered!) To Fraser fell the task of working with the heads of departments to ensure that all curriculum documents and ultimately all work samples fulfilled syllabus requirements and exhibited student proficiency. Now Fraser was the kind of man who trusts his own abilities and systems and looks askance at those of others. He had met several times with the HoDs of the mega-departments, of whom he was one in Mrs Madigan's absence, and had given instructions about how to liaise with subject coordinators beneath them. But were there too many links in each chain? He could not be sure that the liaison happened as it should, that his directives were clearly relayed to those who had to produce most of the essential information. He was concerned about Bob Graham (science et al), a delightful educator for whom administration, he surmised, was something of a nuisance. Taking care of English meant more work for himself; only in mathematics and the arts did he feel that he was on secure ground. It was all manageable but a bit messy, with the potential for too many loose ends and unanswered questions. He spent as much time as he could afford on the matter, allowing for his already heavy deputy's responsibilities. In his mind, they came first: after all, had not Parslow assured him that these inspections were almost a matter of form?

The inspection team duly arrived, at ten o'clock – so that the school day could get under way uninterrupted, said Mrs Klaussen – on a Thursday morning. Her first announcement was that, given her dual role as team leader and Science inspector and the unavailability of the arts inspector until the next day, it would definitely be a two-day operation. Accommodation in the town had already been arranged; Parslow need change nothing. The inspectors' workroom/lunchroom, piled high as it was with evidence of the College's procedures, she pronounced most satisfactory. The team would be delighted to have refreshments brought to them there and they immediately set themselves assiduously to their various tasks. Mrs Klaussen said that her first task would be to check over the headmaster's dossier and chat with him about the school's philosophy of education. They repaired to his study.

As may be imagined, such a conversation was exactly the sort of thing in which Parslow revelled. Mrs Klaussen did have to bring him back to the point more than once, but they spent a delightful forty-five minutes checking that all the required information was there (of course it was!) and highlighting aspects of the College's offering that had undergone change and improvement in recent years. Parslow sent Mrs Klaussen back to her workroom in plenty of time for his own appointment with the builder and project manager for the new boarding house. All was rolling smoothly.

Back in the workroom, silence.

"All going well?" she asked her team and got only grunts in reply. But she had no sooner settled herself in front of the science pile than her English inspector came across, waving a sheet of paper which seemed to contain a long list of green numbered points. Knowing her colleague's love of green as a way of highlighting matters of concern, she raised her eyebrows.

"Finding irregularities, Steve? Already?"

"It's not been done in the way we ask for," he replied. "Or not with some year groups. The information might all be here but it will take a lot of double-checking. To be honest, it's a bit of a mess."

"Press on," she said, "and keep me informed. I'd need to tell Parslow before today is out if there are actual omissions he needs to rectify for tomorrow." She looked around the room, asked for any other problems and got only cheerful smiles. If there was not a general problem, then maybe it was just a matter of awkward presentation of the English material.

By lunchtime, she felt very comfortable. She had been told to be careful by the chief inspector, the one who had had to withdraw, because, until a year ago, science in the College had been ruled by one of the most conservative dinosaurs still in the profession. Especially look at their system of science practicals, she had been warned – but both the stated requirements and the student submissions were excellent. Some of the syllabus choices still looked a bit old-fashioned but the teachers' programmes showed signs of recent updating. There was still much to check but she felt that the new man, a Mr Graham, was up to date in his thinking and in his practices. She paused for lunch feeling quite at ease. It would be a straightforward inspection.

Lunch was a time to stop reading, but it was not down time at all. Rather, it was a time to share impressions, to hear of an oddity in one area of the school that might point to a wider problem for further investigation. But there was nothing to report, not until Steve came in from a toilet stop and brought his page of green jottings over to the central table.

"Still concerned, Steve?" Di Klaussen said. "Let's hear about it then."

Steve helped himself to the plate of sandwiches. This school could cater well, he thought, and then he flattened the page of green jottings out beside him. He glanced down it, and then up, to find Di looking at him in some alarm.

"Come on now, Steve, is it really as bad as all that?"

"As I said earlier, it's a bit of a mess, in the programming of Years 7 and 8 essentially. The student work samples are all fine – there must be some lively minds here somewhere. But the documentation is not so good. It's all been cobbled together. In the more senior years, some of it has been signed off as SB, old style but OK, some by a person called Madigan, generally very good; but the junior years have been signed off by Fraser, who, I understand, is the deputy. All in different formats, with units relating to the syllabus in different ways, so that it's hard to get any overview of how it all fits together. There is a chart that says that everything is covered, but when I hunt for the evidence I run into dead ends."

He paused and reached for another sandwich. So did Di Klaussen – she needed a substantial pause, time to think through how she would respond to this unwelcome development. Eventually, with her other inspectors all looking smugly indifferent, she said:

"I suggest you and I spend an hour on it together after lunch. Then, if we are clear that there is a problem, we both go to Parslow. Both of us, Steve" (he looked nervous all of a sudden) "because I shall need a very exact explanation of what his staff have to do by tomorrow. It's a surprise, because everything else is so clearly up to the mark. I sense a school that is moving forward well; except that it isn't if English is not what it should be."

She looked at her very solemn companion. Steve was normally a firm, decisive man and she was surprised to see him somewhat thrown. She went on, "From what you tell me, the student work is fine, better than fine, and that mostly tells us that classrooms are working well. Have things got into a muddle with too much rapid change, perhaps?"

"Possibly. But I would say that whoever has finally put the papers together doesn't understand how the syllabus works. That could be this deputy fellow."

"I see." Mrs Klaussen raised her eyebrows. "Give me five minutes and then you can lead me through the jumble. I'll make an appointment with Parslow for three."

At five o'clock Di Klaussen sat by herself in the workroom and reflected on a most unusual day. It had had its highlights – an excellent exhibition of artworks, for example, covering all the year groups and suggesting that her arts inspector would have a pretty easy time of it on the following day. She had been introduced to Mr Graham and an enthusiastic young colleague, one Guy Somerville, and had told them how impressed she was with developments in their faculty. The three had spent a very pleasant ten minutes chatting about what could be done to improve the education of science teachers. Her colleagues, all departed now to a local hotel, were, all but one, perfectly happy – they had been well fed and could look forward to a good dinner and a restful night with not even the tiniest cloud on the horizon. They could expect to have everything done by lunch the next day, so it felt almost like a long weekend coming up. They had left, taking a less cheerful Steve with them, and she was left to tidy up and mull over her interview with Parslow.

The headmaster had been jovial, at first. He had expected the interview to involve a summary report on the day from herself, and most of what she had to say was indeed commendatory. But when she introduced Steve as her English inspector, Parslow must have sensed trouble coming and the joviality transformed itself into something darker and more defensive.

"Come now, Mrs Klaussen. Mr Fraser tells me that all the documentation is there. I checked over the tables of recent Year 12 results myself – there is clearly nothing to worry about there."

"That is so. Sometimes schools of this kind preserve relics of the ancient past longer than they deserve but that does not seem to be the case here." She paused. "But the documentation that should show exactly how the syllabus requirements are being met is odd. Steve and I have checked it all as thoroughly as we can – but it is by no means clear. Steve, give us a straightforward example from Year 7 or 8."

Parslow interrupted. "I don't think I'll be any the wiser with that sort of detail." He thought quickly. "I had rather get Mr Fraser in and you quiz him. He knows his stuff – an admirably organised man as deputy and he has been holding the reins in English for a time because our head of department, Mrs Madigan, is away on urgent family business. Why don't I set up something for early tomorrow and you can check it through with Ben?"

Steve looked as though his moment for giving evidence had been snatched from him. Nevertheless, he took up the offer and jumped in before Di Klaussen could respond.

"I would like to do that. I could explain to him more fully just what we find unusual and what appears to be missing." He took a breath. "My clear impression is that there are gaps."

Parslow glared at him – had there been an implication that he himself was not up to grasping anything substantial? – but contented himself with an offer of nine thirty, by which time the school day would be solidly under way. It was then that he had made the offer to Di of a tour of the art exhibition, an offer very obviously not extended to her English colleague. In this way he contrived to end the day on a brighter note and he gained time in which to think ahead – exactly how was he to tackle Fraser? He was, on the whole, satisfied with the man. No, he was not Ralph Langton, not yet, and he could not be expected to be. After all, Langton had operated with a lifetime's knowledge of the College and its practices, sometimes too much knowledge for a headmaster bent on change. Fraser seemed to be organised and dependable. His wife, he thought, had far too much to say, but then there was a part of Parslow that felt that the College would be better off without any wives at all. He was wise enough not to voice such a view. He escorted Mrs Klaussen back to her now empty workroom, wished her a pleasant evening and went in search of his deputy, intending, at this late afternoon hour, to meet the man on his own ground, even if that meant having to be polite to Mrs Fraser too.

"Come in, Headmaster," she beamed at him. It was almost as though she had been keeping watch over her front garden, waiting for – someone. "We were just thinking of a pre-dinner drink. Won't you join us?"

"A very brief one, Sarah; I'm on my way to another meeting." (He wasn't.) "But I'd like to bring Ben up to date on today's visit from the inspectors."

At this moment, Ben Fraser emerged from the rear of the house and ushered his visitor into a comfortable sitting room.

"Some wine, Headmaster? We were about to open this pleasant little pinot gris," simpered Sarah Fraser, affecting what she took to be a very European pronunciation.

"Yes, thank you." He was just a shade abrupt. He accepted the glass and then said to Ben, "Can I take you through the day? There is a point I need to, er, clear up before tomorrow."

Fraser saw, and he said to his wife "we won't be long" in such a way as sent her about some other business. He raised an apprehensive eyebrow at Parslow. "What have our colleagues done – or not done, as I guess?"

"That," said Parslow, "is what I will need you to tell me."

They both took a pause at that comment before Parslow went on:

"The inspectors are delighted with almost everything. Their reservation – it can be no more than that, surely – concerns English, because they tell me that the syllabus documentation is in such a variety of formats that it is hard to see whether it does in fact meet all the requirements."

"Of course it does! Haven't they seen the chart, with every box ticked? It's as clear as it could be."

"They have seen the chart. What they are telling me is that, when they do their own cross-check, they find gaps – or possible gaps. They seem to be saying that the chart is not entirely born out in the syllabus documents and programmes, particularly with regard to Years 7 and 8. And so," he paused again, "I have said that you will meet them at nine thirty in the morning to show them how it all works. That seems the best way forward."

Fraser was uncomfortable. He studied his hands for a long moment.

"Yes, I can do that. I will shift my weekly meeting with the matrons – very useful meeting, that, by the way – and I'll see them in their workroom. I really can't imagine what they are fussing about – it's all there!"

"It needs to be, Ben. You know we can't possibly allow errors in English, of all departments. I wouldn't want news of this to get out, not to anyone."

For some reason he had felt the need to emphasise that last phrase, but Fraser did not react to it.

"There'll be nothing to get out." He produced his most engaging smile, the one used when sitting next to a new colleague at morning tea, and offered a refill of wine. Parslow shook his head and rose.

"No, I must be going. My regards to Sarah; see you in the morning. Come to me as soon as your time with the inspectors is over. I am very keen to have this resolved."

He moved out to the front door and made a hasty exit. Sarah Fraser came through from the kitchen too late to make a farewell.

"He was in a terse mood today. What's biting him?"

"The English inspector, that's who, a pedantic little man, I dare say.

But if I find that one of those English teachers has let me down, has not followed instructions, I'll…"

He faltered, suddenly aware, too late, of Parslow's injunction. But surely not letting news get out didn't extend to one's wife.

"You look as though you need another glass of that wine. Dinner is not for another hour. Come and tell me what it's all about – a problem shared, that's what I always say."

He accepted the offered glass but just sat in his comfortable sitting room and pondered. Sarah was not concerned – give him time and it always came out. She set her own glass aside and waited.

Fraser got through the meeting the next morning, but it was a tense time. He knew, knew only too well, how he had ticked every box on the summary chart without precise knowledge of how those ticks applied to specific syllabus points. He had done the same thing with other subjects and he wondered why no questions were being asked about, for instance, French. He reflected that Libby Caraton was in effect the co-ordinator of that subject and had done all his work for him; whereas in English it had all fallen to him. Damn it, there was only so much that a deputy could be expected to do. He virtually ran the place and he wasn't going to be held to account because of the deficiencies of others.

He left the meeting at ten and headed for Parslow's office, armed with a sheet containing a list of queries and omissions, mostly queries. As he walked, he decided to call for a meeting of the department straight after morning tea, probably in the inspectors' workroom, and iron out the problems on the spot. He would take them off class for two lessons and the whole thing would be solved. Steve the inspector had at least this virtue, that he had provided a very clear list of issues requiring attention. He might be a pedantic little snake but Fraser was confident that he presented no insuperable problem. Feeling more or less confident, he came to the headmaster's ante-room.

"He's on the phone, Mr Fraser," said Mrs Delahay. "He told me to expect you – I'm sure he won't be long."

Fraser was forced to spend – he timed it – four minutes gazing at nothing much; but then Mrs Delahay looked up, said, "Just knock and go in," and he found himself being greeted by a headmaster who looked as though English department detail had been the furthest thing from his mind that morning.

"Ah, Ben, a lovely morning. I've just been arranging when the builders will finally be on site." Then, with a sudden change of direction, "Give it to me straight – is the inspection issue eliminated?"

It was certainly not eliminated, not yet, thought Fraser, but he would not say so.

"I have a little list of matters for clarification re Years 7 and 8," he said and went on to outline his plan for the rest of the morning.

"What? All of them off class at once? Is that necessary?"

The question was snapped out and Fraser made himself take a long moment's pause.

"It will be the most efficient way, Headmaster. If I get them all together, I can check that they are all hearing the same news, are made once and for all aware of the same requirements. That way it won't happen again."

"Exactly what won't happen again?" said a now wary Parslow.

For answer, Fraser waved the sheet of paper at him and explained that he was not at all concerned, that he was just following a sensible procedure. He wanted someone to blame, other than himself of course, and if possible he wanted to blame the whole lot of them. That would distance it all even further from himself and avoid the messy business of focusing on any particular person. So he needed to get them all together. They could jointly solve the problem for him, and then he could enjoy sheeting home the blame jointly too.

"I can arrange the class cover in only a few minutes. Periods three and four will do it. It really will be the most straightforward course."

Having, at that point, little knowledge of the matter, Parslow could not dispute with him.

"Get on with it, then," he grumbled. "Keep me informed."

Fraser hurried to the door and glanced back. Ah yes, a headmaster already focusing on other matters, far too busy to worry for long about him: that is what he saw. He smiled at Mrs Delahay and went off to arrange the covering teachers. They would hate him for it, but bad luck to them!

Parslow heard the outer door close and picked up his phone.

"Mrs Delahay, get Mrs Klaussen, the chief inspector, over here as soon as she can make it – straight away if she possibly can."

He sat back. Something had obviously gone wrong and he had to know the truth of it. Fraser was not telling him everything, he could see that. But what was it all about? He had a good crew of English teachers: he liked them and his students liked them. He did not want to see them held accountable for anything beyond their area of responsibility. He grinned – perhaps he could blame Sam Baker for not leaving things in good order fifteen months ago. The phone rang and that put an end to his chuckles.

Twenty minutes later he was not remotely inclined to chuckle. Plainly, he had made a monumental blunder in leaving Fraser in charge of the syllabus documentation for the inspection. Mrs Klaussen had made it clear to him that the man had only a fragile hold on the niceties of syllabus construction. Pretty obviously, his heads of departments and subject co-ordinators had done their work well; but, in the one area for which Fraser himself was directly responsible, things were in a muddle. Mrs Klaussen was very satisfied with all the evidence of work done in English – she said that he had a bunch of very capable teachers. But she needed solid syllabus evidence of recent developments announced by the SEA, including the call for clear connections between the syllabus and a school's own programmes. It was here, where Fraser had worked on the material for Years 7 and 8, that things got hazy.

"Will Mr Fraser's meeting with you after morning tea, with all his teachers, be enough to tidy things up?"

"Normally we would deal with the head of department," she said and Parslow could only nod. "That would be more efficient, in our view."

He would generally agree with her, he said and explained again the Baker-Madigan-Fraser problem of recent years. She was not impressed.

"Mr Parslow, I have to tell you that areas signed off as SB or Madigan are flawless – it is the more recent material that is not so. Mr Fraser should really be the one to deal with it."

"Well, we've set up this meeting now, so I am not inclined to unset it. I am sure you can give the individual teachers credit where it is due to them and seek their input in removing any difficulties. Now, why don't you come through to the staff morning tea?"

He led her through the bright morning air to the common room and, at a suitable break, introduced her as the leader of the inspection team whose work was very nearly done and who had commented very favourably on so much of the documentation and evidence compiled for them. They had only a few loose ends to tidy up, he said, trying to avoid the eyes of English teachers, who had already been made to feel by Fraser that they were a very loose end indeed. Mrs Klaussen had the look of one who is being misrepresented, maybe not intentionally, and contented herself with a bland comment about how they all enjoyed coming to such a fine school. She left Parslow and went back to her team. As Parslow also left the room, Hector McFadden, Head of Mathematics, touched his elbow and whispered, "English is it, then? Is that why we are all covering their lessons?"

"Nothing of the kind," muttered Parslow, which was all the confirmation McFadden felt he needed.

The Anderson household that evening was, for once, quiet. That is not to say that it was peaceful – far from it. Penelope was asleep. Doug had no duties but Jenny had been out all afternoon and so the hours after her return had been entirely domestic, allowing Doug time to give only a slight comment on the day's events. It was at about eight o'clock that they sat back, both of them eager for the proper debriefing to begin. Jenny knew not to rush. She had tea made for them both and a few squares of chocolate left over from a chocolate mousse recipe that she had attempted, with, it must be said, only fair success. She sipped her tea and saw Doug doing the same. Eventually he spoke.

"We don't like Fraser, do we? We've been a bit suspicious of him, to say the least. But I had no idea he could be so plainly dishonest."

"Tell me more about the meeting, Doug. This Mrs Klaussen sounds OK. She must have known what was going on."

"At times I thought so. But what difference would that make? She is gone, she has no role to play here."

He reached for a chocolate and gave her a wan smile.

"The meeting itself," he said, "was not so bad. It couldn't be, not in front of the inspectors. They outlined some deficiencies in our programme documents, really areas in Years 7 and 8 that we had to clarify. Fraser divided us into two groups – he was part of neither and pretended to supervise – and we made the adjustments. Flem and I were on Year 8 with a guy called Steve something or other and we answered his questions easily. If somebody had asked us those questions earlier then the whole matter would never have arisen. But Fraser hadn't asked – I don't think he knew what he was meant to ask. It was all his fault, but when it was all done, an hour at the most, he asked us to follow him into a nearby classroom that was empty."

She saw her man's colour rising. He put his mug down, looked at the chocolates as though they might be explosives, squirmed half up off the sofa and sat down again.

"And that's when he shifted the blame onto you lot?"

Doug clenched his fists tightly. "You bet he did. Let me see what I can remember of it: 'Now listen, team, this should never have occurred. I explained over and over what was required and I marked it on the chart as all done, in good faith. I do not like to be let down in this way, not by people I like to think are good and competent teachers. When you get instructions in future, you all make sure you carry them out. Understood?'"

"The pompous prick!" said Jenny. "You must have all reacted – you had to."

"Blaize was redder than I've ever seen him. Maya was nearly in tears. I was so angry I just glared at the man and Flem – well, who knows with Flem? – had a smile of contempt. I thought it was contempt, anyway."

"Flem is always playing games of some sort, Doug. You can't actually dislike Flem, but you can't trust him either."

"I can do both!" It was said with both vehemence and bitterness, hence the unusual ambiguity. Jenny held out her hands to him and he took them.

"Why? What happened?"

"I was so angry I couldn't speak. As it happened, I was closest to the door and I just walked out. Yes, I know it was cowardly…"

"It was nothing of the sort," she murmured.

"… but I couldn't breathe in there. As soon as I was in the corridor, I stopped. Blaize and Maya came out, gave me a pained look and went the other way. I moved back to the door, to sound off, or do something, I suppose. It wouldn't have done any good, but I had to say something."

He paused. The corridor, the open door, the way sounds echo in a place like that, were all intensely before him.

"I didn't go in. Because I heard Fraser's voice – 'it's all right, Flem, I know I can rely on you.'"

"You're joking! He can't have said that?"

"I know what I heard," he snapped back. "Flem came out and saw me. He gave me an odd look, and then that smile of contempt. The same smile as before. I wanted to hit him – oh, I didn't, don't worry – but I turned my back on him and left. So you see, I never spoke to Fraser and he thinks I've just run in fear."

"So Flem and Fraser are in league then?" said Jenny, not really knowing where she wanted to take the conversation from there. "What on earth would make a pact between those two?"

"I have no idea. I've seen them in animated discussion once before, but I thought Fraser was just laying down the law."

Doug gave a heavy sigh. It was essentially one of despair. All of a sudden both of them hated the place; and yet both knew that Doug did not hate his work in that place. Most of the time he loved it, but this was not the first time, as they saw it, that the institution had devalued him to the point where he could no longer see how he could properly belong.

"You must be an amazing teacher, to have got through the rest of the day," she said lovingly. "Who did you have to teach?"

"Just Year 11 after lunch. I never even went to lunch – I just came back here to be alone because I couldn't trust myself to speak to anyone. Then I collected my things for Year 11 and went across. At the end of the class I saw Blaize going in to his room for Period six but we did not speak. We'll have to at some point."

"Yes, I think it would do you good. Sounding off to me is one thing. You needed to do that; but you also mustn't cut yourself off from the others. You may need to support each other."

He looked at her anxiously – he had not been thinking about further repercussions – but said, "Young Maya will need support, that's for sure. She's probably thinking she'll be fired. She lives with Libby, which will be a help, but so will some reassurance from within the department."

He sat back with another great sigh. But then he altered.

"I'm going to write down an exact account of today, all of it, while it's fresh in my mind."

He had jumped up, but Jenny said to him, "For what purpose, Doug? How would you use it? Or is it just to make you feel better, to write it out of your system? If it's that, I'll give you half an hour, no more. You are not going to dwell on this all evening."

"OK, thirty minutes max." He took a pad off his desk, put the date at the top of a page and in no time filled three scribbled sheets. Jenny had left him to it and had gone to the kitchen, though she kept an eye very firmly on the time. She was pleased when, before the half hour was up, she heard music. He had picked up Verdi's *Requiem* and had gone straight to the 'Dies Irae'. She smiled – the day had not squashed him entirely, then. The monumental music thumped its way through the house.

Allan Parslow also reflected on a most unusual day. It had been unusually busy and unusually varied, even for a headmaster. Arrangements with the College's building contractors continued smoothly and a phone conversation with Greg Donald had gone well. But now: he had before him a draft report from Mrs Di Klaussen which made it clear that the inspection was over and that continuing accreditation was assured. There had been the fuss about English but, as he put together the pieces as he understood them, he felt strongly that in fact it had not been an inspection problem at all. No, it was more complicated, possibly worse, than that. It was a problem with his deputy.

He looked at the brief report in front of him and thought back over his conversations, those with Klaussen and those with Fraser. What did he know?

In nearly every way the College was in excellent shape and gained a hugely commendatory report from the state authority.

In English, teaching was going well – often very well.

A lot of the English documentation had been fine, but not the parts personally signed off by Ben Fraser.

Klaussen had told him that, at the meeting, his teachers clearly understood their syllabi.

No blame could possibly be laid at the feet of SB or FM, not on the basis of the documents signed off by them.

But Ben Fraser plainly wanted to blame the English teachers.

Parslow was determined not to let him do that, but he could not immediately see how he was to protect them and not undermine his deputy in the process. He should never have agreed to Ben as a stand-in head of department, especially with an inspection happening, but it was too late to worry about that now. He had not heard from Felicity Madigan in over a week now – time to be in touch again and see if he could arrange, or hasten, her return. But that did not solve the Fraser problem, not if he had behaved unjustly to some good teachers. Parslow pulled himself up at that point: had he himself never behaved unjustly to at least one of them, young Anderson? But that was in the past. Let it go and focus on the current problem.

He tidied up his desk at the end of a long day. The afternoon had been so busy that he had seen no more than ten minutes of the First XI. Now, what had he heard? Baxter, 8 for 176 at the close of play. It promised well for Saturday. The tidying done, he walked out to the oval. To stand, in darkness, in the very centre of the oval gave him one of his favourite moments; perhaps the best of all, because all was laid out before him. It was after nine, somehow not quite dark, but serene, and it was all his to command. He became aware of music, fierce music but apparently coming from far off. "That must be dreadfully loud close up. I wonder what…" but the thought drifted away from him and he went back indoors.

By the lunch interval on Saturday, spectators of the cricket might have felt rather less optimism than Parslow had on the Friday evening. Baxter had gone on to 220 all out, thanks to lusty hitting and fast running from their final pair and then had the College struggling at 2 for 24 when the break came. But for a dropped catch and a fumbled run out the situation might have been considerably worse and the College team ate a gloomy slice of pie or sandwich, aware that their chance of defeating that most arrogant of opponents was slipping away. Well, they had two or three solid batsmen left: knuckle down and who knows, they said to themselves.

If the spectators felt a similar despondency, they hid it very well, behind hampers full of food and champagne. In small groups or larger clans, they chatted jovially in the warmth of the day, on holiday, as it were. Perhaps the parents of the two College batsmen already dismissed looked as though their enjoyment of the day had been cut short but they were convivial with their neighbours on the boundary, swapping drinks and sharing quiches. Nothing could mar their general sense of bonhomie for long.

One family had positioned itself just off from the sightscreen at one end of the oval, because the father was convinced that, when his son's turn to bat came (it was still the fall of several wickets away) he would be perfectly positioned to catch a beautifully lofted six. While he talked proudly with the deep mid-wicket group, his wife had collected around her a number of women more interested in fashions and in fashionable talk. They dissected the apparel of the Baxter parents, of both sexes, and found it wanting. They passed a brief opinion on the state of the grounds and were just moving on to the College staff when they were joined by Sarah Fraser. They admired her hat, offered her a glass and seemed to feel that she was one of them. Naturally this pleased Mrs Fraser no end and she relaxed into the conversation.

"My Alex's maths is coming on well this year. He seems to have decided that he can do maths after all, which is a relief."

"I've never had to worry about maths at this school. Other subjects maybe, but never maths."

"Absolutely. You know, one year Simon had to suffer English under an old buffer called Simpson. He simply slept through it – I mean Simon but possibly Simpson as well."

Those who remembered Joe laughed heartily at this.

"It's good they pensioned him off at last. I don't know all the present crop, but I understand that Mrs Madigan is being missed."

The speaker clearly was not aware of Sarah Fraser's connection with the temporary head of English; perhaps she knew her only as the wife of the deputy. But others did know, and there was a moment's silence.

"Both my boys have had Mr Anderson. He knows what he's about."

"I suppose so. I met him once and thought he lived on some other planet."

"Oh, English teachers are often a bit wafty like that."

"They certainly are," came in Sarah Fraser, who could hold herself in no longer. "They all seem pleasant enough, but I'm not sure that the College can rely on them. It is a good thing that Ben is watching over English at the moment, with Mrs Madigan away. Otherwise English might have caused the school to fail its inspection. But Ben soon had it in hand and all is well, thanks to him."

She paused and smiled complacently, allowing the other women time to absorb the full genius of her husband.

"I tell him not to take on too much," she continued, "because he nearly runs the College as it is." She gave a sympathetic sigh, unaware that her listeners had all returned assiduously to their champagne.

"I do like this carrot cake. It's more – how shall I put it? – more carroty than some."

"The boys are going back onto the field. I hope we see some good batting."

There was no further talk of English, or of Mr Fraser. Sarah had no idea that she had overstepped a crucial line: you could make fun of past eccentrics as much as you liked, but the College must stand firm. The women's brigade was good at smug ridicule of things they considered not to matter, but they saw the College as upholding all that was dependable and worthy. Scoff at individuals, if you liked, because that could be jolly – but always preserve the good standing of the school! However, Sarah walked away feeling thoroughly satisfied that the Fraser esteem would now be at a higher point than ever.

The deep mid-wicket group had been discussing the cricket, mainly because it included three or four boys who could talk of nothing else. Attached to them was Hamish Fanning, there as a friend of another boy and given a hearty lunch when it became clear that he had no family down for the day. Hamish was not much good at cricket but he still found the game fascinating, at least from a statistical point of view, and he had taken up the job of the team's scorer. When the first of the opposition team had come back to the field, he excused himself and began to walk back to the scoreboard. To get there, he had to pass behind the sightscreen, where he stopped briefly to say hello to a friend and his father and, as he stood there, he heard some of the remarks made by Mrs Fraser, whom he recognised, and the other women, whom he did not. He found it hard to focus on the kind enquiries of his friend's father because of what he was hearing: "Anderson... on some other planet... English teachers wafty... can't rely on them... English failed inspection..."

His ears were burning, and not with curiosity – it was more like outrage. He had heard parents behave in this high-handed, scoffing way before – it was often like that if they dropped in on Charlie, his father, at their home in town. But that was just silly people showing off. This was the deputy's wife running down some of his favourite teachers. He glanced at his watch and explained that he was due at the scoreboard. He hurried away but then looked back in time to see a smiling Mrs Fraser disengage herself from the group. He looked at her with distaste and began to wonder what, if anything, he could do in response. He was appalled and felt for some reason personally affronted on behalf of Mr Harry and Mr Anderson and the others and he began to ponder and to plan. But then he was at the scoreboard, in front of his scorebook; the game began and thoughts of Mrs Fraser had to be put aside.

By Monday Doug had recovered his equilibrium, at least to some extent. Over the weekend he had experienced moments of the most intense frustration, amounting to anger, and he was for a time immobilised by the feeling. But he had taken Penelope for a couple of long walks, one away from the school grounds and one around by the copse. There were no dead animals of any kind in his path and he experienced a kind of peace in the shaded meandering patch of woodland, enough to come out on the other side feeling substantially refreshed. He could face Monday.

Classes, as always, were the least of his worries. He was prepared, and he made himself work up some enthusiasm, so that, if his buoyant manner was a little forced, only he knew it. Years 12, 7 and 8 were taught with increasing levels of animation, with the last lesson before lunch being Year 9. They would go back to that eerie night scene in the *Mockingbird*, with Bob Ewell half-terrifying Jem, and they would scaffold an essay topic on darkness versus light in the novel. That should keep a bright class moving along, he thought.

It didn't quite happen that way. Sam Quick, in particular, was not to be diverted from his crusading spirit of the week before and it soon appeared that he had assembled a party of allies. Their reasons for making the alliance Doug doubted, but he was left in no doubt at all as to the force of their opinions.

"We can all see the racial prejudice stuff in the book," said Sam at the earliest opportunity. "It's pretty obvious, but we think behind it all is underprivilege and that's what we want to focus on."

There were many encouraging nods and semi-affirmative mumbles.

"If one group were not privileged over another," responded Doug, "then racism could hardly exist. We are really talking about the same thing."

"Maybe," said the boy, thrown briefly off his stride. "But everyone talks about racism these days. We want to stand up for the less well off in society, make a real difference to them."

"That," said Doug, "is a worthy thing to do, whether you read *To Kill a Mockingbird* or not. But we are reading it now…"

He was interrupted. "So you'll support us, sir?"

"Support you in what?"

"In our crusade against underprivilege. Can we count on you?"

Doug smiled tolerantly at his bunch of fourteen to fifteen-year-olds.

"I'd want to see the particular issue or cause first, you know. In principle, of course I support you. Now that that is clear, let us get back to our study."

The boys exchanged knowing glances and subsided. They felt that they had made a point. Doug led them through the chosen scene and then tried to draw matters together with examples of light or darkness in the novel. By the time the board was half full with the students' suggestions, it was clear that darkness was winning. He had to push some alternate points – take another look at Mrs Dubose, he suggested – and by the end of the lesson he felt that a lot had been accomplished. The framework of the essay was clear enough and they would submit their work on the following Monday. He had one more lesson to teach after lunch, but no staff meeting or other duty. He decided on a run and then time with Jenny and Penelope. Friday was by no means a distant memory, but he had conquered the rage, with the boys' unwitting assistance, and now he felt good about plugging on. The teaching had revived him, as it had done several times in the past. He could even face the dining hall.

CHAPTER THREE

Term One almost done, the afternoons starting to draw in, the mornings much crisper: there was a general feeling that the school year was moving on and things such as the memorial service for Robert Fitzpatrick, in reality only a few weeks in the past, were ancient history and rather more readily forgotten than the achievements of Egypt, Greece or Rome. Even an event that had set the College's spirits in a whirl, a frenzy of excitement – a thrilling two-wicket win over Baxter, the final four being triumphantly fielded, though not caught, by a parent down by the sightscreen – had ceased to be mentioned, except by that jubilant parent. *Sic transit gloria mundi.*

It was, from the boys' perspective, downtime. Mid-year exams had not yet appeared on their horizon; summer sports had given way to a brief season of cross-country running, so that the paths of the College were pounded daily, but by only a few with true enjoyment. Even a single five-kilometre loop is a brutal punishment for those not suited to such exercise, and the College had many of those. The football coaches encouraged their prospective squads to run with determination, to build up their fitness for the season in terms two and three. But, with holidays coming, even those boys found it easier, and friendlier, to pause here and there and share holiday plans. Of course, there was Ryan of Year 10 who aimed for three loops a day at an ever quickening pace, but he was going to Nationals later in the year, so he didn't count. The rest took it easy, unless Peter Gryce, coach of the first XVIII, insisted on leading a run, in which case great energy was expended for the return of little pleasure or improvement in fitness. Well, the boys said, term would soon end.

The staff were of the same mind. They taught with dedication but, as in week ten of any term, there is a tendency to wrap things up, to complete the marking of assessments and thus to rule a line under some unit or other, be it Mesopotamia or the solar system. Doug Anderson, therefore, ruled a line under *To Kill A Mockingbird*: classwork was complete, the assessment task (an ingenious one, he thought, because it had been his turn to set it and he had decided on the diary of Calpurnia, the astute silent watcher of all the events) marked and returned, a couple of anti-racist poems offered to the boys in class-time and the burst of enthusiasm for an anti-poverty crusade forgotten. If he and Jenny considered anything (other than Penny, of course) in the evenings, it was their destination for a week away as soon as term finished. They went with Jenny's suggestion, a stretch of coastline because that was what they loved most and as far away from the school as would be convenient with a little child. Mallacoota, she said, would be a 'forget about it all' place and a villa overlooking cliffs and beach was just what they needed. With barely a week to go, therefore, the Andersons, like all the staff, were content to play out the term quietly and comfortably.

Even week ten, however, can bring its unexpected complications. On the Monday morning, at the morning tea break in the common room, Doug sat, as he often did, next to Libby Caraton and was happily filling her in on all Penelope's triumphs over the weekend when they both became aware of Ben Fraser standing before them. He had a cup of tea in one hand and a plate with a slice of cake of some indeterminate sort in the other and so, unable to make use of either, he bent to a low table nearby, freed his hands and then smiled warmly at his colleagues.

"I am sorry to interrupt – but may I have a word with Libby?"

"Of course, Ben," she said. "What can I do for you today?"

Was there an indefinable stress on the last word, as though this were not the first time for such an interruption? Doug made as though to rise, though he intended to stand close by, but Libby got in first: "I'm sure it's just for a moment."

"It is indeed just for a moment. But if Doug will give me his spot for that moment, I will explain." Nobody moved, and he continued, "It concerns just yourself."

It was Libby who rose. "Doug has only been telling me of Penelope, who, if he is to be believed, should be enrolled in Year 7 at once. But we have finished our conversation, so what can I do for you?"

Doug reddened a little at Libby's absurd exaggeration of Penny's accomplishments and he too now rose, feeling that the situation was becoming ridiculous and intending to move right away. Fraser gestured at the seats but Libby remained standing. She looked at him with barely disguised suspicion.

"I only wanted to pass on my thanks for your hard work on all the foreign languages material a couple of weeks ago. It was highly commended by... the relevant inspector."

"I'm glad," she said, smiling at his apparent forgetting of the name. Then, wanting the conversation to be entirely professional, she added, "the whole language programme is making ground; at any rate we have stronger senior French classes than I have seen in my time here."

Fraser looked at his tea, now cooling but out of reach on the low table and then, hearing a bell ring, said, "Yes, we do. I'm sure. Full marks to you. And I'll seek your help on another plan I have in mind – but that can wait."

It looked as though Libby would have to squeeze awkwardly to get past him but he made no move.

"If that's all then," she said and gestured him out of the way. She walked firmly away, but Fraser bent down, retrieved his tea and cake and sat down on one of the vacated seats. As he munched, he watched Libby move across to the door, where Anderson seemed to be waiting for her. She nodded at him and then they went their separate ways to class. Fraser, who did not have a class, nodded also and continued to munch, but he seemed to lose his appetite when Hector McFadden, Head of Mathematics, sat heavily next to him and commenced a complaint about all the extra classes he and his maths colleagues had been made to supervise of late. At that point, even Fraser longed for the term to end.

He had, however, not forgotten the events of morning tea. At the end of period four, when staff and students alike were thronging to the dining hall, he stood where he knew Doug Anderson would pass and beckoned him over.

"I'm going to make this only a quiet, friendly warning, Doug, really just a comment, not a warning at all."

"What on earth are you talking about?" said a bewildered Doug, who was having great difficulty adjusting his focus from Tim Winton with Year 11 to the smiling man in front of him.

"I should have thought it was very obvious. We have all seen how often you sit with Miss Caraton. And then this morning I see you reluctant to leave her side and blushing like mad at some private conversation you have had. It does not look good and you ought to take care. I know Jenny thinks of Libby as a friend, but that only makes it worse. Be sensible."

There is a level of outrage that makes rational communication utterly impossible. They were standing just off to the side of a busy path, but where soft voices, such as Fraser had used, would not be heard. The colour drained from Doug's face and he glared viciously at the deputy.

"You nasty-minded sleaze," he hissed at him. "Take a look at yourself!"

"That's all I want you to do. Just a friendly warning. Now let's go in to lunch."

Fraser walked back onto the path, joining the throng, so that nothing more could be said, even if Doug had wanted to. But he just stood, immobilised from the shock of the incident, when a voice sounded next to him.

"You don't look too good. What was all that about?"

Doug stared wildly and Flem followed up with a suggestion that they go in to lunch.

"I hope he chokes on it," muttered Doug, somewhat irrelevantly, as it seemed to Flem.

Doug turned abruptly and walked away from the dining hall. Flem stared at him, shrugged his shoulders and went on in. He never missed lunch and he could always ask Fraser about it later. Doug could certainly be emotional, but this was way over the top.

Matron South was in danger of being genuinely grumpy. As a person of busy actions but of few words, she was often terse. But the boys loved her for it, as when they knew that they had left her laundry room in a mess and told each other that Matron would be on the warpath again. She had, as they all knew, the determined warmth of one who cared for them in every way she could. Given that she did care, then, true grumpiness was generally out of the question – but no longer. The boys got scowls instead of mock anger, barked commands instead of brisk requests and even hasty treatment at her surgery hour instead of her time and her patience. Honestly, they might as well have gone to the san and been treated as just one of the mob.

Matron knew all this and she was fast becoming angry with herself. She saw herself going about her duties in her usual methodical way and she knew that all that needed to be done was being done. But something was missing from it – some kind of camaraderie had ebbed away, leaving her without her normal happy satisfaction that things were not only done, but were well done. She knew she was being unreasonable, even with the prefects on whom she seemed to be relying more than ever. She had snapped at one of them only the night before because the supper things were late in being brought back to her kitchen. She should not have snapped, because Barney Custance, in the House for once, had delayed the end of supper by collecting his prefects together for one of his talks about initiative. She had been severely annoyed with herself, but, being unused to bouts of self-analysis, she could not work out what was causing her malaise. And so, wrongly, she simply blamed herself.

Doug Anderson was in the House on the Tuesday night of the last week of term and he set about his duties in no better frame of mind than did Matron. Instead of outrage, a feeling he had communicated only too forcibly to Jenny, he now felt a deep, settled gloom. The thought of the coming holiday would make him buoyant for five minutes, but then a feeling of foreboding, or of the school laying in wait for him, made the thought of the terms to follow almost too much to bear. He came on duty trying to tell himself that he could still relate to the boys, but it was a dour Mr Anderson who oversaw a boring study time, doing his rounds in a purely matter-of-fact way, helping here and there without any of his usual zest. Because they just wanted term to be over, the boys assumed that he felt the same and that all would be back to normal once he had had a refreshing break. But Doug was not feeling nearly as resilient as that.

In the middle of the evening he paid his customary visit to Matron to check on her supper arrangements. She seemed scarcely to notice him and he had to repeat his question. She roused herself.

"I'm not quite myself this evening, am I? Please excuse me. Maybe you'd have a cup of tea with me. I imagine the House is settled; and if it's not, we can set the prefects on it, tell them to use their initiative."

This speech stirred Doug sufficiently from his own lethargy to realise that this was not their accustomed Matron South, that something was seriously amiss.

"The House is fine, and a cup would be lovely," he said. She busied herself and he waited, to see what would be forthcoming. She placed two mugs on the table and sat opposite him. She did not know what she wanted to say, or even if it was wise or proper to say anything at all. But she had to speak, and friendly young Mr Anderson was just the right person, one who, she hoped, would affirm her and tell her that she hadn't really lost it after all.

"I hope the tea is fine too," she began and watched him sip at it. "You know, Mr Anderson, when Mr Baker left the school many of us thought you would come into the House. Oh, it's none of my business, I know, but I wish you had."

"We didn't think, with a baby and all, that it would work. The House might have swamped everything else." He tried to speak calmly but her comments brought up too many uncomfortable memories of being misunderstood and unvalued.

"You were probably right. But Mr Anderson, things are not what I was used to. Mr Baker brought trials with him, as I know only too well, but he made the House buzz with life. He could be tough but he was tough while being in the midst of everything. Now…"

She faded. It was one thing to remember, fondly almost, a past housemaster and another thing entirely to speak adversely about the current one.

"Is there anything I can help you with?" asked Doug, moved by the sight of a solid woman doubting herself, though he knew not what assistance he could possibly offer.

She shook her head and went in a different direction.

"I don't see all that much of Mr Custance. We don't seem to operate as a team."

That remark struck a chord with Doug, who knew what it was to feel the strength of two people operating in exactly that way; but he also knew how disastrous a fractured team could be. She could have been talking about English.

"Do you know," she continued, but it wasn't a question, "that on Sunday afternoon Mr Custance suddenly decided that the prefects should organise a clean-up of the grounds around the House."

("Fraser has been in his ear, I reckon," muttered Doug to himself.)

"So he grabs whatever prefects are around and tells them to pull the House together and get it done. Hamish is a sensible boy and he divided everyone into four groups and off they went. Phil Oxbury is a good soul, but a bit vague," (Doug nodded in agreement) "and he took a group out the back of the House. It never occurred to him to think of gloves. Anyway, poor Henry Lau got a very deep glass cut, in a nasty spot between two fingers, and I did what I could but it needed a stitch or two, so I took him to the san. Obviously I had to tell Mr Custance – I must do that if a boy visits the san for any reason – and do you know what, he laughed it off: Tell that fool of a prefect to use his brains, he has plenty, he said, and would not discuss the matter with me any further. I was amazed."

She stopped, amazed at herself, perhaps, for such a long speech. Doug looked at this agitated woman and felt he was getting a little closer to the core of her disquiet.

"Is young Lau all right now?" he asked.

"That's not the point," she snapped at him. "Oh, I am sorry, Mr Anderson, I just feel that it's all wrong. Mr Custance might have known that I have all the necessary equipment and here I was, available if he wanted me. I would never have allowed boys to clean up, outside or inside, without gloves and without some instruction about taking proper care. It need never have happened, not if I'd been involved from the start."

And there it was. Baker had been testy and often dictatorial; but he had included Matron in the House and now she felt marginalised, as though her identity were being cast aside as no longer relevant. Matron South had to feel that she was crucial to the life of the House and now she had her doubts. Doug wondered whether Custance was setting her aside by design – it was probably more from looseness born of laziness. Custance really wanted the House to run itself without too much effort or guidance from him. Hence all the talks to the prefects about using their initiative. But it was a dangerous approach to take in a House with boys as young as thirteen. Custance was wanting them to be what they couldn't be, not all the time at any rate; and worse, he was setting aside an admirable matron in the process. She was right about one thing – Doug would not have run the House that way!

"You must know, Matron," he said, attempting to offer the only help that came to mind, "that we all value you and what you do for the House enormously. The boys wouldn't know what to do without you."

It was meant kindly but it was taken the wrong way.

"That's just it – they didn't, did they?"

The frustration surged from her again and Doug felt flummoxed and embarrassed. He heard a knock at her kitchen door.

"That will be the boys for the supper trays," he said and went to let them in. As they carried the trays away, he said to Matron, "Let's go down and make it as jolly a supper as we can. Come on."

She came, and they did, and they were both glad that they had done so. The boys' chatter made them cast aside, for a time, their frustration and their misery. Though so very different, both knew that their feelings arose out of the College itself, from a sense that they did not belong to it as they had thought they did and as they still so deeply wanted and needed to. For a time, therefore, Matron entered into banter about whether her cake tonight was as good as last week's; and Doug touched base with a couple of boys whose history essays had been overwhelming them earlier in the evening. He was happy to learn that a draft now existed and would he please drop by and look it over after supper. So it is that to maintain unceasing anger is impossible for us, whereas to absorb oneself in honest details sustains us, at least for a time. We can put aside the horror, perhaps even convince ourselves that it wasn't so bad, that it can be contained. But it bides its time and bursts out afresh when it is ready.

Tuesday had begun well for Allan Parslow but it did not end so. After a day of patient planning, he deserved, he felt, an evening of quiet. But at five, when he went out into the ante-room to thank Mrs Delahay for the day and to tell her what he planned for the morrow, she met him with a large envelope and a greatly puzzled look.

"Something for me?" he said. "From whom?"

"I suppose it's for you, Mr Parslow. It is unaddressed. A minute ago, as I was packing up, it was slid under the door" – she pointed to the outer door into the quadrangle – "but when I opened it, I saw nobody."

She passed the envelope over. To Parslow's feel, it contained only one or two sheets. His mind being full of his own plans, he spoke briefly to Mrs Delahay and went back into his study, placing the envelope on his desk and commencing his own tidying up. But when he sat down to run over in his mind the work he should take home and his tasks for the following day, his gaze fell on the envelope. He slit it open and took out a single typed sheet headed 'Petition'.

"What silly games are they playing now?" he said aloud, with no one there to hear. "Wanting a second pool, or less homework, I suppose."

But his comfortable irony quickly evaporated as he began to read:

We the undersigned students of the College, knowing the College to be replete with resources, and knowing that there are many in the community and in the world in desperate need, call on the headmaster to halt the building of a grandiose boarding house and to divert funds to a worthier cause, namely, the alleviation of poverty and underprivilege wherever it may be found. We believe this will add to the College's standing as well as being good in itself. To be commenced without delay.

There followed the names of some twenty students, a hasty glance telling him that they came from Year 9. But he scarcely took the names in as he rushed back to the ante-room and, finding Mrs Delahay gone, rushed back to his study and dialled a number.

"Ben! I'm glad you're still about. Come by my study please. Yes, right now, please."

He slammed down the phone and, with ever rising colour, awaited the arrival of his deputy. A second pool he would have laughed off but the effrontery of this petition needed to be dealt with firmly. He would see that it was done.

Ben Fraser could read the signs well enough and he knew that this was a time for offering his headmaster unequivocal support. So he said that it was indeed no laughing matter; it struck at all the College was aiming to be and, yes, he would go round the houses this very night and get to the bottom of things.

"I know the bottom already – I want the essential culprits. I expect you to parade them before me tomorrow morning. But come and tell me tonight, at whatever time, what you find."

Parslow spoke tersely and then sent his deputy on his way. That his grand project should be traduced in this way was appalling and he finished his tidying up in a very bad humour, ill at ease, because, he realised, he had no idea how far it had gone. What if a copy of the petition had been sent to the press? He could not expect Professor Donald to overlook such a disaster.

Angrily – and this was unusual in such a determinedly optimistic man – he made his way to his residence, thinking of his comfortable sitting room, its beautifully polished piano, its shelves of books and photographs, its easy chairs. But though he reached his residence, there was neither comfort nor reassurance to be found there; for, slid between the screen door and the locked main door, was another envelope. He groaned, assuming it was a second copy of the obnoxious petition, and he simply added it to the pile of papers he carried and went inside. But wait a moment – this was a different envelope, letter size or DL as Mrs Delahay preferred to call it, and not the A4 size that had contained the petition. With a feeling of something close to doom he ripped it open. As he read the single typed and unsigned page, his expression went through rapid changes of astonishment and disgust and his colour once again rose dangerously.

The headmaster ought to know that Mrs Fraser, wife of his deputy, sees fit to run down the College's English teachers to parents, insinuating that her husband is really running the College. She speaks openly at the edge of the sports field and her manner is offensive and malicious.

Parslow was stunned. The note was very vague as to details and yet he felt strongly that it was all too accurate. It came almost certainly from a student – 'run down the College' sounded like a boy's phrase to Parslow – and yet in its very terseness it was intensely literate. He already had his doubts about Sarah Fraser, which was precisely why he had given Ben a mild warning when they discussed the difficulties of the English inspection. But surely that awkward moment was well in the past. Or not? He couldn't work out the timeline but he would certainly give his deputy a very stern word or two when he came with news of the petition perpetrators. What an extraordinary finish to the day!

Parslow could not face even the staff area of the dining hall and, with the meagre provisions he kept on hand, he concocted a simple omelette. By seven thirty he was impatient, by eight wildly so, and he jumped rapidly to the door at about ten past eight.

"Come in, Ben. I've nothing much to offer you this evening." (Fraser breathed a sigh of relief.) "But I hope you've something definite for me."

Fraser, as he often did, said nothing at first. He allowed himself to size up the headmaster's mood as he followed him into the sitting room. He made a commonplace remark about the piano and then, at Parslow's gesture in that direction, settled himself into an easy chair.

"Now then, what's the news?" was the terse demand. To Fraser it sounded particularly abrupt, but then he could not know that there was a second, much more awkward, matter to discuss.

"Well, Allan, I think it's fairly clear what's behind it all. It has started with a small group of Year 9s, some of our brightest, who have decided that we should be a social justice institution rather than a school. I am convinced that the petition hasn't really gone anywhere, not yet, and I think the protagonist, Sam Quick, will withdraw it when you talk to him. I also…"

"He will most certainly withdraw it," interrupted Parslow. "Not that withdrawing it amounts to much if lots of others know about it."

"Certainly some others know of it – one class only, I think – but it has not been made public. I rather feel that the boy Quick was testing the waters."

Fraser paused to gauge the effect of that before playing his trump card.

"He'll find himself in very hot water," exclaimed an increasingly testy Parslow. "But you said one class in particular. How is it a class matter?"

"I was coming to that," and Fraser could barely suppress a smirk. "I am going to suggest that you not be too severe with Quick," (Parslow's eyebrows shot up) "because the whole idea, I suspect, came from the way their study of *To Kill A Mockingbird* has been organised, I might say manipulated, by their English teacher, Mr Anderson."

Fraser sat back comfortably, ready to assess the effect of that remark. He knew well enough that he had re-interpreted Sam Quick's evidence to suit himself – or, maybe, had added to it so as to give it more impact, more bite. He saw, but could not read, a most worried frown that appeared on the headmaster's face.

"Anderson, you say? A mostly reliable fellow. I wonder what got into him."

Fraser could not resist it. "Reliable? I'd hardly have thought so. I had to give him a gentle warning only a few days ago about his unseemly behaviour with Miss Caraton."

"Oh don't talk nonsense, Ben. The man's as devoted to his wife as any man can possibly be." He brushed aside an attempted rejoinder. "But I wonder if his general feeling of dissatisfaction has caused him to…" and Parslow became lost in his own musings. They went something like this: probably Fraser and Anderson dislike each other because of the inspection mishap and Anderson feels he was unfairly blamed; Fraser could be exaggerating, but then if Quick says that his teacher was involved…

"Bring me Quick," he said, coming to a rapid decision, "as soon after eight in the morning as you can, unless his first class has an assessment, not likely at this stage of the term. I'll find young Master Anderson, confront him with the petition and see what he has to say for himself. OK?"

"Certainly," said Fraser with some satisfaction. "I've already checked the boy's timetable for tomorrow and it's only art first up. I'll intercept him in the House or at breakfast."

He made to get up. It had gone well. You didn't have to know Allan Parslow for very long to realise that, should he refer to a member of staff as master, then that person should feel very nervous indeed. But then he was a little thrown.

"Stay a moment. There is something else that has come up. In fact, it has been an evening for unexpected, and in this case, unsigned letters. Here is one left for me at the residence. You won't like it, but I feel I have to show it to you."

He reached back and across to his desk, where a sheet of paper, face down, had been inconspicuously waiting its turn. He knew it would provoke an outraged reaction but, handing it over and then watching the colour rise dramatically through Fraser's neck and face, he perhaps assumed embarrassment was the man's strongest response. He was wrong.

"Anderson again," burst out the deputy, screwing the paper into a ball and hurling it back at Parslow. It fell gently to the floor. "The scurrilous, the vicious, the dishonest... creep! To attack my wife in this way when he hasn't the guts to face up to me!"

Whatever Parslow was expecting, this was not it. Fraser's response made what he wanted to say even more awkward. But first he had to respond to the charge against Doug Anderson.

"Why Anderson, Ben? Do you have any evidence that he would take such a line as this?"

Fraser thought back over the scene in the common room, Anderson obviously shielding Libby Caraton from too close contact with himself. That was why he had engineered the scene near the dining hall: to create distance between Doug and Libby and to leave more scope for his own intentions.

"He is certainly capable of underhanded, of ungentlemanly behaviour. I reckon I've seen that." He hadn't, but then Ben Fraser was quite capable of interpreting as illicit any behaviour that threatened his own plans. "Anyway, who else could possibly have a motive for such an appalling piece of tripe as this?"

"Ah, you think he might have a motive, do you?" said Parslow and very quickly waved aside an interjection. He went on: "I don't think it's a staff member at all. It's not their style. No, this is someone else – it could be a student or a parent who has overheard something they didn't much like. I will make no comment on the letter's accuracy or otherwise, but I do ask, no, I insist that you speak very firmly to Mrs Fraser about discretion. I made the same point, in a veiled way, I admit, at the time of the inspection. Whoever wrote this," and he bent to pick up the paper, "has heard something and has reacted in defence of people he or she likes. Please discuss with your wife how vital it is that we don't inadvertently undermine the good standing of the College. I shall take no further action at all. I will not confront Anderson with it, because I have no evidence against him and because all I know of him suggests that he could not do such a thing. Therefore, you will not confront him with it either. He need never know that this... communication... exists."

Parslow straightened out the sheet of paper, folded it neatly once again as if to preserve it from further violence and looked at the understandably shaken face of Mr Fraser.

"Let us say no more about it," he said softly. "But please have young Quick at my office in the morning. I'll be there from seven thirty onwards."

"May I take…?" said Fraser, reaching a hand for the paper. "So that all is quite clear."

"No, I don't think that will be necessary. I shall destroy this, as I destroy all unsigned communications. You know well enough what it says."

Fraser dropped his hand. The glow of satisfaction that Doug Anderson might be hung out to dry on account of the students' petition had evaporated. He had planned a cosy evening with Sarah, expatiating on the stupidity of a young English teacher. Now he could say nothing of that, and instead, this! He had been studying the carpet, but now he glanced up.

"Until the morning, then, Headmaster." He turned to go without further words.

"Yes, Ben, that will be fine," said Parslow as gently as he felt he could. And then, when Fraser had departed, he fell to further reflection. Anderson? No, a lot of nonsense. Anderson's knowledge of the petition? Very possible, and he must be told to focus on the job he was paid to do and not encourage gullible students to overstep the mark in such a heinous fashion. He would know more when he saw Sam Quick and, confident that he could read a student accurately, he decided to dismiss the matter from his mind until he could see the boy. Unfortunately for Parslow, the matter refused to be dismissed and bubbled to the surface of his consciousness two or three times during the night. It was enough to make any man grumpy.

Fortunately for Mr Parslow's temper, his blood pressure and his digestion, he was in a much better frame of mind by the middle of Wednesday. He had been determined to be firm, but not severe or unpleasant, in his interrogation of Sam Quick and he left the boy, who still had time to get to art, at which subject he excelled, feeling that nothing very damaging had actually occurred. The boy obviously knew why he had been summoned and his demeanour, as Parslow saw, was a blend of determination to stand up for his rights, whatever they might be, and fidgety anxiety as he sat before the head.

"Well, Sam," began Parslow, "let's get straight to the point. I have a paper here which purports to be a petition but which I find very disturbing, because it is based on all sorts of wildly inaccurate assumptions."

He paused and observed. Yes, the boy had registered the force of that last remark. The basis of the petition was thus undermined and he could move on to what really concerned him.

"Am I right in thinking, Sam, that you had a more or less leading part in concocting this?"

The boy had prepared for this question and steeled himself to reply.

"Yes, sir. It came out of our English work – not directly, I mean – and we all felt that we had to take a stand."

He stopped. Somehow, he knew not how, he instinctively realised that it might be better to say less, not more. He was too astute to ramble on.

"I can only applaud a desire to see social justice achieved," said Parslow, when he realised that he would have to lead the discussion after all. "And there are all sorts of ways of achieving that – our bursary programme is a case in point. But it is not reasonable" (with heavy emphasis) "to assume that, instead of being what we are intended to be, a fine school, we give away our substance to others in a willy-nilly fashion. That won't work at all."

"But that's not what we…"

"… intended? What you have written amounts to the same thing. And so it discredits the College – is that also not what you intended?"

The boy blushed deeply. "No sir, not at all. We only wanted to see our school do more good in the world."

"I'm sure you did. But you, and the others, have gone about it in an unwise, and a false, way. And because it is false. I want to see this petition withdrawn. How widely has it been circulated?"

"Those who signed it have a copy – and your copy. That is all." He breathed deeply, sensing that he had come to the heart of the matter: withdrawal of the petition, not punishment, was the head's purpose. But it was not to be so simple.

"And your English class, Sam? They presumably know about it. And your teacher too – Mr Anderson?"

"Other boys were part of our class discussion, but only those who signed know about and have the petition. And Mr Anderson has no idea…"

"Now hang on there." Parslow looked even more intently at the boy, to gauge his next response. "Didn't you say to Mr Fraser that the whole… plan… came out of Mr Anderson's teaching? That he had somehow inspired the project?"

Sam gulped and felt that the chair might give way beneath him. He suddenly saw it – I'm here to dob in Mr Anderson. That's why the head is being so gentle with me. His spirit rose but he could not, in his passion, be as coherent as he wanted to be.

"That's not how it was. I… we… Mr Anderson wanted to discuss racism and we said it was all about poverty and Mr Anderson agreed with us but he…"

Here the lad ran out of words. But Parslow knew his next move.

"Sam, did, does Mr Anderson know of this petition? It's a simple question."

"No, sir. He never knew. And I bet he still doesn't, because he would have come gunning for me if he found out."

The boy attempted a grin, a very weak one. Yet Parslow knew that what Sam had said was almost certainly true. An idealistic boy could easily be inspired by an engaging teacher, leading to results the teacher certainly never intended. He felt he had got what he wanted.

"Thank you for that clear answer, Sam. Now, I want all the copies of this paper left with Mrs Delahay by the end of recess this morning. I want your promise that it *will* be all, that no further copies will be made, and that the whole matter is totally finished. Do I have such a promise?"

Can a boy gulp and breathe more easily at the same time? If so, Sam did it. "Yes, sir, I promise all that." He had escaped, in such a way that his parents need never know about it, or not yet; and, in a vague way, he hoped that he had caused Mr Anderson to escape too.

"Then that is all. You still have time to get to art, I believe."

The boy glanced at his watch, surprised at the headmaster's knowledge of his daily movements.

"Art is good, is it?" pursued Parslow.

"Yes, sir, it's great. At the moment we…"

"Then go and enjoy it." A pause. "But Sam, think – and make very sure that you do all that you have promised."

Sam stood, the vision of what the art class was doing suddenly dispelled.

"Of course, sir. May I go?"

He got a nod, and he went. Parslow sat back. His anger at the petition had quite gone. After all, if his boys could not have outbreaks of mistaken idealism now and then, what sort of a school was he running? They might, like Sam, wish to make a grand statement but they rarely gave a thought to consequences. He would alert Doug Anderson to the issue, but so as to attach to him no hint of blame; and he would instruct him not to pursue the matter with the class or with Sam Quick. If the matter was dead, let it remain so.

And now Fraser – what on earth was going on with him? Or between him and Anderson? Parslow was convinced that Fraser had deliberately misrepresented Anderson's part in the petition, or rather, that he had misrepresented what Quick had told him. To suit his own ends? But what could they possibly be? His reaction to the business of Mrs Fraser and the anonymous note had been so sudden, so ferocious, so extreme, as Parslow was inclined to see it, that it must have been very personally targeted at Anderson: but why? This would need a lot of thought. Perhaps a discussion later on with Anderson himself would shed light on the matter. He looked up the young man's timetable.

His discussion with Doug Anderson made matters better, and worse. He came upon Doug at the end of the morning tea break in the common room, where he and Peter Gryce were laying out a schedule for the football season to begin in the next term. Anderson was explaining how he would encourage his squad to play and Gryce was dictating precisely how his squad would play. If a boy was promoted from the second team to the firsts, thought Parslow, a confused understanding of the game would inevitably result.

"I'm sorry to break in on this, gentlemen. But Doug, could you pop across to my study in, say, ten minutes?"

It was said as casually as he could manage and Gryce, one of the most determinedly one-track people God ever created, merely grunted at the interruption. Doug raised his eyebrows but Parslow merely smiled and moved on. Ten minutes later, therefore, Mrs Delahay ushered Doug in.

"Ah, Doug, thank you for your promptness. I hate to keep you from hearing Peter deliver the whole season, kick by kick. Perhaps this year there won't be a flood to interrupt his plans."

Doug relaxed at the banter but knew that he was not there to discuss the methods of the first XVIII coach. Parslow motioned him to a seat and began.

"Doug, I need to lay a situation before you. You need to know about it but do nothing about it. Just be aware."

Now thoroughly mystified, Doug tried to look understanding, and failed.

"I can see you aren't with me. Well," and he drew out the petition from a file, "this paper was left for me yesterday. It originates with Sam Quick of Year 9 and it might have received some impetus from your classes on the Mockingbird. If it did, I'm assuming that bit was quite accidental. Tell me, did you know anything of this petition?"

Doug collected himself and tried very hard to think of Jenny: always pause before speaking.

"Of this petition, Mr Parslow, nothing whatsoever. Sam, and some others, were determined that the novel should inspire us all to attack poverty, that poverty was what Harper Lee was, or should have been, concerned with. I remember saying," and he coloured as he thought back over the class, "that of course I supported their idealistic wish to crusade against poverty, and then we went back to what I had planned. I had no idea that Sam was going to fire off like this."

Without thinking about it he smiled because, deep down, he liked what the boy had done.

"It really is no laughing matter! Imagine if it got out. But I think I have stopped any chance of that." Parslow sat back, observed how his sharpness had removed the grin, and continued: "We all of us endorse idealism in our students. This outburst, however, could have been disastrous, for all of us. Now, as I say, you are to do nothing, because the issue is buried and I want under no circumstances to breathe fresh life into it. And I do not hold you responsible for it – but you did need to know, so that you could be ready to head off such nonsense another time if necessary."

Uncharacteristically for Parslow, he sighed heavily. Doug thought this meant that the discussion was at an end and made to rise. But no:

"You are, Doug, a good, a better than good, English teacher and the boys respond to you well. I would not like to see you unhappy here." (Is he about to tell me to go and be unhappy somewhere else? thought Doug.) "Tell me, is there anything wrong between you and Mr Fraser at the moment?"

The question was blunt and direct. Doug almost gasped at it, so unexpected was the thrust. Once again he coloured and felt himself grip the chair, to feel its steadiness.

"I suppose the inspection," he began but then halted. He could not go on.

"Yes, but I'd have thought that was behind us. Anything else, anything of a personal nature?"

How could he know? Or was it simply that everything in the College environment was personal, deeply so? But he could not venture down the path of Fraser's comments about Libby Caraton, it would have been too humiliating.

"I suppose we are just very different," was all he could manage.

Parslow allowed quite a long pause, to see if anything would follow. Eventually he said, "I do not want anything I've said this morning to upset you. As I've said, with respect to the petition, you had to know, for future reference. But that is all. I just want you to go on doing the fine job you are. Have a good day, Doug. And remember, the football season isn't all that far off!"

Doug rose. This was the man who had tossed aside his English ambitions with barely a glance. "No, I don't think that's in the school's best interests." And was he now trying to sound concerned, fatherly almost? Doug could not trust him and he made his way back to the common room, to retrieve a pile of books for marking, mightily confused: nothing had happened, he had not been even gently reprimanded, and yet a feeling of being totally ill at ease and misunderstood rushed up at him as though it would choke him. Curse the

Mockingbird, curse Year 9 and curse this horrible place where everything went wrong, everything was soiled. He knew he was over-reacting but he could not help it.

Penny was a little restless that afternoon. Just restless, Doug thought, and then wondered if he was seeing in her what he felt in himself. It was all too easy, he reflected, for moods to be shared, just as one might catch a cold or something worse. There was already a chicken casserole in the oven and he said to Jenny that he and Penelope would take a walk. He received in response a smile indicating that such a plan might be good for both of them before she went back to some notes of items in the gallery due for rotation. He would leave her for an hour, he decided, and do the cross-country runners' loop. A brisk walk pushing the stroller might be just what he needed.

He sang to his little daughter as they went along. She would smile as she recognised the childish tunes and sometimes she would babble along with him. She was very good at insisting on 'Again!' On this occasion, the grand old duke of York got a thorough airing. As they reached the copse, however, Doug became aware that the demand for repetition had ceased and, looking down, he realised that she was sound asleep. He blessed her for that, at the same time fearing that it might mean a rather later than usual bedtime. But she looked so peaceful and he paused in his pushing just to gaze at her. The copse, the sleeping girl, the gentleness of the whole situation moved him in some way and, just for a moment, he shared in its peace. I wish I were Coleridge, he thought – I'd write so well about this moment.

He moved off, still half in his reverie and rounded a sharp bend in the path as it wound through the copse. Suddenly, he was arrested by a strange sight – perhaps two strange sights – but it took him some seconds to connect them. In the middle of the path, not fifteen metres away, a cat was toying with a bird. Or what had been a bird. Perhaps it had been a magpie, but the cat was ripping and tearing at it energetically. At risk of waking Penelope, he was about to yell at the cat and move towards it, if only to clear his path, when he became conscious of the second sight. Just off to the side of the path, a boy was moving, quite stealthily, towards the cat; he was carrying some kind of net. In a moment, remembering the earlier incident of a dead cat in much the same spot, Doug left the stroller where it was and advanced rapidly and noisily.

"Hey! What's going on here? What are you thinking of?"

The boy, startled, looked up and saw Mr Anderson. Something of perplexity and horror flashed across his face. Doug knew the boy – William O'Connell, a lad new to the College this year in Year 8, a member of the House. He was a quiet boy, quiet rather than secretive or withdrawn, Doug would have thought, but only timidly sociable in this his first term. He straightened up and came right out with it.

"I only wanted to save the bird, but I am too late. Cats do an awful lot of damage to birdlife."

He spoke as a crusader and Doug realised that underneath the reserved exterior something much tougher was at work.

"But what about the cat, William? You were going to trap it in that… thing, were you?"

The boy stared angrily. "And what if I was?"

"And you've done this before, William? Maybe a couple of times? And did that mean killing the cat?"

"But this copse," and he gazed lovingly around at the now disturbed patch of woodland, "ought to be the birds' place. It's not for feral cats."

"I don't think you can take it on yourself to…"

It only takes a few minutes during which a stroller is at a standstill for a sleeping infant to be aware of the fact and to object. Penny cried, and Doug did not finish his sentence. He dashed back to the stroller, calling over his shoulder for William to come along with him. But William dashed off in another direction, cutting straight through the copse and making pursuit with a stroller impossible, absurd. Doug heaved a great sigh, knew that his walk was finished and went as quickly as he could to the House. He had to tell Custance of the incident and also that the boy might have run, he knew not where.

"A pity you couldn't have brought him in," said Barney Custance with the air of one whose life has been made unnecessarily difficult. But, as Doug seemed about to object, he followed with, "No, with the child and stroller you couldn't, I understand that." At least, thought Doug, the man had acted promptly. It was close to dinner time, the House was full and Custance had quickly found prefects who went out in search without knowing why. They found William O'Connell, minus net, simply sitting by the side of the oval, waiting, he said, for the dinner bell, looking utterly unconcerned.

Doug saw the boy come into the House. Custance brought him into the study, said that he would take over from there and sent Doug on his way. Doug, who was normally one to see an issue through to its conclusion, was only too glad of the dismissal. It wasn't that he trusted Custance to deal with the matter sensibly; but he was relieved to be able to collect Penny from Matron's and get back home to Jenny. Something was weighing very heavily on him and he knew he had to talk it out. The incident in the copse, the angry, determined boy, the dead bird, and most of all the net, seemed to him to represent a malaise, infecting House, department and school in a way he did not understand. Home was the only safe place he could see in the muddle of his life in the College. Home he went.

Little has been said of the chaplain of the College, for the simple reason that there is little to say. He performed his duties sensibly, with decorum and gentleness; but not only were his sermons utterly unmemorable, so was the man. When, therefore, he came to Allan Parslow a week before the end of the term to present a term's notice and give the news that an opportunity had come up in New Zealand where he had family connections, the headmaster's heart leapt within him. It leapt with anxiety because finding a chaplain is never easy; but it leapt with excitement because the resignation created an opening, a chance to do something new, a chance to offer to the boys and to the College community a fresh understanding of the school as one that did more than nod at Christ as at an old, but often ignored, friend. Indeed, Parslow half-hankered after the job himself – what sermons *he* would preach – but recognised the impossibility. So he had immediately notified Gregory Donald, who smiled down the phone as he shared in the eagerness of his headmaster and who said that, as it was a matter of general significance, he would see that all council members were informed at once. Thus the news got about pretty quickly.

A week later, on the last day of term, a day of packing up and of leaving classes, sports, house and hall behind, a day of holiday good wishes and glib farewells, the Rev Charles Herbert came, by appointment, to see the headmaster. He had asked for only fifteen minutes in the middle of the morning and Parslow had squeezed him in before his end of term address to the staff. He fervently hoped that fifteen minutes would do and, though he often kept people waiting if he thought they deserved it, the staff did not deserve it on this occasion and would rightly resent it if he delayed their departure. Both men, on this occasion for different reasons, were happy to omit pleasantries and their conversation went as follows.

"Headmaster, it may seem irregular my coming to see you without having gone through our chairman first. But I have a particular reason for doing so."

Parslow thought it best to look grave and muttered something like, not bad news, I hope.

"Not at all. Well, actually, that is for you to decide." (Parslow wondered where on earth this was heading.) "I have been in my parish for a decade or so. It is a job I still enjoy and in which, so people tell me, I do good things. However, Rebecca and I are beginning to have discussions about our doing something quite different…"

("If he's leaving, why not just tell Donald?")

"… something different from parish work. Then I hear that the post of chaplain in the College will soon be vacant…"

("Good God!")

"… and so I have come to see you this morning. I come, I assure you, in the most preliminary way, to ask you if you would even consider it a possibility, that I might leave the council and come to join you on the staff…"

("Well, well! It could possibly…")

"If you think it not suitable, then I shall move no further in the matter and will think of other possibilities. But my period of association with the College has shown me how much I like the place. I think I have something to offer, but it is up to you to say whether such a move is feasible, or not."

Herbert sat back comfortably and looked frankly at the other man, glad to have got the main point of the visit off his chest. He sat content to wait for an answer, aware that, preliminary or not, he had dropped something of a bombshell. Parslow smiled and broke the silence.

"I am very happy to say that the matter is worth pursuing, Charles. If we do pursue it, then we have to talk to Professor Donald at once, and he will have his own opinions, I am sure."

He paused. This would be a chaplain to be reckoned with. He could not see Charles Herbert sitting on the sidelines of the College: he would insist on being a fully involved member of staff. But then, that was what Parslow felt that he needed. The man, if not young, was sports-minded, he knew, and that was always a good thing, a way to keep one's feet on the ground if one's main job was to point to something up in heaven. He continued:

"Why don't we find a time over the holidays for the three of us to meet and talk this through? It would still be a case of committing nobody to anything but it would tell us if there is a way forward or not. What do you think?"

Charles Herbert thought it was a good plan. It was not a knockback, which was all he wanted at this stage. There was still a lot to think through, for both him and for Rebecca, but he would relish the chance to do that thinking.

"At this point, Headmaster, this is all very confidential to the two of us, or to us and Professor Donald. If things look like progressing further, then I will need to see my bishop. But until then, only the three of us, eh?"

"Of course, Charles. And now I must go and address the staff, a kind of sign-off for the term." Then, as an afterthought, "Would you like to sit in on that meeting? Some of the staff know you and I would say only that you had dropped by for a chat. The meeting lasts only twenty minutes or so."

Herbert felt that it might be instructive and so allowed himself to be led to the common room and to be introduced in a pleasantly vague way. He listened to Parslow, assessed the reactions of the staff as best he could and felt in no way put off. After the meeting the two men shook hands and Herbert moved out to the oval, standing for a moment to take in the prospect of what might possibly be his next home. No, he said to himself, don't assume anything yet!

For Doug and Jenny Anderson, two days of misery ended the term.

Jenny felt that, if it were not for the week at Mallacoota commencing on the Saturday, Doug might have been in a state of real despair. She understood fully his anger at Ben Fraser and his frustration at matters involving the English department, of which he should, she thought, have been the head. She realised also that things in the House were not going well; but she had struggled to grasp how a boy, a cat and a dead bird had sent her husband's mood tumbling from dissatisfaction at the way he was treated to a deep and general hopelessness. He could not explain it to himself, much less to her, no matter how much he wanted to. So, for all their talk since the Wednesday evening, Jenny had got no further with Doug than to sense a powerful disturbance, a feeling that he had wound up in the wrong place and would be better off out of it.

It was in this dispirited state that Doug attended the staff meeting on the Friday morning. He sat through it, barely listening to a word, though he did spark up when the headmaster announced that Felicity Madigan would be returning to her job as head of English at the start of the new term. Parslow himself was clearly pleased about this and he exhorted his staff to welcome Felicity back after a most difficult personal and family time.

That announcement caused the several English teachers to congregate and to share their reactions. Only Flem Harry seemed nervous about the change; most were positive, feeling that to have a proper head of department – Fraser had clearly not been that – would be a real and tangible benefit. Thus the common room was all but empty when the English teachers broke up and went their various ways, Doug out to the oval as his quickest way home. It was there that he came across Charles Herbert who was just getting into his car.

"Ah, Doug, have a good and well-earned holiday, all three of you."

"We'll try, Reverend." was all the response Doug could make. It caused Herbert to shut the car door again and to come closer to a man he thought was, generally, temperamentally optimistic and cheerful.

"You look terribly down. Are Jenny and Penelope all right?"

Doug managed a smile, as he always did at the mention of his daughter.

"Yes, they are fine. Penelope is doing wonderfully well." He stopped there but, on seeing a raised eyebrow, went on: "No, it's just this place.

I'm sick of it and I think it's sick of me. I really feel it's time to move on."

He was a generation older than Doug and he had had plenty of experience of moving on. In fact, was that not exactly what he was contemplating when he had come to the College this morning? But his years of experience had taught Herbert one thing about moving on, something that seemed to run counter to intuition. As he saw it, we move on best when we are happy to move, happy with where we still are, not miserably eager to get shot of a place. He placed a hand on the young man's arm.

"It can be good to move on and I have no doubt you will do so, at some point. You are not Mr Chips. But do so when you have truly assessed the situation and feel good about it – and, I should add, when you have something positive to go to."

"You're right there," said Doug with half a grin. "But this is not a good place in which to feel useless."

"No place is. But are you? Above all, do your students think you are? I'm sure they don't."

Doug looked gratefully at this man who could know nothing of the day to day life of the College. He was a kind parish clergyman – how could he understand a place like this? But his comment had touched on something important to Doug.

"Jenny says that too." He paused and then felt that he owed the man a better response, even if he was only a remote council member. "Yes, I guess I'll plug on. But it won't be out of a feeling of belonging."

"I am sorry to hear you say that. But plug on by all means. And when you're in the classroom, relish it, because that's where you will make the greatest difference." Then he changed to a brisker tone. "I must go back to parish duties, but I hope we meet again soon."

Doug nodded and they parted. Herbert's car drove away, leaving Doug in sole possession of the oval, if he wanted it. He would tell Jenny of this conversation, because she trusted Herbert as she trusted almost nobody else who had to do with the College. Then they would pack and get ready for a longish drive the next day. Five or six hours it would take, more depending on how many stops they had to make for Penny. He thought of her and smiled, and then he walked home just a little brighter.

Yes, he would tell Jenny of his conversation with Charles Herbert, including the bit about his students not finding him useless. Maybe that was enough to cause one to plug on.

CHAPTER FOUR

The beginning of a term should be exciting. We are refreshed, we are eager say the students, as do some of the teachers. Often they mean it. But it is not the whole truth, especially not when the new term threatens to continue, maybe to prolong, the agonies of the old. Doug had had that encouraging conversation with Charles Herbert on the last day of Term One and he felt ready to plod on; but, and he put it to himself in exactly this way, would it be anything more than plodding?

He had, he told himself, much to be thankful for and much to which he might look forward with some degree of eagerness. There was the football season, of course, almost two whole terms of indulging in a passion he could never explain, let alone justify, but which was immensely real for all that. He could even put up with Peter Gryce, whose passion was of the tyrannical rather than of the joyful kind. He felt more relaxed about his English work, essentially because it would throw up no necessary interactions with Ben Fraser. Felicity Madigan had moved back into her cottage in a far-flung corner of the grounds and he had to admit that she interested him. She had verve, a kind of enthusiasm for her craft that had done something to ease away Doug's resentment that the head of department's job was not his own. And anything that did away with dealing with Fraser was pure gold. He was prepared to take on the term, therefore, with as much of his customary energy as he could muster. He would see to it that he did not just plod!

What was more, he did feel better for the time away. The week in Mallacoota had been blessed with fine, crisp autumn weather; the veranda of their little villa had open views of both beach and endless sea; and the local cafes and takeaways were excellent. He had mentioned this last point to a customer in Freds Ocean Fresh Fish (where else should they be from in such a place, and wouldn't an apostrophe have been better?) and was informed that the last three years had seen the little village flourish such that it was now a year-round destination. Hence the need, he was told, for quality. Well, he reflected, the whiting fillets he bought could not have been better. He would pan fry them with some lemon and garlic, a simple salad – no wonder his spirits were reviving as he planned the menu for the night's meal.

The inlet at Mallacoota, a huge drowned river valley, gave wonderful opportunities for walking and for getting out on the water. They found the local hiring place and took a boat for the whole day. Armed with plenty of supplies, they spent hours chugging about the inlet, stopping at tiny coves, taking a swim, though not for very long in April, snapping lots of photos and even doing nothing except relax in the sun, keep Penny fed and watered and enjoy the sparkling day. Their time of hire ran out at four forty-five and so, pedantic as ever, Doug had the boat one hundred metres off the jetty when it was only four thirty.

"Don't rush, Doug. Just let it drift for a moment. There's plenty of time."

"Yes, of course," said Doug with an embarrassed grin. But relaxing, when the clock is involved, is easier said than done, and when, at 4.40, he saw the hire man beckoning to them from the jetty, he made haste to get back to shore. Perhaps he made too much haste. The hire man had said something about coming in from straight out, following a path that would avoid a patch of tangled weeds that could slow or even stall the reliable but not powerful engine. Hurrying, Doug made his angle of approach too oblique and, when only thirty metres from the jetty, he felt the engine shudder and the boat refuse to move. He engaged reverse, but to no effect. Jenny gave him a sad, a pitying glance.

"I wasn't taking enough care, I know," he blurted out and then, to her and to Penelope's astonishment, he leapt over the side and began to push the boat towards the clearer way. By 4.55 he had it beside the jetty, where he expected to find a frustrated, maybe a furious, hire man. Instead he found amusement.

"Some people never listen," the man said with mock dismay. "I was a teacher once, so I know that some people never listen." He helped mother and child from the boat. "You weren't listening when I told you about the weeds, were you? City people," he grumbled on, and then: "You had a good day, I bet. A perfect day for the inlet."

Doug had by this time retrieved all their belongings and had managed to navigate the plank. The man offered him no assistance. He decided, therefore, not to be conversational.

"It was a wonderful day. Our little one will be tired, so we'll be off. Thanks for the boat."

The man sensed Doug's embarrassment.

"It's all worked out, mate. You just got a bit wet – that's all."

He grinned at Jenny, gave Penelope a pat on the bottom and went back into his shed, presumably to lock up and finish his day. Doug prepared to trudge the half kilometre back to their villa but Jenny forestalled him.

"It was a good day, Doug. Don't be annoyed at yourself. I wasn't paying attention either."

"But it was my job to be watching," he said with irritation. But then a slimy tug on his left leg took his attention and they both laughed, with great relief, because Penny was solemnly unwinding long strands of seaweed.

"Pretty," she managed to get out, dissolving Doug's tension at a stroke. When the child had completed her labours, they walked on.

"Thai takeaway do for tonight?" he said. A comfortable nod was the reply. The incident of the weeds was put aside, though it was to leap back into Doug's mind more than once in the following terms as he reminded himself that one can almost never experience unalloyed pleasure: weeds abound.

Jenny went back to work in the second week of Doug's holidays, or for four days of it, at any rate. Before the time away, she had been putting the final touches to an Easter exhibition, showcasing works in as many media as she could source. In her absence the exhibition had been opened and she returned to find it gaining huge amounts of attention. She relaxed – there was little for her to do on it now, not until it finished and the packing away took place. So she simply enjoyed it and allowed her mind to focus on later in the year. The director, Sylvia Marriette, would be months ahead of her, establishing the broad outlines of the gallery's exhibitions, so that the more finely Jenny could think through some of the detail of the coming months the better. She sometimes laughed as she watched Doug plan tomorrow's lesson – why be only one day ahead? she thought – but he only laughed back and said that he couldn't finally know what to do tomorrow until he was clear about what he had done today.

On the Wednesday afternoon of that week, however, she came home to find Doug fresh from a long walk to some nearby hills, after which he had collected Penny from the childcare centre and was preparing dinner as he recited 'The Owl and the Pussycat' to her. It seemed a pity to disturb the gentle innocence of the moment but it had to be done. She had to give an answer the next day.

"Doug, I have some news from Sylvia," she said, picking up Penny, not exactly as a shield, but so as not to be left alone with her news. Doug looked up sharply – her manner and the mention of Sylvia both suggested a sudden change and he was not at all sure he was ready for it. He absentmindedly pushed some things to the side of the stove and waited anxiously for her to continue. She saw the tension in him, the movement of the hands back and forth to his dinner preparations and his effort to make himself focus on her.

"You see," she said, "Sylvia has been asked to head up a national project, all about what makes regional galleries work. She'll be great, there couldn't be a better spokesperson for what we are doing. But it means," she knew she had been rushing and now took a deep breath, "it means her taking about three months away to get the project off the ground. You can see where this is heading, can't you?"

Jenny's voice faded. She needed a reaction but Doug's gaze seemed to be fixed on a calendar stuck to the kitchen wall. "So what she wants..."

"I know exactly what she wants," he broke in at last. "And why wouldn't she? You're obviously the best person to run things in her absence." He seemed to come to a decision. "I'm so pleased for you. You've had a bit of experience in the role, way back before Penelope, and this represents another great opportunity." He looked at her hard. "You do want to do this, don't you?"

Still holding a by now very restless Penelope, she came to him and managed a one-armed embrace.

"Of course I do." She moved his face so that he could not fix his eyes on the calendar. "But I know what you are thinking – changes, what it will mean for us day to day, how will all the pieces of life fit together..."

He tried to interrupt. "You know me too well. But I am only thinking of a terrific chance for you..."

"... but we will talk about all that later tonight." She took the child over to the stove and gazed at the makings of a traditional bolognese. "There's just one thing," she said and turned to face him. But first she put Penelope down, ignoring the grumble from the child, and brought him firmly to her: "I'm meant to give an answer tomorrow."

If he gasped, it was only briefly. "Then that's what you'll do," he said. "Yes Penny, Mummy will attend to you. Let me make the sauce."

Jenny sighed as she picked the child up again. Nobody seemed to throw an opportunity like this at him, she reflected. But they had once, and she had urged him to reject it. What on earth had she done?

Penny obliged, for once, by falling asleep promptly after dinner and bath and story and another story, so that they had a good evening's chat. The three months would begin in a month's time. Jenny would check in the morning that childcare could accommodate them; she would tell Sylvia that there must be no weekend engagements, although she knew there might be some nights. It would be manageable, she assured him, and he smiled and said he knew it would be.

"Sylvia might never return," he said. "You never know what lies in store."

"She has already guaranteed that won't happen," laughed Jenny. "No, this is a short-term thing, a challenge for the time being, not for always." She held him closely once again. "You know, we can manage all the threads. There will be no loose ends."

"And because you say so, I'll believe it too." He embraced her hard and the two firm bodies produced their own kind of reassurance.

She made the necessary arrangements with Sylvia Mariette the next day and then the Friday was her day off, as well as nearly the end of the school vacation. They started it as slowly as Penny would permit, with more TV time than they would normally think proper and longer time in the shower. The day was blustery though not wet, the kind of day that beckons you out and urges you back in, both at once. Eventually there was a decision – an early lunch of a solid minestrone and then a trip to the ocean and Gio's café. It seemed silly to hunker down inside.

They left the town behind them and smiled broadly, as though they could breathe more freely, when they descended a long, slow hill that ran down to the sea. Then they lost the sea in a maze of sandhills until they drove up onto a clifftop. Penny had slept for most of the journey but she awoke with the stopping of the car and seemed to recognise the place.

"Sand?" she squeaked in excitement.

"Yes, play in the sand," said Jenny, "and walk on the sand, and maybe splash in the water, if it's not too cold."

This was too much information and was simply met with a more determined "Sand!" Doug had hoisted from the boot what he called his beach backpack. He unbuckled his daughter and the three of them made a very slow progress down the path from the clifftop to the beach. Penny walked well – the slowness was because she had to stop and examine each leaf, each rock, each flimsy bit of shell blown up the path. But when she toddled onto the sand, her joy was overwhelming and she just flopped down to feel how it flowed, grainy but smooth, through her fingers. She protested when Doug insisted they not sit right at the end of the path but the protest was short-lived and for half an hour the child felt sand, pushed and pulled sand, fell in love with sand all over again. Then it was a walk, Penny meeting the waves and toddling away from them and finally up another path and a short walk to Gio's café. By now it was gone two o'clock and the lunch crowd, if there had been one, had departed. They took a good table in the window, not outside in the wind itself, and waited for Gio to be free.

He beamed as he came across to them. Gio was a solid man, in build and in character, and he warmed heartily to customers who kept coming back. Bread, pastries, coffee – he spent his working days immersed in these things but, Doug liked to think, they were really just a pathway to people, an excuse for a good chat.

"Ah, Jenny, Doug, I hoped we'd see you before school began again. It has been too many weeks. And in those weeks," and here his gaze went to Penelope who clung a little closer to her mother's knee at the sight of the looming man, "what a beauty she has become! But why should I be surprised?" Delighted at his compliment to all three of them at once, he gestured towards the counter.

"What can Max get for you?" Then he saw their surprise and followed up with, "Mrs Gio, she is away today. Our Enrico, his little Tom is not so well and she has been there all week. But Max is good, very good."

"Is Tom really sick, then, Gio? A week away for Mrs Gio must mean more than a cold."

"But no, she likes to fuss. All will be well – probably already is."

Doug fell to thinking of how everybody's life must be composed of so many elements. He thought of Gio and his wife anchored to their café and imagined them inseparable from both occupation and location. But actually it was not so: like his life with Jenny and Penelope, theirs was composed of so many threads. Jenny had assured him that they could keep track of them all, that it would become just another routine. But what if Penny were to become ill like Gio's Tom – what then?

He was pulled roughly out of this reverie by Jenny's nudge.

"Shall we try it?" she said. And then, realising he had not heard a word of her conversation with Gio, she continued with, "see what happens with a babycino?"

"No, I'll stick to my flat white, please." But then he grinned and nodded and Gio went away, apparently satisfied.

"You were miles away," she said to him earnestly. "What led you off?"

"It was his grandchild, I suppose, and then I thought of all the bits and pieces that make up a life, especially a family's life. Better to think of coffee and... but I didn't order anything to eat."

She gave him a pitying look and then first Gio, and then Max, approached them, the first with a plate of just warmed croissants and dishes of butter and jam, the other with the coffees. Penny was already pointing at the flaky croissants but then Jenny took the tiny cup from Max's tray and set it in front of the child. She looked astonished and made to touch the froth. Getting a finger full, she sucked and the astonishment turned to sheer delight.

"I guess it won't be the last one," said Doug.

"May she enjoy many more," said Gio and he left them to themselves. It was peaceful: only one other table occupied, by what looked like a retired couple. It was warm and as he spread the butter and jam and enjoyed the sweet, soft flakiness, he relaxed and saw Jenny smiling across at him.

"Whatever you were thinking before, whatever problems, they are nothing when we can have this."

"True. But this can't be all day and every day."

She gave him something between a nod and a shake of the head and they both felt that they could make sense of a complex life. But then Doug had to reach into his backpack for a baby wipe: froth was everywhere!

Term began and so, once again as it were, did Felicity Madigan. She did the rounds of all her English colleagues, thanking them for their work in her absence and contenting herself with merely starting conversations which she knew would have to be taken further, not always to easy conclusions. She had enjoyed her first year, almost a year, in the College but she saw it as a place in which it was too easy to settle, a place in which, if you were not careful, a dozen years might pass by in a blink, without your being aware. For a woman like Felicity Madigan, this would not be tolerable.

She was now in her late thirties and those who knew her liked to think of her as a pocket dynamo. She was indeed short and slight; but she spoke rapidly and decisively as though always ready for the next challenge. It must be said that the person she most liked to challenge was herself but her colleagues quickly realised that such a wind of change blew from her that there would be no avoiding it, no escape. The English teachers, most of them, therefore welcomed her back as someone they could trust after the unpleasant aroma spread by Ben Fraser; but they did not expect a comfortable settling back into routine. In fact, routine was a word Felicity never used.

She did not try to tell herself that losing both parents so close together looked like carelessness. Indeed, the sudden shock and then the winding up of an estate which proved to be unexpectedly complex left her for a time quite exhausted. What she wanted now was to wrap up the past and to stow it away somewhere, to look only ahead. She had already done that with respect to a brief, horribly unhappy marriage from her early twenties – how little she had known of herself then, let alone of Campbell – and now, orphaned and quite unattached, she decided to sweep away past liaisons, eschew new ones, and be a head of department to be reckoned with. Parslow, she knew, wanted her to move forward and to drag others with her. She smiled to herself, reflecting that even a headmaster might get more, much more, than he had bargained for.

The teaching of English got under way, as it had to, and it was only at the end of the first week that she was able to draw her colleagues together. She organised a small Friday drinks occasion in her cottage. It was a small place but it had a very pleasant garden. It was still fine and warm at four thirty and she set up a couple of small tables outside and organised the drinks and snacks. How would it go? She was determined to set a course and they would have to bend their own compass settings to her will. There could be no other way.

Ben Fraser had already indicated that he might be held up by other duties. She felt he was avoiding her, and not simply in order to give her space without the oddity of a deputy who had acted in her place being omnipresent. No, there was in him something closer to embarrassment than to proper reserve, a real nervousness about how others might compare the two of them. She could not see why that should be but she resolved to watch and listen.

Before term had even begun, Flem Harry and Blaize Rascham had appeared at her door to issue a vociferous (Flem) and a sincere (Blaize) welcome. The previous year had told her enough about these two and both of them, for different reasons, she would have been quite happy to see move on. One was a chameleon, not to be trusted; and the other was eager, hardworking but somewhat dull, dispirited it seemed. She knew that a budding romance with the French teacher had not gone anywhere, but if that was enough to weaken a person's resolve and debilitate their teaching, then it was certainly time for them to look elsewhere. Nothing would come of plodding on to nowhere in particular.

The Andersons would come – Doug had accepted her kind invitation to the three of them – and she saw him as very capable, introverted, intense. Once during the previous year she had wandered by the football field on a Saturday and had seen his intensity transformed into a passion that surprised her. He was reliable, probably her best ally, but he seemed to want to keep his distance. She would have to watch that closely too.

Then there was Maya, who shared a flat with the French teacher, now a year and a bit into her time at the College, a young woman in her first teaching position, obviously still finding her feet. Felicity had mentored her quite closely in the early part of the previous year, before her own unwanted absence, and she knew there would be further mentoring required. But Maya had brains and a delight in new possibilities, so the effort would be worth it. And Bert Cleary? There must be some other nook of the timetable that could harbour the rowing master. She had told Parslow this over a year ago and would tell him once more, and once again, until she got her way.

The gathering in her garden was harmonious. The presence of a toddler generally inspires amusement, an easing of professional attitudes and tensions, and little Penelope did her job admirably. Flem Harry also fell into a useful role: he kept glasses filled and made pleasant little quips, just sharp enough to keep people on their toes without coming even close to causing offence. His references to the Taj at first escaped Felicity, until she realised that the headmaster's grand building plan was an easy target, one he felt he could safely hit in company such as this. Would he have risked it if Fraser had been there? She didn't know.

So a couple of hours passed, before evening duties or the needs of toddlers caused the break-up. Their timing was impeccable, Felicity thought, and she expected them all to go more or less together. But Maya surprised her by lingering and it was clear that she wanted to say something that was not part of party talk. Felicity was determined to give her every opportunity.

"Could you give me a hand, Maya, now that the blokes have slunk away. It will take us only a minute to transfer the bits and pieces back inside."

Maya was willing and the job was soon done. She stood in Felicity's tiny kitchen area and leaned against a bench.

"Can I mention something to you, Felicity? I don't know what it means but I'm not quite easy about it."

This is going to be unusual territory, Felicity thought.

"But of course. Can you mention it over a coffee, because that is what I need right now?"

It was one of her few luxuries, the coffee machine and she prepared two mugs expertly, the frothing, as well as the shot itself, just perfect. She gestured to a table and they drew up two kitchen chairs.

"Over to you, Maya. I expect there will be lots of things for me to catch up with."

"It's not quite like that, at least, I don't think it is." She took a breath and a mouthful. "Yesterday, after morning tea, when I had a free period, Ben Fraser approached me. He referred back to the inspection – you'd be glad you missed that – and said that he wanted to work with me on programming, since it was an area in which I lacked experience. Or so he said."

Felicity was already bristling. On what possible grounds could a deputy attempt to take over what was obviously her territory? She let her eyebrows provide both a comment and an invitation to continue.

"He then said we should make some times after school, an hour two or three times maybe, and that he would be only too glad to help, especially since you, Felicity, would have so much to do in settling back in. He was being kind, I suppose, but…"

"You are quite right to have misgivings," said Felicity very firmly. "You and I worked together very well last year and I have no doubt we will again. This is precisely the sort of help I can give – not that you need much. As I recall it, you came to us with a good understanding of how a syllabus document works and how we build a teaching programme from it. I'll tell Ben he is not to come in on this and that I am quite sure you know what you are doing anyway."

Maya looked uncertain. Maybe, Felicity thought, there is more to come, though she had no sense of what it might be. She would deal simply and decisively with the issue – but would it be a simple issue?

"I need to feel," said Maya, obviously collecting herself, "that I can speak to you in confidence."

"Ye-es, but it might depend on what you have to tell me." Oh please don't go there, said Felicity under her breath. Don't muddy the waters with a fascination or some hoped-for relationship!

"You see, Felicity, it can't really be about programming at all. I'm not sure what you know about the inspection, but in fact it was Ben who didn't know what he was doing and we did the work when the inspector pointed out shortcomings. I know more about the matter than Ben does, and I'm sure he knows that."

"Well, then?"

Now came the impossibly hard bit and Maya seemed to shy away from it. "Good coffee," she said, "just like a pro. But that's you." She smiled, the kind of smile that begs for encouragement to go on.

"You said you felt uneasy, Maya. I don't understand that, not yet."

Maya gazed into the empty mug.

"I flat," she said, avoiding eye contact, "with Libby Caraton. She has been terrific all through, a great support. Anyway, last night I told her about Ben's 'offer to help' and she said to be very wary, that he had tried to have one-on-ones with her and she had kept him at a distance. Mr Fraser's married, it should be all fine, but now he's made me feel very insecure and it seems he did the same to Libby." She looked up finally. "So, yes, I am uneasy, but it's not really an English matter at all. I don't really know how to deal with it."

"The first thing," said Felicity, who did know how to deal with things, "is exactly what I said before. I shall tell Mr Fraser that it's not his area and to back off. About his unwelcome pressure, if that's what it is, I can give you support in other ways, such as helping to avoid any chance of a tete a tete. And I can even give you some phrases that are good for keeping men at a distance."

That brought a smile to Maya and the shoulders relaxed a little.

"It's what both Doug and Blaize did at different times for her, Libby tells me – to prevent one-on-one, say in the common room. She says they were great, though I doubt they ran to the phrases."

"They'll work, you'll see," and Felicity took the two mugs over to the sink. "I'll deal with the English bit, and then we'll watch and be very careful. I'll observe your wish for confidentiality, but only for the moment. If things become more unwelcome, Maya, something has to be said."

"Yes, I know that," said the younger woman. "I know, and I'm grateful you've let me talk to you like this. It isn't how your friendly departmental drinks were meant to end, is it?"

Felicity gave a wry grin, and then they were both able to smile.

"I suppose not. But we've worked together on English and we can work together on this too."

Maya rose and moved to the door. "They are good people to work with," she said, "most of them, most of the time."

"Then keep flinging your new ideas at them, and it might be all of the time." Felicity saw her out and returned to the kitchen. But before she could finish tidying things away, she had to have a good think. There was much to think about.

Confident that the regrettable, and irritating, incidents of the end of the previous term were behind him, or had at least gone into a long hibernation, Allan Parslow began the new term in a frenzy of happy activity. What with council papers to prepare – he always tried to give them too much to read, in the belief that a surfeit of information stymies pernickety questions – and supervision of a project manager who was meant to supervise everything and Old Boys' events which were really building fundraisers, he had little time to think of Mrs Fraser's loose tongue or Doug Anderson's thwarted ambitions. From what he had heard, the man had run off and hidden himself in the remotest corner of the state. Perhaps it was not such a bad idea, mused Parslow, and then turned his attention to more important matters.

One of them was a grand College fair to be held in May. Planning for the event had, naturally, begun the year before, for it was to be a logistical masterpiece as well as a College showcase, though neither of those things could hide its true purpose, which was to be the broad community arm of the fundraising. The fair would bring together the widest possible representation of all those connected to the College, past and present, and even, when you included politicians and others of dubious public standing, those whose connection was nominal. The connection of all of them, however, had to be made practical: it must be a connection of cash, not merely of goodwill. Hence the planning many months in advance.

Parslow's College council had been shown the final draft (more final than draft, he hoped) of the weekend's programme and had expressed approval. Even Miss Boots had murmured something close to endorsement. It was certainly an ambitious programme, full of concerts and displays, art shows and sports, endless refreshments, not too many speeches but plenty of opportunity to tour the building site. So it was that meetings in which he had to co-ordinate the activities of all those involved in the event had taken place over the first two days of term. He did not arrange one huge meeting. It would be too unwieldy, and anyway, music director and groundsman did not speak the same language. If you told them that student busking was to be encouraged at certain hours, one would cheer and the other quake. Better to keep such people apart.

He relied, therefore, on Ben Fraser to be a kind of go-between, checking that arrangements made by one group did not cut across the needs of another. This was something Fraser did very well, manoeuvring the chess pieces at Parslow's behest without ever quite grasping the big picture on the board. Not only that, but Fraser had pointed out to him a gap which it would not be hard to fill. Old Boys from every era of the College had responded to invitations and were coming in healthy numbers (one hoped the oldest of them were still healthy!) but Fraser had commented that Old Boys loved to see and chat with the teachers of their own era. Now, for the oldest old boys that was no longer possible, but it was very possible for students of the last twenty years or so. Some such teachers you wouldn't want to invite back. Frank Stanton? Over my dead body! But if the likes of Ralph Langton would make a visit, perhaps even Sam Baker, then those who had seen them as pillars of the College would feel that their links with the past were sound enough. They had to feel that strong link in order to give.

So it was that those two venerable men, who had come together for the funeral of Robert Fitzpatrick, agreed to make another appearance for the sake of the College. Their only stipulation was this: they were guests, but not speechmakers. In the case of Sam Baker in particular, Parslow was only too ready to agree.

It must be admitted that both Baker and Langton knew what was expected of them. They would be there to help Parslow fulfil his dream. Nevertheless, they decided to enjoy the moment, or a weekend of moments and they made contact with each other a month or so before the event. Come and have coffee, Langton had said, and we can have a chat and they had settled on a day just after the school holidays, when, said Ralph, the more obnoxious crowd at Sands coffee shop would no longer be in evidence. They both knew the chat would be a fencing match.

"Glad to see you are still able to walk this far, Ralph. You're not quite done for yet, are you?"

"No more than you are. Still just gazing out the back door at the bush, are you? Or do you ever venture out into it?"

"Not much – not as often as I should. But I've had some time away – went to visit some cousins in Perth. So you see, I'm not fading away, not yet."

"Neither of us wants to, do we? Is that why we are going to this silly fair, to convince ourselves that we are still alive, perhaps even that we still matter?"

Baker took refuge in his coffee for a moment. He could not quite laugh away his former colleague's thrust.

"That's not quite it, surely. I haven't sought this connection, but I think I will enjoy seeing some of the people. I can't help wondering if someone like the older Aylett might turn up, or even Hendriks – remember him! And it would be fun to see how they turned out. We dealt with some interesting people."

"Yes, we did," responded Langton, "but I fear some of them will have turned out to be very ordinary adults. We might have just imagined their brilliance."

It saddened Sam to hear the note of despair. "They won't have to be brilliant. They can leave that to us. But I hope some of them have taken life on. I don't want to discover platitudes."

"No one ever accused you of platitudes, did they! They accused you of many other things." He paused. "Would you be happy to say hello to your old matron again, if you saw her?"

Sam had done so at the time of the funeral and he thought he could again, but he only nodded and finished his coffee.

"Let's walk a bit, Ralph. We can worry about school when we get there. Come on out and tell me about your stretch of the bay."

They paid and wandered out. I pressed too hard, thought Langton and began a brisk description of his shorter and his longer walk, assuring Sam that he felt fully up to the latter, if it wouldn't tire Sam too much.

"You never give up, do you?' Sam barked back, and off they went.

Flem Harry was not easy. Nothing had happened – and that was the problem. Something should have happened by now, but so deep and absolute was the silence that he began to think he had imagined the whole thing. No! That was absurd: he couldn't have imagined those conversations. So why was there no sequel to them? And if nothing happened to Anderson, where did that leave him?

He tried – he'd lost count of the times he tried – to reconstruct the sequence. First there had been the strange behaviour of Doug Anderson near the path to the dining hall. The man had been beside himself, quivering with rage; he'd said he hoped Ben Fraser would choke on his lunch; he'd stormed off after what must have been a very angry, if not noisy, altercation with the deputy. But only Anderson had been in turmoil – Fraser had been in good, relaxed spirits over lunch.

The second conversation had occurred later that day, when he had managed to waylay Fraser some time during the evening, as he was, or so it seemed, heading towards the headmaster's residence. Once again he had been full of chirpiness and had not minded having his altercation with Anderson brought up.

"I came across a very distressed Doug Anderson today, just before lunch. He wouldn't tell me anything but I have never seen him so agitated. I do hope nothing is wrong at home. He seemed to be rushing in that direction."

Harry put it as innocently, as disingenuously as he could. And Fraser, who had not seen Flem approach Doug just after he himself had moved on, took Flem's words at face value. He should have known better.

"He and I had a conversation. You must have run into him shortly afterwards. I tried to keep it as gentle and friendly as I could but Anderson can really be a most unreasonable young man. I hope he doesn't do anything foolish and blow it all out of proportion."

Fraser could act the innocent too and sometimes he did it well. But on that occasion, as Harry remembered it, he must have been too sure of an overwhelming success, because he continued:

"Thanks for the information. It merely corroborates what I knew. But I appreciate your helpfulness, in this as in other matters. Actually, I don't think you'll have to fill me in on Anderson for much longer, not much longer at all."

"Do you really think…?" began Harry, but Fraser held up a hand. He did not backtrack but he was certainly not going to elaborate.

"I can't say any more, and the headmaster is expecting me. Enjoy your evening, Flem."

Harry watched him walk – could it be jauntily? – up the path to the headmaster's residence. He had been prepared, for his own security, to provide Fraser with information but he now began to feel uneasy about how it might be used. A less self-centred man would have been become uneasy much earlier.

Stage three was the stage of the vacuum – nothing at all. He had tried to meet Ben Fraser on the last day of term but Fraser had been elusive. He had started to tell him how thick Anderson and a council member, Rev Herbert, seemed to be, but Fraser had had no time to listen. Indeed, he'd been brushed off as though Anderson was no longer an issue. So what was all that stuff about not having to fill him in on Doug for much longer, as though Doug were soon to be moving (or moved?) on? In one sense, he didn't much care; it had seemed rather far-fetched anyway. The real problem was that he, Flem, might somehow have come to be on the outer, possibly subject to the whims of a deputy he knew he could not trust. And since Fraser was the only one who offered him any protection – certainly not Parslow, and he had grave doubts about Felicity Madigan – it was a protection he could ill afford to lose. But if he had forfeited it – how? And if other wheels were now in motion, what were they? He set himself to find out.

Consequently, he had attended Felicity Madigan's drinks on the first Friday afternoon of the term eager to be useful and, as a useful servant can often be, ready to pick up whatever slivers of gossip came his way. He had served drinks with his customary panache, had observed that Felicity had not responded at all to his Taj Mahal quips, had noticed Maya, obviously troubled about something, linger behind when others went. Of the Andersons he had nothing to comment: a bit quiet, perhaps, a bit too absorbed in the child, but maybe parenthood did that. It was a state he must remember to avoid. Flem finished the afternoon with some distinct impressions and he might formerly have passed them on, especially with regard to Maya. But nothing will come of nothing, he said to himself and, seeing silence from Fraser, for once he too remained silent. He would watch and glean – but risk nothing.

Term was barely two days old, and Barney Custance knew that something was wrong. He prided himself on never being sick and he actually felt more or less normal. But there was that strange little patch, a square of two inches or so, on his side, above the waistline. It was red and he wanted to itch it. It seemed to radiate darts around the body like the filaments of a stingray. His wife advised the doctor immediately and Barney, who liked to take care of himself, went at once. It would just be some skin rash, said Mrs Custance, and she expressed a concern that it might be contagious. Surely there would be some antibiotic ointment that would help it.

"It's shingles," he told her in alarm on his return. He was highly agitated. "I mustn't touch it and rub my eyes or I'll go blind. I still feel mostly normal, except that it does rather sting. The doctor says rest will help, even with what he calls a minor case. I'm going to tell Parslow that I need a week in bed."

His wife gasped and asked about medication.

"Precautionary, as I understand it. Antibiotics so that no infection sets in. Antiseptic hand wash. Being very careful. I must say it's a bit of a shock. I'll phone Parslow now. He can make arrangements with Fraser. But would you see if you can find Matron – I'll have to talk to her."

Matron was summoned from the laundry room.

"Don't come too close," he said to her in a mildly pathetic voice. "I don't know a lot about shingles, but one can't be too careful."

She smiled indulgently and hoped it wouldn't spread.

"Do you mean through the House?" he asked in alarm.

Another gentle smile: "I meant on your body. The torso is not so bad, I suppose. But there are other parts…"

"I know about the eyes," he blurted out. Then he tried to assert calm decisiveness. "There is nothing for it but a week's rest, a week out of action in the House, I'm afraid."

There was a part of Matron South that thought this wouldn't be so very different from normal.

"I am confident," he went on, "that the prefects can run most things. I have been training them to do this and they will rise to the occasion. I need you, Matron, to be the one they report to and then for you to pass on to me a note of anything significant, especially if it will run over to when I am fit again. I hope it's only a week, but you can never tell with these things."

He sat back in his great armchair as though the effort of such a long speech had exhausted him.

"You can look after the House, can't you?" he managed to say.

"Definitely, Mr Custance," responded Matron, who felt not displeased at all at this turn of events. "We shall certainly keep things ticking over for you. I'll see the prefects between sport and dinner. They can each have their tasks, and I think I'll get Hamish Fanning..."

He did not want to hear her long list of ideas. He waved a hand to interrupt her and said, "whatever you think best, Matron. It's in your hands."

Custance rose and steadied himself on the back of his armchair. "Just pop a note, each evening, maybe, under the study door. Only what I need to know, you understand. I can trust you to manage all the rest."

She went to the door and, turning, said, "The House will be fine, Mr Custance. Just you rest; take as long as you need."

It was some time since Matron's step along that corridor had been so brisk and purposeful. Some boys were just coming in from class and she wanted – don't be silly, she said to herself – to hug them. She smiled and said she hoped class had been interesting for them. Delighted, they spread the word that Matron was back on form.

"He's really quite unwell," she said to the prefects at a meeting in her kitchen before they went to the dining hall. "I think we have to face a week off, at least. It's up to us to keep things running. I know I can count on you all."

Too polite to embarrass Matron with a pointed comment, the boys nevertheless exchanged glances that spoke clearly enough. Up to us? – when was it ever anything else, they clearly thought. But if they thought these things, they also admired their matron and entered willingly into her plans. At least there would be a plan – not just a glib "use your initiative, boys!"

They were almost sad that nothing out of the ordinary happened that night. Barney Custance would have been supervising, which meant that the prefects would have done his work for him and reported that they had done it. So the House did its study, had its supper and went to bed; and, at the end of the evening, Matron and Hamish Fanning were standing at her surgery door.

"You and the others have done a fine job tonight, Hamish. If you hear any disturbance, just come and let me know. I'll be up."

The boy thought that Matron did not need to be too self-sacrificing. He told her that everyone was taking it very seriously, even the Year 9s, and that he could see no problem that night.

"The important thing," she said, "is that you prefects keep up with your work. I know you'll help me – but don't let the studies slip, Hamish."

"You can be sure I won't. Good night then, Matron."

Matron watched a sensible, dependable young man saunter off. She had confidence in the boys but in her case it was because she knew she would give them full and clear directions. She knew what was needed. It was past ten thirty but she felt full of energy. The House would run well, and she hoped it would be for more than a week.

It was, though not by much. Ben Fraser, acting, presumably, at the instigation of Allan Parslow, indicated firmly to Barney Custance that enough was enough. Before the end of the second week he was ordered to see his doctor again and to return with a certificate saying not so much that all his signs of shingles had disappeared but that he was fit for work. But during the ten days of his seclusion behind his study door, the House had been in good hands and Matron South had every reason to be content with her contribution. It just showed, didn't it, how effective a sensibly hands-on approach could be!

One of her most pleasing outcomes concerned William O'Connell. She had been told little of the bird and cat incident of earlier in the year, that event having happened when she had felt at her most marginalised. Nevertheless, she knew enough to recognise a withdrawn and troubled boy and, when the new term had barely begun and he showed signs of an unusual rash, Matron decided that the case needed her close attention. She went with him to the san, saw him every day herself and was in constant communication with the mother. She told Mrs O'Connell that it seemed probable that nervous anxiety was behind the rash. Mrs O'Connell thought this very unlikely but Matron persisted in her daily consultations and eventually felt that she was glimpsing the truth. On one occasion the boy, whilst waiting for her, was reading a splendid book of Australian birds and Matron used it to promote conversation.

"But of course I like birds," said the boy. "Who wouldn't? They're wonderful!" He saw Matron smiling at him and took, for him, a considerable risk.

"You don't know about the cats, do you, Matron?"

"I heard some gossip, William, but no, I don't really know about it."

"I killed a couple – over in the copse – feral creatures that prey on the birds. Mr Anderson found me, but at least I'd got rid of a couple."

There was an odd mixture of pride and fear in his voice as he claimed responsibility. Matron needed to tread carefully.

"But I hope you won't kill any more, William. There must be another way. And the school authorities won't tolerate it, I imagine."

William blushed deeply and started to scratch.

"They don't say much. I was sent to Mr Custance and he threatened all sorts of things, but then nothing. Mum and Dad didn't mention it over the holidays, so I guess nobody told them. But Mr Custance said…"

"He said what? Maybe they haven't settled what to do yet."

"No," he said, without making it clear to what the negative applied. But then: "No, it's all in limbo. I feel I could get expelled any day and though I often feel I don't belong here, I actually like it. I don't want to be hemmed in, in town, you know."

"And when you're anxious about that, do you scratch more?"

He began to cry, but then fiercely checked himself.

"I just need to know, one way or the other."

Matron was aware of quite a queue at her door and said that they would talk some more. She saw how crucial loose ends were playing havoc with the boy's confidence and security. She advised him to talk to his mother frankly about it, because that was one loose end he *could* deal with. Much better if he spoke to her first, because Matron knew that she would need to have just such a conversation with her too. She also had to get the College to make its position clear: but how? The obvious course, to go straight to Mr Custance as housemaster, was closed to her, though she realised that she would have to put a note of the matter under his door. Or would she? Perhaps not straight away, as he could not do anything, at the moment. She hesitated to go straight to Mr Fraser, feeling unsure of her reception, unsure whether he even knew of the cat incident. But that evening, Mr Anderson was to be in the House and he certainly did know. She would confer with him.

She found him that evening in the cubbyhole he used as an office when he came to the House for supervision. The boys had been settled to their studies and he was considering whether he could get any effective lesson planning done. As soon as he saw Matron, he gave it up, not unhappily.

"Come up to my rooms, Mr Anderson. I need to talk to you about William O'Connell and we can have a cup of tea."

He followed her with interest, remembering the boy in the copse, and before the jug had boiled, she had filled him in. She was well placed to deal with the mother, she said; but how could she get a clear outcome, so that the boy felt at ease in the College?

"You've written a note for Mr Custance, you say? Good – housemasters are often prickly but they must never be left out of the loop, even when sick."

Neither needed elaboration on that point. In their different ways they had felt, suffered from, a housemaster who felt he had not been informed.

"Mr Custance is the proper one to see to it," Doug went on, knowing it was not the answer Matron desired. "He will be back on deck again soon, surely."

Matron raised an eyebrow but whether doubting 'surely' or indicating that it wouldn't make much difference either way, Doug could not tell. He tried again.

"Do you know if Mr Custance reported the matter to the deputy? If he did, then Mr Fraser could take the matter up himself."

"Well," said Matron, "I don't know, actually, and that's because William doesn't know. Everything's been innuendo in his view, nothing clear at all. That's why I don't see how best to help him."

Doug was reluctant to get too involved. Once before he had been made to feel that he was interfering in an area beyond his responsibility. The accusation had been unjust – then, as now, it was simply a case of helping a boy in confusion – but it had taught him caution.

"I suggest, Matron," he offered, "that you go on doing what you do best. Take care of the boy, reassure him that all will be well. I'll just try to find out where the matter has got to. That will seem natural coming from me, since I was involved at the start. I think I can promise to do that."

She noticed his reticence and respected it, though she understood almost nothing of its causes. So she nodded and smiled and offered more tea; and she felt that she could indeed reassure young William by telling him that Mr Anderson was on the case.

Mr Custance appeared in the House on the second weekend of term, looking, as best he could manage it, rather weakened by his ordeal. He let it be known that he would be in class on Monday but that in the meantime he would simply try to catch up on the last ten days' events. He retired to his study, intimating that so much had piled up in his absence that there was no telling when he would appear again.

In fact he confronted a very small pile of mail and a slightly larger pile of Matron's notes, which she had pushed under his door each evening but which he had felt too ill to peruse. He did so now: boys in the san, phone calls to and from parents, the usual stuff and all of it now safely in the past. He need trouble no further about them. Two of the letters were from professional associations to which he belonged, notifying him of most interesting conferences, one of them in term time. He would need to put his case to Fraser very carefully about that one. The third letter turned out to be from a parent and had arrived only on the Friday, in a twenty-four-hour speed delivery bag. He looked for the sender's name: O'Connell. Both she and her son were a bit odd. He slit open the envelope.

Dear Mr Custance and Matron South,

I am sending the same letter to both of you since it is important that you both understand things about William. He has only just told us, in a long phone conversation, of an incident from last term concerning cats and birds. I needn't go over the facts – you both know them. And I do want, first of all, to thank Matron for being there for William in Mr Custance's illness. William, his father and I have talked before about loving birds but not interfering with other wildlife and I thought he had responded well. It appears otherwise and now he is in this fix. Hence my main purpose in writing: can he, and we, be told clearly what is to be the outcome of the incident at school? Perhaps he has been told, but he isn't aware of the fact and he feels that no one will make it clear to him. You might not realise it but he has very quickly grown to love the school and he desperately needs to put all this business behind him. I ask you to help him, therefore, by letting him, and us, know exactly where he stands.

The letter was signed by Angela O'Connell.

Custance sat back and reflected. Yes, it was true that the cat and bird incident at the end of the previous term had been so odd that he had deferred doing anything about it, partly out of nervousness about how the likes of Parslow and Fraser would react. He had hoped it might all just go away – after all, it didn't impinge on House discipline in any way. But he had, he supposed now, let the boy think that consequences would follow and he justified it now to himself by arguing that the boy had had to be prepared, just in case. So he had done nothing and had thus resolved nothing. He had better see the boy. He would do so on Monday: this was to be his last weekend of peace!

So we approach week three, that time of term when all has settled down, when there is no danger of dreaming ahead to the next vacation or of lingering in the euphoria of the last. In week three, productivity is at its zenith.

At morning tea on the Monday, Doug Anderson, with great reluctance, beckoned to Ben Fraser and asked, out of interest and since he had been the one to come across the case, as it were, where matters stood with respect to William O'Connell. Fraser's curt request for an explanation forced Doug into a brief summation of the events in the copse. He went no further than that, intimating that Mr Custance had perhaps seen no need to take the matter further. Fraser, however, sensing that something of significance had been kept from him, replied that he had an urgent appointment but would follow the matter up directly.

"I'll speak to Barney," he said, "and I'll get back to you if I need to. Just leave it there for the moment."

Fraser hurried away, leaving Doug uneasy, wishing he had never raised the matter. He forced his thoughts ahead to his next class and went to the library for some resources. He did not see Fraser heading briskly to the House; he did not know that Fraser felt extremely, almost frantically, annoyed that such a man as Doug should know something he did not know himself; and he did not know that Fraser already felt some antagonism towards Custance, though that was because of Parslow and the shingles. There was no reason Doug should have apprehended these things, and so he apprehended no danger.

Ben Fraser went to the House, therefore, in no good mood. As he approached it, coming across the Green, he saw Barney Custance sitting on a low brick wall talking to a boy and, as he came up to them, both stood up.

"OK then, William? Be sensible, but we don't need to go any further with this. Off you go – you'll just make class."

Ben Fraser did not know the boy by name, not even by face, and he just nodded curtly as the lad went by. He stood before Custance.

"I'm not happy, Barney, not happy at all."

The suddenness of this took Custance entirely by surprise. His response was perhaps not the best he could have made.

"I'm sorry to hear it. How can I be of help?"

Fraser was nearly dancing on the spot in his exasperation.

"By keeping me informed, that's how. A boy should be suspended, perhaps expelled, and I know nothing about it. But that young man Anderson, whom I…" (he thought better of it) "… but Anderson knows. Does the whole school know? And why was I not told of this horrific business of cats and birds?"

Fraser came to a halt, wanting to go further but knowing that, in an interrogation, you don't say everything at once. He glared at the housemaster and was amazed to see a quiet smile come over his face.

"Oh, that? That was William O'Connell I've just been speaking to. An interesting kid, but he let an obsession run away with him. It won't happen again – in fact, I bet he'll be a model student from now on. I have him just where I want him."

Custance was not nearly as sure of that as he made himself sound. For his part, Fraser was in no mood to consider the matter closed, not when he was just beginning on it.

"Not so fast, Barney. As I understand it, a most serious incident took place – a boy in your house trapping and killing cats. And you didn't think it necessary to tell me?"

"I have been sick, you know, and I felt…"

"You weren't sick late last term. So what have you told the boy? – don't be silly and all is forgotten? I won't stand for that, Barney."

Custance took a step back. He was in need of a pause and he was helped by a Year 12 boy who, issuing from the House, cheerfully told him that the things he needed were in the library.

"Good to see you out and about, Mr Custance."

He walked happily off, having unwittingly made Fraser feel invisible. But he had created a moment or two, which was all Custance needed.

"Calm down, Ben. A boy has done a foolish thing, but it is not the kind of thing we want noised about, which is what would happen if we took drastic action. A quiet resolution, in this case, is the best thing, don't you agree? The general population – or the press – don't need to know about this."

It was a deft stroke, because Fraser could instantly imagine the headmaster seeing it that way too. However, he had to make his point.

"I don't like it, but I'll let your resolution stand. I would never undermine you. But Barney, there has to be better communication than this. Keep me fully informed – it's the only way I can make this place tick along."

Custance might have been a lazy man, always ready for the easy way out, but he was also astute in some things. He knew that Fraser liked to think of himself as in charge of the College.

"You make it tick splendidly, Ben. You know that. If I may mix a metaphor, I didn't want it to tick out of tune."

Fraser was not amused by the attempt at verbal dexterity. "One more thing," he said, unwilling to let the matter go without some semblance of victory. "Anderson: I've known him to be interfering before. What's his part in all this?"

"Simply that he was taking his little girl for a walk and they went through the copse. It was Doug who came across William and exposed what was going on."

"Fair enough," said Fraser. "But I don't see what business it is of his to follow up. I'd keep him at a distance if I were you. I'm not saying watch your back, but…"

He decided to leave it like that, suggestive without being specific. "I must get on to other things. There is a school to run, after all. And Barney," as the housemaster had turned away, "ease yourself back into things, won't you?"

But Custance was not to be conned in such an obvious way as that. He smiled, said that he needed to see Matron and went back into his own domain. Fraser felt at something of a loose end.

Custance did check in with his matron, complimenting her on her work with William O'Connell and ascertaining that Doug Anderson had volunteered to help her out by approaching Fraser for information. He would certainly watch that young man – the boys loved him but, after all, that could be just another strategy.

It may be supposed that many important things were said and done in week three, but there is just one more of real significance if we are to follow accurately the lives of those who lived at the College. It concerned the position of chaplain which, as we know, was to become vacant at the end of the term. Parslow looked forward keenly to the farewell but he had been busy on other aspects of the matter too. A meeting with Professor Donald had taken place at which the chairman had expressed qualified support for the appointment of Charles Herbert, noting that it would be a grievous loss to the council; and Rev Herbert had had a talk with his bishop and further discussions with Allan Parslow. The matter was decided and ready for announcement.

Morning tea, Friday: amidst the clatter of cups and the chatter of teachers, the bell for notices was rung and all heads turned towards Fraser, who normally spoke about daily arrangements. But it was the headmaster who stepped forward.

"I have an announcement to make," he said. "One of great significance for us all."

"We'll miss you," came sotto voce from the back corner.

"No," said Parslow, "even more significant than that." He allowed a pause, during which he scanned the far corner: of some kinds of wit he strongly disapproved. Then he smiled genially. "You heard some months ago that Grant is going to New Zealand in the middle of the year and I am delighted to be able to announce his replacement as chaplain. Some of you will know him and, if I say that his appointment to this role creates a vacancy on the college council, I will be giving the game away. Yes indeed – Rev Charles Herbert will be our next chaplain, commencing, I hope, before the end of the term, to allow for a handover period. He is an energetic man of broad experience and I know he has a real contribution to make on staff because he has already made one on the council. He speaks well and he relates to boys well. I am delighted that he will be our next chaplain, in the great tradition of the College."

What Charles Herbert would have made of that last phrase we cannot say, because he was not there to hear it. What Allan Parslow meant by it is not clear either, but he was convinced that it rounded off his speech in a fine and acceptable way. He nodded to Mr Fraser who, since he had nothing to announce, said, "That is all," and the staff went about their business. For most, the announcement affected them not at all; but Doug Anderson went to class thinking that he would have something quite extraordinary to tell Jenny later in the day.

CHAPTER FIVE

A couple of weeks passed, during which all the various staff, students and other residents of the College got on busily with whatever it was they had to do. They responded, each in his or her own way, to the momentum of the term, which seemed to carry them along irresistibly. Of course, the headmaster considered himself to be the source of the momentum and sometimes Ben Fraser, or even Sarah Fraser, considered the deputy to be the true driving force. They were all deceived, even Allan Parslow: it was the College, others' grand plans or daily rosters notwithstanding, gathering its energies together, making its own pace and compelling others to fall in step, whether it chose to jog or sprint.

At this point in term two, it was a brisk jog and one who found keeping the pace to be perfectly possible, even if fitting in tasks that lay beyond the day's immediate needs was out of the question, was Felicity Madigan. She was happy in her job, re-energised after the wearisome burden imposed by her elderly parents' deaths; but it was two weeks or more before she could find time to confront Ben Fraser on the matter of his unwarranted, and resented, intrusion into departmental affairs. She had kept watch over Maya as best she could, in the common room and at other times and it seemed to her that the deputy must be biding his time. On that matter she felt a little less uneasy but increasingly irritated as head of English. On a Friday morning at the end of week five, therefore, she approached Ben at morning tea and asked for a few minutes of his time. He raised his eyebrows but he had no obvious reason for putting her off.

"Come round to my office. Just give me a few minutes after this gathering to check on replacements," he said, though Felicity knew perfectly well that he would have done that already. "It's an area in which anything can go wrong, without warning, isn't it?" he continued, inviting her, as it were, to join with him in lamenting the onerous weight of the deputy's job. Felicity smiled back, nodded briefly and sat down next to

Libby Caraton. She found, however, that she could not get as enthused about complex tenses as that wonderfully energetic young woman.

The door was open and so she knocked, merely as a courtesy and walked into Fraser's study. It was immaculate: Fraser believed that one should never have more files out of their drawers or open on one's desktop than were strictly necessary for the job in hand. He closed the file which was in front of him – Felicity saw that it was labelled 'May Fair' – and smiled his customary greeting.

"Well, it's almost half-term, Felicity, and you seem to have fitted back in as though you were never away. I trust everything feels good to you."

"It does indeed, Ben." But Felicity was not going to allow herself to be diverted into any idle pleasantries. "But I've come in about one matter which I feel I have to raise."

Fraser sensed her firmness but could not imagine how it could be directed at him. "Can I help in any way? Only too happy, of course."

She would have liked to lash out physically at the complacently steepled fingers in front of her. It was better, however, to ignore the man and confront the issue.

"Ben, it concerns Maya." The fingers tapped rapidly against each other. "She has told me of your suggestion that you help her in programming, but I need to tell you that it won't be necessary. In the first place, it's clearly part of my job, now that I'm back, and anyway, she's quite competent. She knows how the syllabus becomes an outline and then a teaching programme. In fact, it's something we are all working on together. So that's one issue you can, with relief I hope, take off your crowded plate."

His response was to gaze at a map of the College on the wall behind Felicity. "You know, Felicity," he said, and the fingers seemed quite relaxed again, "I feel it to be a big part of a deputy's role to keep in touch with staff, as we are doing now, but especially with younger ones, who need mentoring as they learn the ropes and gain experience. It was clear to me in term one that Maya was still finding her feet. It is part of my job to make myself available, to check that all is well."

He may have felt that nothing more needed to be said, because the fingers now played with the edge of the manila folder. For a moment,

Felicity thought it might have been labelled 'Mayfair', all glitz and not much substance. Again she forced herself to put aside distractions.

"That is all very well, Ben, but not in a matter that so directly concerns me as HoD. I will not be bypassed in my own department in a matter as integral to our operations as this. You must keep in touch with staff as you see fit – as long as it doesn't simply make them uncomfortable – but this is a departmental borderline I must ask you not to cross. This is surely reasonable, and necessary."

She watched him closely. Yes, he was annoyed this time and she guessed it was because he did not want his self-appointed authority to be put under the microscope. She did not at first notice that she had said, or implied, more than Maya had given her permission to say.

"Really, Felicity," said Fraser, "you are getting far too agitated. You do your job – I'm sure you are doing it nicely – and I'll do mine. I think that should be quite clear, don't you?"

For all that he sounded in control, his voice was not quite as steady as it might have been and his fingers drummed heavily on the precious 'May Fair' file.

Felicity stood. She was angry and not fully in control either.

"It is quite clear, Ben. Demarcation is an admirable thing. And when a man of your... experience, standing... is dealing with a young woman, the most strictly careful demarcation is a necessity."

He also stood and came round from behind the desk.

"You spoke just now of borderlines, Felicity. The borderline between civility and sheer impertinence is one you tread rather recklessly, it seems."

"I merely point it out to you. I came, however, about the programming matter and I think I have been clear enough." She let her gaze sweep the room. "Have a... nice... day."

Felicity turned and left him. She left behind her a man who already had his list of troublesome people – Anderson, Caraton, and others – and he was mentally adding her name to the list, at the very top. He was flushed, a little excited, convinced that he would win, already had won. Felicity Madigan too was in the midst of a welter of feelings. She had not intended to bring up the more personal affront to Maya, with its implications of sexual predatoriness; but she had so fumed inwardly, at his arrogance and at his insufferable condescension – "I am sure you are doing it nicely" – that she had felt compelled to defend persons, not just principles. She could not be sure what damage, if any, had been done. Yes, she had made her point but it would now be necessary to watch with the utmost vigilance. She would give Maya a brief account of the interview, would say that she felt that the point had been taken, but would ask Maya to let her know at once of any other approach by the deputy. And those fingers! How she had longed for a machete.

Felicity went back through the common room, more or less out of habit. It is said that in the College a teacher falls into one of two groups – those who check pigeonholes several times a day in case of a new message, and those who never check them at all, assuming that they will always be found and told of something really important. Felicity belonged to the former group, people who feel the need to be in charge of all possible details, and on this occasion she was glad of it. On Mr Parslow's special pale-green notepaper she found a message:

'Felicity, here we are at half-term already. We must catch up. Are you free at about five thirty? The residence. AP'

She was delighted. The note could not possibly be a consequence of the interview she had just suffered. It might even prove to be a god-sent opportunity.

The staff table at lunch that Friday was quiet: not unpopulated, but all those there seemed lost in thought and disinclined for chat. This was odd, because a Friday is normally a jovial day, with the weekend beckoning one to games, to freedom, to the indulgence of at least some unprogrammed time. But Ben Fraser, Barney Custance and even Allan Parslow were all looking inward, assessing potential threats and plotting to defeat them. They were not, however, all strategists of equal finesse and cunning.

Barney Custance had been back on duty and in charge of the House for long enough that many had forgotten about his absence. He was, as was his wont, letting things run themselves under the pretence that he was helping his prefects grow up into strong-minded young men. For their part, the prefects would cheerfully have visited another dose of shingles or some other lingering ailment on their housemaster, so that some sensible structure, as had happened under Matron, could be put in place once again. And Custance had finally realised that this was so.

He had avoided Matron for some days after his recovery, relying only on notes back and forth, wanting to make it clear that he would do things his own way once again. Only the day before, however, matters had forced themselves upon him in the form of a note from Matron saying that Mrs O'Connell had rung twice and hoped to catch him before the day was out. Concluding that it was a mother fussing medically over her son, he broke his rule and went to see Matron.

"I'm sure you can deal with Mrs O'Connell, Matron. What is wrong with the boy this time, anyway? He's not on the sick list, but I know he can just feel a bit odd at times."

Matron South went to turn off a tap left running by the sudden interruption to her routine and then turned back to Custance.

"She hasn't said all that much, but it certainly isn't about sickness. I get the feeling they are planning some major overseas trip and want to discuss the implications with you. When, or for how long, I cannot say."

Custance took this in – yes, he would have to deal with it. He was about to leave, to let Matron get on with her bits and pieces, when it became clear that she did not want to let it go at that.

"At the end of supper last night," she began, "I saw that William and Mr Anderson were having a long chat. I asked later and that's where I got the little information I have given you. Mr Anderson will know more, I suspect, if you want to ask him. After his involvement in the cat and bird business, he seems to be the one young William turns to."

Custance paused at the door. He had heard too much of Mr Anderson since his return – when he *was* in the House, he liked to overhear the boys' chatter – and it irritated him.

"Doug likes to be hands-on, doesn't he? A bit too much in some ways. He needs to see that part of my system, an essential part, is to develop in the older boys a real sense of responsibility and initiative. Anyway, I shall ring Mrs O'Connell."

"But Mr Custance," said Matron, who now felt pushed into some sort of defence of self as well as concern for Mr Anderson, "there are surely times when some boys need a lot of attention. Just sometimes. Mr Anderson seems to recognise those times, as, I hope, do I. When they really need it."

The speech became a little jerkier, less confident, as it progressed, but there was in Matron South a strong determination to stand up for straightforward truths. She was not a philosopher – just a very caring, astute matron. She was concerned that she had said too much but also content that she had finally said something that was of great importance to her. Custance was somewhat thrown. He rallied quickly.

"As do we all, Matron," but he said it without much relish. He waved the note at her, nodded ambiguously and went off to make the phone call. His mind, however, was on Doug Anderson. Fraser had warned him and, little as he liked the deputy, a man in whom he would never confide, he began to feel under threat. And so he sat glumly over lunch, still feeling uncommonly ill at ease, revolving in his head a notion of asking that Anderson be moved to another house, in the interests of keeping him fresh. It was always bad for staff to get stale, after all.

Ben Fraser sat at the staff table pushing a crumbed fish fillet this way and that, wondering if he had the will to tackle it effectively. He was irritated that matters were not falling readily into place for him and his irritation showed in a sudden wish to fling the fish aside. But he restrained himself: if he couldn't control a dead cod, how could he hope to control his staff?

He was irritated because, though he told himself, over and over again, that he had handled the interview with Felicity Madigan earlier that day superbly and had stood his ground as his position entitled him to do, he nevertheless knew that interaction with Maya Cameray, for the time being, had to be put aside. There were times for inciting opposition, so as to win, but, with so much going on at the moment, this was not one of those times. He did not like feeling that there were fences around him, circumscribing his actions, but there it was and he would have to put up with it. He gave the fish an unnecessarily savage poke.

The person he most wanted to blame was Doug Anderson. If he had had no proof, on a past occasion, of Anderson's meddlesomeness, nevertheless he felt it to be there. Anderson would have to be put down, or out. He had once hinted rashly to Flem Harry that it would be out, and soon. Regrettably, he had not been able to pull that off and the thought made him glance furtively at the headmaster, sitting further along the same table: there was a man who refused to see trouble, no matter how plain it was. And Flem Harry – there was another problem! He had confided somewhat recklessly in his source and that very source might transform itself into a threat. Harry was not to be trusted; there was little difference, Fraser thought, between source and traitor, and so communication had been cut off. But the notion of a lurking threat remained.

He remembered, suddenly, how Harry had tried to tell him something about Anderson and Charles Herbert. It had been their last conversation and Fraser had had to cut it brutally short, to push Harry away. But was there something to which he should have paid attention? Anderson had apparently been deep in conversation with Herbert on the day on which Herbert's appointment as chaplain had been announced. Could there be anything in that? He could not tell who had been consulting whom (for Fraser there was no such thing as a friendly chat, for every 'chat' had its subtext) but it was certainly an odd pairing. Perhaps it was another thing to watch, so as to prevent unhelpful alliances. He put that matter to one side, as he did the fish. He bit ferociously into an apple and reflected that in Madigan, Anderson and Harry there were more than enough problems and frustrations, more than any loyal and competent deputy should have to face.

If Fraser faced too many miry issues, Parslow felt that he had faced only one that day, but it was one that made him most uncomfortable. He should have been feeling gleeful, a true master of all he surveyed. The building of the new boarding house was a reality now, not just an idea. By the time of the fair there would be an emerging structure to show to the crowds, who would be able to feel the substance of his great plan, not just gaze at plans and sketches. As for the fair itself, all the key arrangements were made, everything was slotting together like so many jigsaw pieces expertly handled. His council was eager for it to happen and he was sure that it would raise funds beyond even Professor Donald's expectations. But the merest thought of his chairman reminded him of the cloud, possibly the storm that was biding its time.

He had received a letter that morning from Donald and it had begun as he had expected it would: a list of council members who would be available for various times and roles over the weekend of the fair and confirmation that he and Irene would be there for the whole weekend and would he kindly make the visitors' flat available. So far so good. Then:

"I never like to be approached by Charlie Fanning, a man, as we know only too well, of unreliable temper and no great love of facts. But yesterday he obtruded himself on my notice in a way I feel I must pass on to you, though exactly what you are to do with the information I admit I do not know. Fanning had had his boy, Hamish, whom he expects to be Prime Minister at least, up in town for the weekend and he wanted to tell me the gist of their conversation. Now this is Charlie Fanning talking, so we can't take it at face value. Still, according to Hamish, the College is not functioning as it should, partly because Mr Custance is a rather loose housemaster (wasn't he ill, earlier?) and partly because Mr Fraser, our deputy, is self-absorbed ("up himself" was the unfortunate phrase) rather than school-absorbed. There was also a reference to Mrs Fraser but I couldn't make any sense of that at all. In any case, I'd had enough of Mr Fanning firing off in all directions by then and I cut the conversation short. However, if there is any substance to the comments, you have a problem, or a nest of them, and if there is none, that will not stop Mr Fanning sounding off and thus creating one. I look forward to discussing this with you when next we meet."

Parslow had barely attended to the formalities at the end of the letter and, as he sat over his lunch (perhaps just a strong cup of tea and some cake would have been preferable) he experienced a settled gloom, a very rare thing in a normally optimistic man. "A nest of problems?" Indeed there were. And, as with any properly constructed nest, they would need a lot of disentangling.

Custance? He was beginning to feel that the man he had promoted, unwillingly it must be said, was not up to the job. The man liked to advance theories about students' initiative but Parslow himself favoured systems, especially when the manager was as totally and unfailingly competent as he was himself. But how could he confess that the occupant of one of the plum jobs in the College was out of his depth? He cursed inwardly, cursed Anderson for having let him down, cursed Custance for being weak and lazy and cursed Donald and Fanning together for forcing the matter on his attention, and maybe into the public's mind, too.

Then Fraser? Actually, he carried out many aspects of his role perfectly well. The arrangements for the fair were a case in point. They were clearly made and documented, with such loose ends as were bound to emerge neatly tied into the whole. But he was not so sure about Fraser's handling of people. There was nothing definite – but then he remembered the surely excessive outburst against Anderson and the muddle of the inspection. Further, if Professor Donald could not make sense of a reference to Mrs Fraser, Parslow certainly could. It occurred to him that the anonymous letter might well have come from Hamish Fanning. It had been an intelligent, pointed note, from a person with a grievance but who had thought long and hard about the best way to make their feelings known. Young Fanning fitted the profile well – but how was he to approach the boy on such a matter? He couldn't! At least, as far as he knew, there had been no further indiscretions by Mrs Fraser; but, as Parslow finally rejected his lunch, it came to him that as far as he knew might not be far enough. If things were going on out of his range of view, then he was not master of all he surveyed at all. Now, a gloomy headmaster will do no good to a school or to the people in it; but it made him gloomy to decide that all he could do was watch carefully and trust to the fair to turn everything to good. He might have gone on to reflect that in the past there were those who genuinely believed in alchemy, but he didn't. It was not in him to make that leap.

By the end of the day he felt even more perplexed. He had looked forward to the interview with his head of English whom he knew to be bright, energetic, ready to institute change. He was immensely glad to have her back; her absence, so soon after beginning at the College, had been genuinely inconvenient. He had given her some weeks to settle back in – surely half a term was enough time to put any grief one felt behind one – and now he wanted her to press forward. A sociable glass of wine and a good look at the future would bring his week to a very satisfactory conclusion. At least, those had been his thoughts in the morning. By lunch, as we know, his mood had darkened and the time with Felicity, if it lifted a corner of the gloom in some areas, was to intensify the darkness in another.

She was prompt, as he had expected. He ushered her into his comfortable sitting room, offered her a glass of his nicely chilled white and began in the obvious way. But Felicity did not want to wade through a recapitulation of five weeks.

"Headmaster, we both know that certain things here need to change. Why don't we get straight on to them?"

"You're a person after my own heart, Mrs Madigan," he responded. "All right – you start. But I will have my agenda too, as I'm sure you know."

In this way a fencing match began. Her first thrust, that there must be something better for Bert Cleary to do than to teach English – could there not be a unit on boatmaking in the woodwork course? – was met with the bland assurance that he would work on it for next year's timetable. Then Parslow brought up the matter of the inspection, wondering how far she had got in understanding that near mishap, to be told that she thought she knew pretty well what had gone wrong and that, with herself instead of Mr Fraser in the driving seat, such a thing would never happen again. And this gave her a useful opening.

"Mr Fraser seems to think he still has a role to play, though his grasp of English programming is somewhat deficient. He approached young Maya Camaray and suggested he show her how it's done. I have told him to back off, that it's clearly my area not his, and…"

"Are you sure he's not just keeping in touch with a new teacher, Felicity? That *is* part of his role."

"If so," and Felicity was really bristling now, "there are other and much more appropriate ways to do it."

This roused Parslow. Indeed, it shattered his expectation of a pleasant chat.

"That's strong language. Do you suggest something inappropriate?"

"I speak to you in absolute confidence, Headmaster. I am not really authorised to do so at all, but this is important. Maya did not feel comfortable with his suggestion of several one-on-one sessions of an evening and, given that Libby Caraton had also warned her to be careful of the man, I'd say inappropriate is the right word."

She stopped, knowing she had gone too far. She had broken her word to Maya, though she felt that she could trust Parslow to keep a confidence. What was more, she knew she had no basis on which to proceed, except a growing dislike of Ben Fraser. Parslow looked intently at her and then transferred his gaze to the window, all but dark by now.

"I have heard what you have said. I am not going to respond at all at this point."

Fair enough, thought Felicity. At least you haven't shouted me down. She decided to change the topic.

"As for the rest of the department, you have, as you know, a mostly reliable but not very distinguished group of English teachers. I'm happy with Doug and I've no doubt that Maya will be excellent. If Flem and Blaize came to you saying they wanted to move on, I hope you wouldn't stand in their way. That will sound harsh, but I have to be frank with you."

Again she paused, to see if he wanted more.

"You never knew Joe Simpson, did you? I think we're making progress."

"That may be, especially if the tales I've been told are not merely legends. But I have to tell you that Flem is a person I don't quite trust, and Blaize just needs a change, a fresh spark in his life and in his teaching. I like him well enough, but you're never going to have a top-line department with him in it. Solid, but not the best."

Parslow understood: if he was going to keep Felicity Madigan, as he wanted and needed to do, it would only be as head of a truly first-class department. There was, however, no immediate likelihood that he could meet her wishes on this.

"That's been a very frank assessment, Felicity, and I thank you most sincerely for it. A headmaster does not have a magic wand, or a way of creating silk purses. Now, are there ways in which we can more quickly alter the style, if not the personnel. One thing often leads to the other."

"You mean the way we go about the teaching? Most definitely. And you are right – a radical change in style might cause some to seek fresh pastures, mightn't it?"

She smiled at him and for another fifteen minutes expatiated on getting boys to think and analyse, not just to learn. Parslow warmed to the possibilities – change, for him, was of the essence – and he finally let Felicity go convinced that she was a gem of great price. He made himself a cup of tea and sat back in his favourite chair.

What did he make of it all? Her assessment of her department as teachers of English was pretty accurate. Should he try to move any of them on? Tricky! He would come back to that. Cleary? Was there a role elsewhere he could fill, as well as being rowing master? Probably, but she would have to wait until next year. And Harry? Very likely unreliable. He remembered the debating fiasco of the year before last; and he felt fairly certain that Flem's was the sotto voce voice at a recent staff morning tea. And Fraser? Here was a disturbing issue and he fell to wondering how often his deputy's name was going to crop up, always with ambiguous but troubling question marks against it. He could not connect the dots yet. With a great sigh he finished his cup of tea and prepared to go to the dining hall. He hoped to find a light meal there, for the day had weighed him down quite enough already.

Saturday brought with it the first real game of the football season. There had been practice matches, of course, but no crowd flocked to see them. But Saturday's games were to be against Baxter, a bigger and stronger school, one accustomed to handing out football lessons to all their opponents. It was best not to expect too much if you were playing Baxter.

The day was fine and although some underage games were played at various locations around the College during the morning, it was only at midday that the crowds began to assemble. Doug Anderson did not pretend to himself that it was to see his second XVIII perform at noon; rather it was to picnic in advance of the Firsts at two thirty. Nevertheless, it was heartening to see a crowd, mostly of College supporters, break away from their cold collations and champagne to clap a College boy from time to time, even if a thirty-five-point deficit at half-time suggested that a very heavy defeat might ensue.

Doug took his team into their changerooms at the interval and was puzzled at their attitude. For every contest they had won, Baxter had won three or four, and yet the one was all they could talk, or think, about. He wanted to tell them not to be too easily satisfied, that there were many aspects of their play on which they could improve. Just then, however, two people came in, one just to stand by and listen, one used to taking control.

"A really noble effort, boys!" barked out Ben Fraser. "Keep it up and you'll wear the other mob down. I know you can do it."

He smiled and made a gesture at the boys that could almost have been a benediction, though to Doug it felt more like a curse. He did not want merely a worthy effort, whatever that might mean. He wanted them to do the things that they had worked on at training and so he went amongst the group, reminding and re-enforcing, making one or two changes to positions but mostly insisting that their hard-practised strategies must be given every chance to work. When he drew them together, he did not rev them up to make a greater effort but urged them to execute good football. To his mind, that was what made the game so exciting and fulfilling.

He had the pleasure of witnessing some genuine improvement. At three-quarter-time the deficit was forty-two points, to be sure, but both teams had played well and Doug drew his group to the side of the oval for the short break allowed with real enthusiasm. As he did so, he overheard the Baxter coach say to his players that they had loafed for long enough. It was good to get under the other team's skin, even if only briefly.

Fortunately, Ben Fraser was away on the other side of the oval. He and Mrs Fraser were working their way round groups of parents and so Doug had no fear of interruption. He told the boys what had worked, sometimes extremely well, and what still hadn't. He told one boy who was plainly hobbling to put on his tracksuit and get ice for his ankle, so as to prevent further damage, and he sent his team out determined to make further inroads on the Baxter dominance. As he took up his position by the scoreboard, he was surprised to see Charles Herbert approach him.

"You're on the right track, Doug. The boys did you proud in that third quarter, all things considered. You can't really compete with their rucks, so you're behind from the start. But I like the way you're working with them."

It turned out that Herbert had heard a good deal of Doug's (and Fraser's) half-time contributions and had been on the edge of the group at the recent break, too.

"I'll leave you to watch them," he said. "Good luck."

Within ten seconds Doug had forgotten Herbert, because the game began and he had the great joy of seeing some things work better again. If he felt bound to emphasise to his players, half an hour later, that they had lost by thirty-three points, yet he was full of enthusiasm for what they had shown him and, perhaps recklessly, he not only congratulated the Baxter coach on a clear win but told him how much he was looking forward to a return fixture later in the season. Then he reminded himself that hubris was never a good thing. He went home, discovered that Jenny had just got Penelope up from her daytime nap and asked if they would come with him to watch the Firsts, which he was most definitely expected to do. The fresh air would do Penelope good, said Jenny, and they all returned to the oval.

The First XVIII game was not a success, not for the College, and the final margin of eighty points (102:22) ultimately reflected Baxter's willingness to be experimental when the game was already won and their inaccuracy and wastefulness more than the College's determination to hang on. In fact, the more Peter Gryce roared at his boys to play like men, the worse they got: 2 goals 12 to a solitary behind in the last quarter said it all. But that did not stop Ben Fraser from congratulating the boys as they trudged wearily from the field. He then saw the Andersons nearby and murmured to Doug that encouragement was always the right thing. Doug thought that Ben was rather selective in applying that policy and turned away.

As he did so, he came across Charles Herbert once again who, claiming that he needed to get to know the College more closely, had made an afternoon of it. He said hello to Jenny, lifted Penelope up and exclaimed at her size before her cry said that he had gone too far, and turned to Doug.

"I'd like to help out, if I can. You are on the right track. The Firsts' coach, I am sorry to say, is not. But only if you wouldn't mind."

"Of course. I'd be delighted," said Doug, "but…"

"It's all right, Doug. Since my work with the Stars, I've followed coaching and styles of play pretty closely. I'm not a dinosaur, but I suspect your Mr Gryce is."

The both looked over to where Gryce still had his players around him. He was red in the face and he made it clear he was not going to accept a similar performance again. But if you had asked the boys later exactly what it was they had to change, they could not have told you.

Doug and the chaplain-to-be shook hands warmly just as Ben and Sarah Fraser, who seemed always to be together, came past them once more.

"Organising prayer for your team, Mr Anderson?" said Mrs Fraser, quite loudly, and, delighted at her wit, passed on without waiting for a reply. It was as well she did, or she might have heard Doug mutter something about Mrs Proudie.

Charles Herbert thought he could spare an hour on Tuesday afternoon and went on his way. Peter Gryce came by and muttered to Doug that Baxter didn't seem to have their usual depth this year and Doug, no longer sure whether to feel cheerful or sour, took his family home.

There was a sequel, an unusual one. At morning tea on the following Monday, Allan Parslow approached Doug to say that a parent, an angry Mr Trumble, had bailed him up on Saturday and complained that his son had been denied any opportunity to participate in the last quarter of the seconds' game on Saturday. This was a parent who made significant donations to the College and Parslow did not want to put him off-side. What should he say?

"Tell Mr Trumble that Chris came to me at three-quarter-time complaining of a very sore ankle. He could barely walk and I told him to come off and get ice straight away, so as not to cause further damage."

Doug was plainly irritated at the stupidity of the parental complaint, but no more so than Parslow when he rang the influential parent back to explain. "Should have told him to run through the pain. That's what we did in my day, and what Peter Gryce would say, if Chris were in the team he should be in."

Even Parslow could see that the comment about Gryce was deadly accurate. That was the problem.

For the rest of the weekend, Jenny and Doug Anderson wanted to chat about anything but school. On the way back from the oval, Jenny had referred, in a puzzled way, to Sarah Fraser's snide pretence at cleverness but had put the matter aside in the face of Doug's evident frustration. No, much better to leave it alone, and they spent the weekend talking of places they would love to see, cooking (Doug), drawing with, or for, Penny, (Jenny) and enjoying Sunday afternoon drinks with Sylvia Marriette and others at her house in the town. Doug was rostered to be in the House on Monday and he came home, after his duties were done, to a blissfully sleeping wife and child. Both of them felt that by the Tuesday evening they might be able to go over recent events and see where things stood. A little of that happened but the full discussion they had anticipated did not eventuate. In one sense it was not necessary.

Doug was pleased with his Tuesday afternoon football practice. He had treated the boys fairly gently, amused that they should complain so loudly of soreness after their exertions of the Saturday. Chris Trumble had watched from the sidelines, supported by an elegant walking stick and some very prominent bandaging. Charles Herbert had come, for only half an hour as it turned out, but he had been introduced to the squad and had explained briefly what he thought he could do to help. Doug had let him take a small group aside for ruck practice and they had come back enthused about how 'The Rev' had shown them how to outmanoeuvre bigger and stronger boys. So it had been a happy practice, at least until the boys had been dismissed.

"What was that chaplain fellow doing here, then, Doug? Can't know anything about how we do things here, not yet."

This unpromising salvo from Peter Gryce was met with a warm commendation of Herbert by Doug.

"The boys responded well to him. I think we can both make good use of him, next term more so."

"Don't need it," grumbled Gryce. "And don't want it. My boys need to hear one message only, from me!"

Happy enough to keep 'The Rev' to himself, Doug changed the subject.

"Any injury concerns for you, Peter? I'm likely to be without Trumble this week. You probably saw him hobbling about."

"I'm told his father was just the same. No, we came through unscathed and I don't want to make changes after only one outing. Looks indecisive."

Again Doug was content to agree. He ambled home for a shower, for some dinner and some quiet playing time with Penny. Classes for the next day were in hand and so he felt, all round, unusually comfortable.

Libby Caraton was there, playing with Penelope and chatting companionably with Jenny. Consequently, Doug said little more than hello and went for his shower. He was oddly shy of any intimacy with

Jenny in front of others; and he only smiled at Penny, who was utterly absorbed with some jigsaws made of large wooden pieces. He came back fifteen minutes later, feeling refreshed.

"It's been an OK day for you, by the look of you? Tuesday generally is," said Jenny.

"Nothing out of the ordinary," Doug said. "Gryce was grumpy, which means nothing. Year 10 were scatty in the last class of the day, but that's normal too."

Libby looked up from the floor at that. "I found the same, after lunch," she said. "I thought I might bribe them with a French snail race, but…"

"Really? What a great idea!"

"Oh Doug," came in Jenny. "Can't you see she's kidding you?"

He blushed. No, he hadn't realised it, he said, but it gave him a good idea for Year 8 at some point. They stared at him, getting half a grin in response, and then he asked Libby how she was managing half-way through another term.

"I'm fine," she said. "I've got my routines, and because French is a fairly small part of the school's operations, I'm left largely to myself."

"That's because you do it too well for anyone to interfere," said Jenny. "And speaking of interference, is there any update on Maya and the odious Fraser?"

Doug looked as though he didn't want to see Libby put on the spot in this way but her relationship with Jenny was too close for such a question to cause any stress.

"As far as I can see, the pompous ass is lying low, keeping away. Maya told me she'd had a chat with Felicity Madigan and perhaps that helped."

"It's good she feels she can confide in someone in authority," said Jenny and then looked somewhat anxiously at Doug. He was not going to be drawn.

"Dinner smells good. Can you stay and eat with us, Libby?"

"If I do, I'll have to go straight after. Year 12 did a test today. But thanks, I'd like that." She turned back to Penny on the floor. "Let's show Daddy how clever you are at the puzzles, eh?"

Libby turned out the pieces of a hand-painted farmyard puzzle and, to Doug's great relief, school vanished for a time. He kept it at bay after the meal, too, when he read, complete with his own idea of the characters' voices, *Icecreams for Rosie*. Penny loved the exaggerated voices – for some reason, Old Bill Coley became an irate Yorkshireman and the pilot who saves the day a posh BBC newsreader – and to Doug's delight used one of her favourite words, Again!, until it was bedtime. It was all of eight o'clock before he and Jenny settled down with a mug of tea and time for each other.

"Work today was good," said Jenny. "I've now got most things arranged for the spring exhibition."

He smiled at her. They both knew how, for Sylvia, all years began with spring and there had to be a start-of-the-year show in the gallery.

"And it's still all sculpture for this year? Or have you broadened it?"

"I've convinced Sylvia that that's broad enough."

For a moment, Jenny was lost in contemplation of the display as she could already see it. At Sylvia's insistence, it contained two of her own pieces and she and Doug were very pleased at this. He understood her rapt smile.

"You'll be the centrepiece, of course."

"Don't be silly. But Doug, I'm glad it's all nearly arranged, because Sylvia goes to the national project in only six weeks. They have delayed the start of the project by a few weeks – I've no idea why. So, by the time of the spring exhibition…" She trailed off, again lost in thought.

"You'll be in charge? Yes, I know. It will be a great time for you."

"I hope so," she said and then faltered. "I hope it will be an OK time for all of us." She paused again, then, "I **am** looking forward to it. It's a chance, an opportunity."

"And you must grab it and make the most of it. We'll all fit in around it. You'll be able to see how it feels."

His certainty reassured her.

"I want us both to have opportunities, Doug. Do you ever regret…?"

"We're not going there," he interrupted briskly. "It's one thing to see how feeble Custance is – but that doesn't mean I wanted to be there myself."

It wasn't what she had meant but it didn't seem to be the time for might-have-beens. She took their empty mugs and stood up.

"Have you marking to do tonight?"

"No, actually. I'm not like Libby with a Year 12 test to mark. I thought a whole evening off would be better. For some reason," and then he cocked an ear, as though to hear if Penny was unexpectedly stirring, "it feels like a night for celebration. We could start on *War and Peace*, or…"

"I'd rather celebrate in bed."

And so they did.

CHAPTER SIX

Parslow was satisfied that all arrangements had been made. He knew that the concerts and dramatic performances would take place and be of a good standard, because he had dropped in on the dress rehearsals. He knew that the refreshments tent and surrounding area were ready. He knew his various speeches by heart and he had the ceremonial plaque locked securely in his desk. He knew the football matches would take place, though even Parslow was humble enough to admit that he could not control the results. Against St Justin's, there had to be a reasonable chance of victory, he supposed. And he had organised good weather: the forecast for the entire weekend was fine and clear. He felt more or less at ease, pleasantly exhilarated, beneath it all satisfied with the hard work he – and others, he had to admit it – had undertaken. It would be a grand College occasion.

He sat at his desk next to a barely touched ham sandwich and the last few crumbs of cake, sipping his tea and leafing through the programme. Friday, this very afternoon, would be a relatively gentle start to proceedings, he reminded himself, before the intense activity of Saturday and Sunday. He had decreed that classes were to run to their normal routine, through to three fifteen, because he did not want hundreds of boys to be at a loose end for any longer than was necessary. There was to be a giant picnic tea on the floodlit oval at five thirty and then the first performance at eight o'clock. For *A Midsummer Night's Dream,* Libby Caraton had, for the last few weeks, called in the assistance of Felicity Madigan (to young Mr Rascham's chagrin) and the play was being given a sprightly appearance. He smiled as he thought of Cramer in Year 9 (now what was his first name?) as a gangly sort of Puck, too tall, really, but with just the right sort of insouciant energy. He had seemed, when Parslow had chanced to drop in, to be delighted at the confusion he caused, utterly unrepentant, as a Puck should be. It would never do in real school life, of course, but it was fun to see such mayhem.

That reflection caused a frown. He had overheard some staff refer to his May Fair as the May-hem and he had not been amused. "Get thee behind me, Satan," he had wanted to say, with meagre theological relevance, because any undermining of his great fundraising fair could not be tolerated. Jocularity was no excuse: the fair had to be seen as a grand exhibition of all the things that the College was best at and known for – apart from academic results, that is. He was determined to pull it off, to draw immense funds from the old boys and to show to all, once again, how truly it was his school. When it all worked as he planned, the College would shine yet more brightly as the pre-eminent school in the land!

Filled with such noble reflections, he walked out to the edge of the ovals; one was set up to be the refreshment centre and meeting place for convivial chat, the other was marked out for Saturday's football. Fresh white paint on all the lines and markings was an uplifting sight. And then he saw, presumably also checking final details, Mr Hattingly, the property manager, another stickler for precision, though not a man of vision. Well, you wouldn't expect that in a property manager, would you? And one vision, one's own, was quite enough.

"It all looks wonderful, doesn't it?" said a beaming Parslow.

"It does." And then, evincing vision of a different kind, "The tent is an abnormally large one, Mr Parslow. I do hope no big wind gets up."

"Nothing forecast, Mr Hattingly, nothing forecast."

Parslow wandered on with the air of the only one whose forecasts count. He came to the library and, looking in, saw Mr Masterson and what was probably his twentieth century history class. It was a very promising class, much better than the ancient history group. Parslow smiled: he did not like to think of the College as being identified with a bygone era. Look forward – be on the move – keep people guessing, and applauding!

There was actually nothing more for him to do. He passed by the English block – it might be a little tired, perhaps, could be his next major building project, but it would have to do for a while yet – and saw Mr Harry standing on his desk. What on earth could that mean? With Harry you could never tell and often it was better not to ask. He preferred simply to note things, file them away for reference, or use, later on. He passed by Mr Anderson, who must have been enthusing his Year 8s about the performances of Shakespeare, because he had got, presumably from props, a huge donkey's head and was placing it on top of a grinning, though probably embarrassed, boy. Since everyone really wanted classes to be over and the festivities to begin, he was relieved to see teachers engaging their students in positive ways. But from the top of a desk?

The picnic tea – sandwiches, miniature pies and sausage rolls, apples, water – was enjoyed by a mob who left the oval remarkably tidy. This was an area in which Fraser excelled. Parslow knew about his deputy's mania for a tidy desk and office and, on this occasion, could only agree that an army of bins and an army of Year 7s to carry them about and fill them had worked splendidly. Mr Fraser beamed at the Year 7 brigade as though they were in fact parts of *his* performance, a performance to outshine all others in exactness and effect. Parslow let him have his moment of glory – he was ready for much bigger things.

On that same Friday evening, Sam Baker collected Ralph Langton at precisely six thirty and they made the two-hour drive to the region of the College together. They had agreed that they were not needed that evening and planned to drive straight through to their local motel. They began with their usual pleasantries.

"That bugger can sure organise the weather, can't he!" – Sam.

"Things continue to fall his way, it seems." – Ralph.

"Remember your chest of tablets, did you?"

"Do I rattle that badly? Will the weekend add another chapter to your memoirs?"

So for a time they talked about their current lives, of the little things that made it up, things much closer to cabbages than to kings. However, as they got closer to the College, conversation drifted to the times they had shared there and what the weekend might bring.

"Parslow sent me the programme," said Langton and got a grunting nod in response. "So you understand that we are, if not the star attraction" (a snort from Sam) "at any rate meant to be 'on show', available for old students to chat to us. I take it that we are meant to show a lively interest in whatever they have done since school."

"Lively might stretch you out a bit, Ralph." Then, after a pause, "I can admit to you I'm quite looking forward to it. Of course, it depends on who comes, but we did deal with some interesting boys."

Ralph recalled their earlier conversation.

"I suppose I'm quite keen too. But I have got out of the way of thinking in school terms, Sam. It's a long time ago already, I feel."

Sam was disposed to be sympathetic. He said, "a couple of years out is an age. But ten is not so much, and twenty years since schooldays feels like a blink. You'll see, they'll remember it perfectly. We just listen."

"I hope it's that simple. I couldn't stand an inquisition, a post-mortem, on the Cholmondeley prize, for example."

Sam grinned at that, a reference to one of their last 'incidents' together, a skirmish he had unexpectedly won.

"We'll head that one off and remind them instead of days when we used to win at sport. Or days when they never did any homework. Or the trouble they gave Matron."

Sam chuckled comfortably but stopped at Ralph's rejoinder.

"I don't imagine you'll want to talk about giving trouble to a matron. There are so many subjects one needs to steer clear of."

Sam agreed, if not wholeheartedly, and there was silence for a time.

"I don't think there's been a lot of staff turnover, has there? We'll know most of the teachers, I suppose."

"Yes, we will, but I doubt they'll trouble us. We are there for the old boys, and the staff will limit themselves to a few polite phrases. I already have my stock response by heart: 'I'm better than ever. How about you?'"

Sam roared with delight at the implications. They reached the turn-off to the College; it felt strange to pass it by but it was not their destination for the night. They drove on for five minutes, found their motel and made arrangements for the morning.

"Do you know what I'd like to do, Sam, early, before things get under way? I'd like to do a walk of the whole campus. Will you come with me? We could tramp our patch once more. Maybe it will ease us into the day."

Sam took a moment to consider that.

"Yes, all right," he said. "We could leave here early – there's nothing to keep us in this place – and do a tour of inspection, just ourselves. We wouldn't even need to report in first, would we?"

"We'll be incognito, just for a bit."

Sam wondered briefly if Ralph was descending to an old boys' prank, as others would tomorrow. No, he could see the sense in the idea. To pretend that one could just switch on, in full reminiscence mode, at ten a.m. as per the programme would not be wise. He thanked Ralph and they parted for the evening.

The Frasers had enjoyed Friday. They witnessed arrangements that had been carefully made work fluently and were delighted that, when they thanked some of the chief participants – Hattingly, Caraton, the performers – they were dutifully thanked in turn. Sarah was so pleased with Ben's achievements that she rose first on the Saturday morning to bring him a cup of tea in bed. She was in the kitchen, reaching down two mugs and the sugar bowl (Ben would need an extra boost, she felt) when she heard a rustling of some sort at the front door. She listened for a knock, but there was none. She stood still and thought for a moment; then, deciding that she had heard something, a possum perhaps, she went to check.

As she expected, there was nobody at the front door. What was there was a very large bunch of flowers, lying gracefully on the mat.

"Oh Ben, there was no need for this," she said out loud and smiled. It was so unexpected – she couldn't recall the last time he had thought of such a thing. That he had had time to organise it in the midst of all his arrangements for the fair astonished her. She carefully picked up the flowers and withdrew the card from its tiny envelope. She gasped: 'From all your admirers in Year 12.'

She must have let out a shriek for, as she stood there in astonishment, a still sleepy husband came up behind her.

"Did you call out? Flowers? What on earth…?"

Sarah Fraser turned to him with a look of bewilderment and pain. Had she thought more quickly, she would have thrown the flowers away before Ben had known anything about them, but now he reached for the card in her hand.

"What on earth does this mean, Sarah?" He was still dozy and it took him some moments to read her pain. Then he burst out: "Who can have done this? What sort of an animal does a thing like this?"

Sarah was immobilised by the incident. But Ben, fearing passers-by, took her firmly by the arm and soon had her in the kitchen, sitting at the table. He saw the tea, pretty well stewed and not so hot any more, and brought her a mug. He was trying very hard to put the pieces together.

That the arrival of the flowers was totally unexpected to Sarah was patently obvious. Was it, then, a mistake? No – the card bore no name, just the message, but the whole thing was too preposterous for a mistake. So was it students from Year 12? They had no reason to insult his wife in such a way, as the word admirers seemed intended to do. A staff member? Outrageous, and it would not explain the reference to Year 12. It made no sense at all.

"I am sorry that this has upset you so, my dear," he said. "It's all most unpleasant and I will certainly get to the bottom of it. Maybe not today," and he interrupted himself to think through his schedule, "but I will find out."

Sarah was in such a state of shock that she had barely any idea of what he was saying. She was insulted, but she was even more bewildered. She lived with the comfortable illusion that she and her husband were indispensable to the College and that therefore all the College loved, or at least respected, them. Nobody, she felt, could have any reason to attack and upset her in this fashion. She did not run through possibilities, as Ben had done; she simply experienced a profound disturbance, a jolting of her certainties.

"Come upstairs, Sarah. We have to begin the day, you know."

"Please throw these away," she whimpered.

He took the flowers out to a bin beside the kitchen door but he hung on to the card. He did indeed want to get to the bottom of it and the card could be the vital piece of evidence. The less either of them saw of the flowers the better.

They were prompt, as they had trained themselves, over many years, to be. It was only 8.35 and Baker and Langton, having parked well away from the refreshment tent, began their circuit of the campus. Baker wanted to avoid any area near the House and so they headed away from the ovals, passed the groundsman's shed, skirted the back of the pool and the rowing palace and came out near the beginning of the copse. They looked back.

"Except for that monstrous building scar, there's not really much change."

"None at all. But who's going in to the new boarding house? Surely they won't just transfer your old empire there, Sam?"

"It would be unwise, and unnecessary. He could include whatever technology he wants in the House as it stands. He must be hoping to expand."

They looked at each other, each wondering how high the other's eyebrows could go.

"Are you serious, Ralph? Co-education comes to the College?"

"Girls!" Langton sighed it out, as though no words could convey the depth of his feeling.

"Might be a good idea," said Sam, but he got only a glare in reply. He gestured at Langton that they should continue their peregrination.

They took the winding path through the copse and breathed a little easier as they absorbed its quietness. Presently they came across Fred Jones, the chief groundsman, wearing heavy gloves and carrying a sack.

"Hello, Fred. You're not on the track of flood damage this time, I'm sure," said Baker, recalling the famous night of the storm. "How are you, anyhow?"

"It's nice to see you, Mr Baker. And you, Mr Langton. No, no flood. I've just been keeping a watch on this area of late. Lots of dead birds, mangled, probably feral cats coming in from the bushland. You can't have dead birds lying around if people want to take a quiet stroll, can you?"

Jones was going about his work in his phlegmatic fashion, but Sam could barely hide a smile at the notion that, with grand festivities happening at the main school, anyone would really want to stroll. Perhaps an old boy wanting to re-visit smoking haunts but even that seemed hardly likely.

"I must get back to Mr Hattingly, see if he wants anything," said Jones and he went off, swinging his hessian sack.

"We had our difficulties," muttered Langton, "but feral cats is a new one on me." He seemed displeased at such an intrusion into civilised College life.

"If anyone is to deal with it, Fred will. Two of the soundest people in the College, he and Hattingly."

Langton grunted. But then, he had been used to giving orders to such people, not working closely with them. They walked on and ultimately came out near some old courts and the new basketball centre, so that, from a new angle, they once again looked across the sweep of College buildings and ovals.

"There's the tent. Let's find the head and then it will be almost time for us to play gracious listeners."

"That's the first time you've ever so much as hinted that I might be called gracious," said Baker. "I'm not sure I feel it – but let's put on our jolly faces. I hope tea is already available. I need one. But Ralph – no cake, please no cake."

They could laugh freely at Parslow's little quirks now. They approached the tent, where they did indeed find the headmaster, chatting with Ben Fraser. He looked delighted to see his former colleagues.

"Ah, my star attractions – Welcome!"

They both winced.

Sam managed the first response. "It's good to be here, Allan. And hello, Mr Fraser. You both have the school looking a picture."

"Everything attended to," muttered Langton. "Even to the removal of dead birds from the copse."

Parslow did not know what to make of that but Fraser was instantly alert and, hearing that Fred Jones knew all about it, said that he had better find that worthy groundsman. He hurried away.

"He's not quite the calming influence you were, Ralph, but he does a sound enough job."

Langton seemed scarcely gratified by that remark and suggested a cup of tea if it were available.

"Of course, Ralph. Tea – and cakes too, of course." He ushered them into the tent and they joined the very short queue. Langton was immediately pulled aside by an eager old boy and Sam stood gazing about him, until a slap on the shoulder made him turn to see a grinning face he knew he ought to recognise. Yes, Oliver Wriggley, who, in earlier days, would never have dared to slap his housemaster anywhere. Baker sighed inwardly and began his duties.

"Fred! I say, Fred, come over here," called Fraser as he approached the groundsman's shed. "Come here away from any passing ears."

"Is something the matter, Mr Fraser?"

"That's what I need to ask you. Is the copse infested with dead birds or something?"

Fraser wanted to appear as though the matter were of no great significance, but his agitation showed. Fred Jones, however, was never agitated.

"Well, Mr Fraser, I didn't want dead birds, not even a couple, as I've found this morning, where anyone taking a walk of the school might see them. I've been aware of the problem for a week or so, and it's cats, I reckon, getting in from the bushland. The way the bodies are torn open says cats to me."

The evidence was plain to Jones but not to Fraser.

"It's just that it's the same spot where a young boy, O'Connell, was killing cats a while ago."

"I recall that. But didn't he kill cats to save birds? Anyhow, you can tell by the way…"

"Yes, thank you, Fred, I'll follow it up," and Fraser began to walk briskly back around the oval, back to the main throng.

"But Mr Fraser," but it was in vain, for Fraser was on the hunt. "It's cats."

They ended up enjoying their conversations, most of them. Ralph Langton found that those old boys who wanted to speak with, or at, him wanted only to hold forth about how good the good old days had been. If they were truly the best years of their lives, Langton pitied them, and even more he pitied the wives and children he heard about. Nevertheless, it was comforting to hear that fond memories lingered and that he himself was not remembered as either a tyrant or as totally distant, remote.

For Sam, things worked differently. Over many cups of tea, he was reminded of things that he had done, or was alleged to have done, and he found that he could chuckle at the anecdotes, especially if they were apocryphal. Hardly a student from his last two or three years in the House was in evidence, which was perhaps to be expected; but from ten years ago came the Hansom boys, Harry and Hugh, who wanted to relive with him all their pranks, of the kind only identical twins can perpetrate. As the young, or middle-aged, men came and went, taking in a tour of the site or finding others of their own vintage, Sam realised that there was nothing to be afraid of in coming back to the College. He might even do it again, in another decade or so.

Shortly before midday, Allan Parslow and Gregory Donald entered the refreshments tent, fresh from the eleven o'clock tour of the construction site. Nearly fifty former students, some partnered, had come and approved and many of them were exactly the possible donors the College was energetically targeting. Hamish O'Loughlin, the old boys' representative on the College council, would add strength to the appeal at the special tour on Sunday, but for now both men were very satisfied with how things were proceeding.

"They are enthusiastic, that's clear," said Parslow with much rubbing of hands.

"We must keep at them," was Donald's rejoinder. "Many a promised donation never materialises. But you have organised a fine festival, Allan. It is all very encouraging."

They noticed Langton and came across to him. Gregory Donald, in particular, was pleased to see him, knowing him to have been as loyal and as capable a deputy as a school could ever get.

"You look wonderfully well, Ralph. I take it that retirement is agreeing with you. And so, I hope, is your visit to us this weekend."

It was a little too formally expressed but Professor Donald was not the heartiest of men.

"I've had a most enjoyable morning, thank you. And there is so much more to look forward to..." (Donald raised half an eyebrow at the dangling preposition) "... particularly the performances. Are they up to scratch, Allan?"

Parslow, who would not have known how to undangle a preposition if he had needed to, beamed. "The play last night was excellent. Wait until you see Puck. He made my hair stand on end."

"I can see how Lady Macbeth might do that, but Puck?" laughed Langton. "Well, I shall see for myself."

The headmaster noticed Sam Baker trying to sidle, unnoticed, out of the tent and called to him to join them. There also appeared Irene Donald, who had lingered after the tour to chat to other council members. She had even got a word or two out of Cecily Boots and had come with her into the tent. So quite a formicable group was formed, one which Sam was only too ready to leave.

"I... er... I wanted," he said, casting around rapidly for an excuse, "to wish young Anderson the best of luck. I imagine he is still foolishly fanatical about his football and his game begins in a few moments. I might see you all at the oval."

With a neatly rising inflexion, he escaped as quickly as he could, overhearing, as he left the tent, Harry Hansom introduce himself to another old boy as Hugh, with roars of laughter. Sam tried to tell himself that at least some of the old boys had grown up.

Already the oval surrounds were filling up. There were family groups, as always, but for this weekend the groups were merging in unaccustomed ways. Some individuals wandered from group to group, renewing an acquaintance here and there or looking, perhaps a little anxiously, for a place to settle. Sam also wandered, content just to nod or wave and he soon found himself near the scoreboard, where Doug Anderson had stationed himself. It was obvious that the younger man would have little time to spare for pleasantries.

"I'm just walking by to wish you good luck, Doug. I'll hope to catch up with you and Jenny over the weekend, and your daughter, little... er..."

"Penelope, Sam. Yes, that would be fine. The game's just starting."

I never had a passion quite like that, said Sam to himself as he ambled away. Maybe the clocks? Even then, it was an escape from reality. For that young man, football seems to be the only reality. Sad, really. And Sam completed a circuit of the oval, still as unaware of the truth of Doug as ever. He managed to ignore a goal to each team and he just registered a cheery wave from Hugh Hansom: *he* had never had any trouble distinguishing the twins. Simple, really!

The second XVIII game wore away, neither side ever gaining a clear ascendancy. By three-quarter-time, the surrounds of the oval were packed. Almost the entire school was there, including staff and their families, not to mention students' families, old boy groups, and even squads of St Justin's supporters, eager for victory. In amongst it all were the Frasers, spreading cheer far and wide. They came upon the Custances and Ben drew Barney aside for a brief chat, leaving the wives to congratulate each other, and thus themselves, on their remarkable spouses.

Ben jumped straight in, not wanting to waste too much of the day on what might turn out to be a dead end.

"I've been speaking to Fred Jones, Barney, about dead creatures in the copse. Birds this time, quite a few, spread over several days, maybe even weeks."

"Oh yes?" Custance was not making the required connection. "Birds do die, you know, Ben; it happens all the time."

"Not by having their guts ripped out, they don't! Now look here, Barney, remind me of that O'Connell boy of yours. He was the one in trouble over something like this before, as I recall. It was the case you chose to conceal from me."

"Ages ago, Ben. Anyway, he was into saving birds, not torturing them."

"It's in the copse again, it can't be a coincidence." Fraser was so keen to have a culprit that, like the good politician he was, he chose to ignore inconvenient facts. "Today's obviously no good," he went on, "but send him to me after dinner tomorrow, when all this," he waved expansively, "is finally over. Then I'll get to the bottom of it."

Custance doubted that very much but he could not refuse to send a boy to the deputy. Anyway, he didn't want to have to deal with it himself.

"As you like. But it seems very out of character to me." Then, wanting very much to change the topic, he gestured at the field: "The boys have got a couple of goals ahead. Maybe Anderson will have a win. Good for him."

There was no sarcasm in the remark, though Fraser wished there had been. He did not relish the idea of Anderson winning anything.

"Just send me the boy, Barney," he said grumpily, and they rejoined the ladies.

Halfway through the last quarter, things had indeed looked promising for the College second team. They were thirteen points up, the biggest margin of a very tight game, and they were clearly winning more of the ball. Five minutes later the difference was four points. St Justin's had rallied, aided by a couple of bad errors by College players, and only inaccuracy in front of goal had prevented them from taking the lead. Doug could sense his boys panicking and he knew that, if they did, they would surely lose. He felt more or less helpless.

Just then, a ridiculously large pack flew for a mark right in front of him. Of course, any boy with sense would have stayed down to collect the crumbs but, sensing glory, they had all said farewell to sense and to team tactics. The pack rose (not very high) and it fell, very heavily, so that the unlucky College boy who had been the foundation of a now collapsed building was totally winded. He lay stretched out, a very odd shade of grey, and the umpire called a halt to proceedings. Boys gathered round their teammate, even those who had just now conspired to squash him, and then they called to Mr Anderson to come to the rescue. Inevitably, some minutes passed: it takes time to check out a boy who is gasping for breath. A matron dashed into the midst of it all and seemed about to blame the umpire for allowing such a thing to occur, when the boy stood up, wobbled, and sat again. Between Doug Anderson and the matron, they got him, breathing painfully but certainly breathing, to the side of the oval. The umpire seemed to think that he was now in charge again and signalled to the timekeepers that he was about to make a restart. He would have, too, but he realised in time that the St Justin's coach had used the interruption to address his boys in a huddle. This was not quite the thing, and the umpire went over to remonstrate. The further minute lost gave Anderson, who had completely lost track of the game, the time he needed.

"Chris, you're on, not in the centre, go to full forward, send Paddy to the ruck, tell Billy to move to half-back. Spud won't be back on. Hurry!"

It was barked out like a message in Morse code, though, truth to tell, Doug had little idea what he was doing. He was just filling gaps. Nevertheless it had sounded impressive and Trumble hastened to obey. He took up his unaccustomed post, told the others of the coach's new arrangements, and, as the umpire finally began play, he heard a voice – it sounded like his father, he thought with a sinking feeling – bellow above the general crowd noise, "Christopher, what are you doing there? Get into your position, boy!"

Many in his vicinity turned to see a red-faced man gesticulating wildly. Some, sensibly, offered him a drink. But Chris Trumble chose to ignore his father, which was just as well because, having let the opposition full-back easily repel one College advance, he wandered back into the goal square just in time for a long kick to float into his arms.

The father jumped to his feet and shouted, "Brilliant lead, boy! You fooled 'em!" Some in the vicinity offered him another drink. The crowd held its breath and Chris Trumble coolly booted a goal. There was barely a minute to go and even though the umpire, on the re-start, paid two outrageous free kicks to St Justin's players, it was to no avail. Mr Trumble led the cheering, telling all around him that Christopher was the hero of the hour. Mr Anderson and the St Justin's coach congratulated each other on a hard-fought game. The boys of the two schools mingled and shook hands and Mr Fraser was on hand to tell the College boys he always knew that they could do it. For his part, Allan Parslow waited his turn and congratulated the coach. And even the young man who had been winded joined in the merriment, convinced that he had contributed to victory, as indeed, by being flattened, he had.

The crowd experienced further excitement that afternoon, in that the first XVIII played a 67:67 draw against the St Justin's firsts. The two headmasters seemed to find this satisfactory, but nobody else did. And when, at the end of it all, Doug Anderson was heading wearily back home, he was accosted by Mr Trumble.

"I knew the boy had it in him. Stroke of genius on his part, wasn't it?"

"Well, I…"

"Won the game for us, didn't he? Straight to the firsts – he would have won it for them too."

Doug smiled, he hoped not too feebly, and said that selection for the firsts was up to Mr Gryce.

"Rubbish!" exclaimed Mr Trumble. "I've donated heaps of money to this school and I think…"

What he thought, if anything at all, was never explained because a couple of old boys of Trumble's vintage came by just then and suggested a drink or two. He winked grotesquely at Anderson and went off happily. Doug trudged home, wondering just how far the arm of such a buffoon could reach. All the way to the top?

At five o'clock on Saturday afternoon, sport suddenly gave way to culture. There was a second performance of the *Dream,* followed, after a brief dinner interval, by a concert at eight. All of a sudden, raucous cheering had to give way to civil applause, the language of coach Gryce to that of Shakespeare. It would have been interesting to hear Peter Gryce deliver his half-time address in iambic pentameters; but he would have thought such a mode of speech to belong to less robust souls.

It was at the five p.m. performance that Baker and Langton met up again, having pursued different courses for most of the afternoon. After the play, and before the concert, they were both to attend the headmaster's light refreshments on the Green, at which council members, significant old boys and local dignitaries were to be present.

"I expect to enjoy the play, and the concert. Can't say I'm looking forward to what's in between," grumbled Sam as they took their seats in the second row.

"Enjoy the food and drink, then Sam – but not too much of the drink. You're driving me back to the motel."

"I shall be fully in control, as usual."

"As bad as usual, eh? Do we know many of the names on the programme?" and Langton turned their attention to the performance, which shortly began.

It is a play much loved by many, not only for its romantic entanglements, or for the hilarious fifth act, when Bottom and his companions perform a farcical play for the duke, or for the fairy elements, led by Puck; but it is also memorable for the graciousness of Theseus to the players, for, when others would scoff at their ineptitude, it is Theseus (Shakespeare?) who notes that "the best in this kind are but shadows; and the worst are no worse, if imagination mend them." He is able to commend them on a play "notably discharged". It **is** an outrageously silly and incompetent performance – "I kiss the wall's hole, not your lips at all" – and the College audience enjoyed themselves enormously. But it was Theseus, played with both strength and restraint by Hamish Fanning, whom Baker wanted to congratulate afterwards and so, when all the others flocked to Bottom or Puck or Oberon, Sam sought out his former student.

"Well done, Hamish. I like what you did tonight very much. I hope you enjoyed it too."

"I did, and thank you, Mr Baker. I'm kind of sorry it's over – and relieved too, I suppose."

"Exactly the way you should feel. You held the stage…"

But here Sam was interrupted.

"Get yourself ready, Hamish. I'm taking you for a bite before the concert."

It was Mr Fanning, who, turning, realised that it was Sam Baker who had been talking with his son. He scowled. "Hello, Baker. You never thought my boy had it in him, did you?"

Hamish blushed and turned aside hastily, ashamed of such an unfair and ignorant remark. Sam did not answer it.

"Well done again, Hamish. Shall I see you onstage tonight?"

"Just in the choir. I pretend I'm a tenor, but that's fun too."

Sam gave the briefest of nods to Mr Fanning and left the boy to his father's tenderness. Now I know why I don't often want to come back, he muttered to himself. Just then, Allan Parslow patted him on the shoulder.

"It was great, wasn't it? But don't look like a grump, Sam – come and relax over a drink."

Sam collected himself. "If I look grumpy, it's only because I've had to reacquaint myself with Mr Fanning. Poor Hamish! But yes, I did enjoy the play. Now where's that drink?"

"Out on the Green."

And there it was – a beautifully floodlit expanse of lawn, people already attacking the wines and the finger food. They were, every one of them, engrossed in their conversations and totally at ease. Sam stood still for a moment, stunned at his sudden reaction, a reaction of fear that he was still part of it after all. The outdoor scene morphed into the House common room and the presentation of a painting, a year and a half ago. Then he relaxed, because he saw that there was not a clock in sight. He followed Parslow to the drinks table.

The Frasers had managed to put behind them the incident of the flowers and had thoroughly enjoyed their day. Both felt that they were showing off *their* school, and showing it in the most agreeable, even dazzling, light. They had chatted to all the right people, in intervals at football game and concert or at the headmaster's refreshments and they wandered home later that night in excellent spirits.

"The boys all did well, Sarah. Even the choir and the larger ensembles, which are often patchy, not to say ragged, were pretty good tonight."

"They were. I've no doubt they could be better. I was a bit disappointed with the play, I have to tell you. I don't think that young woman director understands her Shakespeare all that well."

Even Ben Fraser could see the inaccuracy, the folly, of that, though he did not penetrate to the jealousy that lay behind it.

"I'll get out early in the morning, with Jones, and see that all is tidy," he said, as they turned in at their front gate.

"Parslow can't stay here for ever, you know," said Sarah, but there was no chance to interpret or respond to that ambiguous remark. Ben opened the door and turned on a light in the front hall. There at his feet, pushed beneath the door, was a small envelope, inscribed 'Mrs S Fraser'. Sarah trembled and went white; but Ben picked up the envelope and ripped it open. It contained a single small piece of card.

'We know you for what you are. From Year 12, with our undying regard.'

The brief typed message said almost nothing, but far too much. Fraser flung it to the floor with an expression of disgust but he did not prevent his wife from picking it up. As she read it, she gave a little scream.

"Burn it, Ben. Burn it please!"

"I won't do that, Sarah." Then, when she looked at him pleadingly, "It's more evidence. I need evidence. But why do this? I don't understand it."

The brilliance of the day dissolved. For him, it left anger and a blunt desire for revenge. For Sarah Fraser, who, moments before, had been imagining herself as mistress of the estate with her husband as headmaster, there was grey helplessness. Totally unable to think critically about herself, she could grasp nothing of the cruel trick being played upon her. It could never occur to her that her own pride, her own indiscretions, had anything to do with it.

"Tomorrow – tomorrow I'll find out," said Ben, but he said it essentially to himself. He had no comfort to offer to his wife.

Perhaps it was a weakish sun that greeted the College on the Sunday morning, but by nine o'clock it had risen enough to show itself above the trees of the copse and to start its work of burning away the heavy dew which a clear, cold night brings with it. It was, therefore, a bright and blissful day that greeted a very dour Ben Fraser when he came out of his front gate and headed for the headmaster's residence. He assumed that he would catch him there at such a time, a full hour before the all-comers' chapel service on the oval at ten. He had with him the two hated cards which had deprived both him and Sarah of any useful sleep during the night. He had every reason to be fiercely unhappy with the way the world was treating him.

Unfortunately, he ran into a bright and beaming Parslow, who was surveying the College from the edge of the oval just outside his residence and who spoke as one who has already glimpsed the pinnacle of success and is assured of ascending to it.

"A wonderful morning, Ben! And it will be a wonderful day, a fitting climax to…"

His speech, which seemed likely to become more grandiose with each phrase, was cut short.

"I really have to show you something, Headmaster. You won't like it – it isn't pretty – but it is vitally important."

"Must it be now?" And then, realising that it apparently must, Parslow went on, "I came out to check arrangements for the service but I can spare a minute or two, Ben, if that will suffice."

"At least let me give you the gist of it," said Fraser, who, now that he had worked himself up to full disclosure mode, could not bear to retreat. He ran through the events of the flowers and the cards, showed Parslow the evidence, brutal and shocking as it was, and waited for a response.

"Have you no clues about this yourself, Ben? It comes as a bolt out of the blue to me, I must say. I've never seen anything like it."

Parslow intended his words to be non-committal. In fact, he did have an idea which he had no intention of sharing, not when a day of College grandeur had been prepared for him.

"I can see you haven't time for it now," scowled Fraser. "But we must get to the bottom of this. It is obnoxious, it is disgraceful, it strikes at…"

"So we will, Ben, so we will," said Parslow in that soothing tone which so easily exacerbates frustration and anger and stirs the sufferer to even testier, fiercer responses.

"I am not happy, Allan, and I shall demand action, severe action."

"Get me the facts first, before you demand anything." He had the satisfaction of seeing Fraser pause and take a deep breath, and so he hurried on. "You can see I can't act on this right now. I don't even grasp what it is all about, not yet. So get me more information, somehow. Now, I must see to things out there and I shall see you at the service in just a little while."

He nodded curtly and marched to where the groundsmen had converted half the football oval into an open-air chapel. Almost immediately his mind turned away from Fraser, but not before it had spared one more thought for the connection, unlikely perhaps, that nagged at him. Well, let that be for now. He reached the temporary dais and began to chat with Fred Jones about the PA system. He had to feel confident that his voice would carry.

Ben Fraser was left standing at the side of the oval. There was nothing for him to do except go home, collect Sarah and make sure they were in their allotted places in good time. Should he check the ushers? No, Custance would already be doing that. And frankly, he didn't want to do anything except mull over the gross insult to himself, and to his wife, of the day before. He walked back to his house in a savage mood.

The service, attended by the College students and staff and by just enough visitors to have made it worth commandeering the oval, was dignified and to the point. Because of the location, music was restricted to two hymns with recorded accompaniment and the choir out front to make a noise, even if the congregation didn't. There were readings, there were prayers for the College and the chaplain gave a short, farewell address, characterising his time in the school as a time of personal spiritual growth and suggesting that it ought to be the same for all the students. They appeared to listen attentively.

Parslow himself brought the service to a close. He thanked all who had attended and told them how, for him, the service was the centrepiece of the entire weekend. It was, he claimed, where the College stood up and said what it was all about. It was a school with a tradition, one which valued its past; but it was at the same time always looking for ways in which it could make a valuable impact on the present, and on the future. Its faith had to be forward-looking in its essence, not content to look backwards. That, he said, and perhaps his speech did not connect all the dots at this point, was why the service stood above all the other activities of the fair and drew them all together. Praise be to God for that! It was a stirring speech – *he* felt stirred by it – and several people, including his chairman, thanked him for it afterwards. Charles Herbert was quite struck by it, by the whole service in fact, and made some mental notes about how services in his chaplaincy might have a somewhat different flavour, and focus.

With the service over, Ben Fraser came to the microphone. It was his duty to remind listeners of the final tour of the building site at eleven thirty, during which an unveiling ceremony would take place. Get there early, he said, trying to sound jovial, because, apart from chairs for a small official party, it would be standing room only. It was not entirely clear whether this was meant to entice or to dissuade and such was Fraser's mood that day that he could not have said which it was himself. Professor Donald was displeased. Could not a more formal and respectful invitation have been given, he wondered. For the time being, he kept his thoughts to himself.

The students dispersed and the visitors, a little like the man from Ironbark, wandered here and wandered there until they were more or less herded to the construction site. There they were told what they already knew – that the new boarding house, with all the latest technology built in, would show the world how convincingly the College led the way in imaginative facilities and thus in the very best education. Hamish O'Loughlin urged all old boys to get behind the project; indeed, he spoke as if they had no choice. Professor Donald said that, from his university standpoint, he could confidently state that the College was preparing students for the tertiary world in the finest way possible. And when he and Allan Parslow unveiled the plaque, which would be affixed to the building when a building existed, it seemed to all present that they were parts of something momentous in the life and growth of education in their state. The headmaster and his chairman of council beamed.

They were still beaming when they sat at what we might call the high table, constructed of trestles, on the lawn outside the giant refreshment tent. Here a select few, which had blown out to twenty or more, were to have lunch. The group comprised council members, senior staff, spouses as relevant, Mr Langton (Mr Baker could not be found) and the local town's mayor, Cr Wilberforce, who had arrived wearing a most splendid chain of office. The conversation was light, breezy, complacent.

"A delightful morning, Mr Parslow," from the mayor. "I haven't enjoyed such an occasion, well, not for a very long time. Will you make it an annual event? I hope so."

"We may not be able to achieve that," from a headmaster shaken to his core at the very thought. "We could not possibly interrupt our normal routines in this way every year. But I am glad you have enjoyed it. Let me introduce you to…", and Cecily Boots had the dubious pleasure of hearing the mayor hold forth for the duration of the luncheon.

"Do you wish you were still part of it, Ralph?" said Greg Donald. "Irene was just saying to me how greatly the school must miss you."

"No, Professor," came the reply. "To each his turn, and mine is over. I am doing very well, as you see, but I could not sustain the pace of College life now."

"It is indeed a frightfully busy place," chimed in Irene Donald, who had earlier remarked to her husband that Mr Fraser did not seem as solid as the previous deputy; and as for Mrs Fraser – but Irene had implied that some things were better left unsaid. She knew they made more impact that way.

Somewhere else on the table, Hamish O'Loughlin was explaining that, great as things were in his day, they were only going to get greater. Parslow looked pleased at this, but less so when he realised that all the man's anecdotes drew the focus back to bygone days. He tried to force a change of direction.

"It was fun then, Hamish, but don't you think we can achieve more now?"

O'Loughlin blinked at Parslow – a combination of the sun and the wine – and offered the opinion that all College boys thought that their own days were the best. Simple-minded as the statement was, it was also probably true and Parslow decided he had better let it pass.

"The concert this afternoon will show you how much we can achieve at our best," he said.

"Ah, music, well, yes," murmured O'Loughlin and reached once more for the wine.

At this point Parslow stood up. He was about to say that it was time for them all to move off to the concert hall when he was forestalled by the mayor.

"Wait on, Headmaster," he boomed. "I know what you are going to say." (He didn't.) "But let me say it for you. Ladies and gentlemen, let us all show our appreciation of a truly marvellous weekend by drinking a toast to this fine school and to a fine future for it: to the College!"

Stunned into obedience, twenty or so people rose and did as they were bid. The toast was drunk, energetically by some and more diffidently by others, and the student ushers began immediately to clear the tables. Between them, Parslow and Fraser began to shepherd the flock to the concert hall. As they moved off, a small woman came up to Professor Donald.

"You will be so good as to escort me to the concert, won't you, Gregory?" It was Cecily Boots. Three quarters of an hour with the mayor had been quite enough.

The concert was just as great a success as Parslow had expected. Much of it he had heard the night before, though some changes had been made to the programme to give more groups a chance to perform. From the moment the first violinist got up – each piece was expertly introduced by a leading member of the group – to announce, as overture, *The Arrival of the Queen of Sheba,* Parslow felt himself glow with justifiable pride. Perhaps he nodded briefly when the choir and band joined for selections from *The Lion King*, and perhaps the orchestra almost let their Brahms Hungarian Dance get away from them. But then two of his music scholars, cello and piano, presented that old favourite, *The Swan*, as though it were new and fresh; another scholar from Year 12 played the first movement of the *Moonlight* sonata most touchingly; and the band was in excellent spirits through *Moreton Bay* and other Australian folk tunes. If most of the tunes were Irish, who cared?

All that was very fine and polished but a little conventional. It was towards the end that Parslow felt his skin prickle. The leader of a group – Six Sax they rather daringly called themselves – announced that they would show what saxophones could do when really let loose and they produced a rendition of an old standard, *Smoke Gets in your Eyes*. There was surprise, then there was rapt applause. The students in the audience stamped and whistled their approval in the most un-College fashion, to Parslow's great delight. They could not have defined it, but they knew they were at a very special performance. Then the six players melted away and a select choir of only twenty-four took the stage. A senior boy stepped forward and said that, rather than end on a grandiose or bombastic note, full of sound and fury, the singers wanted to offer a blessing as their thanks to all who had contributed in any way to the weekend's activities. He stepped back and, in the stillness, Rutter's setting of 'The Lord Bless You and Keep You' was sung with great control, until it faded imperceptibly back into the silence with the last amen. The audience were mute, perhaps stunned by the unusual juxtaposition of the last two pieces and, before they could applaud, the lead singer again stepped forth and beckoned his headmaster to the stage.

Parslow gazed about him with unfeigned delight.

"Ladies and gentlemen," he began, relying on the fine acoustic of his hall to carry his voice, not on any pressure from within, "thus we come to the end of one of the great times in the College's existence. Though you are only a portion of all those who have attended something over the last forty-eight hours, I want to treat you as representative and accordingly thank you, from the bottom of my heart, for supporting us in all we do in so forthright and energetic a fashion. May you all travel home safely; but, before you do," and here he held up a hand to forestall any over-hasty departures, "it is right that we all join together in congratulating these singers and all who have entertained us this afternoon." He turned to the twenty-four-voice choir behind him, waved generally about him and said loudly, "Thank you, boys, and well done!"

The applause broke out and went on for several minutes, even if, by the end of it, maybe a quarter of the audience had gone. Parslow had managed the conclusion very well, he felt. It had finished with the students, his students; but in addition, in the ebbing and flowing of idea and feeling in that last piece, he had sincerely felt that the achievements of the College were indeed extraordinary. For a moment, he felt that they surpassed even his achievement of a new boarding house. But then he pulled himself up, thanked the choir once more, stepped down from the stage and accepted the congratulations of all around him. Could it be that he accepted them, not only with delight, but with relief?

We shall not linger over the tidying up and putting away. They are necessary but tedious postscripts to any great occasion. Instead we will leap forward a couple of hours to the living room of Ben and Sarah Fraser.

"This boy you have coming here, Ben, is he your chief suspect?"

"He had nothing at all to do with it, my dear. It is about another matter. I shall see him in the study."

"You never stop, do you?" It was said with pride and approbation. She was about to follow it up with a suggestion that she might possibly be of assistance, for she saw in her husband an unfortunate level of agitation, when there was a knock. She heard Ben answer it, take the boy into the study and close the door. She took up a magazine and pretended to read it, hoping that she would have to do so for only a few minutes at most. Meanwhile:

"I seek information from you, O'Connell, only information; for the moment."

Fraser thought it best to let that sink in and he stood silently for a full minute. The boy sat in the chair to which he had been directed, totally at a loss.

"Now, lad, some time ago you were involved in the mistreatment, the cruel mistreatment, of cats, in the area of the copse. That is so, isn't it?"

The blow has come at last, thought William and, as his thoughts flew to his parents, his eyes filled with tears.

"I can see you know what I mean," went on Fraser, relishing, in his excitement, the role of the stern interrogator. "And in the last little while, maybe a week, or more, other creatures have been found dead in the copse. What can you tell me about that?"

The boy paled even further and shook, but something in him stood firm.

"Nothing, sir. I haven't been in the copse since... then."

"So you say. But it is too much of a coincidence." Fraser was working himself into a fine state of outrage; but, with all that had happened over the weekend, he did not control it as he might have. "You've left it a while, so as to throw us off the track, haven't you? Come on, boy, make a clean breast of it, nasty as it is."

"Nasty? I don't know what you mean, sir, I truly don't."

"Yes, nasty. Innards torn out, quite brutal."

Somehow the boy registered a gap – he was not being given a full or fair account.

"Torn out of what, sir?"

"Birds!" shouted Fraser, making Sarah jump in the living room. "Heaps of them. Jones is finding them all the time."

At that, William O'Connell stood up, now red rather than pale.

"You don't know me, sir, do you? I love birds. I would never harm any bird, not for anything. Ask anyone. But I know what would – feral cats. The very ones I was trying to dispose of. Go and accuse the cats, sir, not me!"

The boy was beside himself, with both fury and distress. He had a vision of the copse littered with his precious birds, things of beauty, even to the most common pigeon. He glared at the deputy.

"Calm down, boy, calm down," said Fraser, trying very hard to show restraint. And then, as though to save himself from looking any more foolish, he added, "I had to try you. Of course I did." There was a pause, and then, "You can go now."

Sarah Fraser was aware of a student hurrying out of the study and slamming the front door behind him in a most impudent fashion. She rose and went through to the study, to see her husband staring out the window, breathing heavily.

"So he was not the one you were after?"

Fraser turned to her and his normally firm voice was edged with panic. He was beginning to realise that agitation over one affair had caused him to burst out, grotesquely, in another, even though the two were quite unrelated.

"I lost it, Sarah, I lost it." Then, after a pause, "What is happening?"

By this time, many of the participants in the weekend's festival were, unlike the Frasers, comfortably settled down at home. The Andersons, though ready for bed themselves, had still to settle Penelope and to allow Libby Caraton to debrief for an hour or so as the energies stirred up by the drama wound their way through and out of her tired body. Parents had driven home; students had tried, mostly unsuccessfully, to remind themselves that it would be classes as usual in the morning and to remind their matrons, mostly successfully, that a supper of May Fair leftovers would be most welcome. Sam Baker and Ralph Langton made the drive up to the city in companionable silence, Sam declining, because it was getting late, the offer of tea or something stronger.

"I didn't know you were allowed anything stronger, old man."

"For special occasions, or special people. But since neither applies, I'll just say goodnight. And many thanks for driving. I could have done it, but it was much better with you."

They stood beside Sam's car and shook hands.

"We have more in common than we let on, Sam."

Baker understood the truth of that. But he found it so terribly hard to open up to anyone. He didn't know how to begin.

"After all we've been through together, that ought to be so," he grumbled. Then he relented, just a little: "I will say this. We understand each other fairly well. I would like…" but then he faltered at the sight of half a smile on Langton's face. He took refuge in a caustic comment about the Hansoms who still thought they could fool him.

"None of them could fool me, Ralph."

Langton looked at him in pity.

"They did it to us both, all the time. What you haven't realised, old friend, is that we helped them do it. Goodnight, then. I'll phone and invite myself to your hideaway. Until then."

Baker climbed back into his car and drove away. But he only drove a block or two; then he pulled over, trembling. Was it all an act, and the students, like himself, merely actors? He thought back over the weekend.

He remembered how he and Charlie Fanning had taken pains to snub each other after the play; and then he thought about that day's lunch on the oval, when he had deliberately missed being part of the headmaster's party so that he would not have to act the part of the irascible old housemaster. He remembered how he had passed by the Andersons with their picnic on a blanket by the oval. He had looked at their little daughter and Doug had beckoned him over, to his wife's obvious amazement. Surely Doug Anderson was not acting a part: he taught English with sincerity, he helped boys all he could (Sam's mind jumped alarmingly to Robert Fitzpatrick) and he was devoted to wife and child. No, Doug was no actor. And neither, he suspected, was that fellow Charles Herbert who had wandered by to join the Andersons. So Ralph couldn't be right, not entirely. But perhaps he was right about Sam, who was now too tired to take that reflection any further. He drove on home.

Any good festival must have a post-mortem, held as soon after the event as possible, so that memories are fresh and so that the maximum amount of time for forgetting before the next festival is created. Accordingly, and to the dismay of those he summoned, it was to be on Monday morning – the very next day! – at seven thirty, over breakfast. At least at that hour of the day they were safe from cake.

They assembled in the council room and Parslow at once informed them that he was asking for responses under the following headings: quality of the programme, efficiency of the arrangements, suitability of events for old boys, food and drink. The matter of financial success he would discuss in private with Delaney the bursar.

By means of this method, Parslow was given views of every stripe and hue, enough to convince him that his fair had contained something for everyone. The meeting endorsed everything and queried everything. The music had been just right but might have been totally re-selected to great advantage; the food was plentiful and appropriate but it failed to meet the peculiar needs of almost any age or ethnic group; and so on, except that the football was pronounced a disaster, on the grounds that St Justin's should always be thrashed or what was the world coming to. After something over half an hour, Parslow called an end to tea and muffins, thanked all for their input and asked Ben Fraser to stay behind for a moment. They had another matter to discuss.

"Have you made any progress in finding the author of those reprehensible notes?" asked Parslow when the room was clear.

"Not yet," Fraser was forced to admit. "I have no leads. I've spoken to each of the housemasters and they deny all knowledge. But it is an outrage, and when we do find out..."

"Yes, yes, you've told me what you expect. Now, Ben, I have an idea about it but it is only an idea and, I fear, unprovable. In fact, I am pretty sure I don't want to prove it. The consequences would be dire. So I'm telling you to leave the matter in my hands and to trust to my judgement. I will be discreet and I will not be hounded into drastic action. That's how it has to be."

"You mean a cover-up! I can't accept that. It's neither right nor fair."

Parslow did not answer. He looked steadily at his deputy as though to say that there would be no shifting him on this matter. Eventually, he said:

"You have had a hard time of it lately. Custance tells me of your attack on O'Connell, badly misjudged, I think; and this business with Mrs Fraser has been just too much. Look, we have only two weeks of term left and we will plod through them together. You will go on being thoroughly efficient with day to day arrangements, but you must leave this other matter entirely to me."

Parslow got up and walked round the huge council table to his deputy.

"Let's get on with it, then," he said and ushered Fraser out. Each went to his own study and, as far as anyone observing might have known, an effective school routine was resumed.

Parslow sat himself down to continue with his own reflections, before the really important meeting with Delaney. For him, the weekend had been a tremendous success. Professor Donald and all his College council were in agreement on that point. Aim one – get people enthused – was achieved; now for the second part – get the money in.

But what of this other business with Ben and Sarah Fraser? There was indeed a streak of malice in it. Normally, he would investigate thoroughly, but, as has been said, in his heart he did not want to. He recalled the note left for him once before, warning him of Mrs Fraser's indiscretion. He recalled Greg Donald's summary of Mr Fanning's comments, obviously gleaned from Hamish; and he felt it very likely that Hamish Fanning was either the sole perpetrator or the ringleader of this last incident. He could confront the young man and he would probably get at the truth. But the inevitable consequence – expulsion – would be a ghastly thing. The public scandal Charlie Fanning would stir up could not be tolerated, not just now, and it would only make matters more difficult for the Frasers. No, he would let the matter lie, except that he would find a way to let young Fanning know that he knew. Perhaps that would prevent any further 'pranks' which might have the effect of forcing his hand.

Having thought it through thus far, Parslow felt more at ease. He buzzed his PA and asked both for Mr Delaney to come in and for an early morning tea.

"Cake at this hour?" asked a smiling Mrs Delahay, receiving an apologetic grin in return. She had brought in some letters, all of them unstamped, left the day before, so they would be letters of congratulation, enthusing over the glories of the weekend and praising beyond reason the part their own sons had played in it. That was fair enough, he supposed. But his feeling of pleasure faded very fast, as soon as he had read the first letter: "It's clear Christopher should be in the Firsts. Please see to it. Trumble, a significant donor."

CHAPTER SEVEN

Sometimes, there is no point in denying it, the weather persists in being neither one thing nor the other. Such a condition can, of course, apply to more than just the weather – to a person's behaviour, for instance, or to the performances of a football team – but it is indeed the case that, at the start of term three in the latter part of July, the weather could not settle to anything in particular. Days would appear to offer sun and calm, only to degenerate into freezing winds, icy showers, possibly small hail; and if calm conditions returned, it would be after dark, of no real use to anyone. There was no putting the pieces of the day together in any satisfactory way at all.

Conditions such as these do not make school life easy. From the moment students returned on Sunday afternoon (Parslow liked to feel that classes got off to a brisk start, no messing around at the start of the term) they contended with damp clothing and fickle tempers. Staff arrived to class grumpy and peevish as though the weather were a personal insult, and even matrons berated their charges, not only for bringing mud into the houses but for allowing mud to form in the first place. Routines were resumed easily enough, but beneath the surface there was uncertainty, a very deep well of discontent.

For headmaster Parslow, the vacation time had been no vacation at all. He had never planned that it would be. There was the building to keep an eye on, and there too the inconvenient weather played havoc with the schedule. There was continual writing of letters to pursue donations, many of them promised at the May Fair but, as Donald had hinted, disturbingly slow to materialise. There were papers to prepare for his College council, projections for the following year, processes for allocating boys into the new house, when it was ready, notes on some staff issues that troubled him. On top of that the mail kept flooding in, most of it routinely dealt with, in one case potentially interesting and useful.

The letter came from a teacher at Chaddlehangar School. What an absurd name, Parslow thought, and he reached for an atlas, which was of no use, and then for a UK book of road maps, left over from a trip some years ago. There it was, set deep into the south-west corner of England, close to the market town of Tavistock, and not too far from the mysteries of Dartmoor, Baskerville country. A certain Mr Millane was seeking a year's experience in Australia and he wrote with his principal's blessing to enquire whether any English teacher from the College would be willing to make an exchange with him. He could offer not only an interesting school environment but a comfortable house on the outskirts of the village, a mile or so from the school and in a most scenic part of the country. He knew that these things take time to arrange and he suggested a period of the next northern hemisphere school year, starting in late August. He would come with his wife and one small child and he was sure that both the education and the environment of the College would suit them all perfectly. Would anyone be interested?

Parslow received this letter on the last Friday of the vacation and he immediately fell to thinking. Felicity Madigan had made it clear that she would welcome a refreshing of her English staff and here was an opportunity. If it was, initially, only for a year, one never knew what that might lead to. He would need to satisfy himself that this Mr Millane was the right man to introduce into the department; but, assuming that for the moment, whom should he send to Chaddlehangar?

The two Felicity Madigan wanted to move on were Rascham and Harry. His first thought was Flem Harry, a man of some quirky genius but one whom nobody quite trusted. He guessed that Ben Fraser thought well of him and he assumed that quirky genius was exactly what UK schools loved. But to send someone so oddly unreliable as Harry? No, it would not do. So Rascham, then: a nice but not inspirational young man, one needing an injection of something fresh in his life, the kind of man who might go to England, fall in love and never return. If he was not brilliant, this Mr Millane might not be either. He would write to the Chaddlehangar principal to check that out, and he would see Felicity on Monday and tell her of his plans for young Rascham. In this way Parslow felt his mind jump ahead as he organised people's lives for them, even making them into the kind of people who would suit his convenience. On this occasion, his mind was leaping too far, too quickly.

He saw Felicity Madigan in her spare period before lunch on Monday. He handed her a copy of Mr Millane's letter, so that she could get at least some impression of the teacher she would be acquiring and, as soon as she had glanced through it, made his suggestion, or, rather, what he would have called his decision.

"We shall offer them Rascham. I think he would fit their needs well enough, and you have told me how much he needs a fresh start. This would offer it. Suits us all, don't you think?"

Felicity looked at him quizzically. She saw his thinking and she was now aware enough of Parslow's ways to know that he saw all his staff as pieces of his giant jigsaw. She had no intention of fitting into her spot as easily as that.

"I'd like us to pause and think a bit further, Headmaster. The name that immediately sprang to my mind was not Rascham, but Anderson."

She watched his reaction and was pleased to see that it was not entirely dismissive. At the same time, he didn't simply deviate from his original thought.

"I imagined that you'd be glad to be rid of Rascham for a year, if not longer. You said, about him and Flem Harry, that I ought not stand in their way if they wanted to move on. Here's an opportunity."

He made it sound as though she would be foolish not to take it.

"I certainly wouldn't want to foist Flem onto an unwitting school," she said and saw Parslow grimace. "But can I go back to Doug for a moment? I know it's a bit more complicated for him – he's not single after all, but then neither is Mr Millane – but he's the one who most needs it."

"I don't quite follow that."

"I'd be surprised if you didn't." She paused, her head just a little on one side, as though asking him to confirm her surmise. She went on. "You have in him a very good teacher who feels that the school, quite unfairly, is out to get him. He's only still here, I suspect, because of his wife's job in town, which she loves. But he feels unappreciated. It goes back before my time here, I know that much; I suspect it has something to do with my job, and I know it has something to do with Mr Fraser. I don't see that it affects his teaching, but I do observe, and I do listen. Ask him, Mr Parslow. It would be a fine opportunity for him; and let me deal with the other two."

She paused. Parslow did not respond at once. Nobody had ever spoken to him like that. It had not been rude, or aggressive; but not even Professor Donald, who could come to the point very tersely, offered an assessment that threw him back on his heels quite like that. After the first shock, he was grateful for it.

"You would lose Anderson for a year. Is that a problem?"

"No," said Felicity, "not if this Millane fellow is up to scratch." She hoped she had not gone too far. "And I think it would be the fairest thing, to offer it to Doug." She allowed herself a mildly ironic smile. "After all, he might knock you back, mightn't he?"

This woman has found out, or has surmised, far too much, thought Parslow.

"I shall ponder what you've said. Naturally, I shall find out more about this Mr Millane, but I might ask Mr Anderson to give the matter some preliminary thought, as it were. In his case there will be logistical considerations, and I have no idea how it will impact on Mrs Anderson." He sighed at the mere thought of a spouse needing to be considered. "I'll raise it with him. And thank you for your input. I had looked at it differently – as you saw."

Felicity did see. She was comfortable that she had responded correctly. Now she would watch but not push. For his part, Parslow wrote immediately to the principal (*he* would never be a principal!) of Chaddlehangar School to check out Millane's credentials. He did not want a goose, or someone simply running away from difficulties. At least the letter was that of a sensible man. And it was all very well for Felicity to think of fairness – he had the College's reputation to protect. And that bit about the College being out to get Anderson – nonsense! He paraphrased a favourite line: "Think not what the College can do for you, but what you can do for the College." He smiled happily at that.

Back in the middle of June, Jenny Anderson had begun her stint as acting director of the gallery. It was to be for three months and she meant to enjoy it. Indeed, from the first she did enjoy it, even though her role was essentially to hold the fort. She was fascinated to see how much bigger the view of the whole operation was from her acting director's seat. She had thought she knew most of what went on in the gallery but she had been wrong. All sorts of issues – of procedure, of personnel, of reporting to those who provided the funds, and of possibilities for the future – were now coming her way and she was expected to deal with them. Sylvia did not just organise exhibitions, Jenny reflected; there were many more aspects to the job than that. She threw herself into it with energy, and with relish.

One thing though: she was a little late, a couple of days only, for her period, an unusual thing for her. She would give it two or three more days before telling Doug. Even if she were pregnant, she would hope to get through the next two months, but she could not be sure of it. And then there would be more change, more elements to cope with. No matter if deep down she longed for it – change was still unsettling. She started to count months and arrived in March; sometimes a hot month, but not the worst. She sighed as she drove into the College grounds and wondered if Doug was in from his football yet. Yes, of course, he would have showered and gone to pick up Penny from the day care. The evening routine would descend upon them. She did not know if she would be up to much chat after that.

Jenny had barely unpacked her few things and filled the jug when she heard Doug at the door. She heard him put away the stroller, heard "Yes, give that to Mummy", and then the eager little footsteps. She saw Penny, saw her hold out a crumpled sheet of paper filled with random scribblings of crayon and somehow she knew it had been a good day. Doug joined her in the kitchen, asked whimsically whether the crumpled sheet would figure in the next exhibition and got out two mugs. Tea now, thought Jenny, then all the evening routine, and maybe there will be time to share our days after that. But what if that evening routine were to be doubled, she asked herself.

She was not, however, prepared for the sharing which took place. When Penny was safely asleep, they sat back comfortably together and Doug gave her one of his mysterious looks, always preparatory to… something.

"What?" she said. "Something out of the ordinary?"

"Well, yes. Parslow stopped me at morning tea and said he wanted me to consider something. It's a possibility at this stage, just a possibility."

He saw that he was only confusing her.

"He gave me this, a copy of a letter that has come to him from the UK. Just read it," and he handed her the paper. He sat back to watch the reaction. It was not slow in coming.

"He wants you to go to England for a year? Wants us to go?"

"I don't know whether he wants it or not." Doug was judicious in his assessment of the situation. "He has asked me – us – to think about it and let him know if we are interested in following it up." He looked steadily at her. "I only said that we would certainly discuss it."

He waited. He had so many questions himself that he understood why Jenny would have even more. At least, he thought he understood.

"Oh, Doug," she gasped out and flicked through the letter again, as though it might tell her what to say. "A year, a whole year, beginning when, next July? Or August?"

He nodded; he was smiling.

"And you think this might be good, don't you?"

"Well, yes, but it has to work for you, for all of us, doesn't it?"

At "all of us", Jenny's eyes filled and her resolution of waiting two or three days more fell away. He held her close.

"We could do this," he said, "and enjoy it. But it has to be right for both of us. Penny would just be coming for the ride."

"But what if it's not just Penny?" she blurted out, so that Doug nearly jumped off the sofa. "What if...?" and she looked pleadingly at him.

"Are you sure?"

"No, I'm not sure. It's only a day or two, but I have a feeling..."

Doug sat down and held her, then kissed her so as to stop his heart from bursting. He looked at the eyes, still wet, and he said, "Let's talk about that. This other thing," and he pushed the letter to the floor, "can wait."

"Can it?" she said. "Do you have to give an answer?"

"Not straight away. By the end of the week. But Jenny, if you are pregnant, that will be wonderful, just so wonderful."

Words might have been his profession but no more would come, not just then. He made her tell him about months and when, soon after, they went to bed, he lay awake for some time, calculating. He knew he had to be in the House the following night, Wednesday, but that still gave Thursday night for a good discussion, before he had to make some sort of response to Parslow on Friday. It was all very rushed – and it might all come to nothing. Parslow might find that this Mr Millane was useless and reject the whole idea. But he hoped, he fervently hoped, that all the pieces would come together.

It will come as no surprise for you to learn that the Frasers were not happy. Not that anything further had occurred: nothing at all, since the weekend of the fair, had happened which might have caused their anger and frustration to keep simmering away. The point was that it didn't need anything – all it needed was nothing from the headmaster. Every day of the last two weeks of the previous term Sarah Fraser had asked, in words or with an eyebrow, whether there was action or at least news of potential action. There was nothing. And now, at the start of term three, there was still nothing. No change, no promises, not even hints. It was unfair, and it was grotesque. If the man had a lead, or a suspicion, or even a gut feeling, let him act on it and put the two of them out of their misery. If the culprit was found and thrown out of the College, they felt they could continue. If not? That was not clear to them at all.

Parslow had not put the issue out of his mind. He did feel that he had many more important things to do; but he had to assure himself that there would be no further incident, no further cruelty, no demeaning of a silly but pathetic woman. He deeply regretted having hinted to Fraser that he had his suspicions. It was done, however, and now he had to make sure that nothing further occurred. He had to be able to show that he had stopped the deception, once and for all. Thus it was that he 'invited' himself to the House for supper on the Wednesday night, just after term had begun. He would be out for a wander and he would just drop in. He did so, soon after half past eight, when he judged that a break in the House's routine would not matter all that much. He ran into Doug Anderson.

"Good evening, Mr Parslow. You'll be after Mr Custance. But it happens to be my night on duty, so you'll find him in his residence."

"No, I don't need Barney, or yourself, though I hope you will spare me some time after morning tea on Friday. No, I'm just out and about. What's tonight's routine? Is there supper?"

"At nine. I'll be winding up the compulsory homework time soon, but you could look in on the studies until then. You'll find some boys still hard at it."

Doug did not think that the some would amount to many at all, not below the senior years, anyway. But a headmaster, he supposed, could do as he wished.

"I will. And I will speak to the boys over supper. Just a short something, but it needs to be said."

He walked away, leaving Doug wondering what ghastly behaviour by a boy or boys had caused Parslow to make a special visit, in order to say a short something. He had no idea and he put the matter aside. It was time to send the rostered boys off to help Matron.

Supper began in a most subdued fashion. The boys cast sidelong glances at each other, wondering what it was all about. William O'Connell, unusual in so many ways, wondered which one of them was to be Annie Johns. He was pretty sure it would not be himself. After some time for eating, Doug stepped forward.

"Listen in, please," he said and paused for barely a moment. "It is a great pleasure to have our headmaster with us this evening. He needs to talk to us – sit or stand as you are, and be still."

Doug tried to melt back into the supper table; and yet he was, as the boys were, eager to hear whatever it was, whatever was so portentous as to bring a headmaster out in this unexpected way.

"Good evening, boys, and welcome back to term."

Parslow paused for a long moment. He gazed about the room, only partly to prolong suspense, but also to be sure that he knew just where a certain Year 12 student was standing. Yes, with others of his year group, along the far wall. Perfect. He made as though to speak, paused, and finally began.

"I pride myself on being headmaster of a school in which all are treated fairly, decently, and absolutely without malice of any kind." Another pause. "We all know this to be crucial when we compete against another school in sport, or in debating, or in whatever it is that is one's passion. We try our very hardest, but we never show contempt, or unfair aggression, or any kind of malice."

He emphasised the last word again and let it sit there for a moment.

"The same is true of relationships within the College. I know you will tease and joke at each other – but if I ever heard of malicious bullying, or malicious gossip, I would act swiftly and decisively. If I ever discovered malice directed at *any* person in our community, student or adult – we are all equal in the eyes of God – then I would be angry and I would act. Have I heard any such thing?"

Another pause, though everyone knew the answer to the question. Why else was he here?

"I think I have; and so, I suppose, I am putting somebody on their guard. Tonight I want you all to know exactly how I feel about these things; you need to know so that, if I act, there will be no surprise about what I would have to do."

Enough, he thought, bring it to a close.

"I have the greatest faith in this school. It is a fine place, full of fine people, as indeed is this House. But even the finest of us can act badly. I trust that nothing will now happen to call my faith in the school, or the House, or any individual in the House, into question."

His eye swept the room, moving more slowly when it came to the Year 12 group, only one of whom, trying desperately to control his feeling of terror, was actually looking at him. He nodded, as though satisfied, and then turned to Doug Anderson and Matron South.

"I always knew the House put on a fine supper. Thank you for letting me share it with you."

He walked past the supper table, stopping only to pick up a lonely piece of cake, and was gone. The residents of the House looked at each other, more or less mystified. Doug tried to restore normality by collecting the rostered boys and insisting that supper be cleared away as quickly as possible. He urged them all to go back to their studies, or to get ready for bed; but, on a sudden impulse, he asked Year 12 to stay behind. When he had them by themselves, he spoke briefly.

"I do not know any details at all, concerning what the headmaster has said, or implied. However, if any of you has anything, anything at all, to tell to me, or to Mr Custance, I think it would be better to bring it forward now, rather than wait in hope of permanent concealment. Now, I know work is descending on you in torrents, in this your last real term amongst us. So let's get on with it."

It will be apparent that Doug had not grasped what Parslow had actually wanted to achieve. How could he? He sent the boys off, though he was aware that, in twos and threes, they paused in corridors to wonder aloud about what they had witnessed. They gathered that the head thought he knew something and had hoped either to flush out the culprit, or… But at this point, like Doug, they could go no further. They wandered to their studies, and Doug decided to check on the junior dormitories, as a way of drawing the day to a close.

An incident such as this must have its sequel, perhaps several. One was that, by subtle questioning, the boys of the House discovered that Parslow had not visited the other boarding houses to make a similar speech and so they said not a word of his tirade, as they thought of it, at them. The silence was absolute. A second was that Hamish Fanning, taking the next day a twentieth century history test for which he had studied solidly over the vacation, made such a mess of it that Mr Masterson suspected a nervous collapse from overwork. He even mentioned the matter to Parslow who contented himself with offering to a puzzled Masterson the following advice: "Tell the boy from me to put the past behind him." Yet a third sequel was that Custance was furious that the whole debacle (his word) had taken place in his absence and he took it out on Doug Anderson by refusing to look at or speak to him for weeks. Doug found that he could put up with that.

As we have said, Doug began a tour of the junior dormitories, wanting to calm the House down before the evening got too far advanced. He came across Matron South near the Year 7 room and she stopped him.

"I'm just going to move amongst the younger boys for a while, Mr Anderson. I hope that is all right with you."

Her deference was quite unnecessary, Doug thought, and he said that he was only too glad of the assistance. He headed towards Year 8 and found all of them gathered into one of the two smaller dorms.

"I'm going to be turning off the lights very soon, my friends – get yourselves ready for bed. Back to your own dorm, you lot." He was about to move on when he noticed one boy not taking part in the general conference. It was William O'Connell, sitting quietly on his own bed, seemingly lost in thought. Doug pulled a straight chair across and sat down next to him.

"Hello, William. I haven't had a chance yet to touch base since the holidays. How are things with you?"

"Ah, oh, fine, Mr Anderson, just fine."

"That doesn't sound very convincing," said Doug, trying to give an encouraging smile and draw the boy out. He ventured, "You've not been made anxious by this evening, have you?"

He was relieved to see an answering grin.

"Oh that. Mr Parslow wasn't getting at me. I think I… but it wasn't me." Then he sensed that he had given a hint of a kind and wished he hadn't. "No, I was just thinking of Mum and Dad and the holidays."

"Was it a good time? I hope it was."

"It was, mostly." And then the boy relaxed his shoulders. He needed someone to confide in; he couldn't keep it in for ever. "I told them about how Mr Fraser saw me last term and accused me of killing birds." Even now, those words were hard to say. "Mr Fraser didn't know much about me, I know that, but to be accused of…! And they have written to Mr Parslow to complain, I suppose, and I think they want to come and see him about it. And I know people think I don't fit in here, but I really don't… want…"

He could not go on.

"I don't know much of this business of you and Mr Fraser, William. But I do know you and your love for birds. And I also know I can trust you to be truthful. You're one of the straightest people around here."

The boy looked as though that might not be of much help.

"But what if, out of it all, they decide I'd be better off somewhere else?"

"Then you must speak up for yourself. And I can speak up for you too. I can tell Mr Parslow that the College needs someone like you. You do think you can trust your parents to understand you, don't you?"

Doug knew he had not been able to find the right words, but William O'Connell didn't seem to mind. He had at least one ally in the place and that was all he needed. Their discussion by the bed had come about accidentally, as the most valuable discussions often do.

"I'm on your side, William, and I can speak for you. But I think you will speak very well for yourself. And now I must go to Year 9 before they create havoc."

He got up and moved the chair back to the wall. The boy still sat on his bed. Another boy came and stood nearby, obviously waiting for Doug to leave. He looked at them both.

"Get ready for bed," he said. "I'll put my head in in fifteen minutes."

He went out into the empty corridor, stopped and let out a huge sigh. He did not want to get enmeshed in anything that concerned Ben Fraser – and now he had promised the boy that he would. Another muddle! As he stood there, Matron South approached from Year 9.

"Did they take a lot of settling down in there? I'm not surprised."

Doug looked at her and tried to switch back to the events of earlier in the evening.

"No, Matron, they were fine. Young William needed to talk."

She smiled warmly and said, "I'm glad it was you who wandered in, then." And then, as though there were a connection, in her mind at least, "I don't think Mr Custance will be happy about tonight. Who is going to tell him about it?"

"The boys will, I suppose. But it is really up to Mr Parslow." And then he made a decision: "Whatever the issue is, the less we interfere in it the better. We'll just get on with things, as we always do."

Matron nodded, but even as Doug said it, his mind floated back to William O'Connell. If the boy himself wasn't Mr Parslow's target, then he had a shrewd sense of who was. He was an interesting and perceptive lad. Doug wondered how it would all play out.

Doug arrived home at the agreeably early hour of four thirty on Thursday afternoon and found, to his surprise, Jenny also at home, having cups of tea with Libby Caraton. A sudden squall of rain and light hail had curtailed his football practice and for once he had not been sorry – he and Jenny needed time for discussion. But Jenny was home early because she had begun to feel particularly seedy; and Libby, noticing Jenny's car drive in, had come over anticipating a quiet chat without Doug. Thus nobody quite got what they had anticipated or desired.

In half an hour, Jenny and Libby had already covered the main topics of interest. Knowing Libby's discretion, Jenny had explained why she was feeling suddenly nauseous without feeling ill and also that they were considering a year away, from the middle of the following year. This had made Libby reveal that she felt it was time to think about moving on from the College; indeed, if the Andersons would not be there, there would be little left to support her and make her stay longer. At this point Doug entered.

"Afraid of a drop of rain, were you?" said Libby in more or less false mockery.

"Hardly. But I did take advantage of it, I have to tell you."

He glanced at Jenny and the briefest of nods told him that she had shared their two big items of news.

"After all," he continued, "we have a lot to talk about."

"You do," responded Libby. "I'll leave you to it. But it seems to be a time of movements, or near movements. I was just about to tell you, Jenny, that Blaize put in an application a couple of weeks ago, to move way up to Queensland, as far as he could go, I guess; and now he tells me he has withdrawn, as soon as they said they wanted to interview him. Is he too afraid to move, to act – or what?"

Jenny shook her head; she seemed to want to sit very still. Doug was just about to comment that a man could have more than one iron in the fire, but he thought better of it and got up.

Libby forestalled him. "Tell you what. You two chat and I'll go and fetch Penny. I'll see you in half an hour."

"That would be wonderful, thank you," muttered Jenny, who would not have been the one to go out anyway. "Do you want some tea, Doug?"

He noticed that hers was untouched and, when Libby went off, he changed his clothes and made himself a mug before returning to the sitting room.

"Interesting about Blaize," said Jenny. "Can he not tear himself away from Libby, do you think?"

"You'll laugh at me, Jenny."

She was very ready to, but he looked serious enough. He went on.

"I'm not very quick to notice things, but I have begun to wonder whether Blaize and Maya…"

"Oh don't be…" she interrupted, and then, "Oh, I see. Do I see?"

"Let it be, Jenny. Don't say a word, not even to Libby. Especially not to Libby."

She nodded. "I understand. Now, let's use what's left of this brief half hour. Are you going to see Parslow tomorrow? What will you be saying to him?"

By the time Libby returned, they had resolved that, without making a firm commitment, they were prepared to hear more. Doug felt keen, and Jenny felt too much inner turmoil to be sure of anything.

"I can say," he concluded, "that we need to know a lot more in terms of logistics, of what I would be expected to do. Of housing, and everything like that. That will buy us a little time." He paused. "I am sorry the sickness has hit so suddenly. And so early. At least it removes doubt – doesn't it?"

His question was so hopeful that Jenny had to smile at him.

"I guess it does," she said. "You're a great one for wanting to remove doubt, aren't you? And don't you dare quote Othello at me – I couldn't manage it just now, and I am *not* Desdemona."

He kissed his fingertips and planted the kiss, like a blessing, on her forehead just in time to hear Libby's car return.

"I'll entertain Penny as much as I can," he said.

She smiled wearily: however much Doug tried, the little girl could not be kept from crawling over Mummy.

Doug Anderson and Parslow had their conversation on Friday morning, as arranged. Doug left it feeling comfortable and just a little excited. A process had been begun and yet nothing was set in concrete. He had said nothing of Jenny's likely pregnancy – there was no need, not yet. They both agreed to say nothing publicly until there was something definite to say and the conversation had ended with Parslow hoping that the overseas plan would come to fruition.

"It will be very good for you, and you for them," he had concluded.

Thus it was that the members of the English department were all feeling positive, optimistic, sensing good possibilities lying ahead. Actually, almost all of them. That same Friday, Ben Fraser asked Flem Harry to drop by his study once he had finished his lunch in the dining hall. Flem looked surprised but nodded and went on munching. Fifteen minutes later he found Fraser at his desk. The deputy attempted to be chirpy.

"We've all been so busy, Flem, that we haven't touched base for a long time. I'm sorry about that – I hope you don't feel I've been ignoring you."

"The fair swamped everyone, and then we've been on holidays," said Flem as he sat himself easily opposite Fraser. He felt the man's tension, but there was no reason why he should feel tense himself.

"I'm starting to work on... various matters," began Fraser and he patted a large manila folder. "It's all very... but it leads me to ask you a question. It's this: how is Felicity managing as head of your department? Are you all a happy mob? I see some things, and I have my small bit of English teaching; but I would welcome your perspective. It's always valuable."

For Flem, it was as though he had to keep himself from being sick. The performance he had just witnessed, he felt sure, was total bluff – total crap, in fact. There was a pretence of great plans, but the folder would contain nothing but Ben's bits and pieces about staff. The man was conjuring with 'various matters' for Flem's benefit, but Flem would not bite. His instant reading of the situation told him that, for some reason, Fraser felt vulnerable but Flem was not about to help him. In fact, he felt quite sure that to be on Madigan's side was preferable, as things stood now.

"We are a very happy group," he began. "She gives a good lead and is always encouraging. She's been back long enough for you to see that. I'd say we've struck a really top-class head of English, wouldn't you?"

He threw it back to Fraser as though to force the man's hand. He was quite adept at this sort of game, but so was the other.

"I'm glad to hear it. Relieved, if I may say so. She went through such a hard time. I need to feel there's the strength in her for what I have in mind."

"But that's all in the past, surely?" Flem was at his briefest. "I see her as moving forward very confidently. There is nothing to concern you about Felicity."

He had aimed that last sentence as a direct challenge. As he read it, Fraser *was* concerned and Flem felt that he wanted to feed that concern and watch it grow. He could not have said exactly why he felt this, but he did know which side he intended to be on.

"That's reassuring, most reassuring," and Fraser took a deliberately surreptitious look at the top paper inside the folder. "It's good to hear this from you, Flem. I was a bit anxious for Felicity because... well, I can't say any more. You understand. But you've been very helpful."

He stood up, so that Flem had to stand also. But Flem thought that the screw needed another turn.

"She's very clever, and very determined. The kind to carry all before her. An excellent HoD, Ben," and Flem nodded and left as one who has the greatest confidence that his teaching department, if not other parts of the school, is in good hands. It was, but it was most unusual for Flem to declare it to be so.

Fraser sat back down. He knew all this about Felicity and, though she annoyed him by her brazen independence, she did not threaten him. But the conversation, for Ben, had had nothing to do with Felicity Madigan. He had wanted to see if he still had a willing stooge in Flem Harry. What had he discovered? Obviously, that the young man had deserted him, had decided to play some other game. Let him play it, thought Ben; he would exact his revenge at some point, he felt sure. But it was a difficult time in which to operate without allies, Fraser also knew that. He did not look forward to the rest of the year.

On Saturday, at the end of that first week of term, the College football teams went to play those much-anticipated return fixtures against Baxter. It will be as well to avoid useless suspense: on a blustery day, before an alien crowd and, or so it was claimed, on an oval too much like a circle, the College teams were both soundly beaten. It was a day of worse gloom than that of the earlier encounters. The margins were greater, and there was no third match, no chance even to dream of possible revenge. Both Parslow and Fraser travelled up for the event and both suffered grievously at the hands, or should we say the tongues, of the Baxter executives, who made it plain that this was the proper order of things. The principal of Baxter was even heard indulging in an unfriendly quotation – "God made them high and lowly, and ordered their estate." Parslow found the day neither bright nor beautiful, but any sharp retort would have been out of place. He held his tongue and fumed inwardly.

Doug Anderson was bitterly disappointed. His boys had given him their best efforts and for patches had seemed to be holding their own. But in each quarter a burst of four or five goals in quick succession deprived them of any confidence and the final margin was close to twenty. He shook the opposing coach's hand after the game and reflected that his comments earlier in the season about looking forward to a re-match had been made to look ignorant, juvenile. It was simply that he did not have at his disposal the overall strength and talent to compete against more polished opposition. Mr Gryce's Firsts, even with Trumble playing, suffered a similar fate and came away a very bedraggled bunch, in spirit if not in uniform. By halftime they had seen that Gryce was at a loss, had no further resources or strategies to call on, and, feeling the full force of their predicament, they had seemingly given in. This, it may be imagined, did nothing to improve Gryce's temper on the bus back home.

Between the two games, Parslow had gone to console coach Anderson. He too had seen the College boys succeed for brief periods of time and he tried to make the most of a very slender positive.

"They worked hard for you, Doug. I trust you will not let them be too downhearted."

"No, Headmaster, that's not my way, is it? But it will take them a little while to recover from such an awful drubbing. Nobody likes being made to look second rate."

"While I think of it," and Parslow decided to try a different topic, since there was nothing to be gained in dissecting the bones of a defeat, "it may be that you are not here for much of next year's season. Do you have a recommendation? Who should take over?"

As he hoped, the question sparked Doug's interest and brought forth a ready response.

"In terms of knowing the game and knowing coaching, the answer is obviously Charles Herbert. It would be good to see him involved in such a way. But if you want the truth, Mr Parslow, he should be coaching the Firsts." He paused, then added, "but you might find that a little more difficult to manage."

There was irony in his voice, an unfamiliar note to Parslow, but the headmaster took it up.

"More difficult indeed. Lifting up Olympus, as you Shakespeareans might say." (Doug had not been about to say it but he grinned at the allusion.) "I do not imply that knives might be used, by the way. But Peter Gryce is closely identified with the role."

Doug wanted to say that that was the trouble but stayed silent.

"Thank you, Doug. I shall give your comments some thought. I am not one who is afraid of a challenge."

He left a deeply wondering Anderson and moved off to the special spot from which he was expected to watch the Firsts. Doug muttered, "Good luck to you" under his breath and organised his boys to make an encouraging reception committee for the Firsts when they took the field. It was the only cheering they received through a long and wearying afternoon.

Parslow and Fraser had driven up from the College together. Fraser had let slip that he had never seen Baxter. He was keen for an afternoon right away from the campus and accepted Parslow's invitation to come in his car readily enough. Conversation had been light and scattered on the way up but Parslow was determined to use the return trip for talk more substantial.

"Well, that was all pretty depressing, Ben," he began, once they were on the road home. "A school of our size has to learn to accept defeat – but we should never accept surrender."

Fraser gave him an uncertain look and began, "Well, the boys…" but Parslow waved the interruption aside.

"Oh, I know it wasn't their fault. They did what they could, most of them. We were outgunned. But has Peter had his day? I don't see the boys responding to him, not as they once did."

He let the suggestion hang there – Fraser could take it up as he wished, or not. He did.

"Well, what are our alternatives? Anderson fares no better," (Parslow winced: this was plainly not true and he was reminded of Fraser's dislike of Doug from an earlier issue) "and I don't see any other staff member equipped to take it on. We may have to stick with Peter Gryce for a time yet."

Parslow sensed some odd kind of smugness in that final sentence and he became brisk.

"I don't know about that, you know. I understand that Charles Herbert has a first-class background in sports coaching and administration. He was with the Stars. Doug thinks Herbert knows the game very well."

"Oh, really," came an irritated response. "I hardly think... Look, the man's only just joined us, and in a very specific role. I can't see him being taken seriously as the senior football coach."

Parslow took advantage of a crowded merge on to a freeway to remain silent for a moment. His deputy did seem to have a way of taking a stand against some people. But why in this case?

"He has helped Doug already, I understand, and knows what he is about."

"I don't see how someone so new can know the school and its ways. If he is allying himself with Anderson, then I smell trouble."

"I can't see how he is allying himself with anybody. Yes, he is new, but he won't be in a year's time when next season comes around. Still," and he wanted to leave the topic for now, "let's see how the rest of this season pans out. We are in no rush."

He felt Fraser breathe more easily in the seat next to him. He reflected that the deputy was himself still fairly new, in College terms at least; in this school, ten years was as the blink of an eye. The feeling nagged at him, not for the first time, that he had landed himself with a deputy who was administratively strong enough – although there had, he reflected, been some serious administration shortcomings at the time of the inspection – but very deficient in his understanding and management of people. He began a conversation on the progress of the new boarding house, a topic on which Fraser could only be supportive. The necessary miles rolled away and they were home soon enough. Parslow thanked his deputy for his company and his thoughts and resolved that he would not repeat such a drive again.

Some younger age-group games aside, it had been a very quiet afternoon at the College. Being the first weekend after a vacation, very few students took leave, but still there was a gentle, sometimes breezy, often drizzly, atmosphere. It was a day for being indoors, for getting things done, such as the final touches to one's first sermon for Sunday chapel. The Reverend Herbert was engaged in just that task. He wanted to make a good impression and, as was his habit, he was determined to be as thoroughly prepared as possible. Consequently, his wife Rebecca had decided to leave him well alone and to immerse herself in reading of her own. She was a historian by training and she hoped to try her hand at historical biography. They had just had an early lunch and she was ready to get stuck into Oliver Cromwell when there was a knock at the door.

"I'll get it, Charles," called Rebecca and she opened the door, afraid that she would not, new as they were, know her visitor. But she did know her, from only a recent introduction – it was Sarah Fraser.

"No, I won't come in," said Sarah, "for I'm on my way to the Custances. But I hope you'll come and see me over afternoon tea this afternoon, say about three. It would be so good for us to get to know each other. Don't you feel it like that, in such a big place?"

"You're very kind," said Rebecca Herbert. It was not a particularly large school and she had no idea what Mrs Fraser expected her to feel. But, incoherent though it seemed, the offer was sincere, she supposed, and she said she would be only too glad to come.

"That's fine, then. See you at three. I'll be on my way. There's so much to do when Ben's away."

Rebecca watched her walk away in some bemusement. Was the woman dotty or had it all been a performance? She heard Charles calling, wondering if he was needed?

"Not at all," she said. "It was Mrs Fraser asking me to go over for afternoon tea. I'll go, of course. But it was an odd invitation – or perhaps she's just an odd woman. Perhaps she needs to feel that I will be on her side, or something like that."

Charles looked at her with mild concern. "It sounds like a day for treading warily. You've had to do that in parishes for years – you'll manage."

So it was that, in the midst of quite a squall, Rebecca Herbert turned up the path to the Frasers' residence at what she judged to be a suitable time – three minutes past three! She was welcomed effusively and was led into a comfortable, and warm, sitting room. There were magazines, there were flowers, and a small selection of books of travel: Rebecca assumed it was a room carefully designed to look casual. Sarah Fraser saw her take in the room at a glance.

"I hope you can make your house as cosy as we've been able to make this. The College is generous in its housing, I must say, for us senior people."

"We feel well taken care of," said Mrs Herbert blandly. "It is a big change for us, and yet I feel that we shall be part of the College in no time. Charles is very keen."

"I know exactly what you mean. And there is so much for him to do. Now, let me bring in a tray. Will you have tea, or coffee?"

They settled that and other gastronomic matters and then, over a sandwich and a hunk of fruit cake, resumed their conversation.

"Tell me a little of where you've come from, Rebecca. I dare say church life has been full of labours, just as school life is."

What a quaint woman, thought Rebecca.

"Yes," she said. "You know," and she paused reflectively for a moment, though whether it was in longing for the past or in joy to have left it behind would be hard to tell, "I rather think that I will have fewer calls on my time. A clergyman's wife is treated as part of the congregation's property, a part of the deal, if you know what I mean. I take it that a school chaplain's wife can fall into the background a bit more."

"And will you like that? I like to feel that I am part of a team, with Ben."

Her complacent tone told Rebecca that, for Sarah Fraser, it was her intention to be the leader of the team, even if from behind the scenes. She did not want to be seen in that light.

"This is a big chance for Charles," she said. "It's his opportunity to take his gifts for ministry into a different sphere. He will make his impact – and I will be more retiring. I've already made up a course of reading, the seventeenth century mainly, and I look forward to that."

Not being able to think of anything that had happened in the seventeenth century, Sarah left that topic alone. She reverted to Charles Herbert.

"He will have a lot to do, as you say. The demands of chaplaincy are considerable. All those services, for example, things like the choir to manage. He will be very busy."

Was the woman rambling again? Sarah was becoming increasingly wary, but she could not let that last comment stand unanswered.

"Once one is attuned to a place, the services nearly run themselves. They are not the key. No, Charles will want to be fully involved in the whole life of the school. The pastoral role is what he loves most."

Sarah Fraser looked down at her cake and seemed to finger it gingerly.

"I have always thought that a chaplain's place is in the chapel," she said.

Managing not to gasp, Rebecca offered the view that a parish clergyman's role went out more broadly into the community; it wasn't confined to the church building. Then she went on with her own cake, waiting to see what would follow. She did not have to wait long.

"In a school such as this, as I'm sure you will find out, we all have our places. There is an expectation, I suppose, that we will stick to them."

Rebecca thought that this had gone quite far enough.

"You seem very successful in terms of flowers. I've never been much of a gardener, but I'll have to try. We've space enough."

"Your predecessor did not do much in that line. The soil here is good, if you want to give it a go. But the winters can be quite severe."

"As we are finding out today. And our parish was only just a few miles away. Well," and she glanced very deliberately out the window, "there seems to be a break in the blustery weather. You have been most kind this afternoon, but I think I shall be on my way. I'll go and see if Charles has his sermon under control. You must tell me how you find his preaching."

Sarah followed her to the door. She clearly wanted to have the last word.

"We'll go on with our chat another time soon, I hope. We must keep in touch. It's so good to have you here."

Rebecca Herbert made the five-minute walk back home wondering not about her husband's sermon but about how she could tell him that the deputy's wife had a very firm view of a chaplain's place and expected him to stay in it. He had been right to tell her to tread warily and she was just a little concerned that she had not been wary enough.

The chapel was full, very full, for the Reverend Herbert's first Sunday service. This was not because an eager crowd had assembled to see and to hear him – it was simply that almost no one was away on the first Sunday of term and so staff, students and even some spouses and family members all crammed in together. It was rare for the chapel to be full even to the very edges of the rows and for even the seats behind pillars to be taken, from where one saw almost nothing. Unfortunately for the boys in those seats, one could still be seen.

There was a tiny chaplain's room in which Herbert could check his robes, pray and be calm. He had done all those things, in good time, and he had been informed that he should enter and take his seat as soon as the bell began to ring. Then, when it stopped ringing, he was to stand and commence the service. He would have liked to enter through the body of the chapel but he was not about to alter tradition before he had really begun. There would be time enough to plan such things.

Outside there was a small, sheltered courtyard. It was not for the students to use; rather, it was a gathering place for guests or for anyone who, it was felt, should be escorted into the chapel. It was also used by the choir when they needed to process in, but on this occasion, not a grand or festival Sunday, they were already in their places inside. There were just two figures in the courtyard, Parslow and Rebecca Herbert; the Headmaster felt that he should escort her to her place on this significant occasion for her and her husband. Boys were still bustling in at their doors, so he had a couple of minutes to spare. He looked round at the pleasant, sheltered little space.

"I like the quiet of this little nook," he said. "There are not too many such spots in the College."

"I've seen only a fraction of the campus yet. But yes, this is a place apart, isn't it?"

"I hope you'll see plenty, and soon. It is a grand school. How are you settling in? Quite comfortable in the old house?"

She gave a tight smile. "It is most comfortable, as I'm sure you know. And everyone has gone out of their way to be welcoming."

She was not inclined to say more, but Parslow was in conversational mood.

"So you've met a few people during the week? That's excellent."

"I have," said Rebecca. "Just yesterday, in all that squally weather, Mrs Fraser came to invite me for afternoon tea. That was… good of her."

Parslow did not register the hesitation.

"A nice, comfortable way to meet a number of ladies," he said.

"Oh no, it was just the two of us. Getting to know each other." Rebecca was cautious, but she wanted to judge the Headmaster's response, so she went on. "She seems to be a person with decided views about the College."

Now Parslow was on the alert. He stopped thinking about staff wives having afternoon tea, a matter of no interest to him in itself, and began to assemble in his quick mind the various ways in which he had heard about Mrs Sarah Fraser.

"The Frasers are only in their second year themselves, you know. Ben Fraser is an excellent deputy – organises many things most capably for me."

"I was introduced to him the other day, but that is not to say I know him. Mr Parslow, I did feel a little awkward when Mrs Fraser more or less told me that a chaplain had a clearly defined role in the College and should stick to it. I'm sure your school is not quite as rigid as that."

There was a response, in the sudden twitching of the head and the gaze shifting skywards as Parslow considered his next move. He said:

"I want Charles to feel he can make his own role, not simply slip into a predetermined one."

They both smiled and Parslow stepped across to the chapel door.

"Yes, all the boys are in now. Let me show you to your seat."

So some things are very predetermined, Rebecca thought, as he led her in. Just then the chapel bell began to sound and she saw her husband enter. He was his normal, composed self and she wondered how this particular service would help him to make his role.

Charles Herbert had chosen to do so in the most obvious and direct way – by self-introduction. His talk, hardly a sermon, followed an anthem by the choir, on this occasion *Zadok the Priest*. The choir presented it in a stirring fashion, though it was a little too heroically grand for the moment, Herbert felt. He rose to address the school feeling that he was going to appear just a little ordinary after all those resounding hallelujahs and amens. But he set his own tone and carried it through with quiet conviction.

He told them a little of his background, football and all, implying that he could tell them stories of many famous players of twenty years previously, if anyone cared to ask. He told them of how he had pursued his ministry through sport and in various parishes, most recently one only a few miles from the school. And it was only fair, he said, that the students of the College should know that he stood before them as a man of solid faith in God and in the hope of salvation through Jesus. He assumed there would be some listening today who shared his faith, and some who did not. But, he said, at least that gives us something to talk about, something more significant than the weather, or maths homework, or even life away from school, important as that was.

He told them that they were not getting a normal sermon that day – well, they would have realised that already. However, he wanted to tell them his plan. For the rest of this term he would talk to them each Sunday on a different parable, mostly from Luke's gospel, and he wanted them to know why, so that they could follow his thinking. Firstly, he said, they are great stories. Each is a story that makes a clear point, very sharply. And on top of that, they are remarkable in that they dramatise an interaction between what it means to have faith and how that faith works in everyday life.

He paused – perhaps that last sentence had lost them. It was complicated, he knew that. But he sensed that many were looking at him as at a new kind of chaplain, and he went on to say that he had decided to start, next Sunday, with probably the most famous of Jesus' stories, that of the prodigal son, and he hoped they would enjoy exploring it with him. That was all: he introduced the final hymn and moved back to his place. The chapel was too formal a place for him to judge reaction; that would come later. He breathed deeply. He had made a start, his way.

Parslow had invited some more or less senior people for drinks in the council room after the service, so as to introduce the Herberts more informally to a cross section of the school community. There, the chaplain was congratulated and told how well he had challenged the boys. Have I challenged you too? he wondered. Or doesn't that matter here? Everything was smiles and conviviality, and Rebecca Herbert was surrounded by welcoming faces, so that it was easy to ensure that she was not left alone with Sarah Fraser. When it was over, Parslow repaired to his study.

He wanted to ring Professor Donald. The College chairman would visit him on the following Wednesday, but he wanted to raise a matter before then and let Donald mull it over for a few days. Before he rang, he assembled his thoughts. As they had over the vacation, they mostly concerned the Frasers.

Firstly, he was beginning to think that he had made a poor choice in Ben. There was the muddle of the English inspection; there was a willingness to take a set against a colleague – the man's judgement of Anderson was weird – and now he had unleashed false accusations against the boy O'Connell. William's parents had been to see Parslow only two days earlier and a most uncomfortable conversation it had been. Parslow had had no choice but to promise to speak to his deputy further – he was at least able to say that he had already done so briefly – and it had been no problem to assure the O'Connells that William's place in the school was secure. At the personal level, then, Fraser seemed to be… well, not all that steady and reliable. That was a huge problem.

Then there was Mrs Fraser. She liked to interfere and speak her mind when she should not: that was clear. Was it simply about wanting to laud her husband's excellences or was there something malicious in it? She had been treated despicably in the incident of the flowers, but what lay behind such a brutal action? And now, with Mrs Herbert so very new, to be saying, even by innuendo, that a chaplain should know his place and stay in it: it was not acceptable, and it could turn out to be very damaging.

What to do about it all? He had not faced anything like this situation before. When he came to the College, Ralph Langton was already a deputy of long standing and he was utterly honest and reliable. He did not regret losing Langton, but he did regret that the replacement, accompanied by a loose-speaking wife, was so inferior. He decided to lay it all, a mixture of facts and impressions, before Professor Donald. Together they would establish a process – Donald was particularly good at that – which would in itself be reassuring. He picked up the phone, determined to attack this disturbing matter and lay it to rest. The first part might be easy enough: but the second?

CHAPTER EIGHT

The gymnasium, also used as the basketball centre, away on the far side of the ovals and then further, was the venue for the annual football presentation evening. The season was over, a season of which the best that could be said was that it was a mixed success – that is, there was a small element of success mixed with a considerable amount of failure. It was never going to be a brilliant season, though one senior coach had had hopes, and the other delusions, of something more wonderful. Nevertheless, presentation evenings are there precisely for the celebration of what *has* worked out well and there had been just enough worthy moments to constitute celebratory material. So the players, coaches, parents and College executives gathered determined to say, publicly at least, how splendid it had all been and how promising was the future.

The gym had been given a festive look. Pennants, team photos and other honourable memorabilia of the past were on prominent display. They helped to justify the occasion for, if one examined them closely, one saw that the wheel had turned from empty years to magnificent ones in the past and would surely do so again. There was a table containing ribbons (for all), medals (for the captains), and trophies for the boy in each team judged to have made the most significant contribution to his team's whole season. These awards were at the discretion of the coaches who, it was said, gave votes after each game. Mostly they did: what was even more remarkable, they consulted their votes before determining and announcing the trophy winners.

Staff sat together at one long table for the meal, while parents and boys sat together at a dozen or so more smaller ones. This time-honoured arrangement raised an issue. It raised the said issue every year and every year Allan Parslow declared his inflexible unwillingness to change. He had decreed that no alcoholic drinks would be served on any occasion when boys were present, no matter their age. If they could not be served alcohol in public, they could not be served it at the College either. Several parents resented this bitterly, in a couple of cases so much that they had taken their sons out for rousing lunches earlier in the day. This eased the bitterness and raised the noise level.

We need say very little about the formalities of the evening. Peter Gryce spoke more or less incoherently and was loudly cheered. Doug Anderson spoke more intelligently and the members of his own team listened, but the Firsts and their parents felt too superior to take even perfunctory notice. The award for most significant player in the Firsts went to the team's full back, presumably because he had had most work to do, from start to finish of the season. In the Seconds, the award went to that Sam, aka Spud, who, by being flattened, had led inadvertently to a win over St Justin's. It may be assumed that he played a good part in other matches too.

When the formalities were over, the staff mingled amongst the boys and the parents told each other how splendid their sons were. This meant that the two staff wives present were even more than normally at a loose end. They were there, Jenny Anderson and Sarah Fraser, in support of husbands who had to be there, but they knew almost no one else and could not enter easily into conversations about the football. Jenny was wishing that Rebecca Herbert had come with her husband, so that she would not have been left, after the dessert and the coffee, to the trifling conversation of the deputy's wife. She bore it as best she could and was immensely grateful to Charles Herbert, who made a threesome for a brief time and who inquired after her pregnancy. It was a simple enough inquiry, but it was enough to break the thread of Sarah's lengthy narration of Ben's excellent exploits.

At another part of the hall, Mr Trumble was in fine form.

"You've got a ready-made captain here for next year, you know, Peter. He is like his dad, a natural leader and organiser."

Even Peter Gryce was not to be manipulated as easily as that.

"Ah, Mr Trumble, I may have lots of terrific prospects, lots of them. We can't rush into next year yet."

"I should hope so," came back Mr Trumble with a guffawing bellow. "I hope you've got many who can play. But you only need one captain and Christopher's your man." He clapped Gryce, who assumed that Mr

Trumble had been one of those who had needed a strong lunch, on the shoulder and continued, "I should know. I've watched him all these years. Why, I remember in the Under 13s."

Gryce wondered whether Trumble knew his boy at all, a fringe player for the Firsts, pleasant, eager, obviously dominated by a boorish father. He excused himself and went to find some parents who might simply congratulate him on a job well done. Trumble found that he was not far from Parslow and decided that he had better impress on the top man his feelings, or decisions, about the leadership of next year's Firsts. He felt in a strong position to do so.

By this time, Jenny was feeling that she had been made to participate in applause of Ben Fraser for long enough. It was getting close to ten o'clock and, though Libby as babysitter would always be flexible, she felt it was time for her to leave. She caught Doug's eye as he chatted to boys about what the Seconds could look forward to next year and especially about the role that the chaplain would play as coach in the latter half of the season. He recognised Jenny's anxiety to leave and mouthed 'two minutes' at her. She at once stood up and began explaining to Sarah Fraser that she felt rather tired.

"Anyway," she said, "we need to be relieving Libby Caraton pretty soon. She is marvellous at looking after Penny, but I wouldn't want to keep her too late."

Sarah Fraser also rose. "I quite understand, my dear. It has been so nice to have this quiet chat with you. We are obviously aware of many of the same things."

Jenny doubted all of that little speech. Particularly, she had no idea what those 'same things' might be.

"There is just one more thing, something you may not be so fully aware of. How could you be?" Sarah spoke quickly, she was suddenly intense and she came stealthily around the corner of the table. "It's an awkward thing, but I would not feel easy in myself if I kept it back. I know that Miss Caraton can be of immense value to you, and I'm told she is a more than adequate teacher. You see, however," and her voice hushed even further, "there were one or two occasions early in our time here that she made, well, quite improper advances, to Ben. Of course he handled it superbly, as he always does. But I do want to warn you about her. It would not surprise us if she tried the same game with Doug, and…"

Jenny had to interrupt her.

"I have no fear of Libby at all. She is a great friend, totally to be trusted."

"Yes, I know, my dear, but…" and Mrs Fraser seemed prepared to leave it hanging like that. The unspoken is often more suggestive than the bluntly stated. Jenny, however, could not so leave it.

"Mrs Fraser, there are no buts here. I know my husband, and I know Libby."

"I'm sure you do – well, your Doug, at any rate. Now I must let you be off; you mustn't overtire yourself."

She uttered the last sentence just as Doug came close enough to hear her. He nodded at her, with a smile for her kind consideration, and then he registered that all was not well with Jenny.

"We had indeed better go," he said. "I hope we find Penny sound asleep. I've said all the thank yous and goodbyes I need to."

He took her hand and, with another smile and nod to Sarah Fraser, led her out into the night. It was very cold, with a stiff breeze adding to the chill. But they were only five minutes' walk from home.

"Sorry to leave you with that silly woman for so long. I suppose it was all right?" He was hopeful, not unduly concerned. But Jenny could contain her fury no longer.

"She is an abomination!" and she went on to tell an increasingly irate Doug of the last five minutes' conversation, if that was the word; five minutes which served to blot out all the inanities she had suffered while Doug had been chatting to the parents. She wanted mostly to speak of the unsavoury comments about him and Libby but she did not overlook the unguarded comment that suggested that Fraser had been in these situations before.

"Does she speak out of jealousy, or spite? What is behind it?"

He was silent for a moment or two.

"She may suspect her husband, I suppose. But this is one of the most malicious slights of all time," he got out. "There is something about both Frasers that hates us, and hates Libby. I suppose we don't fall in with their wishes, play the game their way." And then he burst out, "I loathe their games!"

"So do I," said Jenny, holding tightly to his arm as they neared their house. "Now, not a word of this to Libby."

"Of course not." He paused. "But this is outrageous beyond belief and beyond putting up with. Parslow is going to know of this."

They stopped a few metres from their front door and Jenny looked steadily at him in the pale light of the distant security lamp.

"Are you sure? Can you do that? I understand why it *should* be done – but will Parslow see it your way?"

"I'm not sure I care what he sees. He isn't a fool, and he has been more generous to me of late. I think I have to say something."

She gave him a sudden kiss.

"Good on you. I'm sorry – this will have wrecked your night."

"No. Well perhaps a bit." He gave her a kiss in return just as the porch light came on and Libby Caraton opened their front door.

There was a large and comfortable sitting room in the Herberts' house, called the Big Room by Rebecca but intended as a kind of clergyman's meeting room, on the assumption that a College chaplain would be regularly meeting with groups of people. Charles Herbert's predecessor had used it as his private library and study, where he would pore over his collection of Australian spiders and beetles; he had not needed or wanted a room for meetings. For Charles, however, it was a room in which he could comfortably seat twelve or so and he intended to use it often. He began by using it for Sunday evening gatherings at which, over supper, he and Rebecca would invite some students to tackle a topic of interest. Big topics for the Big Room, that was what Herbert intended.

Students generally like a novelty, especially when it is accompanied by food. Nevertheless, they were somewhat suspicious of this innovation. In their experience, chaplains were elegant and eloquent figures, entirely removed from everyday life. But here was a chaplain, plus wife, who got excited about football, who was known to tell a Year 10 class that they had better put the syllabus aside for a moment to discuss something more important and who now wanted them to chat to him about ideas arising from that morning's sermon. He must have assumed they had listened to it. It wasn't long before they did.

"But, sir," a bright young spark had said at an early gathering in the Big Room, "you don't seem to worry about how exactly we've ruled our margins, or even if the date is at the top of each page. Our standards will slip."

Herbert had affected a resigned helplessness.

"Inevitably. Remind me to give a sermon on dates and margins some time, won't you?" And then, more briskly, "But I think we should be much more interested in why the son wants his inheritance, all of it, right now. Would you be like that?"

The question was thrown back at the boy in such a way that he could not avoid it, not without seeming weak, and he was not the type, as Herbert suspected, to risk that. And so a lively conversation got under way in which, as the boys reflected later, they had revealed more of their hopes and dreams than they had intended to do. Somehow it had just happened that way.

On this particular Sunday evening, eight weeks into the term, Herbert had invited the senior members of the chapel choir to his gathering. He had begun, while sausage rolls and chocolate cake were served – in matters of food, the Herberts were practical, if not imaginative – by thanking them for so splendidly keeping alive the tradition of Anglican psalms and commenting on how delicacy and energy could exist together in such a composition. This was safe ground, the boys thought, inasmuch as psalms were an enjoyable exercise, a performance that, for them, made little connection with the rest of school life. But then, all of a sudden, Herbert wanted them to say what was the point of the psalm, and they had no idea.

"I ask myself that question every time I open the Bible, or any other book for that matter. Whenever I prepare a sermon, or a class, I have to ask that question. Now, this evening for instance."

There were many things he wanted to ask them about the service in which they had participated. Rebecca calmly kept the food coming, and we will go back to that service for a moment.

As we know, Charles Herbert had declared that his sermons for his first term in the College would focus on some of Christ's parables as found in the gospel of Luke. On this particular evening, he had wanted to show how a relationship with Jesus could be both encouraging and confronting at one and the same time. Was that not true of many aspects of life, he had asked them. He had chosen a small story from chapter thirteen, one of the many which envisage the kingdom of Heaven. In this story, many seem to assume that, because they ate and drank with Jesus, had shared a good time with him, they would be accepted, by virtue of their own friendliness, as it were. But Jesus warns them that they might be told that he did not know them because, after all, they had never really known him. Superficial jolliness, Herbert had said, was fun – all of us enjoy it, because we are generally wanting to feel easy about things – but it did tend to obscure the heart of the matter. And that was, clearly, whether one had really responded to the master of the house. Without that response, there would be no admittance.

"But you see," he had concluded, "that is not much to ask, is it? A personal response to Jesus? And isn't that the heart of the matter?"

He had been leaving the chapel after the service when he passed by a small group of staff. Had they been waiting for him? He could not tell.

"That was strong stuff, Chaplain," said Ben Fraser with a hearty smile. "Did you intend it to be so uncompromising?"

Some nodded uncertainly. Flem Harry smiled as though in agreement.

"I am encouraged that you all appear to have listened so attentively," said Charles, not altogether pleased at the sarcasm he heard in his own voice. He suspected that the deputy hadn't actually listened at all and that made him keen to get away. He did not wish to be provoked. "As I said, things can be both encouraging and confronting sometimes. I hope I was encouraging."

"It was all rather 'join us or darkness', wasn't it? That could easily alienate a lot of the boys."

"Not join us, Ben, never that," said Herbert. "It's join Jesus, not us." He wanted to say that Fraser was making exactly the same profound error as the misguided people in the parable, but that would not have been polite. He moved away, though he heard Fraser laugh and Flem comment that the chaplain had told them at the start of the term where he stood and that Fraser ought not to be surprised.

"Come on, Ben, let the man be himself," were the last words Herbert heard. He went home, resolved to ask boys that evening if they could identify the heart of the matter. He would enjoy sharing food and drink with them. But could they probe their feelings more deeply than to consider whether it was good cake?

"You will do all kinds of big things – you will vote, you will probably bring up children – I hope you will often ask yourselves about the heart of the matter, the point of it all."

There was silence. They took refuge in munching. Then Sebastian, an energetic but not always accurate tenor, decided to risk it.

"But, Mr Herbert, when we vote, won't it be more of a balance, weighing up pros and cons? That's not what you told us in chapel: only the pros mattered there."

Herbert beamed at him, delighted that there was to be a genuine discussion.

"You are very perceptive. We should weigh up different matters before we cast our vote. Do we?"

He looked eagerly around the room.

"I think most people just make a gut response," said another, which was also perceptive, and true; but the truth was undercut by a rather loud burp, as though to indicate that gut responses could be of various kinds.

"Is that gut response the same as the heart of the matter, or is it something different?" said Herbert when the laughter had subsided, and for half an hour they had an enjoyable discussion, throwing ideas and feelings this way and that, resolving little, perhaps, but stimulating thought, which was all the gathering was meant to do. Charles and Rebecca tidied up afterwards.

"Somehow you get them going and they don't realise it's happening," she said to her husband in full appreciation of his gentle gifts.

"It was the boys that did it." He chuckled, and it seemed he had forgotten his earlier tenseness caused by Ben Fraser's misinterpretation of all he was trying to do. But, as he got ready for bed an hour or two later, he found himself wondering what was the heart of the matter for the deputy; or for that odd young man Flem Harry. Well, it would keep.

On Monday morning, Allan Parslow emerged from his residence into a morning full of the promise of spring and his step was its briskest, one might almost say its jauntiest. He had spent a profitable weekend, in that he had conducted interviews of students entering Year 7 the following year and had found them to be an interesting bunch. Somehow, it seemed to him, boys of eleven or twelve were becoming more self-assured, more outspoken even, year by year. They all wanted to take part in everything, to excel at most things, to be leaders, every one of them. It was as though they had all been to some coaching college for prospective students. He grinned at the preposterous notion. Well, they had all been bright and eager enough. It would help enormously if at least some of them would turn out to be good sportsmen, footballers especially. He could see them already, some of them, in his new boarding house, responding to every challenge, ready to set the world alight. He had been like that, once.

Parslow smiled contentedly as he marched across to his office. Yes, he had enjoyed those interviews, more than he had enjoyed the Saturday night football presentation. He had sat through tedious speeches, Gryce's especially, and he had been talked at by the likes of that ass Trumble. Would the boys he had interviewed turn out to be like their parents? Some of them would. They would lose that eager spark of enquiry and adventure and would become self-satisfied, boring, men of overblown, grandiose... he couldn't find the right word. But then, when they were forty or fifty years old, they were not his problem. He put them aside, and, pausing to look round at his domain, his eye fell on the chapel. A good appointment there! Rev Herbert had once again spoken well on Sunday morning. He was forthright (so am I, grinned Parslow) and he was already getting the boys engaged. It was odd: he wasn't a brilliant performer, seemed to eschew drama, any histrionics or flights of fancy, but he was intelligent in his probing of issues and boys. He was utterly sincere and he knew how to connect with the world of the students, who would learn more from him in a week than they had in all the years of... Well, let that be. He had been a good man too, in his hermit-like way.

He entered his office and opened the diary. There were two early appointments, one with Doug Anderson, to finalise arrangements for his exchange with the school of the absurd name, and then one with Miss Caraton. He frowned: he could foresee no good reason for that appointment, not one that would turn out to be convenient. He prepared a list for Mrs Delahay, the formal letters of offer following on from his weekend interviews. At eight precisely there was a knock at his door and he got up to admit Anderson. Why did the young man always have to look so tentative? It rather seemed as though he were going to pull out of the adventure. For Parslow either way would do.

"Come and sit down, Doug. Our business won't take long. Did you have a good weekend? All well at home?"

Parslow felt a twinge of guilt. He had once tried to manoeuvre the young man, for the good of the College, he felt sure, but it had not worked; and now he was determined not to push but to let Anderson make the running.

"Yes, thank you, Mr Parslow. And, as you say, our business is simple. The answer is firmly yes, we want to go to Chaddlehangar, starting July next year. Jenny and I are clear that it will be a good thing."

They had spent some of Sunday evening discussing how much else Doug should say. He was still not entirely sure how to play it.

"I am glad," responded Parslow. "It will be a great opportunity. We will miss you, the boys especially, but you will enjoy the challenge. And Mrs Anderson? And your little one – two by then?"

Jenny would have been highly suspicious of the headmaster's apparent warmth and concern but Doug took it at face value. He relaxed.

"Jenny will miss her work, but she knows she can come back to it. And England has its attractions for an art curator. I think this has come at just the right time."

He had been thinking of Jenny when he said that, but to Parslow it sounded as though the man wanted to escape, was relieved to be getting away from the College for a year. There were, however, many months until then.

"You are obviously keen to go, Doug, as you should be. A change in one's teaching is often beneficial. But is it more than that you want?"

Parslow looked steadily at the man before him. There was something Anderson wanted to say, something he needed to get out. What could it be? It couldn't be simply ennui because his football season was over. He asked whether Doug had enjoyed Saturday night, or had he too been cornered by Mr Trumble. He saw Doug smile – they were in agreement on that score, then – but the smile faded rapidly.

"I did want to mention something to you, something from Saturday night. It is awkward, very awkward, but I think I have to say something."

Parslow was at a loss. "Something Peter Gryce has said, is it?"

Once again there was the fleeting grin, disappearing before it had time to settle.

"No, it's not about the football in any way." Parslow saw the man edge forward in his chair, summoning courage, as it seemed. "Look, Mr Parslow, there was a brief conversation between Jenny and Mrs Fraser on Saturday night," (Parslow stiffened, apprehensive) "actually a long conversation, because there was nobody else for her to talk to, but only the last bit matters. It was offensive and I, we, think you need to know about it."

Parslow's anxiety grew rapidly. He tried to picture the scene: yes, he had seen the two women talking, chatting happily, he had assumed. He hadn't noticed anything out of the ordinary. Why would he? And why would Doug use such a word – offensive?

"Just as Jenny got up to leave," and Doug took another huge breath, as though steadying himself before diving into turbulent waters, "Mrs Fraser said that she wanted to warn Jenny about something, about Libby Caraton in fact, who has been a great friend to Jenny and was babysitting Penelope that very night. She said, and I am confident I have this correct, that Libby had in the past made improper advances to Ben, which he had brushed aside, and she was worried that Libby would try the same thing with me. She said that she wanted to put me on my guard. It was a malicious thing to say, without foundation."

Doug relaxed – he had said it and was obviously glad that he had. He had felt offended for himself, his wife and their friend and he completely distrusted the 'friendly warning' Mrs Fraser had offered. Parslow saw all this, and in so doing saw why the Andersons might jump at the chance to get away. All of a sudden he had doubts that they would come back. His mind raced to his diary: it could not, surely, be a coincidence that Miss Caraton was to see him in half an hour. He was very keen to bring the present interview to an end.

"I am sorry to hear this, Doug, and I thank you for your frankness. I shall reflect on what you have said."

He paused and saw Anderson ease further back into his chair. Yes, the young man felt he had been heard. They could go back to business.

"We have these letters, formalising your exchange. Here are copies for you. This one needs your signature, below mine, and then I'll send it to Chaddlehangar. Are you ready to sign? You have had the details already, especially about housing."

Doug took his copy, smiled at it, and then took a pen from his pocket. He asked for the main copy, signed it rapidly and handed it back to Parslow.

"I hope I have not been out of order this morning," he said. "I felt it was important."

"You have done the right thing. You will understand if I don't comment on it right now. But I'm glad you have spoken directly to me."

He stood and Doug followed suit. Moving to the door, Parslow looked round at his English teacher and felt an unaccustomed interest in how life might turn out for him. He held out his hand and Doug shook it, only a little hesitantly.

"The wheels are now in motion, then, Doug. Enjoy your day, won't you."

The interview was suddenly over and Doug found himself in Mrs Delahay's ante-room. She was now at her desk and he said a brief good morning to her. He had plenty of time to ready himself for the first lesson. It would be a relief to go back into a world, and to materials, that he knew well and trusted. Debriefing with Jenny would come later – for the moment, he was happy to be going to Year 10.

He left behind him a very puzzled – not merely puzzled, but angry too – headmaster. Every time the name of Mrs Fraser was brought before him it turned into a problem, a problem with some unpleasant, some unsavoury element to it. Whether she was the victim or the perpetrator, the same repellent aroma was there. He had spoken to Ben about his wife but there seemed to be no way of controlling the woman's tongue. In putting it like that, though, Parslow was making the matter far too simple. He could not know anything of the underlying jealousy and frustration working away in a person who had to tell the world that her husband was perfect. Sarah Fraser felt that, unless Ben's position was unassailable, hers could not be safe either. She was in a trap composed of both loyalty and jealousy; but all Parslow could see was a loose tongue. How could it be otherwise?

He returned to his desk immensely irritated. In fifteen minutes or so Miss Caraton would come, presumably to tell him that she was leaving and he would know why, though he could not let her know he knew. Uncharacteristically, he longed for openness, for an end to games, appearances, manoeuvres. At least he had the grace to smile at himself, briefly and ironically, for every day involved a manoeuvre of some sort.

When Libby Caraton was ushered in by Mrs Delahay, therefore, he played it calmly. She was not tentative, but determined and clear about her needs. She told him that it was time for her to consider moving on. The College had given her a wonderful experience but, ultimately, boys only could not be her preference. She wanted to advise him that she intended to put in for a position as a teacher of French in a very large co-educational school and she wanted to place his name on the list of referees.

"Of course you may do that. I would think it advisable." He looked steadily at her. "I understand your reasoning. You have contributed most excellently here, but one should never stay in one's first school for ever. I would, however, like to feel that you have found the College congenial, that you would not be thinking of leaving us for reasons of personal… unhappiness."

Libby stared at him. What on earth could he mean?

"I have tried to increase the number of women on staff; but it cannot always have been easy for you, feeling a little isolated, perhaps…"

"You are right, Mr Parslow," she responded, feeling that now at last she saw his point. "The College does not always make it easy for young women, though we have a lot to offer. I had much the same conversation some time ago with Helen Meiklejohn."

She saw him wince and was quietly pleased. He did not take it up, however.

"I should imagine that your application will come across as a very strong one. Please keep me informed. I do want you to know how much I have valued your teaching in French. You've quite transformed the subject in the eyes of the boys – and even in the eyes of some of their parents."

They both grinned at that. There was really nothing more to say. Libby had been almost startled into a frank discussion of some of the people and practices of the College but had accepted that they were talking about women as a minority; and Parslow felt that he had opened a door, but he was relieved that they had chosen not to go through it.

"I hope things will be clear for you sooner rather than later," he said to her. It would all be very inconvenient for him. He still felt that the Frasers must in some way be involved in her departure. He would lose a fine teacher and have to deal with a deputy, and a Mrs Deputy, who seemed to set everyone's teeth on edge. In thinking this, Parslow only partly understood what was going on. But a head with such a complex organism as the College to run could never fully understand all the currents of personal feeling that swirled and eddied beneath his carefully maintained surface. He was not out of his depth; but he could not fathom the depths of others' lives.

It would be prudent, Parslow felt, to bring Professor Donald up to date on these matters. He could wait until Friday, when council would meet, but it was always better if he and Donald had thrashed matters out before they got to council, if indeed they needed to. He decided to reflect for a day, in order to feel comfortable about exactly what or how much Donald ought to know. Probably everything, since he had brought Fraser issues to the chairman's notice once already, so that this would not come as a complete surprise. On that occasion, Donald had advised 'watch and wait', essentially do nothing, so as to avoid any chance of public embarrassment at a sensitive time. But a tactic of treading softly seemed pointless now to Parslow. There had to be a resolution, or his state of exasperation might continue, indefinitely. He would reflect for one day more and ring Donald in the morning.

He didn't, because his chairman rang him first.

"Just touching base before Friday, Allan. I have all the papers, all satisfactory, nothing controversial. Is there anything else? And I have one piece of news."

"I was going to call you this morning," said Parslow, in his determination to confront the Fraser issue sliding over Donald's last statement, one on which he would normally have seized. "I want to raise a matter which is probably not for council, not yet, at any rate, but it is for you. You will remember our brief discussion of Mr Fraser, our deputy, and Mrs Fraser and some unfortunate things that were being said, and done."

It had come out in a rush and he paused. He heard a grunt, which, with Donald, signified that he did remember and was not going to like what followed. He didn't, and when Parslow had given his account of Sarah Fraser's words to the wives of both chaplain and English teacher, Donald came in abruptly.

"I acknowledge that she is not our employee. Nevertheless, this must be stopped. It is probably contained at the moment – but it is like a bushfire, with unexpected embers blown here and there and you can never tell when her words will start a spot fire somewhere else." He was thinking rapidly. "How about this? On Friday, Irene comes down to the College with me. While we have our meeting, instead of leaving her in your residence, we arrange for Mrs Fraser to entertain her quietly. If I brief Irene, she will have a calm but very pointed chat with Mrs Fraser. She has worked with me before in a similar way. She will be unofficial, in one sense, but abundantly clear. Mrs Fraser needs to hear that her words will actually damage her husband's position – I suspect she thinks they will bolster it. I can vouch for Irene's absolute discretion. It's worth a try. Do you think that Mrs Fraser will take it appropriately?"

Parslow was trembling. Worth a try? Well, possibly, but he had not intended to widen the circle of those who knew, not yet, not in this way. He had to admit, however, that his attempt to work through Mr Fraser had failed, at least partly because of his own inept handling of the flowers business, his revealing that he had a suspicion but would not disclose it. He could not have acted openly on it, not in any way that would have satisfied the Frasers. He had stopped young Fanning, if it was him, from committing any further atrocity, and that was something, but it was not enough. With all these thoughts whirling mercilessly through his head, he said:

"It will have to be delicately done, and…"

"No, it will have to be clearly done. It won't be rude, but our meaning must be plain. These loose and possibly malicious comments must stop."

"… and," but here Parslow changed course, "and will Irene speak to just Mrs Fraser, or to both of them?"

"Just to Mrs. It will start off as the most ordinary chat between two women connected to the school. When it is over, they will not be friends, but that is of no account. They may never meet again."

Parslow was used to working with his chairman in ways that were open, collaborative, genial. He had never before had to confront the true ruthlessness of the man.

"What you mean is, Mrs Fraser will be told that she must shut up or they must both leave."

There was barely a pause.

"Exactly. Do you have a preference?"

Parslow gulped. It was all proceeding too quickly.

"I've had the man for less than two years and in himself he is mostly satisfactory, so…"

"Then I think you should hope they go. Cut your losses. If all you can say of your deputy in a school such as ours is that he is mostly satisfactory, then you are better off finding a new one. It is not like you to be uncertain on such a matter, Allan."

There was the hint of a rising inflexion at the end of his sentence, so that Parslow could almost take it as a question. But he knew that it wasn't.

"Not at all. I am just thinking through possible consequences. Shall we say, then, that you, Irene and I meet at four thirty in the residence, to talk through things? I shall have Mrs Fraser come and pick her up before five, when we go to our meeting. If their discussion is brief, how is Irene, so to speak, to be retrieved? I don't want her to feel embarrassed."

There was a short laugh.

"I'll see to it. You need have no fears. Now, I have a meeting shortly, but before then I must tell you one other piece of council news. You might like it – or not, possibly."

Parslow was at a loss.

"You may remember that Hamish O'Loughlin, the old boys' rep on council (I hate the notion of representatives, very undermining) had indicated that he expected to be posted overseas at some point. It has all happened suddenly and his posting is to begin in a couple of weeks, so that Friday will be his last meeting with us. No great loss, I should have thought, but he has told the Old Boys' Association and there is already talk of who their new representative might be. They will elect him, another stupid arrangement. We should be telling them who we think is suitable."

"Once their man is appointed, Greg, he is bound by council confidentiality, just like the rest of us."

"Quite so," said Donald and then he paused. "I have my sources," he went on, a little more slowly now, "and they tell me that very energetic lobbying is going on to ensure that the new man on council will be a chap called Trumble."

Silence, for many seconds, and then a laugh of sorts from Parslow.

"The man is a pompous ass."

"That has never stopped anyone from being elected – to anything!"

"They had better be told to think again."

"I cannot control their election." He spoke with sorrow, as at an unfortunate malfunction of an otherwise tolerable system. "Well, I'll see what I can do. I must go now, but we'll chat further on Friday. I may have more news by then. And as to the Fraser matter, we must confront it. Irene can work wonders."

He rang off, leaving Parslow trembling. Fraser – Trumble – why was he not in control as he used to be? He looked at his diary, hoping to find something reassuring on his list for the day. He saw the two asterisked points. Normally they would have been just what he needed:

*final check of council papers.

*remind staff, one term's notice expected.

All very ordinary, and all very unsettling. He decided to walk through the new boarding house. That would be soothing.

Hamish Fanning had recovered. When he attempted to sleep, he did sleep. When he went to his desk, the work flowed, mostly quite easily. When he sat in class, he was able to focus, more or less as he always had, which, as he acknowledged to himself, was by no means all of the time. But he asked pertinent questions and he took notes in his own idiosyncratic fashion. Consequently, when Mr Masterson passed the headmaster at morning tea on Wednesday, he was able to report that Fanning had scored full marks in an impromptu quiz the day before. He was mystified by Parslow's response, yes, I thought he would.

If it ever happened that Hamish paused to reflect on what he had done to Mrs Fraser, he felt totally comfortable. She had deserved it and his conscience was clear. What had thrown him was not guilt but the awareness of impending disgrace. The headmaster knew it all – but how? He was in no position to put all those facts and impressions which Parslow had received together, and so to the boy Parslow's address to the House had come as a shock of the most profound kind. And then the message relayed through Masterson – that had confirmed that the headmaster knew but it also told him there was a reprieve, providing nothing further occurred. He tried to fathom the headmaster's reasoning here but again he failed. How could it be otherwise? He had no idea of Parslow's feelings towards the Frasers or of how heads spend their time worrying over building fund contributions. Even more significantly, he had no idea that a person like Parslow could actually be afraid, deeply afraid, of the storm which Hamish's own father could breathe into life if he were faced with the discipline, perhaps the expulsion, of his brilliant son. He knew his father carried on a lot and could be rude, as he had been to Sam Baker; but it did not occur to him that his father's blustering reputation had, in large part, saved him. He did feel safe. Parslow knew and was not going to act; nobody else knew, or could.

On the same Wednesday on which Mr Masterson had reassured the headmaster, Hamish was the prefect assisting on duty in the evening. He had planned to prepare for an English essay under test conditions the next day, but then he consulted the roster and discovered that it was Custance who was, ostensibly, on duty in the House. Bother, he said to himself, or something stronger. If it had been Anderson, he could have run his thoughts past a relevant teacher and then got on with his preparation, because Anderson would run the House. His job, at worst, would have been to collect the boys on the supper roster. But Custance would tell him to grow up and show a sense of responsibility – which meant, do the man's job for him.

At seven o'clock he began a tour of the younger study rooms and was pleased to see that both Years 7 and 9 had been deluged with maths homework. All praise to the maths department, he thought. He saw Mr Custance go into Year 10 (he would pick the easy one, thought Hamish) and walked on to Year 8. It was ten past seven and there was no sign of anything other than a corporate chat. He called out "Desks!" and was amazed to see that it worked. On some evenings, they just laughed. He was about to leave and get on with his own work (could he start an essay with an assertion that the Romantics were a bit thin-skinned and precious? Probably not) when he saw, near the door, William O'Connell at his desk, staring at his beloved encyclopedia of Australian birds.

"It's a great book, William, but it's study time."

"All right. But Hamish…?"

Hamish stopped. This curious lad wore an eager expression; he seemed about to say something and then thought better of it. He felt obliged to ask.

"How are things, William? OK here? And at home?"

"Oh, I'm fine," said William. (Did he look eager, or mischievous, or what?) "I was wondering how you were going."

Hamish blinked. What an odd question from a Year 8 boy! "I am good, though I won't object if you prepare an essay on Romantic poetry for me. How about it?" He moved away, so that the voice, softly, came from behind him.

"It *was* you, wasn't it? The person Mr Parslow was getting at that night. I'm sure it was you."

Hamish's heart lurched and the blood rushed to his face and neck and then as suddenly disappeared. He should have just walked on but he couldn't; he had to turn and face his accuser. Or was it not like that at all?

"Don't worry, I wouldn't dream of telling anyone. I don't know what it was all about – I just know that you do. That's why I asked how you are. For days afterwards, you hardly looked any of us straight in the eye."

"I can't imagine…"

"Yes, you know what I'm talking about. But you seem to have recovered, as far as I can tell. I'm glad. You're one person who actually talks to me. Not many do." William patted his encyclopedia. "Not about things that matter to me. So you need have no worries. I'm on your side."

Hamish managed a smile, an anguished smile, with some admixture of relief.

"You do your work, and I'll go and do mine," he said. "We can talk about birds at supper, if you like."

He got a nod in response and went on his way. He was halfway to his own study when he came across Barney Custance.

"There you are, Hamish. I wondered where you'd got to. I've settled the younger ones. That's where I expected to find you."

"I was in... Year 8 didn't seem to have much... I must get on with my English." The words came falteringly and Custance stared.

"Come on, lad, get a grip. Or are you unwell?"

He wanted only to get away from a housemaster he knew he couldn't trust.

"I'm fine. Just thinking about an English test essay for tomorrow."

"As you should. But don't forget about tonight's responsibilities, either." Custance gave his encouraging smile and went back to his own study. Fanning sighed. There would be no coherent revision of those wretched Romantics tonight. He smiled at his own alliteration. But then bits of lines – tumult, prophesying war – came to him as more fitting to his mood at that moment.

Back at his desk, he reached for his notes (not many of them) and his annotated anthology, thick with marginal scrawlings. What would the essay be about, he wondered. A straight nature topic? Probably not, because Mrs Madigan liked the more cryptic poems. He was young enough to find the Grecian Urn very cryptic. These Romantics loved to allude to all manner of clever things, so that it was hard to hold all the threads together. Suddenly he slammed the anthology shut. That, he thought, is precisely what I always thought I could do, manage all the bits and pieces. He felt threatened, ill at ease, not sure where one thread twisted its way around another. Damn O'Connell, he thought. Just when he had it all together again, the boy had let off an explosion of doubt. Could he trust him? He thought he could. Could he do anything to reassure himself? Not a hope. He went off to disturb one of his mates. He was at a loss how to feel. The people he should have been able to go to – father, housemaster – were useless to him. It was all a muddle, he thought, but he did not realise that several figures on the campus, headmaster included, shared his confusion.

Two venerable colleagues – ex-colleagues, but colleagues in retirement – had been drawn together by the May Fair and had continued to meet up. It was Ralph Langton who led the way, because he was more honest about his own needs than Sam could be. So he arranged further coffee and stroll occasions and once took the train up into the hills to visit Sam in his hideaway. He was pleased to see that Baker was relaxing with him and even more pleased – perhaps astonished would be better – to receive a phone call from him.

"Ralph? Listen here, I've got an idea."

"Dangerous things, Sam, especially coming from you. I don't think I ought to listen."

"I want you to consider this one." Langton heard a deep breath taken and then Sam seemed to launch into a prepared speech. "I want you to consider being a partner in a tour of the stately homes of the United Kingdom. Yes, it's indulgent, but there's a good deal going which only applies to two people twin share. The price is outrageous for singles, but there must be space they want to fill for doubles. It would start in only three weeks and we'd be away for three weeks in total. It looks marvellous. Do you think you…?"

Here the prepared speech ran out. What Sam wanted to give next was a personal plea – would you come with me? – but he wasn't good at the personal plea.

"Hang on a minute, Sam, I need a whole lot more detail than that. If I'm to spend three weeks with you, it will have to be something very special. I need to know…"

Sam could not listen further. "I'll see you at that Sands place you love in two hours. I'll have all the material. Then we can book…"

"Has it got anything to do with clocks?"

"Of course it has. Two hours." Sam hung up.

Therefore, in the same week that produced anguish and confusion for Hamish Fanning and for several others, Ralph Langton and Sam Baker were spending the night in a hotel room at the airport prior to an eight a.m. flight the next day.

"This is a barren room, isn't it? The ones on the tour had better be an improvement on this."

"I suppose so. I think the rooms will be the least of our concerns." And when Sam raised an eyebrow at him, Ralph continued, "What of the weather? It can rain for weeks in England, interminably in Wales."

"We are two nights only in Wales, for Carnarvon, which isn't a stately home anyway." (He spoke as though that fact had a bearing on the weather.) "I've checked for a week ahead, Ralph; it will be fine August weather."

Sam beamed at the thought of their adventure. Everything was in place for the kind of tour a fit man in his sixties would relish.

"I know. And I intend to enjoy it too." Ralph paused. "You know, this trip has us moving far away from our shared past. Maybe we stayed too long in that place?"

Sam considered.

"No, it felt right at the time. I'm content with that. I'm not trying, as I told you, to write it all down any more. Parslow would be pleased to hear that. But I've no need to dwell on it now. It's all out of my system to the point that I no longer need the memories." He let a moment pass. "Well, perhaps the odd one, of an interesting boy, or a scrap with you, something like that."

This time it was Ralph who took a moment to weigh the other's words.

"It's taken you a while,' he muttered.

"Yes, I know. The other day I got a brief card from old Masterson, the only one who wants to keep in touch. He's due for long service leave and is planning to travel. I suspect he's more adventurous than we are – South America, Cuzco, that sort of thing."

"He is younger and fitter than us, Sam. Than I am, I should say. Still, I have my doctor's letters and all my travel insurance is done."

Sam took no notice of that.

"As an aside, he told me something interesting. That young man Anderson is going to do an exchange to a school in the south of England. Have you heard of a place called Chaddlehangar?"

"Hah!" squawked Langton. "It may almost have reached the twentieth century by now. It was said that boys in the upper sixth at Chaddlehangar had to address each other as Mister. Anderson will be perplexed. And that wife of his will think it a madhouse."

Sam reflected, and then came out with, "I'm glad he's doing it. We were all too obsessed with the College. Years went by in the world outside and we virtually missed them. He's doing the right thing."

"As are we," said Ralph, for whom missing the world outside had been his aim for far too long. "Now, I've been reading up a bit about

Blenheim; the world didn't pass that place by, despite appearances. In fact, Blenheim might claim to have run the world."

Sam relaxed. They would chat, have an early night, and then begin their own small grand tour. School could safely be left behind.

Friday afternoon should not be a time for meetings. The end of the teaching week should be the signal for some gentler time, something close to winding down. There should be time to visit the staff social 'pub', have a gossip, let things drift a bit. One deserves a break, after all, between classes and weekend sports. Friday afternoon should be left free.

Not only was it the time set down for a council meeting, which didn't operate according to the College timetable anyway, but also, unfortunately, for an English department meeting. The trial exams of a fortnight before had been assessed and a meeting was necessary to finalise marks and grades so that reports could be written. Felicity Madigan could find no other time when her teachers were all available. Friday afternoon it had to be.

"I'm comfortable with the spread, and the borderlines," Felicity said as she drew the meeting to a close. "You have all you need for report writing. Don't spend all weekend on it."

They grunted assent, relieved that the business was done by five o'clock. It had been a brisk and efficient meeting.

"You have guided us through the maze splendidly, Felicity," said Flem. Doug looked up in astonishment, but the others continued to stare at their papers. He thought he caught Maya in a sidelong glance at Blaize Rascham but Blaize was determined to be uninvolved. Flem, however, was not finished.

"I cannot remember a time when the marking and moderating have gone more smoothly. Hardly a disagreement, let alone our usual acrimony."

"That's a bit strong, Flem," said Doug. "We are not an acrimonious bunch."

Flem gave him a pitying look, as though to one whose memory was seriously defective or who had chosen to bury the inconvenient truth.

"Not too strong at all," he asserted. Then, turning to Felicity, "We all thank you for your guidance and encouragement. Why, the whole process made sense, for once."

"It's the same process I used last year before my absence," said Felicity quietly. She knew that Flem's remarks were really a slur on Ben Fraser, from whom he obviously wanted to distance himself. Fraser did not teach Year 12, so Flem's tactic must have seemed to him safe enough at this meeting. She put up a hand to forestall a rejoinder and said, "It has all worked well and I thank you all for that. Now, is there any other matter that needs raising?"

Flem seemed to have forgotten that it was Friday afternoon.

"Hardly a matter of urgency, but a suggestion, if I may, Felicity."

His unctuous deference to his head of department was nauseating, Doug felt. Felicity decided to ignore the tone and see what absurdity he would present.

"I'm thinking of next year, the future in general," he said, as though addressing a mighty conference, "and I'm wondering if we can't restore Henry James to our booklist. One of the greatest writers and one of the most distinctive voices. Our boys should know about him, don't you all agree?"

They by no means agreed. Maya had nothing to contribute, having not read any James herself. Blaize gave her a comforting look. Doug took up the charge.

"Come off it, Flem. James is fine for us, not for the boys. They can't engage, it's too alien."

"James alien? You can't be serious. Now, Felicity, I really think…"

"I'm with Doug on this. What, after all, don't you know, would they find? She brought it out wonderfully, perhaps too wonderfully. As a consequence, her interlocuter failed to register how deeply she had seen through him, through all of them, as it were. Oh she could be superb, even if the audience could not grasp the extent – or was it the depth – of her grandeur?"

Flem blushed furiously and Doug patted him on the arm. "I think you've got your answer, Flem. Well, I'm off to pick up Penny." He looked at Felicity, received a gentle nod and gathered up his papers. Others did the same. Flem lingered.

"Felicity, I thought I was making a serious suggestion," he said.

"Did you? Did you really? Flem, almost everything about you is a performance, and a carefully calculated one. I assume that what we've just seen was one, too."

It was a brutal speech, Felicity realised as she uttered it. She was responding not so much to his suggestion of James, easily enough put aside, but to his obviously ingratiating attitude towards herself. She could not trust the man and it was time he knew it.

"I... I am surprised at such words from you," he said loftily.

"There you go again, Flem." She took stock and made her decision. "Look, Flem, you're a very solid teacher with a fine grasp of the subject. I like that. But you're not part of the team, are you? Whose side are you on this week, Flem? Have a think – and think also about opportunities away from this place. It is too insular for you – it's not doing you any good."

Flem would not take it.

"I think you've misunderstood me completely. Deliberately? I cannot tell."

He picked up his stack of papers and moved to the door. Turning, he arranged his face to be more pained than angry. "Yes, misunderstood. I'm here for the long haul."

He left Felicity sitting at the table in the meeting room.

"I doubt it," she said under her breath. "I doubt it very much."

"Shall we go across to my house, Mrs Donald? I have things ready for some tea. And some fruit cake, perhaps? If I say so myself, I make an excellent fruit cake."

In the brief introduction in the headmaster's sitting room and now as they walked around the edge of the oval, Irene Donald had seen enough. She did not relish her assignment. On the other hand, she never refused her husband's requests and she felt little pity for the overblown actress who was gushing around her. Did Mrs Fraser really think she was to be won over with such simple-minded nonsense?

"That will be most welcome," she said. "But first," and she paused in her strolling, "I wonder if we might sit on this bench for a few moments. I always enjoy this view of the grounds. I am not often here when it is so calm."

Sarah Fraser was surprised. She had looked forward to a cosy chat in her own living room; but, if the wife of the chairman was a little eccentric, she would know how to handle her. They sat on the bench and gazed across the green playing fields.

"It is a wonderful school," said Irene Donald. "You and Mr Fraser have been here, what, nearly two years now?"

"We have. We feel very settled. And Ben has done so well. I am very proud of him."

"And he of you, I have no doubt." That drew a smile one could only describe as coy but Mrs Donald went straight on. "It must have been different, coming to a school where everyone lives together, as well as works together. For myself, I wouldn't find that attractive. Greg has his work at the university and I like to get out into the community. I would feel cramped, I suspect – but you don't?"

"But there are so many different things I can do here. I like to think I am a real help to Ben. We are a team."

"I think I know what you mean. I suppose you have to go to sports nights, things of that kind, to accompany Ben. It must be tedious, sometimes. All those men with their sporty talk and no other women to talk to."

She gestured at the field, as though those tedious men might still be running around out there.

"Oh no, Irene. (I hope I may call you Irene.) There are staff wives, and parents, and I chat to them. It's all part of flying the College banner, you see."

"I do see, and I suppose I do something of the same at university functions, except that I don't know most of the people there. That might not be a problem for you. But I resolve not to enter into the affairs of Greg's world – it's not my place."

"You would think differently if you actually lived amongst it. Here one is part of it. One actually sees so much."

Sarah Fraser was becoming eager. She had a ready listener, one it would be useful to impress. But for Irene Donald, the time had come. As she had listened, and it had been with readiness, she had formed a suspicion based on Mrs Fraser's frantic need to be everywhere her husband was.

"One can see things but not become involved in them. We may talk freely at home with our husbands but that talk must never go out into the school life. Just as he will be told things in professional confidence that never come home to you."

Sarah knew better than that and smiled complacently. This Mrs Donald was a dull old thing after all. She was about to assert her prerogative, her right to know and be involved, when the chairman's wife went on.

"I suppose there are people who are drawn in because they need to keep an eye on the husband. And maybe they have cause. I feel very sorry for them."

Sarah Fraser sat very still. Was she being told that her husband was a philanderer? And that she knew it? This was not the conversation she had been expecting to have. It was all untrue. Ben was just occasionally diverted... and she had to help, and not let him ruin things.

They had both been gazing across the playing fields as they sat next to each other on the bench but, with her last words, Mrs Donald turned and looked straight at her companion for the afternoon. She saw Mrs Fraser twitch.

"But even if one did suspect, or know – even then, to fall into any kind of school gossip is disastrous, isn't it? We have to be above all that. I have known of cases where a man's career has been severely jeopardised. It is one thing to tell him off at home, but quite another..."

She paused and gave a thin smile. "But I don't know why I am running on like this. You are in no such position. And I suspect that all you say to others is motivated by a desire to laud Ben to the skies. Just as it should be. You know he has an important role to play. As do others, of course. So we support our husbands but never run anybody else down – they have important roles, too. Like your new chaplain. I'm told he is a most interesting man. But here I am dominating the conversation. Greg tells me I do that sometimes. But I promise I won't if you can lead me off to that nice cup of tea and a slice of your cake. It's almost dark, we have sat here so long."

Irene Donald stood and took a step or two towards the oval, as though to take a last look at her favourite prospect. She had to give Mrs Fraser time. She had watched her closely through that last long speech; she had seen the twitch, the colour coming and going, and she was sure that her words had hit their mark. She was less sure of how the other woman would react. She had to give her time.

Sarah needed it. She had come through an uncertain time in the College and she prided herself that she had done so with aplomb. Now, in a moment of panic, she felt as though an X-ray machine had been used on all her most private thoughts and motives and, what was much worse, that the X-ray results had been pinned up on the school noticeboard for all to see. She understood that she had been given a very blunt warning and that somehow Ben was being warned too. The panic rose in her and she fought it down. She would provide this odious woman with tea. Not only that, she would put up with her for the next hour or two, for however long the bumbling council people took over their affairs. A blunt talk with Ben, then, which was what she needed, would have to wait. She steadied herself and rose. She would have liked to say something splendid but could think of nothing. She would have to play the role of kind hostess for a while yet, hostess to a woman who had obviously been sent to harass and insult her. Yes, that was what had happened. She seized upon some fragments of courage.

"Yes, tea is what we both need, I suspect. This way."

She turned her back on her opponent, leaving her to follow in the gathering gloom. She wished the paths around the College were not so well maintained – or the insufferable woman might trip, might break an ankle. With such invigorating thoughts as those, she marched ahead.

At the Council meeting, at least, the agenda was transparently clear. They examined the finances, looked approvingly at next year's enrolments and heard with a twinge of regret that they might lose an excellent French teacher. Most of them, however, simply assumed that the College was a desired goal for any teacher, so that replacements would be forming a queue to seize the golden opportunity. Parslow allowed them to think so.

"And now," said Professor Donald, "we must be prepared to wear both an auspicious and a drooping eye," and he gave himself a small burst of silent applause, while most of the others looked blankly at him, "because we are about to farewell our old boys' representative, Hamish O'Loughlin. Hamish, you have served us well and faithfully over the last four years and we want to thank you most sincerely for that. Now that your work is going to take you to the other side of the world, we congratulate you just as we affirm how much we shall miss you. It has been a pleasure to have you working with us."

It had been too formal, he knew that, and yet it seemed right for the man. O'Loughlin had done the minimum required. In the past, the much more difficult Stan Li had been a better conduit to the old boys' network. The council wasn't losing much. O'Loughlin made a suitable rejoinder – it, too, was nothing much – and Donald felt he could go back to business.

"As you all know, the College Old Boys' Association are the only ones who elect a representative to this body. None of the rest of us represents anybody – we serve only the College. And, as Hamish has so ably exemplified, once the representative is accepted onto the council, he follows the same rules of confidentiality and discretion as we all do. From time to time the council has other old boys as members, so that the official 'rep' is, ultimately, just one of us." He spread his arms collegially. "It is, of course, up to the old boys, through their association, to nominate a new representative. At our next meeting, I expect to be able to tell you who that will be."

"Oh, I think that's pretty clear already. Wally Trumble has been canvassing votes and I'm told he has it sewn up. There can be no doubt about it."

O'Loughlin's tone might have been that of a man presenting bad news. It was not welcome news to Parslow, even though he had been warned of it earlier.

"Mr Trumble," he said, "has a son in Year 11 and is well known here at the school. He has been a great supporter of our fundraising efforts."

That sounded positive to those who, as yet, knew nothing of Mr Trumble's boorish manipulations. They smiled.

"Well," came in the chairman, "we will have that confirmed before our next meeting. We come now to other business."

The meeting meandered to a close. There was nothing to concern them, the members thought, and they went their various ways feeling quite content. Headmaster and chairman stayed behind, feeling somewhat less content.

"Come on, Allan, it won't be the first time we've had an ass on our council. We'll manage him. But I think I should move straight on and retrieve Irene. There's a limit to how many cups of tea she should be made to suffer."

They shook hands. Parslow said goodnight to Mrs Delahay, whose minutes he would check on Monday. He began to tidy up the room. It had been a very easy council meeting. What troubled him were the things going on out there, in the school, not in this cosy council chamber. In here, it was essentially official and very controllable; out there it was real and increasingly messy. Quickly he collected his things, locked up and went back to the residence. It was a good house, and sometimes it provided a way of closing the door on the irritating muddle of College life. Then he pulled himself up: No! He would not allow himself to see it that way. His house was a place for quiet planning, for working out how to maintain control. He went to see if there was any of that nice Old Boys' port left, as though to fortify himself for the job ahead.

Flem Harry spent the evening at home. A Friday night at home, without seeking any company at all, was a rare, even a strange thing for him. He told himself that he simply felt like it. That was all. He could get on with his reports, as would others, so that there was no point in trying to meet up with anyone. He took the second half of his favourite quiche from the fridge, assembled some salad and treated himself to a very drinkable Sauvignon Blanc. Then he put all his report information on the table and sat down to face the writing.

But he didn't write. He thought, and he considered his next move. He knew he was sailing in treacherous waters. He had been told that, off the north coast of Scotland, the North Sea and the Irish end of the Atlantic collide, creating immense danger, unexpected whirlpools, even if the surface looks calm enough. It is the same here, he thought, but I am a canny enough sailor to survive, to come out on top. Maybe it was that very danger, or rather, the complexity of things which called for all his cunning, that inspired him. Well, if he was to be the supreme strategist, he had better know about all possible obstacles and devise plans to deal with them.

To Ben Fraser he gave barely a thought. The man no longer troubled him. That very morning, as they had walked out of the common room after morning tea, he had said quietly to Ben, "So Libby's probably off?

Had to get away from your attentions, did she?" He was convinced that he had Fraser where he wanted him.

Anderson was off to England, to the school with the preposterous name, for a year; Blaize plugged on, a non-entity; the headmaster seemed pre-occupied, probably with his great building plans. Let him play with such toys if he wished. That left only one problem area.

He poured another glass of wine, a most refreshing drop. Maybe he had overplayed his hand with Felicity Madigan at the English meeting, but he had wanted very badly to see how she would react. She had put him down, very firmly, which was more or less what he had expected. The whole incident had helped him to size her up, to get a realistic estimate of his adversary. Should he worry about her clear hint that he should leave the College? She could not actually threaten his position and, in his vanity, he saw himself as her most exciting teacher. Why, she had almost admitted as much. So he was safe: but how to let her know that he knew he was? How to let her know that she had no option but to – what was that vulgar expression the students used – to suck it up?

Two more glasses of wine and no reports later, he felt no closer to a solution. Maya, it seemed, was protected by both Blaize and Felicity – for different reasons, he supposed. For all his clever sailing, he had put himself at odds with all of them, one way or another. He could move on Fraser once again, he supposed, but would it be worth the bother? He had spent a couple of hours in solemn reflection and yet he could congratulate himself on no brilliant plan of campaign. He poured the last glass of wine and searched for his recording of Verdi's Requiem. 'Dies Irae' – that was pretty much how he felt. And bugger the reports!

But if you had told Flem that, in stressful moments, he reached for the same musical consolation as did Doug Anderson, he would have been horrified at the coincidence! For Flem supposed that he would never be cowed by the day of wrath – he would revel in it.

CHAPTER NINE

He came to consciousness suddenly – but only partially. He was certainly not awake but he was aware of some things: of needing to stretch out but being unable to do so, of a strange scratchiness in his throat, of thirst, of a weight on him, somewhere, he did not know where. Gradually, and as though through a shifting mist, he became aware of a sheet (it can't be mine, it doesn't feel right) and then of pale pink walls in a room too big for any he was accustomed to. He made as though to put out a hand to his bedside table, but he couldn't see the table and his hand was not ready to move. Not yet. So he just lay.

Fragment by fragment, the pieces started to reassemble themselves. There had been drizzly rain, and he had gone to inspect works in his new boarding house. Up to the second floor, talking with Hattingly and the plumbers. Then what? A sudden gush of water – a burst pipe? How could there be a burst pipe? And he had hurriedly stepped back, had forgotten the steps were there, had fallen. There had been a cry, himself or Hattingly he didn't know, and then nothing. Nothing until now. He lay there, awake enough to suppose that someone would explain the rest of it to him eventually. There being nobody around, he just lay there. Perhaps he dozed.

He awoke more fully the next time and once again he wanted, very badly, to stretch out his right leg, but he couldn't. That same feeling of a weight oppressed him. He looked round, moving his head a fraction as he did so, and became aware of a person inspecting a contraption by the side of his bed. At last he understood – a nurse, a hospital, an injury from that fall in the boarding house. He looked at her.

"Hello, Mr Parslow." She came closer. "Are you aware of what I'm saying to you? It's good to see you awake. Lots of people have been asking after you."

She smiled and seemed to expect a response.

"I hear you," he managed. "St James' hospital? But when…?"

He tried to move, even to drag himself up, but the nurse put out a hand to restrain him.

"Don't push against the bed. Not yet. You'll need help. The doctor was in half an hour ago and she will want to know that you're awake. You must lie quite still – I'll be back directly."

She moved out of his line of vision and he heard a door swing shut. He realised that he would have to submit to lying there, for how long he could not know, but his mind, now active, was in a whirl, trying to establish a time sequence. For aught he knew – his mind must have been active for he relished that 'aught' – it might be many hours since the fall. School holidays – the second week – Thursday morning: now afternoon? How bad was his condition? He moved a hand and felt his leg, the one he so much wanted to stretch. It was no longer made of flesh.

"Damn!" he said out loud, just as the door opened, and then two figures stood at his bedside, the nurse from before and another woman. She introduced herself as Dr Ackroyd, on duty for the afternoon shift.

"So it is only Thursday afternoon," he muttered. "Good. Not much time lost."

"I'm afraid not, Mr Parslow. It's Friday afternoon, almost evening." She brought a chair to the side of the bed and seemed to settle in for a discussion. But Parslow was too agitated.

"What do you mean, Friday? What happened to Thursday?"

"You were concussed, basically. There was an operation, anaesthetic. But please lie calmly…"

(What an absurd thing to say to me, he thought angrily)

"… and I shall try to fill you in. OK? Are you up to it?"

"Up to it? What on earth do you mean by that?"

"Mr Parslow, you are, essentially, a very lucky man."

"Huh!" which she ignored.

"You have experienced an extremely bad fall. In it, two major things happened. You sustained concussion, but, as far as we can tell, no lasting head injuries; and you have a badly broken leg, which necessitated an operation and a pin and plate. The leg is in a full plaster, but you have probably worked that part out for yourself."

She paused. The nurse was smiling, perhaps expecting him to be pleased. Parslow was not pleased.

"So you've had me out to it for a day and a half. I can't be away from the school this long. It's quite impossible."

"Your surgeon, Dr Zafin, will explain further. But I must warn you, Mr Parslow, that, with a break like yours, the period of rehabilitation will probably be several weeks. You will not be back at work straight away."

He wanted to sink back into the bed but he was already sunk.

"Impossible," he muttered, more feebly this time. And then: "Professor Donald? Does he know of this?" He tried to make his eyes do a full circuit of the catastrophe that was his body.

"Yes," came in the nurse. "He has rung every couple of hours. He has been most concerned."

"Get him, get him!" Parslow blurted out. "I want to see him at once. On the phone? No, not the phone. He must be here."

"Take it easy, Mr Parslow," said the doctor, aware now that her patient would not in fact be an easy one at all. "Nurse, see if you can make contact and bring the man up to date. How far away is he, do you know?"

Parslow butted in. "Two hours at most. Less, the way he drives. Get him here!"

"I think we had better sedate this patient, Nurse."

That achieved the desired result.

"Not on your life!" Parslow made a huge effort, of mind if not of body. "I will not be sedated, but I will be quiet. But I must see Donald."

The nurse went on her mission and Dr Ackroyd took the customary readings. She gazed down at her most unwilling patient.

"We'll make you more comfortable shortly, and we'll arrange some food." She paused. "I beg you to understand: you've had a very bad fall and you must take time to recover. We'll help you all we can but you will have to be realistic. And sensible." Another pause. "I'll be back."

There was no time for him to respond. The doctor, unfortunately he thought, was determined and knew her mind. But how was he to remain calm. The College – his College – needed his hand to guide it. It could not be left to – and he groaned aloud – to Fraser! Or worse, to Mrs Fraser. He simply could not be absent, not for a few days, let alone weeks. It was all very inconvenient.

Parslow paused in these ramblings, because both nurse and doctor had returned. And, yes, they did make him more comfortable. They offered him a sandwich – had they never heard of cake? But what he wanted was news of Professor Donald.

"He is still in a meeting at the university. We left a message. But his wife answered at home and said she would expect them both to come down first thing in the morning."

"Not until tomorrow? No, no, no!"

The nurse smiled at his exasperation. "What? Do you expect the school to disappear, on a Friday night in the vacation?" She patted his cast. "Keep this as still as you can. Can you now reach the call button?"

He could, and he was left once more to his impatient self.

"So you see," said Professor Donald at the end of half an hour, "we could not do anything until we could see how you would come through it. People will be coming back on campus in droves over the weekend and we will have to make an announcement; but I am very glad to be able to talk it through with you before we do. Irene sends her kind regards, by the way."

Parslow was much more collected by Saturday morning and was able to undertake the conversation in no worse than a semi-recumbent position. He winced at the thought of an announcement.

"It's such terrible timing," he said, as though anyone might arrange the timing of such an accident. "I have to be there, I have to be in charge. I cannot tolerate the thought of Fraser running the College for weeks, half a term, maybe more."

"Quite. The trouble is, Allan, that he is your deputy and a deputy is meant to depute. I suppose he is back now, from wherever his holiday took him…"

("The second week only, in Brisbane.")

"… and he will be expecting to act in your stead."

Parslow winced again.

"But, outrageous as it will seem to you, I have a suggestion to make."

Donald waited. Parslow knew his chairman well enough to know that this would not be an idle thought, but rather something he expected to see put into action.

"Come on then. You know I'm not afraid of left field."

The chairman settled himself, aware that his suggestion, sound as it was, would not have sat well with Parslow in the past.

"Now," he began, "I think we can make the case that, at this unfortunate time, the less disruption caused to the College the better. If Fraser acts as you, and somebody for him, and somebody else for that person, then disruption – looseness – grows exponentially. Whereas if a trusted old hand could be persuaded to fill in for you, to hold the fort only, for six weeks or so, then the rest of the College can move ahead unhindered. It all makes sense."

"I don't think Ralph is…"

"Neither do I. He is much better than he was. He has just managed an overseas trip. But his health would be a real concern. That is not true of Sam Baker, however."

There was a sharp intake of breath from the patient and Donald reached for the water. Parslow waved it away.

"It might be possible," he said, "but there are many risks. He was not as universally liked and respected as our dear Langton was."

"I know that." Pause. "And yet he might be well received, just to hold the fort, given the alternative."

Parslow nodded. "And he and I could hold regular conversations. I wouldn't be out of the loop."

"I suppose you could," responded Donald, repressing any hint of a doubt on the matter. "Do you agree? Shall I approach him?"

"Do you need my agreement, Chairman?" And then, sensing that his words sounded ungracious, given that Donald was trying very hard to remove a potential disaster, he added, "I am grateful for your thinking on the matter. Fraser will not like it – he might leave us in protest."

"I've thought of that, too," said Donald.

Thus it was that, after a brief phone call simply to announce his arrival, Greg Donald called on Sam Baker at his home in the hills. There were preliminaries to be worked through, concerning Sam's trip – Donald said that in England one need go nowhere except London, which shocked Sam, for whom York had become the place never to be missed – and his general wellbeing. Then followed an unusual conversation.

"Do you know of Allan Parslow's accident of a few days ago?"

Sam had to admit he knew nothing of it. Donald filled him in.

"And now I come to you in need of help. There are reasons, weighty reasons, why upsetting the whole College and having Fraser, our deputy, act as headmaster for a time, is not our preferred course of action. As I say, my visit is in order to seek your help. Will you come and be acting headmaster of the College for a while, probably half a term or a bit more? Allan and I will be very grateful if you will."

Whatever Sam Baker had been expecting, such an offer was not it.

"You're joking!" he burst out. "You want me? After all Allan did to make sure I couldn't even be his deputy? I've never heard…"

"Well, you're hearing it now. It is my suggestion but I have Allan's full agreement. I very much hope you'll come along with us in this."

"What of Langton?" said Sam, still casting about him for solid ground.

"He isn't physically up to it, and you know it."

Sam did indeed know it. Their trip had been a huge success and he had valued Ralph's companionship more than he knew how to say. But every so often the pace had needed to slow, or Ralph had needed a rest day.

"Yes," was all he could say. He gazed at his bushy outlook for a moment. He had got very used to it, in nearly two years of retirement. On their trip, he and Langton had talked about how they had moved away from the College, didn't need it any more. And yet…

"How could it be made to work, Professor?"

Donald smiled warmly, for, if it was now a matter of mere details and procedures, then he felt sure of the outcome.

"As I see it," he began, and within half an hour they had a plan in place. They would move Sam into Ralph Langton's old flat which was still fully furnished on Monday and Sam would take up the reins straight away. Could he come tomorrow down to town and spend the night with the Donalds? Then the two men could be at the school before eight o'clock and make an official announcement. Meanwhile, Donald would speak to Fraser. There was an odd part of him that looked forward to that interview, that skirmish.

It took Sam fully an hour to collect himself after Donald had gone. He began to organise the few things he would need to take when suddenly he remembered Ralph Langton. He reached for the phone.

"You'll never guess what has occurred this afternoon, Ralph."

"And you agreed to it, I hope. It is a good plan. Greg Donald's mostly are, you know."

"You knew all about it?"

Langton smiled as one can only when talking to a mouthpiece.

"The dear man called me. I think he didn't want me to feel passed over. Of course, I told him not to be absurd."

"About me?"

"No, about me, you fool. Enjoy it, Sam. A month, maybe two, with Parslow breathing down your neck from his rehabilitation: you're made for it!"

Sam was not too sure how to take that.

"Thank you for your good wishes. I think they are well meant."

"Enjoy it, Sam. You deserve it, so enjoy it."

That was all, but it gave Sam some confidence. Anyway, he said to himself as he went on packing, I've always enjoyed a joke, the blacker the better.

The Frasers had gone to Brisbane for a week. Why Brisbane? They could not really say but, with most southern visitors, in search of warmer weather, settling on various parts of the Gold Coast, they had wanted to make a statement by being different. They had no idea what that statement might be.

During the last week of term and the first of the holidays, they had revisited, dissected, analysed and poured scorn on the visit of Irene Donald. They called it Irene's mission, since she had obviously been set up to do it, willingly enough, they supposed, perhaps even gleefully. So much contempt had been directed at the Donalds, and at Parslow, by Sarah that it seemed to her husband that only the bile sustained her. For his part, Brisbane for a week should have been a chance to escape from the misery and the uncertainty. Sarah, however, would not allow it and they spent a week at museums, cinemas and cafes reliving and detesting virtually every moment of College life since the May Fair. He couldn't stop the torrent and so, on their return flight late on the Saturday, he told her that he was minded to give Parslow a term's notice at once. There was no point continuing. He might have added, and no point in your endless tirade, which will only make my job more intolerable than ever.

It was as though Hattingly had been waiting for them. Barely had they taken their luggage out of the taxi than he strode towards them.

"Mr Fraser. Mrs Fraser. You've been out of circulation and we weren't sure how to contact you. But I have to tell you that Mr Parslow has had a severe fall and has been in hospital since Thursday. He'll be OK, eventually, but Professor Donald tells me that he might be out of action for a while. With term starting on Monday, you need to know."

There was a long moment, during which the Frasers stared at each other, weighing up the possibilities. Sarah spoke first.

"This is terrible, Mr Hattingly. What happened?"

"It was in the boarding house, the new one," but Fraser interrupted.

"Time enough for all the details later. But what has been done? We have term beginning, a school to run. Where is Mr Parslow now?"

Sarah saw it at once – he was switching immediately into acting headmaster mode. Much as she wanted to know, and relish, all the gory details of Parslow's fall, she accepted that they must wait. In fact, she needed to slip quickly into a new role herself.

"There will be lots to do, Ben. But you always manage; and with people like Mr H to help..."

She felt quite regal, ready to dispense favours. Hattingly did not notice.

"He is in St James', out of danger. But the message I must urgently give you is that Professor Donald will be here at nine in the morning to see you. He asked me to be sure that you got this message."

"And Mrs Donald too?" Sarah was quivering with a sudden, eager rage.

"He did not mention her," was the only reply.

"It is necessary that he and I should confer," said Ben grandly. "It would not be necessary if the head were to be away for a day or two; but it could be some time, I think you said. Weeks?"

"As to that, my information is very vague. But it's clearly not to be a matter of days." Hattingly liked all details to be precisely set down and the uncertainty irked him. However, he had now given his crucial message. "I'll leave you to settle back in. Naturally, I'm around if you need me."

He moved briskly back down the path, followed by, "We know we can rely on you, Mr H." The empress herself, he muttered and left them to it.

The Frasers unpacked swiftly and energetically. Then Sarah urged an early night – it was already after ten – in preparation for a chairman coming, as she supposed, virtually cap in hand. The very chairman whose wife had so insulted her. Vengeance would be gentle, but sweet, very sweet.

Gregory Donald drove to the College unsure how long his meeting with the deputy would take. It might take an hour, he thought, because sensible, College-minded people would need time to thrash out details. On the other hand, he might be thrown out after five minutes. He could cope with that.

Their first exchanges were brief, unctuously polite on the part of Mrs Fraser. He was offered tea or coffee, to refresh him after his journey.

"Perhaps in a few minutes," he said. "Ben, we need to have a few words."

He looked in the direction of Fraser's study but Sarah was determinedly guiding them through to the living room. Ben looked as though he were not sure which would be preferable.

"Sarah," he said, "just prepare both. Professor Donald and I can begin."

She bustled merrily away, making sure that connecting doors were open so that she could hear the conversation. Fraser showed the chairman to a comfortable seat and took one opposite. He rubbed his hands together.

"Well, Professor, this is a bad business. I have heard only a very sketchy outline of it, from Hattingly. How are things with our headmaster?"

"It might have been very bad indeed. Thank God it is not so. There was concussion, but that has passed; there is a badly broken leg, an operation to put things back together. There is to be a period of rehab, lasting perhaps half a term."

"We will cope. A school like this always does. I shall be getting the team together – this afternoon, if they are available – and we will begin term almost as normal."

He placed some stress on the almost. It would not do to sound as though the absence of a headmaster left not a ripple of disturbance. Gregory had to intervene.

"You will indeed be very busy, I have no doubt. And that brings me to the essential point of my visit. Mr Parslow, and I, and those of the council I have been able to contact want as little disturbance to customary roles as possible." Fraser was nodding wisely – he would see to it. "We want you to continue in your role as deputy headmaster, seeing to all the many things you see to, with nobody needing to step into your position, and nobody else into that person's, and so on." Fraser had turned deadly pale. "We have arranged for Mr Sam Baker, who worked here for many years, sometimes as deputy, to come in as acting headmaster for the necessary period of time."

There was something of a crash from the kitchen and Ben saw, though she was directly behind Donald, his wife appear in the doorway, her face a study in disbelief. Donald was continuing.

"This, in a period of uncertainty, will make the least disturbance. Mr Baker will need all your support, of course, but the whole College community knows him and will feel that all is going ahead predictably. It enables…"

He was interrupted by an agitated Mr Fraser.

"But hold on there, Professor Donald. I am the deputy headmaster, the one who acts for the head in his absence, whether that be planned or unplanned. It is in the nature of my role that I step in here. It should not, it cannot, be otherwise."

If Donald had thought that he would carry his point easily, he now had to re-think. Fraser, he saw, had been determined to be a formidable acting head.

"In many cases you would be right," he said, as calmly as he could. "But in this case, stability demands a different course of action. I have spoken with Mr Baker…"

"… before you had the courtesy to speak to me?"

"… with Mr Baker, while you were still on holiday, and he has agreed to come. So he will be the acting headmaster, charged simply with keeping things ticking along, as it were. And you will go on doing all that you do, so that the daily running of the College goes ahead unimpeded. It is the best course of action, and it has already been put in place."

Twelve hours of happy anticipation were swept away at a stroke and in their place was the bitterness that had so dominated the time in Brisbane and the weeks before that.

"It seems to me, Professor, that you are going out of your way to show no confidence in your deputy. I shall take it that that is what you are doing."

"If that were so, Mr Fraser, I would not be asking you so firmly to continue as you are. I would take a quite different approach."

Fraser understood the threat implied. "I shall take the matter under advisement," he said, recalling a phrase from he was not sure where. His wife came forward, minus tea-tray.

"This is not…" but she faltered and stopped. Energetic and positive in good times, Sarah Fraser did not know how to respond when certainties were stripped away. "No, I do not see how you can…"

Donald stood. "I shall forgo the coffee on this occasion. I have a meeting with Mr Baker this afternoon," (he said it very deliberately, to underline the decision already made) "and so I had better get back to town. I shall be down again tomorrow. I need to ask you to ensure a meeting of all staff in the common room at eight in the morning. Until then, I take my leave."

There was no need to show him to the door. Donald was relieved to be out of the place. He left behind him two stunned people, one bitterly regretting a lost opportunity to shine and one now convinced that there was no way forward for him.

"I shall call the meeting. And then I shall write them a letter of resignation."

All of a sudden, Sarah Fraser snapped back into something like her normal mode.

"Do the first, Ben. Wait a month or so for the second – cause them greater inconvenience that way."

He managed a smile. "I am sorry for you more than for me, Sarah."

She was deeply moved by the simplicity of his words and tried to think how she could let him know that.

"Oh Ben," she said. "Where did it all go so wrong?"

Sam Baker sat in the headmaster's office – his office, for the time being – and reflected. It was ten o'clock and he needed a pause. He had told Mrs Delahay that she could bring him tea as often as she liked but under no circumstances cake. She seemed to agree that this was a sensible course of action and went to fetch him his first mug. Well, Sam, he said to himself, what exactly has happened?

He and Professor Donald had met the staff, nearly all of them, at eight o'clock. Donald's speech had been brief and to the point. Parslow's situation was already well known. The point of his remarks, his reason for being there at all, was to make it plain that Mr Baker, whom many of them knew so well, would be in charge for as long as necessary and that he, the chairman, relied, as he knew he could, on all others to go about their business with as little disruption to the life of the College as possible. Some, Sam noted, had grinned in his direction; as many had looked in some puzzlement in Ben Fraser's direction, but he had gazed steadfastly at Donald, as though fully attentive to what was being announced. Sam suspected that, knowing it all in advance, he actually heard very little.

Sam had responded, briefly, efficiently he hoped, saying only that he answered the chairman's call with enthusiasm and looked forward to working with colleagues old and new in the weeks ahead. He might be here just to hold the fort, he had said, but he knew the complexities of the College well enough to understand that he would need the help of all of them. He would do his best.

Some old hands looked wonderingly at him, hoping, perhaps, for some flourishes of Baker's grumpy wit. Custance, he saw, looked particularly sour. Newer colleagues nodded wisely. Flem Harry smirked. Anyway, it was time to get the school day under way. In classes, Sam said, teachers should make the position quite clear to students and then get on with lessons. For his part, he wanted to address the school and was calling for a brief assembly, fifteen minutes, no more, straight after the last class of the day, in the chapel. Please make sure, he said, that all students come directly there, not via their houses. He thanked them all for their support (did he have it?) and sent them on their way. He and

Donald shook hands, the chairman departed, and Sam looked across at Fraser. It had to be faced, and at once.

"Ben, if now is convenient for you, we should talk. We have to know where we stand, don't we?"

It was not really a question.

"Give me five minutes, and I'll be at the headmaster's office." He couldn't bring himself to say, 'your office'. Sam registered the phrasing, nodded briefly and let the man collect himself. That was what the five minutes were for – he wanted to arrive in his own time, not appear to be led away.

When Fraser entered Mrs Delahay's ante-room, Sam had been going through the diary with her. The sight had made Fraser wince, as though with a sharp stab.

"Let us call a halt to this, then," Sam said to her. "Come on through, Ben, we have much to discuss."

"I'm not at all sure that we have," said the deputy, much to Mrs Delahay's amazement. Nevertheless, he followed Baker and they sat in the two easy chairs by the coffee table. Sam had not yet had time to attend to it and the litter of brochures, plans and notes about the new boarding house stood out plainly.

"Is all this," and Fraser gestured at the piles of paper, "on hold then? Is it now considered an unsafe worksite?"

"Probably just for today. I am to see Hattingly and the project manager at noon and they will fill me in. I hope there will be no delay."

Sam considered this a pointless start to their conversation; he had to move straight to the key point.

"I cannot pretend, Ben, that our situation is anything other than unusual. A deputy normally stands in. Professor Donald and the council, and, I gather, Allan Parslow, though I have not seen or spoken to him, see it differently on this occasion. I understand if you feel put out, but you have no need to be put out with me. If it's a case of half a term or so…"

"Put out is a bit mild, isn't it? I have been most deliberately snubbed and insulted, without any attempt made either to conceal or to explain. All this nonsense about ensuring stability – mere words, of course, a cover-up."

Fraser had spoken, not quite calmly, but steadily enough and there was a part of Baker that felt for him. He knew nothing of what might have poisoned the relationship between Fraser and Parslow, if poisoned it was. The two of them would have to sort that out sometime, after Sam had gone. For now, he simply had to insist on full acceptance of the arrangements as they had been laid down.

"My only role here," he said, "is to act as headmaster for as long as is necessary. That I shall do. Yours is the longer role, I assume. But, during my stay, we must keep our roles absolutely distinct." He paused to take in the man sitting opposite: proud, vain perhaps, needing constant endorsement probably. "It has to be that way, Ben. I shall, in effect, be making that clear at this afternoon's assembly when I tell the school how much I rely on you, and others, as well as on the boys themselves, to keep things going well, more than well. We both have to see it the same way."

Fraser was gazing about the room, looking longingly at every inch of it, at every cabinet and every picture. "Publicly, I can acknowledge that," he said, trying to control the edge of bitterness, "but I will never *see* it that way. You cannot expect me to."

He had tried to make it challenging but it came across as petulant. Sam did not want to go much further.

"For the moment, I shall make do with the acknowledgement. And that needs, publicly, to be unequivocal. Now, I have to get to grips with certain things and you have the daily business of the College to attend to. I shall set up a time for tomorrow when we can go through the calendar as we know it for the next month or so, so that I do not overlook anything." Again he paused, just long enough for him to determine that he would want Mrs Delahay at that meeting. He then decided to risk one more step. "Ben, you and I barely know each other. Can we at least shake hands?"

Baker stood, and then Fraser, most uneasily. Probably, Sam thought, he wants to preserve his distance from me. He kept his hand out and slowly, unwillingly, Fraser took it. The shake might have been perfunctory but to Sam it was far better than a parting in blunt acrimony.

"Have a good day, Ben," he had said and then reflected that a comment like that didn't deserve a response. At any rate, it didn't get one. As Fraser left, Sam turned to look back at the coffee table. He had barely begun to tidy away the various papers, putting them carefully to one side in case they should be needed for his midday meeting, when Mrs Delahay appeared at his door. She held it somewhat in the manner of a sentry defending her post.

"Mr Custance is here and is asking for just a few minutes of your time." And then, seeing a flicker of non-recognition pass over Baker's face, she had followed up with, "Mr Custance of the House."

Sam recovered quickly and went over to her, gesturing that she might step back.

"Thank you, Mrs Delahay. Do come in, Barney. It is a pleasure to see you."

Custance eyed him warily. They had worked alongside each other, they knew a good deal of each other's strengths, and weaknesses, but they had never been friends – their ideas about running a house had been too far apart for that. Sam assumed he had kept well hidden his scepticism about Custance following him in the House. He needed, he knew, to treat the current senior housemaster with respect.

"Well," he began, motioning Custance to the seat so recently vacated by Ben Fraser, "we didn't expect this, did we? How are you getting on?"

Barney Custance very pointedly did not take up the offered pleasantry.

"I won't hold you up, Sam. I waited until I saw Ben leave, I wouldn't have wanted to butt in on him…"

(Or butt in on me? wondered Sam)

"… but it is as well you know how things stand. It won't be only Ben – for many of us, this is a terribly wrong move. He should be acting, not you, and other roles juggled so that everyone gets a chance. The younger members of staff won't know, or care; but lots of us do care, and very deeply, too. Just so you know."

More bitterness, Sam thought, this time from a wanted-to-be acting deputy. He had acted in the role himself, more than once. It wasn't much fun but he knew it was seen as important.

"I would not have come in answer to Professor Donald's request if I did not also care, care about the College. Oh yes, two years ago I was relieved to be leaving it. You were there then, you saw it all. But now, Barney, I want to serve the College, and I will do so as asked. It's what we all need to do – no more, but no less."

Custance stood up; there was clearly nothing more for him to say. Nothing that would achieve his aim, although, as Sam reflected later, Barney had never been too sure what his aims were. As deputy he would be a disaster, unless the sole measure of success were the ability to delegate.

"I've said what needed to be said, what you needed to hear. Just think about it, Sam."

"Certainly I shall," responded Sam firmly. "As I shall think about how all of the staff will co-operate with me. Embittered you may be – oh, don't bother to pretend – but that is something for you to take up with Allan or with the professor. For now, we work together, as we've been asked to do. Let's get on well, eh?"

He held out a hand, but all he got was, "I don't think you understand anything," and Custance left.

So it was that, at about ten o'clock, Sam sat in the headmaster's office, his office for now, and reflected on the events of the morning. Had he been blunt? Yes, certainly. Had he been too dictatorial? He hoped he had been civil and reasonable. But just then Mrs Delahay came in with tea and said that Miss Caraton had dropped by.

"Show her in," said Sam, calling up his memories of an enthusiastic French teacher with a gift for getting students to perform in ways they had not thought possible. She had strong opinions, he remembered, but she was definitely the future. She came in carrying an envelope.

"I won't interrupt you for long, not on day one," she said with no preliminaries. "But in order to give you a term's notice, it has to be today."

She held out the envelope and Sam took it. His expression soured and he tried hard to bring it back to neutral at worst.

"Do sit down, Libby. You catch me on the hop. So you are to leave us? I am very sorry to hear it."

She sat, reluctantly it seemed.

"I am sorry it has to be this way. Mr Parslow and I had discussions last term and he knew this was on the cards. If I had been seeing him today, there would have been no surprise."

"I do hope…"

"Look, Mr Baker," she interrupted, "Sam, I've had a good run here but it's not the place in which I should stay for ever. I've enjoyed it – nearly all of it – but I need wider experience. The position in Sydney gives me that. Please believe that I have learnt a lot here, but that I need to move on."

Sam sensed that they were well rehearsed lines, delivered as a director might have ordered, and that, in all likelihood, there was more to be said if only he could feel his way to the appropriate question.

"I'm assuming," he said, "that Mr Parslow will be back before you leave. It would be good for him to have a thorough exit interview with you, because you would have valuable perspectives, I think. I understand that such a talk isn't possible between the two of us today."

Libby grinned.

"I'll tell Mr Parslow what I think he needs to hear. Perhaps."

She stood and Sam, his tea untouched and half-cold by now, stood also and thanked her for her promptness, her adherence to good process.

"I thought it necessary. You may find not everyone here values good processes. But thank you for your time."

She was gone. Sam, not realising he was doing just what Allan Parslow did at moments of stress, went to the window and gazed out over the grounds. All was still. The College seemed unruffled, yet Sam felt that he had walked into a more ruffled, a more unsettled, school than he had imagined. Of course, that could be no bad thing. He remembered how part of him had wanted no change, predictability, a settled order, but he had also seen how that could not last. If Parslow wanted to move ahead, perhaps it would have to be with a new team altogether. But some of his team were new and they seemed to be part of the problem. What was more, it was disastrous to throw out what was good and needed to be preserved. He pulled himself up: he was thinking of the future, not just of holding the fort. With a sigh he went back to the desk and flicked open the diary to a yearly calendar page. He might be here for six weeks; but it would be very wrong of him to think in terms of a longer future in the College. He hadn't wanted to leave, not back then, but he had brought it on himself until it had been his only option. Holding the diary firmly, he contemplated the weeks of term four and then looked out the window again. He would keep things tight for five or six weeks. It was already a point of honour with him that he should do so. But, as he gazed, he saw not playing fields, but deep, dark bush.

For her part, Libby Caraton was content. It was done, officially, and could now be made public. Jenny and Doug knew, but so far none of the others, not even Blaize, who seemed a bit remote of late. She would tell her few close colleagues at morning tea. She had Year 11 in the following lesson, so there would be no hanging around, no need for discussion. Especially since there was really nothing to discuss. She didn't know whether she felt exhilarated or empty.

She walked into the common room in time to see Doug and Blaize warmly shaking hands and both smiling broadly at Maya. She realised later that she had registered the first of these impressions more strongly than the second and, in her own departing frame of mind, had assumed that Blaize had finally made up his mind to move on. She went across to join the merriment and saw that Blaize had that same look, that remote expression, as she called it, that she had noted before.

"Well, you all seem full of delight – at...?"

Blaize drew Maya more firmly into the little group.

"You see, Libby, over the holidays, Maya and I have become engaged."

He let it just hang there, without further comment. Libby had to respond.

"Well, congratulations," she managed. "This is wonderful news." And then, as she assimilated the tidings and took in Maya's radiance, she said, "I am so delighted for you both." She paused but they only beamed at her. "It must have been quite a vacation, then."

Maya reddened, but Blaize was unflappable.

"A memorable one in every way. And now we can plan – Easter next year, we think."

"Wonderful!" she exclaimed, but her heart was not in it. "My news is not nearly so surprising. I've accepted at Redwych and I've just given Sam my formal letter. So I've got just this term to go."

Maya was first with congratulations, not surprisingly, since Doug already knew and Blaize did not quite know what he felt. He just smiled at her and nodded. Just then, Sam sounded the gong for notices. Blaize and Maya sat down together and Libby suddenly felt out of it all. Yes, she thought, this is what happens when you decide to move on: in the interim, it's as though you don't exist.

Doug enjoyed a precious late afternoon hour at home before he was due in the dining hall and then the House. Jenny, back into her normal, which is to say flexible, routine, had collected Penelope on her way home and she and Doug, as they sorted out the child's daily debris and arranged dinner, chatted about a most remarkable day in the life of the school.

"You gave me a hint of it a while ago. You must be more perceptive about such things than…"

"… than you ever suspected? Perhaps it was just a lucky guess."

"Yes, I suppose so." Doug looked a little crestfallen at that and she came and threw her arms around him. "I hope they'll be happy. It seems so sudden. Will it work for them – here?"

"It's worked for us, being young marrieds in a place like this." But then he had to attend to Penny, tugging at his leg and insisting on being part of the hug. Doug sat on the floor with her and let her flop all over him. "How was your day, anyway?"

"Very manageable." She grinned at him. "Not exciting, a little predictable, but with one or two problems to solve. Which I solved. I don't need the extra adrenalin rush just now. It was fun, but I can manage very well without it."

At four months, she was showing quite clearly. He understood her and understood, too, how she would eventually crave that extra excitement once again. But then his thoughts veered off in a different direction.

"I wonder how the stress will tell on Sam Baker. He took care of today's meetings well enough, particularly the talk to the school in the chapel. But some people have made it obvious that they resent his being here."

"I should be one of those, given our past interactions. I might say, *we* should be."

Doug would have none of it.

"He'll be much better in the role than Fraser," (enthusiastic nods from Jenny) "and he's behaving very sensibly. I'm perfectly happy to work with him – not that I'll actually need to, not much."

He wondered whether he had changed, or whether Sam had. Perhaps in not quite two years both men had had a chance to grow in perspective.

"You're too generous, Doug. But let's make the most of it – anything other than Fraser."

Penelope's demands grew more strident, as though she were agreeing vociferously with Jenny's last statement.

"Come on, my little blossom. I've just time to give you your bath before the dining hall."

Jenny watched them go. She hoped his state of equanimity would last. There was bound to be change. All this coming and going. That made her think of Libby. Now that it was real, she realised just how much she would miss her. She sighed, and listened to the chuckles and splashing from the bathroom.

The evening began well. Even Year 9 settled down to some work. Doug did not expect it to last long, not on the first day of term, but it gave him time to move about the House and particularly to check in on some Year 12 boys. They had returned to school for a bare two weeks of refresher classes before the final exams were upon them. They could polish up both skills and knowledge, Doug felt, but they couldn't polish knowledge that had never existed for them. He hoped to find them well prepared. He found Hamish Fanning lounging back in a chair before unopened books.

"Well, Hamish, I'm glad to see you looking so relaxed. I *think* I'm glad to see it."

Fanning smiled comfortably.

"I'll get down to something. I'm just not ready to think about economics, or English, or any of it, not right now."

"You were deep in thought about something, just a moment ago."

The boy stood up.

"Not this, Mr Anderson," and he gestured at the books. "It was a conversation I had yesterday with Dad. It was about," and he spoke portentously, "The Future."

Doug felt pretty sure where this was heading. "And did you see eye to eye on that subject, Hamish?"

"I knew you'd understand," said the boy. "Maybe we came to a compromise. Dad wanted to pigeonhole me in economics/law, and he thinks Sydney is the only place. But I know I want to do international relations and UNSW is the place for that. I'm trying to work out whether I can face the double degree of international *and* economics, just to please him. I suppose I could start it."

Doug smiled at the way the lad was shrewdly working out how to circumvent a vain and pompous father.

"It's the international relations that fires your imagination, then?" He made a wry face. "Not the greats of literature?"

"I don't want greats, Mr Anderson. There's much more to be said for Winton than for most of your greats. How can they speak to me?"

"You are right, Hamish, that's what's important." It was gently said. "And will Dad accept your compromise?"

Hamish frowned. "He'll have to. If I get good enough marks, he'll enjoy boasting about that so much, he might not even notice." He paused, shrugged his shoulders. "Then he'll get used to it and move on. Hell, he even got used to Bill being no great scholar." Bill was now caretaker of a golf course. "I've never seen him so happy, more than when Dad tried to force him into accounting. Dad fires up, but then he accepts things and moves on. Thank goodness!"

Hamish would never know how Charlie Fanning's tendency to 'fire up' had caused Allan Parslow not to risk a confrontation over matters concerning Mrs Fraser. What the boy needed to do was to move on himself, move on from a school that puzzled and exasperated him as much as it buoyed him up.

"You'll make a great success of the international course," said Doug. "But please make sure you make a great success of the exams first."

"I'm well prepared." It wasn't arrogance. "I've had my bad patch, a term ago, but I think I'm under control now." Anderson was moving to the door. "I'll be fine."

Doug reckoned he would be. Even allowing for the various forces in his life, pulling him in different directions, making it hard to know exactly where he was heading, and why, the boy would come out on top. Then Doug realised he might have been reflecting about his own life: where, exactly, would he come out?

After discussion with Matron, Doug advanced the supper by fifteen minutes. Most of the boys had long since run out of work and so he allowed them time to chat, warning them that he insisted on no noise near the Year 12s. He took the supper helpers back to Matron and saw that all was tidied away. When she dismissed them, she asked if he would like another cup of tea.

"I'll need to see that the new Year 11 prefects know what to do," he said, but then he realised that she actually wanted him to stay. "But there's time for that – a quiet tea would be excellent, thank you."

"I wonder if Mr Custance wants to see how those new prefects go," said Matron. She had her back to him as she poured water into the pot, the one she used for just herself or one visitor. Doug could not see her face but he caught a slight tremble in the voice, the kind of hesitation that suggests an uncertain offering of a comment that involves some risk. Then, when she poured the tea and turned to him, he saw it, unmistakably. He said:

"I had thought he might look in tonight. But he saw the new prefects in his study straight after dinner. He would have told them to use their initiative." Doug gave an ironic smile and his words gave Matron a clear opening, if she wanted one.

"That's OK then, I suppose." She hesitated again, but followed it up eventually: "He saw me, just in passing, this afternoon, and told me not to fuss over the new prefects. As though I would fuss!"

Doug saw that she had been deeply hurt. She had taken Custance's comment to mean, don't get involved, know your place. He had probably intended precisely that.

"I am sorry to hear it, Matron," but she cut him off.

"I would have liked to offer guidance though I knew you were on tonight and would do it better." She was honest to the core. "But to see me as an irrelevant fusspot..." She turned away from him and Doug did not know what to say. Where was Jenny when he needed her? She would have come in with, "Tell him he's a fool and you'll go on doing your job as you see fit." He was about to risk just that when she cut him off again.

"I shall leave at the end of the year." Doug gasped. "Oh yes, I must. I'll give notice. And to think I have to give it to Mr Baker, who once..."

Doug knew just enough of what had gone on two years previously to say, "I think you might find a rather different Sam Baker from the one you used to know in the House. It seems the time away has taught him to reflect. But Matron, must it come to this? You are such an essential part of this place – there must be a better course." His thoughts flew back to a conversation with Charles Herbert by the side of the oval. With surprise he found himself in the role of the encourager.

As Matron looked at him, she thought she saw a man still young enough to believe that things would work themselves out, somehow. She had no such faith, in Custance, in the College, barely even in herself.

"No, I've made up my mind. And there are openings for…"

It was she who was interrupted. The door flew open.

"Mr Anderson, I can't get Year 8 to settle at all. It's mayhem out there."

Doug sighed. As he stood, he apologised to Matron for an abrupt departure and promised to return. He followed the distracted Year 11 boy, Rannulph (always Randy, unfortunately) Morris, along the corridor to the Year 8 dormitory, to discover, quite quickly, that there was no chaos at all. The boys of that dorm were perfectly civil and polite – it was just that they were taking no notice whatever of Morris. Their view was that he should earn, not expect, co-operation, earn it by being tested, and they were prepared to test and meanwhile to withhold such co-operation for as long as they deemed necessary. Doug saw a long term in front of the boy.

It turned out not to be an easy, early night after all. Doug was partly to blame – he simply enjoyed chatting to the boys. It was all of ten when he remembered Matron and, with the House at rest except for some seniors, he took himself back to her flat. He would refuse more tea, he decided, and get back home, but the question of tea or not evaporated: Matron's door was shut and the lights were off. He had never seen it thus before at such an hour. Sadly, he shook his head and walked slowly back to his tiny office to collect his things. He had intended to use the evening to go over the next day's lessons but that was a job still to be done. He sat for a few minutes, just to check that no late noises arose, and looked over the entries in his journal. He would manage. He was beginning to doubt the wisdom of *Julius Caesar* for Year 10: not the most exciting play, full of people manipulating other people and the only true idealist turning out to be utterly incompetent. Was that too harsh? He smiled as he wondered which of the staff of the College he could cast in the principal roles, but he decided that they would all insist on being either

Antony or Octavius. Unless, of course, the headmaster would see himself as Caesar – "But always I am Parslow!" At that point he gave it up and went to bed.

It was only the next morning, at morning tea, that Custance said to him, "It seemed a quiet night in the House last night. Morris was happy when I saw him this morning. I knew he'd do well. Best just to let them get on with it without fuss." He paused for a mouthful of tea. "I indicated that to Matron. We don't want her doing their job for them." He raised an eyebrow at Doug, as though seeking confirmation that Matron had understood and had acted correctly.

"I think she understood you very well, Barney. I might add…"

But Sam was ringing the bell for notices. Custance smiled and found himself a seat. It is just as well, thought Doug – I would probably have said too much.

That same day, Matron South completed her morning routine with her normal efficiency. The House was tidy, particularly the laundry; two Year 7 boys with sniffles constituted her entire sick list. She had seen Mr Custance look in on some Year 12 studies but she had avoided him. He wouldn't even notice the avoiding, or notice her at all. Had she ever asked him in for tea and a bun? Once or twice, early on, but refusals don't encourage further invitations. She returned to her rooms and took up the letter she had composed the night before. She read it over, nodded grimly, found an envelope and sealed it. It was a little after ten. She might still catch Mr Baker before the morning recess break when she would be needed in the House.

For Sam Baker it was the second time – and he had been barely more than twenty-four hours in the job – that he was confronted with a member of staff bearing an envelope. The first time had been disappointing, but this time he was aghast. Surely not, he said to himself, as he motioned Matron South to a chair. He risked being jolly.

"Well, Matron, a new term and the House running as perfectly as ever?"

He was unprepared for her bluntness, but time away blurs the edges of things.

"No, it isn't." Then, aware that such a response would not do and was not central to her purpose, she said, "Mr Baker, you will understand that I might have expected to be speaking to Mr Parslow. Still, I hope I can say I'm glad to see you. Even if," and she proffered the envelope, "it is to tell you that I shall be leaving the College at the end of the year. There are many reasons but, really, it's just time for me to go. There is my letter – I trust it will be satisfactory."

Sam took the envelope, glad that opening it gave him a moment or two to think. He looked up at her and, to her surprise, she saw in him an expression of sympathy.

"I am sorry to hear this, Matron, and I know Mr Parslow will be too. You have been one of the most faithful members of the College staff." He paused, then: "But I can honestly say that I know something of how you feel." No, he thought, I can't go there. "We had good teamwork going in the House, until I spoiled it. But I did enjoy working with you. Have you any plans?"

She was relieved to find the conversation turning to practicalities, because the comment about working with her had all but wrecked her composure.

"There are a couple of positions going. I am considering what might suit me best."

"A school would be mad not to snap you up." He regretted that phrase and attempted to soften it: "I'm sure the right position will appear for you. But is there no way I can…?"

"No, Mr Baker. My mind is made up. Like yourself, I know when I can no longer be as useful as I want to be."

It was a shocking statement. He leaned towards her.

"Matron, I cannot pretend to understand much of what lies behind what you have just said. But, believe me, if it's a matter of usefulness…"

He noticed her pull a tissue from her sleeve.

"I'm sorry. I won't say any more. Only that you will be a sad loss to the College. A very sad one."

If his last remark was intended to calm her emotions, it failed. Matron South stood and, unbelievably, held out a hand. He took it and was pleased with the firm shake. Immediately she moved to the door, took one look back at him and went out. Passing Mrs Delahay, she mumbled, "I didn't know when I was well off, did I?" Perhaps it was as well that Baker did not hear those words.

Instead, he went to the window and gazed out. Because the academic standing of the College was strong, he felt assured that a good replacement for Miss Caraton would present. It would be much harder to find such another matron. He wondered what on earth had gone wrong. The implication that she felt useless could never apply to the boys. To Custance? It came to him that he might risk a quiet chat with Doug Anderson. Perhaps their relationship was not such that the young man would tell him anything. Still, he would try, for there had to be something in all this that he should know. He would make no announcement until he had done that. Meanwhile, he would ask Mrs Delahay for some tea and would instruct her to admit no one bearing an envelope.

Sam worked through the rest of the day's business – another on-site meeting with Hattingly and others, where he was assured that the new house construction could safely proceed, lunch with the new prefectorial team, some of whom he remembered from his last Year 9, a polite phone exchange with Professor Donald – and decided that, at three thirty, he would wander about and see who noticed or came to speak with him. For a short while his wanderings were aimless and solitary, but eventually he was aware of a figure watching him and, turning, he saw that it was Flem Harry. He waved, or beckoned, rather, and Flem came across.

"Good afternoon, Mr Acting..."

(That's not very polite, grumped Baker to himself.)

"... I'm glad to see you have survived the first two days. I hope we haven't all made it too gruelling for you."

Sam had sat through many English department meetings with Flem and he was not about to be baited.

"How are you, Flem? Did you have a pleasant break? And yes, indeed, it has been a great joy to come back, even if for a regrettable reason."

"Just so long," said Flem with an ironic lift of an eyebrow, "as not too many of my esteemed colleagues have told you that you shouldn't be here. Some of them are self-absorbed enough to think so."

Was the man totally blind about himself? Sam gazed at the fields, letting Harry think there was to be no response. But Flem, who was close to despair at his own standing in the school, had to try one more throw of the dice.

"We all know Mr Fraser's, and Mr Custance's feelings. I would be surprised if they hadn't communicated them to you, forcibly."

"Now look here, Flem," came the response. "You and I know each other, warts and all. Go about your teaching life – you still do that well, I imagine – but stop trying to manipulate the lives of all around you. Fair enough?"

Flem thought it not very fair at all. He had only tried to help. But even he knew that going further would be disastrous. He tried his pitying smile.

"Have a good afternoon, Sam," he said and stalked off.

Was it like this when I was here before? Sam asked himself. Surely not. He wondered if the Andersons were at home. It would be sensible of him to congratulate Doug on his exchange to Chaddlehangar. He wandered to the Green, keeping his eyes strictly averted from the House as he went. Meanwhile, Flem was trying to console himself with the thought that the acting headmaster had become dreadfully out of touch. But a nasty suspicion was nagging at him: he might be the one out of touch.

"Hello there, Doug. I thought I might catch you at home on a Tuesday out of football season. How are you? And you too, little… er?"

"Penelope, Sam."

"Yes, of course. My word, she does look well."

He is trying too hard, thought Doug. Where could it all be heading? They had met on the Green, just near the Andersons' cottage, as Doug, having collected Penny from day care, was just about to go inside. He had no option but to invite Sam in and was then surprised at the ready acceptance.

"Take a seat in there, then; or come to the kitchen and I'll put the kettle on and unpack Penny's things."

"I won't take your time," said Sam. "I wanted to tell you personally how pleased I am for you about the Chaddlehangar business. I think it's a splendid opportunity. I wish I'd had the gumption to do it thirty years ago."

Doug, taking the comment at face value, replied that he was very pleased to have such an opportunity and that he and Jenny meant to make the most of it.

"Of course, it is a big undertaking. We will have two children by then."

This was news to Sam and so, by the time the tea was ready and Penny was set up at her own little table with milk and slices of apple, he had heard all about Jenny's time as acting director of the gallery and of the baby due in March. Doug was beginning to wonder what else he was meant to talk about.

"It's been a bit of a whirlwind, these two days," said Sam. "I suppose I expected that. But there have been surprises. Doug, can I ask you, has our dear Matron South been happy of late?"

Doug looked at him in astonishment, his mind racing to catch the implications. He began to mumble he knew not what and then, realising that Sam could not have asked the question without some definite reason, something to prompt it, said, "I don't think she's happy at all. Still a great matron, but not getting her old satisfaction out of a job well done."

Sam sipped his tea.

"It will have to be public in a few days, I imagine," he said very quietly, "but please keep it to yourself for the moment. That's important. She has tendered her resignation, for the end of the year. I was stunned."

Doug trembled. He thought over what she had said to him the night before. She had been agitated, severely so, but he had not thought she would act so suddenly. Sam waited for a response, looking keenly at Doug all the while.

"I think, Sam, that she feels marginalised. Not a full part of the operation, just a menial, almost a bystander. It goes without saying that the boys don't see her that way. Not at all."

He didn't want to say any more. It wasn't up to him to comment directly on Custance, though he knew that in effect he had. Sam knew it too.

"I must move on," he said. "I should call on Barney." He got up and went to pat little Penny on the head, but she flinched. Doug smiled.

"You have to be prepared to take your time. You can't rush her."

He accompanied Sam to the door and watched him stomp across the Green towards the House. Formerly Sam's House, Doug reflected; and though it was still a fine place, he reckoned it lacked the zip of Sam's day. But it's not up to me to sort it out, he said to himself: I'd rather get dinner ready.

Charles Herbert had discovered the virtues of the six-minute mini sermon. On Wednesday mornings, the school assembled in the chapel for a brief service – hymn, reading, short talk, prayer, all in fifteen minutes. Someone must have decided that the residents of the College needed a brief mid-week booster between the major Sunday inoculations. Herbert's first reaction, the reaction of a parish clergyman who likes sermons to be developed at some length, had been to think of Wednesday mornings as useless, but he very quickly saw that they could make a great impact. In the first place being brief, they were not resented; and secondly, one clear point, perhaps a revealing illustration and a one-line catchphrase could be made very effective. He had grown to love Wednesday mornings.

The boys never knew what he would say. They had got used to some sort of series or continuing theme for the Sundays, as in the significance of Jesus' parables. But Wednesday's talk, being little more than a thought for the day, could be anything. They realised that the Rev enjoyed surprising them.

"I want you to consider," he said on this occasion, "whether you have ever truly forgiven somebody for a wrong you think they have done you." He waited – he never simply repeated a sentence, not being a mere politician who thought that twice, or even thrice, made the point a stronger one. All it did, thought Charles, was show that the speaker had nothing else to say. So he waited, as though allowing them time to answer his question.

"Of course, you may have forgotten things, but I don't mean that. I mean taking a firm decision not to keep hold of a wrong, not nurturing it so that it stays fresh in your mind. You might, by the way, ask your English teachers why I think of Miss Havisham at this point." A few students chuckled, a few more groaned. "No, what I mean is this: have you ever felt wronged but been able to say, not merely that you can put aside the action, but that you are holding nothing against the perpetrator? Even more than that, can you say that you made a great effort to seek out and be reconciled with the wrongdoer? That would be forgiveness!"

He referred them briefly back to the reading, from *Matthew*, chapter five, and then looked round his congregation. He did not let his gaze linger, except perhaps when it came to the rows of staff at the rear and sides of the chapel.

"Because, you see, there is a real point to this forgiveness. If it makes you feel better, that's fine. But it is actually expected, as a necessary part of being forgiven ourselves. By next week, I want you all to have looked very closely at what we call the Lord's Prayer. You'll see what I mean."

A prefect read the prayer of the day and Herbert walked out, to wait at the rear door of the chapel. The boys smiled at him as they passed, but not a staff member said a word.

CHAPTER TEN

The College council met twice per school term, once on the first Friday and once more, a movable feast, later on. But even the College was capable of adapting to circumstances: taking into account Parslow's absence and the fact that Sam Baker had barely begun to act in his place, Professor Donald moved the first of those meetings to the end of week two. Some worthies of the council nodded wisely, some reluctantly altered their diaries and Miss Boots, when she recovered from the shock, silently commended her chairman's sense of compassion. For his part, Donald was happy to make the change, inasmuch as the first Friday was Irene's birthday. She may not have been entirely happy to see him depart for the College yet again.

In any case, Donald was determined that it should be a brisk, even a brief, meeting. Financial report, enrolment report, building report – that should do it, he thought, reckoning that he could keep any other business to a minimum or, better, defer it until Parslow was fit to attend. Parslow, unfortunately, felt that he was fit already and a somewhat testy phone conversation occurred early in the week.

"Greg? I heard from Baker last week of the deferral. Excellent. I shall be there."

Silence.

"I'm feeling quite well. I need to keep up with things."

Donald now had a rejoinder ready.

"Sam Baker will keep you fully briefed on the meeting. I am going to keep it snappy – it will be an information checking session, nothing more."

"And I need to hear that information first hand. Baker might edit it, probably thinking he's helping me, but he'll only make me anxious."

Donald took a steadying breath. "Then take a pill, Allan." Then, when he felt that Parslow had snorted in derision long enough, he said, "Baker is there as acting headmaster. You can't both be there, and we have appointed him, remember, to act in your stead. You haven't got a medical clearance…"

"I'll get one tomorrow!"

"… a clearance to be at work, certainly not on the campus. Take your time away as a treat" (more derisory snorting) "and, if you can't do that, then make yourself accept the arrangement we have put in place. As others have to."

Parslow took in the force of those last words. Yes, some of them would relish making life difficult for Baker. So be it. Then he realised he was no longer attending to Donald.

"… so I will say that the rehab has still about a month to run. Unless you have news to the contrary."

"No," groaned Parslow. "That's about it, I suppose. And I feel so well, except for the leg."

"That's the whole point, isn't it? Stick with it, Allan."

Donald smiled grimly as he planned out what he would report to the council concerning the headmaster. He would have liked to say that all was going smoothly – perhaps he would say it, since the others would simply take his word on the matter. He rang Baker and confirmed, in the most businesslike manner, exactly what the meeting would say and do. Baker thought that Donald was dictating the minutes in advance. Had that been so, then the minutes would have needed re-writing in the light of the actual meeting.

Enrolments were strong, very strong, making the building of a new boarding house look like a masterpiece of prophecy. As a consequence, the financial projections were excellent. So much for two thirds of Donald's agenda. Then came Baker's report on the progress of the building itself.

"We lost no more than a couple of days, four if you count the weekend. We were already a little behind the original schedule because of bad weather earlier in the year, but the builders have worked hard to recover those days, or most of them. You will see the project manager's summary: the building ready for the fit-out in December, landscaping of the surrounding grounds before and after the Christmas break, permission to occupy by mid-January. And the long-range forecast suggests mostly favourable weather. I have to say, from my own inspections, that it all looks wonderfully impressive. You will be able to have a grand opening at some point – but I'll stop there, because you will want to discuss that with Allan Parslow."

"Indeed we will! All very encouraging but, as Mr Baker says, we might defer discussion of further detail until Mr Parslow…"

He was suddenly interrupted. Cecily Boots nearly made a 'tut-tut' noise but just restrained herself. All the others looked in amazement at the unexpected voice, a new one, that of Mr Trumble.

"Do we know yet who is going into it? Time is short and these things have to be decided. I never like things left to the last minute. That produces mistakes, and I…"

"Thank you, Mr Trumble," came in Donald, assuming that one interruption deserved another and holding his hand up, like a traffic policeman, to indicate that he had the matter under control. "It will be best for us to wait until Allan can tell us what he has been doing on that matter. I can tell you that the process is well under way, but I do not want to burden us, or Mr Baker, with it tonight."

Normally, that would have been quite sufficient. Perhaps Mr Trumble did not see things in the normal way.

"I should have thought," he grumbled, "that this body would indicate its wishes to the headmaster. Then he would carry them out. So we do need to discuss it tonight. Now, I have some thoughts on who should lead…"

Donald reflected that he had already had one conversation with Mr Trumble about the role, and limitations, of the council. He had clearly not got his point across. He would try again, even if it involved a public rebuke.

"We guide overall directions. Hence we approved the building itself. We delegate to the headmaster management and implementation. That is why we will go no further with the matter at this point. I hope that is understood."

Some of the council members looked chastened, quite unnecessarily, for they had not tried to usurp the headmaster's powers. Trumble, however, had his own agenda.

"My constituency, if I can call them that, want me to inform them," he began grandly but he got no further.

"No, you may not call them that. The Old Boys' association elects a person to join this body. When that person – yourself – joins the council, he is there to assist the work of the council, and not to represent any other body. Thus, he would observe council confidentiality and acknowledge that reporting to the wider world comes either through me or the headmaster, as appropriate. That is how we operate, Mr Trumble."

His antagonist, however, was not to be overridden. He had looked forward intensely to his first meeting, had looked forward to showing them that he was a force, not just a cipher. He wanted to direct matters, and whether he understood those matters or not made no difference to him at all. Perhaps it was because he was following a more personal train of thought.

"I should have thought it a matter of vital, indeed, reputational, interest to this body. And another thing," and here it became apparent that his agenda was not the one circulated, "I understand that, in this College, the good advice of parents concerning the university and career choices their sons make can be set aside at the whim of a teacher. Now, what do you all make of that?"

Because it was not on the formal agenda, most of them made very little of it.

"That was a sweeping statement, Mr Trumble," came in Sam Baker, who felt that he had been silent for too long. "Do you have any…?"

"Not only is it sweeping, it is not on our agenda. We shall pass it by. Now…"

"… any evidence, do you mean, Mr Baker?" said Trumble, ignoring the chairman's ruling completely, almost with a glorious disdain, if anything about such a preposterous man deserves to be called glorious. "Of course I do. There's a young boy called Fanning in his final year and his father tells me…"

"No!" exclaimed a by now very irate Greg Donald, who was close to being rattled. "No, we are not here to discuss Mr Fanning, or his son. Mr Fanning knows how to communicate with the College. We will not discuss tales he spreads behind our backs."

All of them knew that that was exactly how Mr Fanning operated and they saw that he had a willing accomplice in Mr Trumble. That man, purple in the face at the vehemence of the chairman's outburst, was about to re-enter the fray when a small voice to Donald's left, a voice unused to participation, chimed in.

"A point of order, if you please. I feel I must put a procedural motion."

The others stared at Cecily Boots. It took Donald a moment to take in what such a motion might do, but then he caught her drift.

"A moment, if you please, Mr Trumble. A procedural motion takes precedence. Yes, Miss Boots?"

"I sense… well, I am afraid that… I move that our meeting be adjourned until our headmaster can attend."

Her motion might have been a cruel snub to Sam Baker, but he knew procedure too and beamed at her.

"Is there a seconder?" asked the chairman. There were six. The vote was taken and Donald closed the meeting. He did not actually congratulate Miss Boots on her cunning, or even on her good sense. He merely smiled at her and said to them all that he would confirm the date of the next meeting when he had certainty about Mr Parslow's return to work.

"Stay a moment, Sam," he said as the others, relieved or frustrated as the case may be, left the council room. "May I just ask you to follow up whatever that was all about. Fanning is a dangerous man and I want us to have the facts before us."

Sam knew only too well the malice of Charlie Fanning, just as he knew the decency of his sons. He nodded and said that he would phone Donald in the next few days. The chairman departed, wondering if there were council regulations anywhere about excluding unhelpful members. That left Sam to lock up, which he did, reflecting that, in his single attendance, he had probably witnessed a council meeting like no other. He would enjoy telling Parslow all about it.

Sam sat on the Fanning matter for the weekend and nearly all of Monday. He knew he had but one course of action open to him – to make an approach through Custance. It was what he would have expected – demanded! – in his own days in the House and yet he shrank from involving Custance. It was not merely their interview of a week previously that troubled him. No, it was a growing distrust of the man himself, or rather, of how he went about things. How would he react?

Sensibly? With indifference? He did assume that Custance would want to keep Charlie Fanning at a distance, so maybe he could approach the man on that basis.

On Monday afternoon, with the weather gods beaming down on the College as on the most picturesque of places, he tracked Custance down in the House. The boys were at athletics – too strong a word for what some of them did, in Sam's opinion – and Barney was at leisure. I would have been catching up on the marking, not lazing about, thought Sam, and then remembered that he needed to make the approach in as friendly a manner as possible. This was not always easy for him. He heard Langton's voice in his ear: "Steady on, Sam, don't burn your bridges from a distance." As if he ever would!

Custance was actually in his study. He opened the door to Sam and ushered him in.

"What on earth brings you here?" It was not the most promising of beginnings.

"That splendid boy Hamish Fanning brings me here." Then, seeing a look of blank incomprehension on Custance's face, he said, "or rather, the threat of Mr Fanning brings me here. Do you know the man?"

"Enough," was the terse response.

"Barney, there is a new man on the College council, one Mr Trumble, the new Old Boys' appointee," (Custance snorted at the name Trumble) "and the delightful Mr Fanning has been getting in his ear about the school undermining the father's choices about what uni course Hamish must do. It's probably nothing, because Mr Trumble likes to sound off and make himself important, but with Charlie Fanning involved you never know where it may lead. Can you check it out for me, ascertain the facts? Or I can talk to the lad, whichever you think best."

Sam was trying very hard to respect the housemaster's position, though he doubted if he would have received the same courtesy from Parslow in times past.

"I'll see him after dinner. I don't want to upset him, not with exams so close, so I'll dig gently. I'll fill you in in the morning."

Custance spoke as the one calling all the shots and Sam decided to accept that, for the moment. But, as he turned to go, he heard, "this business of Matron is inconvenient." Sam turned back abruptly. "You haven't yet made it public Still, I'm not fussed. She pampers the boys; she's not the one for me. I don't know how you stood it."

It took a lot to deprive Sam of the power of speech, even temporarily. He made as though to go, but then said, "The boys will miss her."

Custance shrugged. "They'll get used to a new one quickly enough. I'll be in touch on the other matter."

It was an obvious dismissal. Sam left a quietly complacent housemaster and stood sadly in the corridor. The school was a madhouse – Parslow injured, a matron feeling useless, a race to have the new house finished, despite his optimistic words to council. He went to the door of the House and, as he gazed out over the Green and listened to the silence, it struck him. Suddenly, with a brisk step, he turned back into the House and marched along the familiar ways.

"Mr Baker!" said Matron South. "I heard steps and knew it was too early for the boys. Well, I am…"

What she was remained unspoken. Sam was too full of his great possibility.

"Is a cup of tea possible, Matron? I had to see Mr Custance for a few moments, and then I had a thought. Have you a moment?"

Matron caught the eagerness in his voice.

"As I said, the boys won't be back for half an hour. Yes, a cup of tea," and she led the way into her tiny kitchen. To Sam's eyes, nothing had changed. All her gear was as neatly stacked as ever. He sighed but then recollected his mission.

"Are there any firm plans for next year, Matron?"

"No," she replied, somewhat defensively, Sam thought. "No, I'm going to take my time." She gave him the briefest of smiles. "Perhaps I'm putting it off. I know you'll have to announce it soon." She poured the tea and waited. It was not in her nature to give too much away.

"I've been wondering if, maybe, a change of plan could…"

"No, Mr Baker, please don't. I've made my decision."

He remembered when he had made his own, two years previously. There had been no turning back then and no one, especially Parslow, had so much as hinted at a change of mind. He understood her, but he had to proceed.

"I am not going to suggest you stay here, in the House. I am not blind and I know you need to feel genuinely part of a team." She blinked at him and wished that this had been the Baker of once before. "But I do wonder whether, instead of leaving us, leaving a place in which you are so highly valued, you would consider becoming the matron in the new house. A fresh start, and under a new housemaster, I assure you."

She was silent. It was too much to take in. He plunged on.

"Since nothing has yet been announced, not made public, then…"

"Then I could withdraw my letter. Yes, I see that." She pushed away her barely touched tea. "Can I get you anything to eat? I have some rock cakes, I think." It sounded absurd, she knew that. She needed time.

"No, thank you, Matron. I only wanted to plant the idea. I can't expect an answer immediately. If you would be so kind as to think about it and let me know – I would be very pleased."

Exactly what would he be pleased about, she wondered. She simply gave a nod and agreed to think. Sam got up to go and Matron barely registered it. She was not in shock, but she was overcome by having gone through an unexpected, and new, experience, that of being acknowledged as valuable by a person in authority. That the acknowledgement had come from such an unlikely tongue had stunned her; but, as she became aware of his footsteps receding, stomping off as she had been used to hear him, she smiled and reached for the tea.

And what of Sam? He was, perhaps unexpectedly, thinking of Ralph Langton. Enjoy it, Sam, the former colleague had said, and, just for a moment, he had. He had enjoyed the possibility of openness, of wanting another person to feel valued. Too often in his career he had wanted to manipulate, to arrange others' lives, to leave them no room to move in their duels with him. It felt good to do it differently. Yes, he thought, two years of perspective could make a mighty difference.

If Hamish Fanning was surprised to see his housemaster enter his study that night, he did not show it. Housemasters could go where they liked, he supposed, and there had to be a first time for everything. But the conversation not only surprised him, it infuriated him. For the entire length of it, only a few minutes, Custance gazed steadfastly out the window.

"So, young Fanning, it's all going well for you, is it?"

"I think so, sir. The exams will tell, but I feel OK."

"And after that? University? I somehow imagine you in law."

This was Hamish's first moment of shock and exasperation. "No, I don't think that's me. I really want to take an international relations course. I may have to combine it with economics, to please Dad. You won't tell him I said that, will you?"

"I don't think I'll need to." Custance stepped about the room but kept his eyes fixed on the window. "Your father seems to feel that someone has been talking you out of law – father feels undermined. Still, if it's your preference...?"

"No one has been trying to talk me into or out of anything, sir." He was adamant, and offended that his own deep wish was being misconstrued. "That's the course I want, at UNSW. I mean to get into it too. I was telling the same thing to Mr Anderson the other night. Dad will just have to see it my way."

"Don't get agitated, lad. I hear you. Now, you keep at the study. I like to see a boy with real purpose."

Hamish nearly added, 'and initiative', but thought better of it. Somewhat tentatively, he said, "I know Dad speaks out too much, but he'll be fine, especially if I do eco as well."

He looked back at the folders of notes on his desk. He desperately wanted the conversation to be over. For Custance it was over – he had enough in order to report back to Baker. So when Hamish looked up at the sound of his study door closing and saw that he was once again alone, he sighed and felt a surge of annoyance at his father's meddlesome ways. His book was open at the Ancient Mariner. If Dad were an albatross, he thought, I just might shoot him too.

"So you see, Sam, I'm not going to defend Mr Fanning. He can be a giant nuisance. He has a bright and determined son. All I'm saying is, that the only staff member it could possibly be is Anderson. He is the only one, according to Hamish, who has discussed the matter with him. Nobody else, as far as I can tell."

Baker was greatly vexed. This was not information that he needed, and the smoothness of Custance's delivery of it made him suspicious.

"Teachers discuss lots of things, especially with seniors. But is Hamish saying that Anderson was pushing for a particular outcome? Or just listening, which is what I rather suspect."

Telling himself that his job was to protect the boy's interests, Custance tried to be equivocal.

"As to that, I couldn't say. If you want to probe the boy still further, go ahead, but I don't think it advisable, not so close to the exams. The only staff member involved has been Anderson."

Both men, for very different reasons, were content to leave it there. When once more by himself, Baker sat back and frowned. Was Custance putting more weight on the boy's mention of Anderson than was justified? He thought so and had decided, more or less, to tell Professor Donald that the boy knew his own mind and we should all applaud him for that, when the phone rang.

"It's Mr Parslow on the line, Mr Baker. Shall I put him through to you?"

There were no preliminaries.

"I hear from Greg that that ass Trumble made a nuisance of himself at Friday's meeting. I did not like the appointment. Has it stirred up any real trouble for you?"

"Good morning, Allan. You sound full of beans this morning."

"It's because I'm full of beans that I need answers. I'm quite well enough to do battle with any Mr Trumble."

Sam grinned: is it possible to be jumping out of one's skin while still in rehab?

"I suspect Mr Trumble will go on being a nuisance. Or rather, he will try but you and Greg Donald won't let him, will you? On this occasion, Trumble has had Fanning in his ear – an abominable combination – and he thought he could fire Fanning's ammunition. But they're blanks, Allan."

"What on earth do you mean? Just talk in plain English, man."

"I'll tell you exactly what I will tell Professor Donald. In Hamish Fanning we have an intelligent and very honest young man, who knows his own mind, who doesn't want to be pushed into an uncongenial course by his father. I wouldn't want to be pushed around by Charlie Fanning either."

A snort of agreement came over the line. "Quite so. So there is no substance to this story of a teacher undermining the parent and pushing the boy?"

Baker took a deep breath. "No," he said. "As far as I can tell, there is no truth in that at all."

Soon afterwards he gave the same message to Professor Donald, who was greatly relieved by it. "I shall find ways to tame that man's bluster," he had said. As far as Baker was concerned, the matter was finished.

That evening, as Doug Anderson walked into the House, Custance, whose study door was open for once, beckoned to him. He might almost have been lying in wait, Doug thought.

"Good evening, Doug," as though the encounter were pure chance. "I don't want the Year 12s to be discussing university options just yet. It takes their minds off the exams. And much better to let them talk it over with their parents. Stay out of it, if you don't mind."

Doug was surprised. "As you wish. You know how they like to chat. They're just thinking aloud, really. But I certainly won't initiate it."

"Absolutely not. I don't want the likes of Mr Fanning saying that we interfere."

"Hah!" laughed Doug. "That man hasn't a clue. Not about his own son." He paused. "Hamish will do well without any interference from us."

"Make sure of it, then." Custance seemed displeased. He was not going to side with one as unreliable as Mr Fanning; but he would have liked to put Doug Anderson more firmly in his place. He ended, scarcely relevantly, with, "especially young Fanning!", gestured to Doug to leave him and shut the study door.

What on earth was all that about, thought Doug. Then he remembered the brief conversation with Hamish Fanning of a week or two previously. He had not pushed Hamish, not in any way; the boy had already made up his mind. But something was wrong if Custance was agitated by it. Had the boy indicated to his father that he had discussed the question with Doug himself? Got his support, perhaps? It was possible and Doug, who knew nothing of the events of the council meeting, spent the rest of the evening avoiding the Year 12 studies, gloomily reflecting that, no matter what he did in the place, it always turned out badly. Badly for him!

Doug would have given much to avoid the debate. There was, however, no getting out of it. The syllabus in Year 11 called for a friendly debate between classes timetabled together and it happened that Doug's class and Ben Fraser's formed such a pair. Doug might have relished the idea, especially since Felicity Madigan had arranged the topic, that Australian poetry is always unmistakably Australian, but he resented being forced into any show of co-operation with Fraser. He had accepted the affirmative for his class and they had enjoyed considering universal themes and distinctively Australian points of view. He did not think their case was a strong one, especially since Fraser taught the most able Year 11 class, but the point of the exercise, as he saw it, was in understanding the poems, not in victory as debaters. It was as well that he took such a view, because, in purely debating terms, Fraser's class won handsomely. The two classes had opened up a double room and, at the end of the debate, there still being some minutes until the bell, Fraser asked the group if there were any questions, about anything at all. For a brief moment, he was seeing himself as the grand master of the estate. But no one seemed to know what manner of question he expected and there was a long moment's silence.

"Come on," urged the deputy. "Carpe diem, boys."

Most looked even more bemused than before but one of his class was brave enough.

"Well, sir, I was wondering about the chaplain's reference to a Miss Havisham. What should we know about that?"

"Ah, yes," said Fraser and he manufactured a little extra time during which he ransacked his memory. "Our chaplain loves to tease us with out of the way questions. Now, as I remember, in Dickens' *Great Expectations*, Miss Havisham is a very eccentric old woman, the mother of Estella, with whom Pip, the main character, is hopelessly in love. She is a weird old lady, stuck in the past in some way." He looked casually at Doug. "Anything to add, Mr Anderson?"

"Well, yes, possibly. Thank you, Mr Fraser." Doug was obviously ill at ease. He did not think he was being set up, but you could never quite tell. "Yes, you see, Miss Havisham is not Estella's natural mother; she adopted Estella when she was only a baby. If I understood Rev Herbert correctly, he was talking about holding a grudge. Now, Miss Havisham was jilted on her wedding day and lives on into old age preserving that moment of anger and betrayal. So I," but here Doug became aware that Fraser was staring venomously at him, "so I think that might have been the connection."

He began to tidy up his papers and Fraser dismissed the boys to morning recess. When the room was empty, he turned to Doug.

"So you thought you'd be clever with your little lecture and make me look stupid into the bargain. Heaven preserve me from colleagues (with heavy irony) such as you!"

"I explained the chaplain's reference, accurately, I think. I did not put anyone down."

Doug felt himself to be unjustifiably on the defensive. The anger rose up in him and, when Fraser began with, "Now listen here, Doug," he could contain himself no longer.

"No! You listen for once. I will not be misrepresented in this way. It isn't the first time and I've had enough of it. There was a question, which you bungled and then threw to me. It's not my fault if I gave a better answer." He took stock and decided there was no point. "Why can't you just let me get on with my job?"

Fraser produced his smile of unctuous pity.

"You poor young man," he said with an ineffably patronising air. "You can't take any advice, can you?" And then, after a long look, more sternly: "Be very careful, Doug."

Those last words were the only part of the conversation which Felicity Madigan heard as she came into the room. She had hoped to hear about an energetic debate but any attempt at a pleasant chat, she saw at once, would be dreadfully out of place. She looked anxiously at Doug.

"Is everything all right here?" And then, at Fraser, "That sounded unexpectedly threatening."

Fraser simply stood his ground, as he felt his seniority entitled him to do, but neither man said anything. Doug was too close to being overwhelmed with fury, outrage, than to do anything more than gesture vaguely with his anthology of Australian poetry and mutter, "It was OK." He hurried away, to his own house, because he could not face the society of morning tea.

"He really does blow up over nothing, you know. I think his class was not really up to the debate. Perhaps that upset him."

"Come off it, Ben," Felicity said. "If they weren't, it wouldn't be because of Doug. And no simple matter of a class debate would cause that level of anxiety. What did you say to him?"

"Morning tea now, I think. I have an announcement to make." He smiled comfortably, closing the matter, as he saw it.

Felicity was not about to be thus brushed off. "No, wait a minute, there must be more to it than…"

"Don't you presume to cross-examine me." He glanced at his watch and then glared at her. "Morning tea."

He left her standing there. She should have been stunned at his rudeness but she wasn't. Poor Doug, she thought, and went to the common room, thinking that a quick chat over a cup of tea might enlighten her. But Doug was not there.

Charles Herbert's absence on the second Wednesday of term was caused by his taking the funeral of a former parishioner and so his next talk, the follow-up to that of week one, was delayed. But it had all been prepared and he saw no reason not to proceed as planned. There was too much ill feeling, sometimes under the surface, sometimes bubbling into view, for him to ignore it. He wanted to tell the school, and especially the staff, that in times of change and uncertainty such feelings were unproductive, damaging, potentially dangerous. Yes, he would speak out; and he felt that it would do the boys no harm to hear it, even if it wasn't really about them on this occasion.

"Well, my friends," he began, when the chapel had settled after a reasonably strong rendition of the hymn, 'Forth in thy Name, O Lord, I go', "I trust you have all done the homework I set and that you all know at least something of Miss Havisham." He gazed round, giving them time to remember. Then he painted the picture – the wedding dress fraying to a tissue that would one day catch fire, the wedding cake complete with mice, the shoes, the decay of the house and the ferocious determination to nurture her sense of ill usage.

"Her inability to forgive, to come to any sort of reconciliation, even with her own heart, ruined her and it harmed the foundling she brought up as a thing to mould into a means for despising men. Thus she spread misery all about her. Read it for yourselves. But consider this: if we hold our anger, our grievances close to our hearts, nourish them and keep them actively ruling in our souls, then we harm all parties, and especially ourselves. To hold out the hand of brotherly love and at least to seek a resolution to our problems is to offer the possibility of healing for all, it is to nourish re-growth, not torment. It is, amongst men and women, the image of what God wants of us in our relationship with him. We forgive, as a way of declaring how much we need forgiveness, a forgiveness offered to us through Jesus."

His voice had sunk lower in the last sentences. Well may the boys have been puzzled. Perhaps they sensed that he was only marginally speaking to them. Perhaps they saw him as speaking out of some deep personal crisis. If so, they misjudged him; but the staff, most of them, did not. Some looked interested, some were angry at his presumption; and Doug, sitting in one of the side aisles, was moved to wonder if there was any possibility of reconciliation with Fraser, or with the College at large. If he couldn't achieve such a reconciliation, what then? It was not Doug that Herbert had wanted to challenge – but, as so often in schools, the target we hit is not the one at which we have taken aim.

Herbert finished by telling them that he was going to introduce a new song, or rather, an old one, 'O Brother Man, Fold to Thy Heart Thy Brother', which he hoped they would enjoy. He sat down and, through the closing prayer, those who glanced up at him might have thought him a little pale, even exhausted. But then he strode to the door and greeted the boys with his customary energy. Once again, however, the teachers found it easier to avoid him.

On Friday afternoon, there was once again an English department meeting. Well, hardly a meeting – one item to tick off and then drinks. Felicity Madigan needed to finalise the booklist for the following year so that ordering could be done in good time. She could simply have authorised the list herself but she wanted to make one or two additions and judged it better to ask for comment – brief comment, she said to herself as she thought of Flem Harry holding forth on the merits of Henry James. So she decided to combine a brief meeting with drinks at her house. Bert Cleary had said he could not attend and Felicity found she could accept that with equanimity.

They gathered around her small dining table. Her lists produced little comment.

"There we are then. I wanted you all to see these lists, partly as an aid to preparation for next year, but also so that you could make suggestions. But if you're all comfortable, I'll go ahead with the ordering."

Felicity was delighted at the simplicity of it all. She got up and moved to the kitchen bench where drinks and snacks were already laid out. Flem immediately rose to help her. Blaize moved to a settee and beckoned Maya across, but her mind was still on the meeting. She couldn't switch off as easily as he could.

"We'll enjoy those texts, don't you think, Doug? I hope I can get the students to enjoy them too."

"You'll have no trouble doing that, Maya." Doug smiled at her and got up himself, as though to signal that the meeting was closed and that it would be good to relax, change direction as it were. But a voice came from behind him.

"Will it suit you, Doug? There's no Dickens for you to lecture us about."

Doug froze, just for a moment, and then decided to let it pass. He moved across to Blaize, still with his back to Fraser, when to his surprise he heard anther voice, Flem's.

"Come off it, Ben. Just because he knows *Great Expectations* better than you do. Let it be and let's have a pleasant drink."

Fraser began to bluster. "I have no idea what you mean, Flem," but then he saw Felicity, who was rapidly putting the pieces together. She was about to urge them to think ahead to the end of the year and holiday plans but Fraser was too exasperated at how his shaft aimed at Doug had misfired.

"I do sometimes have to remind colleagues of acceptable protocols and it seems, Flem, as though I might have to remind you, too."

"Don't be silly, Ben." Flem was grinning impishly. "Have you forgotten that our boys do talk. Your blunder about Miss Havisham is all over Year 11. Doug is not the one at fault here." He picked up a bottle. "Felicity, your choice of wines is superb. It exactly mirrors my own!"

"That," she said acerbically, "might well be the only way in which we are so alike." Then, gesturing at the bottle, she added in a milder tone, "that Mornington Peninsula vineyard is run by friends of mine and I like to support them."

She began to hand round plates of food and motioned to Flem to do the same with the drinks. Her colleagues responded eagerly, because to indulge in refreshments is often a way to break tension.

"Have a glass, Ben," said Flem. "I really do recommend this stuff."

"You would!" growled Fraser, not sure what exactly his sneer was meant to convey. "What? Is it another local passion of people who can't see the big picture as I can? Wine for little people, is it?"

Felicity came across to him.

"Please don't insult us all in my house. I value my colleagues, good, hardworking, intelligent people. I'm starting to wonder if I can say the same for you. Won't you just join us and be happy, for a bit?"

She had tried to make her last words more encouraging, of a softer tone, to get him to drop the pompous, angry mood. But –

"I have to say it as I see it, Felicity. And from my position as deputy, I have to say that this English department…"

"… is a bloody fine one, as you well know. Or it was, until you stepped into it."

Flem had often been a risk taker but this was a considerably bold roll of the dice. Felicity made an attempt to deflect his words. "I don't know what's got into us," she said. "Let's try to…" but it was no use. For Fraser especially, things had gone too far.

"I will see you, young man, in my office on Monday morning." They all wanted to laugh at him. His gaze fell on Doug Anderson. "But it's you, isn't it, always at the bottom of things that go wrong."

He put down his glass and made to leave But Doug, his face burning, had come to feel that if he didn't at once respond he would see himself as a coward for ever. Felicity put out a hand as though to arrest him, for he had stood up, but he was not to be stopped.

"You really have it in for me, don't you? I have no idea why. Why must you and Mrs Fraser go out of your way to offend me and insult me? Why did you tell me that day that I was getting too close to Libby Caraton? Why did Mrs Fraser have to tell my wife that Libby was trying to come between us? You're mad, both of you."

He was quivering with rage. Unaware of some of the other ways in which Fraser, desperate for control, had tried to undermine his position, Doug had nevertheless fixed on the one topic that some of the others there would understand. Maya had turned brick red, to Blaize's astonishment. Felicity was agitated and looked at Maya. Flem was undeterred. He decided to be crude.

"I think many of us know, Doug, why he would see fit to implicate Libby. It's because he couldn't hit it off with her himself. That's it, isn't it, Ben?"

Fraser turned to Flem, still glass in hand, and for a moment it seemed as though he would make a melodramatic gesture and fling the precious Mornington Peninsula red all over his former spy. He managed, however, to put the glass down, none too gently, so that some of it spilled out. Then he swept the room with his eyes, expressing, he thought, sorrow more than anger, though that was his true emotion at that moment, directed at himself and, in a way he only partly understood, at his wife.

"Cretins!" he said, and they gasped afresh at the viciousness he barely attempted to disguise. He left abruptly. Felicity's first action was to shut the door he had left open and then she turned to face her English department. Part of her wanted to cry at the ruin of her pleasant Friday afternoon; at the same time, she felt that she understood enough of the cross-currents of feeling for her to begin to repair the damage.

"I'm so sorry," she began. "I think some of you, maybe all of you, understand where all that came from. We can talk about it now, or we can have a drink, or we can just…"

"Go home?" said Doug. "Yes, that's what I need right now. I'll be off."

They wanted to re-assure him, tell him how much they respected him, but Doug was gone before anyone found the right words. Blaize and Maya got up also and all of a sudden it was just Felicity and Flem. He shrugged his shoulders at her, as though to say, these things sometimes happen, not my fault.

"I don't know," she said to him, "whether to thank you or not. You certainly brought things to a crisis. You're not going to spend time worrying about Monday morning, are you?"

It was barely a question – she knew he wouldn't.

"I don't think it's me who should worry about Monday, do you?" Flem was calm, utterly convinced of his own invulnerability. "Can I help you with all this?" He gestured at the barely touched refreshments.

"No thanks, Flem. I'll leave it until later. I'll make a coffee now and have a think."

It was a dismissal, not exactly what he had expected, but he nodded. He said, "I hope some of our friends can have a weekend not thinking about it."

He went and Felicity sat down suddenly. She had to think about it; and the first thing she found herself thinking about was what poor Doug was going through, had been going through for some time. But it was merely a reflection of her own miserable marriage when she wondered how much of it all he would tell his wife.

One of the many strange things about school life is that, in the midst of turmoil, interludes unexpectedly appear. Not that all of College life was in turmoil. The boys, for example, would have been most surprised at such a notion: they attended class, played sport, sang in the choir and got on with things. But as Sam Baker drove up to town on Saturday morning, he reflected that turmoil quite accurately described what he was seeing. The College was a seething whirlpool of staff anxieties and he had no idea how to control it. He was travelling alone to St Justin's, Fraser having called in to say he was most unwell and could not manage the Grand Inter-schools Athletics Carnival. Baker was pleased. He would take the opportunity to check in at his home in the hills and then drop in on Ralph Langton afterwards. If he stayed the night with Ralph, he could still drive to the College in time for chapel on Sunday. It meant a lot of driving, but it also meant a break and after three weeks (was that all?) he needed one.

He had been told that another two, just possibly three, weeks would see Parslow back in the school. Baker felt that, whenever it happened, he would be only too happy to hand the reins over and pull out. He smiled as he remembered how much he had once craved for a head's job, how the time had somehow slipped away and he had felt passed over. In those days, he had resented being nothing more than an acting deputy. Now it seemed to him to have been a great deliverance. If the job involved dealing with Fraser, Custance, Trumble; if it involved losing fine teachers and, almost, an irreplaceable matron; if the teaching community could not be kept happy, then the head's role was onerous beyond endurance. Or perhaps it called for a certain kind of person, a Parslow, who revelled in all the crafty manipulation of others' lives. In retrospect, he had done well to confine himself to English and housemastering, where he could be useful and do his job well. He thought he had, mostly, and he was glad now that he had not risen to a level beyond his real abilities. But then, perhaps teaching young people *was* the real job, even more than what a head did. He didn't know; but these were his reflections as he drove to St Justin's, after a mere three weeks in his acting role.

The day at St Justin's nearly produced a comical success. By a remarkable fluke of the order of events, the College did well in the first round in the field and the first three track events. Then the rain began, the programme was suspended and a resumption, for a time, looked doubtful. Therefore, Sam observed to his fellow heads, if the results of the carnival had to be declared at this point, the College had won the day, with St Justin's second. The Baxter head smiled grimly but perhaps he had a better meteorological sense than Sam. After half an hour, events resumed and there was very quickly a return to normality. At the end of the carnival, Sam felt it was only proper to congratulate the St Justin's head, for the host school should not, if at all possible, come last. He did not bother to congratulate Baxter – they were quite smug enough already.

So he checked on his mountains house, spent a friendly and relaxing evening with Ralph Langton and arrived back at the College in good time. He noted that the Frasers were not at chapel and was informed that Ben was still unwell. He went by their house but there was no answer to his knock. He wondered what that all meant for Monday morning. He would have liked to visit someone on the campus but did not know if he would be welcome. Instead he read and found himself pondering the following: *We have strict statutes and most biting laws, the needful bits and curbs for headlong jades.* He laughed: we have no such thing, he said, and went for a walk around the campus. All was quiet, even in the copse. He returned to his book but got no further than *man, proud man, dressed in a little brief authority.* He would take care not to be such a man. But some others he could name were definitely like that.

Monday morning, bright and clear, the kind of day on which a school community flourishes. Baker, determined that, should Parslow's return be suddenly brought forward, he would not be found wanting with the essential work, was at his desk soon after seven and had soon planned out his day as precisely as he thought feasible. He saw in his diary a meeting set down with Fraser for nine thirty. This was to be a calendar meeting, checking on arrangements for the end of the current year, beginning preparations for end of year assemblies, things of that sort. It would be utterly, almost unbearably, routine – but would it even happen? He would have to wait and see. In the meantime, he settled to a pile of letters offering enrolment to certain families who had left it rather late and would, in all likelihood, leave other things, such as payment of fees, rather late too. Mrs Delahay entered with his first mug of tea.

"It is a fine day to be sure," she said and seemed prepared to leave after that wonderfully mundane statement.

"No word from Mr Fraser, by any chance?" he muttered to her retreating back. "He has been unwell, as I understand it."

The faithful secretary turned back. "He has not called to cancel." She uttered these words as though they precluded any outcome other than Fraser's attendance. "But he is not due for forty-five minutes."

Baker plodded on with the administration of the College, work which would once have afforded him a soothing kind of satisfaction. How I have moved on, he said to himself, and how differently I see many things now. His eye fell on a cheap chain store clock on a bookshelf and he felt his heart ache for something that was his, something that told him that there were, had been, could still be significant moments in his life. He got up and went to a radio that stood by the window. Maybe some background music would soothe him. He was about to turn it on and so had his back to the room and the door on the far side when he heard a small cough.

"Gazing over your domain, Mr Baker? Enjoying it, I trust." The feeble attempt at irony was too pathetic to be answered but, as Sam turned, he saw Ben Fraser, pale, gaunt, trying to summon up a smart comment but looking drained of all energy, drained, as it were, of will, and life.

"You poor man, you do look ill," Baker blurted out and came across to guide his deputy to an easy chair. Taking one himself, he leant forward and asked Fraser if he was indeed very unwell. "I knocked on your door yesterday but got no answer. I didn't quite know what to think, but now I see how sick you've been."

He stopped there, thinking that his concern deserved at least some response. After a couple of moments, during which Fraser's gaze swept the room to take in all the paraphernalia of greatness, he managed to speak.

"A nasty virus, and I suspect Sarah has it too. But I would never let something like that interfere with my work." He paused, wanting that last statement to be enough, to say all that needed to be said about him as a worthy teacher and administrator. But Baker responded by raising a curious eyebrow and Fraser went on: "It's come to a point of no return, Mr Acting Headmaster. There's no use pretending. I'm not wanted here and I no longer have any inclination to fight against that. I had thought to be a useful person, not the target for humiliation. I have decided to go at the end of the year – in fact, two weeks before the end of the year so that I don't get caught up in wearisome formalities, hypocritical thanks for someone who is loathed. Don't look surprised – you must have expected this. You, Donald, Parslow, you probably engineered it, all three of you."

It was urgent that Baker intervene.

"I hardly think that is why our headmaster fell down those stairs, Mr Fraser. But seriously, must it come to this? Cannot you and Allan Parslow work through matters on his return?" He doubted whether anyone would actually want that but he was also calculating the enormous impact of an absent deputy at the climax of the year.

"I shall see him just long enough to tell him what I think of him." He reached into a jacket pocket and handed Baker an envelope. "This states that I will finish no later than the end of week eight of this term, but possibly earlier, at my own discretion and depending on my health. I am in touch with my doctor already. If that's not acceptable, then bad luck. I really have no more to say."

He made as though to rise but Sam put out a hand, he hoped not too formally or dictatorially. Fraser sank back into the chair. He was truly washed out, unable, now that he had spoken his piece, to see beyond the next few seconds. But Baker had to.

"I hear you," he said, "and I have great sympathy for you, seeing you in this sad condition, which clearly involves more than a virus. But I have to know some things, Ben: are you actually on deck for the next month or so? Or on extended leave? The role, as we both know, is too vital to be left totally up in the air."

There was an attempt at a laugh, which as suddenly evaporated. "Vital, indeed! No, I have done all that I can. I can no more."

"You're not in Hopkins' plight," muttered Sam under his breath, annoyed, somehow, at the irrelevant quotation. "But not only do I have to know where I stand – something must also be said to the staff. I can tell them that you are very unwell and that we must struggle on without you for a bit, to see how you recover. But I can only do that for a week at the most, and then I will have to make an announcement. You have, after all, given me a letter of resignation. I shall have to announce that too."

"Do as you please," said Fraser. He looked truly beaten. He had spent the weekend reflecting on the disastrous English meeting and the more he thought the more unwell he had become. He now felt as much of a wreck as he looked to an outsider. "I have been sick, and so has Sarah. Poor woman, she thinks I have come back to work today and praised me for my fortitude and devotion. She does not know of... of..." but he could only gesture at the letter. "I shall go home and tell her what I have done. And may God have pity on us both, because this school won't."

He rose and almost staggered to the door.

"And then I intend to be most unwell, definitely not in evidence for our departure to be gloated over." He attempted a defiant look, all but broke down and stumbled out through Mrs Delahay's ante-room.

Baker sat there, trying to assemble the pieces. Some things he knew, and some he suspected; yet he felt that there was much that he did not know. He had stumbled into an unworkable situation and it flashed absurdly across his mind that perhaps Parslow had fallen down those stairs on purpose, just to give him, Sam, some grief. This is no time for pointless speculation, he then said, and he jumped up. He moved to the desk, looked at that day's page in his diary, crossed out lunch with the College captains and called Mrs Delahay. There was much to be put in place, and that in haste.

Some two hours later he had substantially reset his day, had rung Professor Donald, whose dry chuckle sounded all too sinister, and had spoken at some length with Allan Parslow. Parts of that conversation, too, suggested that headmaster and chairman had foreseen this eventuality and had been quietly arranging for a Fraserless future.

"You never told me, Allan, that things had been going as badly as that. There are elements in all this I should have known."

"Not at all, Sam. They were hunches, feelings, and now, surely, something else has happened, something to precipitate this sudden resignation."

There was an implied question there, but Sam had no answer to it. They turned their attention to practical matters.

"From what I've seen," said Sam, "my two best allies are Madigan and Graham. I like them and they are sensible people, even if one of them is highly passionate."

"So were you, once, Sam," came the caustic reply, "but I entirely agree with you. You can't rely on Custance…"

"… I'm very well aware of that!"

"… and the two you've named will get things done. Now listen, I am pretty sure that I have this week and next week in rehab, but after that I should be clear. I expect to come back on campus on Saturday week. I assume that's OK with you."

Baker tried not to breathe an audible sigh of relief. "I imagine we can make that work," he said. "I'll cover whatever needs to be done myself today; over lunch I'll meet with Madigan and Graham, and then I shall expect to make an announcement tomorrow. That seems a right and proper way to do things."

He had lunch with those two colleagues, English and Science, and then met with them again after classes. He was very satisfied with those discussions and felt confident about the next two weeks. After that he would be happy to throw it back to Parslow. Felicity Madigan had given him some insight into her unhappy departmental gathering of the previous Friday and by half past five he felt that he was putting most of the pieces together in a roughly coherent fashion. He decided on a walk around the campus. It would clear his head and it was still a magically bright and beautiful afternoon.

It was about six o'clock that he came across a small picnic party, three Andersons. There was a blanket set out on the Green, a couple of folding chairs, and a meal of quiche, salad and some sort of muffins. Little Penelope, who was happily munching away at her suitably deconstructed slice of the quiche, was the only one of the three to be facing in Baker's direction as he strolled towards them. He hoped he was being inconspicuous but the child, with mouth full, pointed at him and he waved cheerily back. Perhaps here was his chance to relax in company without having to force the issue.

Seeing their daughter's gesture, Jenny and Doug turned and saw Sam, now standing some twenty metres away. He would have noticed Jenny turn away again and attend to Penny, but Doug half rose from his chair and called to Sam to join them. He did so, very willingly.

"I was just needing a wander to clear the head," he remarked. "This looks like a very comfortable place for dinner. On such an evening as this."

He smiled genially and Jenny, looking up from Penelope, saw to her amazement a man desperately wanting to be invited to make one of them.

"Penny loves to do this," she said. "Maybe it's not what we would choose, but we manage." She paused and he continued beaming. "You might like to join us, if you don't mind perching on the rug."

He certainly didn't mind and promptly sat down, knowing that it would be much more difficult to heave himself back up again. Something about levers darted through his mind, which only caused him to smile more. He was hardly a Falstaff!

"The quiche is good, Sam. Please have a slice – there's tons. But the only drink on offer is water, I'm afraid."

Sam accepted readily. "This is very kind of you. I didn't intend…"

He seemed unsure of how to complete the sentence but, to his surprise, Jenny saved him the trouble.

"I'll nip inside and get an extra glass. And the grapes. You chat."

She was gone in an instant. Doug looked across at Sam, half

sprawled on the rug, and he wanted to ask, is this an accident, or have you something you need to say? But Sam was trying to engage Penny with a bear he had found on the rug, a bear provided with its own plate and mug. The child took one look at him and edged away, clinging to her father's leg.

"Do I still have that effect?" growled Sam. "Nothing much has changed, then."

"Yes – and no," said Doug reflectively. "You have, Sam, if it's not rude of me to say so. You used to frighten me too, you know. But perhaps that was my fault."

"Did I?" said Sam with mock alarm. "You see, when I was a young teacher in the College, I was terrified of the old hands. They loved it, loved frightening me out of my wits, and I suspect I picked it up from them, as a survival mechanism, you might say." He had been talking in the child's direction, perhaps so as not to look straight at Doug, but now he did. "I don't think you'll ever play it that way. You certainly don't need to."

Something made Doug blush. "I couldn't terrify the boys, even if I tried. Perhaps," and he sensed that this was somehow the moment for confidences, "that was a part of why I didn't want the House. Only a part, you understand."

Sam discovered that he was enjoying the conversation. It was causing him to be more honest about himself than he had been for much of his career. "I think now that you were right to refuse," he said. "It was fine for me, grumping my way through it as I did. But your gifts are of another kind."

Doug became aware of Jenny approaching from behind Sam. She paused, glass and fruit in hand, as though she did not want to interrupt something that might be important. Neither she nor Doug had ever come across a gently reflective Sam Baker before.

"You love your work, or most of it," he went on. "I've always known that. It is vital that you should go on loving it, because that's what makes an impact on the boys. We ask them to absorb knowledge, and some of us ask them to grow in understanding; but what they really absorb is us, our way of thinking, the kinds of understanding we make seem important." He seemed embarrassed and picked up the bear, shaking it merrily at Penelope, to no good effect.

"You see, I've done it again," he laughed. "Keep doing what you're doing, Doug, here, or in that Chaddlehangar place, or wherever it may be. Don't stay here for ever, don't do that. Despite appearances, you might turn into another Sam Baker."

He made as though to rise but Jenny, who had heard much of what he said, came briskly across, picked up the child and plonked the fruit bowl, glass nestled in amongst the bananas and grapes, in front of the two men.

"I'm going to get her ready for bath and bed. You two sit on."

She smiled warmly at Doug, who looked in wonder at a woman who could overcome her dislike of Sam so generously. He told her so that night, and he also told her that the Sam she had abhorred was a former Sam, that some great change had come over him in his time away.

"Maybe he had to go away, if he was ever to understand himself," said Jenny.

"I suppose so. It's made him much more sympathetic to others, in all sorts of ways. Do you know what he said at the end?"

"Don't tell me he actually praised you?"

"No, he hasn't got as far as that yet," replied Doug, feeling that it was himself who couldn't speak the truth on that point, not yet. "No, he said that he was so pleased he stumbled across us, that it had done him good."

"Stumbled? Nonsense!" laughed Jenny. "I think he needed some ordinary company. With all the rubbish he puts up with – Fraser and all that – who can blame him?"

"Perhaps you're right. But, do you know what?" She raised an eyebrow. "He hasn't a clue how to approach Penny."

Jenny chortled and something made her pat her swelling body. "At least he tried. May he sleep the better tonight for that."

CHAPTER ELEVEN

The end of a year, a decade, a millennium: we all tend to see them as vital moments, the wrapping up of one thing before another can begin. But this is an illusion. One day is Wednesday and the next Thursday. No more significant change occurs in the movement from December 31 to January 1 than when any Wednesday passes on to a Thursday, at any time of the year. Yet we cannot help but invest starts and finishes with a great weight of importance. G. R. Elton tells us that, despite appearances, 1485 and 1603 were not in themselves crucial years, not at all. Certainly, the English monarchy changed hands and those dates do delimit the Tudor period of rule. But they were not the years in which decisive actions were taken. Our love of beginnings and endings, particularly endings, causes us to want to wrap up periods of time far too neatly. On the contrary, the flux of life, of human wishes and interactions, works powerfully against any simple, tidy parcelling up. We should not put a year away in a drawer on December 31 as though it were done with. But we still try to do so.

In schools, the urge to consider one year as quite finished before commencing another is, if possible, even stronger than in the world outside. It is so strong that any forward-looking principal will commence the wrapping in October, when his or her staff cannot even glimpse the finish line. Allan Parslow's injury, which delayed his return to the College until almost the middle of November, forced him to delay this satisfying concluding and leaving behind. On his return, he had no option but to pick up the threads of the year still in progress and it was not until the start of December that he allowed himself the luxury of ruling a line under the messiness of one year and thinking himself into the altogether different one – he would insist upon it – to follow. Even as he ruled that line, however, he saw only too clearly how some matters refused to be bound within the confines of a neat package. Despite his heroic efforts, there were loose ends.

When he came back to school, he was still hobbling with the aid of a stick. He felt well – he was well – and the operation and weeks of rehabilitation had done their work. It only remained for the leg to strengthen, to get used once more to doing what it had always done. By the first week of December he was able to throw away the stick, walk a lap of the oval, hold a meeting without needing to be settled in one place. Things were getting back to normal.

Normal? Had they been anything else in his absence? One of the most unsettling things that can happen to a headmaster is to come back from time away only to find that he has been barely missed, that the school has run efficiently and well without him. Perhaps Parslow had felt some of this in his handover interview with Sam Baker. They were seated in the living room of the residence, away from the busy-ness of the office, comfortable, relaxed. Parslow did not feel all that relaxed.

"It was very strange for a while," Baker was saying, "what with resignations and a deputy out of action. But that was probably a blessing. The whole place seems to have run much better without him, without him and his wife, I should say. They exist, but they are not here. And Felicity Madigan and Bob Graham are doing a fine job. You'll find you can pick up the reins smoothly enough."

"Has it really been that smooth, Sam?" Parslow began to think through all that he had heard. "A shambles of a council meeting, wasn't it? I like to feel that I'm on top of those folk at least."

"Or that you and Greg Donald are together, I imagine. Look, the man Trumble is determined to be a nuisance but he is only one voice and can be outvoted, as Cecily Boots so adroitly demonstrated. Your worry is more what he can do and say outside council. That could spell trouble, especially if he lets that monster Charlie Fanning manipulate him."

Parslow sighed. "Fanning's time as a parent is nearly up. If Hamish does well, he will have nothing to grumble about. I shall be very pleased to see the last of him."

"The boy was happy with his exams. My great hope for him is that he gets well away from father."

Parslow nodded and was silent for a moment.

"There will have to be a deputy," he began cautiously.

"Not me, Allan. Don't go there!"

"No, not you." (Was it said too glibly?) "But I am wary of another outside appointment. And I don't think that Bob Graham really fits the role, not entirely. Could Mrs Madigan?"

"Are you asking me, or have you already made up your mind?" Then, seeing Parslow nettled by that response, Sam followed with the opinion that Felicity Madigan would do it very well. "Will she want to? I'm not sure she's ready to give up English. And if she did, how do you fill that spot? The obvious internal is going to be away for a year."

Sam felt some degree of pleasure in being able to raise problems he was not called upon to solve. But Parslow had to solve them, even if he was not yet ready to take up the reference to Doug Anderson.

"I'll chat with Greg Donald about it. Since we have an interim arrangement in place, I can always lengthen that interim, if I want to."

Sam noticed how others' lives were still circumscribed by what Parslow wanted. He said merely, "Yes, you can take your time."

The conversation wound up with thanks to Baker for all that he had done in the head's absence and an assurance that the chairman would repeat those thanks when he appeared at staff morning tea the next day, after which Baker would drive away. Parslow was civil enough to express the hope that it would not be for ever.

"You create the event and Ralph and I might just come again." He paused and smiled gently. "We get on well, now."

"Yes, well, that's good, I suppose." Parslow had lost interest and Sam went to pay a couple of farewell calls. He thanked the two interim acting deputies, for whom he had developed real respect and then for some reason he called in on the chapel, as though to say farewell to it. Charles Herbert was standing in the entry porch, looking up the aisle.

"Sam! I'm glad you've come by. I had it in mind to hunt you out today. To say thank you, and to wish you well."

They shook hands, two entirely different men who could still see the worthiness in each other.

"And I need to thank you, Charles. You've been one of the highlights of my time here." Then seeing a look in response of considerable surprise, he went on: "You can't really grasp how differently you've done some things, and to such good effect. I think the Wednesday morning talks have been a revelation."

The chaplain nodded, almost as though to himself. "They can be used to make a point," he said.

"A point indeed! Some of the staff will never admit they need to be more forgiving – but you certainly made them stop and think."

A pause.

"You were gazing at something when I came in."

"Yes, I was," said the chaplain with a grin. "I was telling myself that it was time for a change, and better now, to give it a few weeks of trial before the year runs out."

Sam looked interested.

"From my very first Sunday," Herbert continued, "I've wanted to enter the chapel for a service by walking up the central aisle. I'm not quite sure why. I'd just feel more natural about it. Rather than feeling like a peg being shoved into its slot. I shall give the head a warning of it, though."

"Always wise. Do it, Charles. Do it and feel good about it."

Sam left the chaplain contemplating his grand departure from custom. He could see the man making a huge impact, if he could keep Parslow onside. He wished him well.

Out in the sunshine, the College felt to him warm and comfortable. Sam knew that that was only a surface impression, that many an area of uncertainty still existed. As he took a last wander, he thought of Ralph Langton. Yes, in a funny sort of a way it had been fun. Some of it.

Meanwhile, Parslow had sat on. He had come back to his home on Saturday and, until tomorrow, he knew that Baker was still technically in charge. Three days had been allotted to finding his feet, reading necessary notes and papers, catching up on things. He had spoken by phone to Donald, had set the next council meeting for two weeks hence and had sounded off vigorously against any incursion into his prerogatives by Mr Trumble.

"As far as council is concerned," Donald had said very firmly, "you need not worry. I have now taken the measure of the man and he will not be permitted another performance of that kind." He let that much sink in. Then he said, "However, you may find that you have a different sort of issue to confront."

"What on earth do you mean?" Parslow's anxiety was clear.

"Well, I gather that the man thinks that his son Christopher is the finest human being ever to grace our school and should be captain of everything next year, including of the new house. I imagine you don't quite see it that way."

Donald barely got that last sentence out before being drowned by Parslow's contempt for Mr Trumble.

"It would be a catastrophe. Nice enough boy, nobody takes any notice of him. He won't be in the new house. It's ridiculous."

"I've warned you. And neither of us should forget the donations. But don't give yourself a heart attack over it."

"I won't. And I'm making sure young Mr Somerville has a good crew round him. The new house has to be a startling success, you know."

"At the expense of everyone else? Well, let that pass." There was some bite in Donald's tone and Parslow chose not to respond. It was good to be back in the cut and thrust of school life, so long as he was the only one cutting and thrusting.

His other significant phone call on those three days of resettling himself was to Ben Fraser. He had asked for a face to face interview but this request Fraser resolutely declined. He wanted to say his piece, to pour it all out so that his feelings would be unmistakably clear (a letter might not achieve that) but he found that he could not steel himself to the sight of a headmaster whom it suited him to blame for everything.

Parslow got through to him after several unanswered attempts and was then forced to listen to the following monologue, or tirade, as he later described it to Donald.

"You know why I'm going – if you don't, you're a bigger fool that I thought. I'm going because, hard as I have striven to do my job, and done it superbly well, you have not supported me. You either undermine me or connive with others in doing so. You're a cowardly man, afraid of ability in others. So you'll go on surrounding yourself with mediocrity and I shall have pleasure in telling the world that under you the College is a mediocre school. And yet, Headmaster," in a sneering tone, "I might have stayed but for the pre-arranged attack on my wife. You gutless disgrace!"

He paused. Perhaps it is over, thought Parslow; but then: "And one other thing. Never, never trust Flem Harry."

Fraser slammed down the phone, presumably to be treated to huge applause from Mrs Fraser, and Parslow sat stunned. Of course, he told himself, the foolish man had chosen to ignore most of the issues that had led to that loss of confidence and support: the inspection, the blatant dislike of Doug Anderson, the tendency – was it more than that? – to get too close to young women. There were so many bits to the puzzle. Maybe, just maybe, the whole episode of Mrs Fraser could have been handled better; but had she not brought it all on herself? He got to his feet, stretched, reminded himself to think further about the reference to Flem Harry, and said, quite loudly, to his grand piano, "I'm well rid of the man." Exeunt Frasers.

At the same time as Parslow was coming back to the College and Baker was leaving it, for the last time in any paid or official capacity, Hamish Fanning was preparing to move out. He had completed his exams, successfully he hoped, with modern history the last of them, a three-hour paper finishing after five o'clock. He spent what was left of the afternoon and the evening saying farewells and telling any who would listen of his plan to commence an international relations course the following year. One such audience was Sam Baker.

"I feel comfortable about the exams, Mr Baker, and now I can forget about them for a while. But I've put in my university preferences and as far as I'm concerned, it's fixed."

Sam smiled at the boundless confidence.

"No further discussion with father about law, then? He's happy with your choice?"

"Well," with rather more hesitation than was usual with Hamish, "he probably still has law in his mind, even though I've tried to tell him otherwise. I'll say it again," with a sigh, "and it might not be an easy conversation, but he'll just have to get used to it. This is one battle with him I'm going to win."

Sam would have liked to comment, to say something about any victory over Charlie Fanning being a good one, but he restrained himself. On one point, however, he was still curious.

"It's your decision and I wish you well with it. I'm sure everyone here will support you, if that's what you've set your mind to."

Hamish gave him a quizzical glance.

"Support me? Guide or manoeuvre me? Mr Custance wondered about that, but I really didn't give any teachers a chance. I remember telling Mr Anderson of my plans but all he did was listen. He never gives anything away."

This time Sam beamed. "You've summed him up very well, Hamish. And I am sure that your astute mind will serve you very well."

After one or two further commonplace comments, he went on his way, delighted that his gut instinct had proved to be correct. But if that were so, what did it tell him about Barney Custance? The man had trodden a delicate path, not supporting the irascible and self-centred parent, but still wanting to see Anderson shoulder blame for something he had obviously not done. That turned his thoughts to Rev Herbert and forgiveness and then to the obvious fact that he should finish his small amount of packing and remove himself from the College. It was all too difficult, too tangled. He would tell Ralph Langton all about it, one day.

Hamish Fanning had another visitor soon afterwards.

"Can I help you with your packing?"

He looked up in surprise.

"William! No, I'm just about done." Perhaps that wasn't quite true, but he did not want O'Connell or any other boy of the House rummaging through his things. Then he saw that he had been too abrupt. "Those books on the desk – you might see if they fit into this box. How are you, anyway?"

He sounded nervous and was annoyed with himself for being so. William fiddled with the books, seemed to examine them and then looked steadily at Hamish.

"It's all right. You've nothing to be anxious about. I only came to wish you well, not being sure when you would leave."

"Yes, well, thank you."

William stood up, lean and gangly. "I've decided to go in for photography. We've been doing it in art."

Hamish smiled. "Birds, I suppose."

"Of course. There's plenty I can do around here. The copse." William's voice trailed away. He did not know how to thank Hamish for taking him seriously, for noticing him, actually. For his part, Hamish was relieved to have the conversation move to safer ground.

"You go for it, William." Then, aware that that sounded rather patronising, he said, "I look forward to seeing your first book come out. It will be a beautiful volume, won't it?"

O'Connell blushed. "One day, maybe." He paused. "I just came to wish you well. I'm... I'm glad you were in the House."

"And I suppose I must thank you. I..."

But William held up a hand. "We won't go there. There's no need."

He went to the door, all of two steps away. He had left it open and now a couple more seniors stood at it, perplexed. Kids from Year 8 were not coming to farewell them.

"Enjoy the photography, William," said Hamish, but the younger boy had already vanished.

"What was all that about?" asked one of the others.

Hamish merely shrugged. He was not about to explain it to his peers, not now. And he would have felt he was betraying an odd, lonely, intense and perceptive boy who deserved better. He was not sure the College could provide it, not for one like William O'Connell.

The Year 12 boys compared notes on packing. Then one said, "Let's call in on Matron."

"You're always hungry, aren't you?" said Hamish to his friend and, relieved to be doing something ordinary again, he joined them. He had intended to drop in on Matron, and what better way than in the security of a group. He closed his suitcase, and then his study door, almost for the last time.

If Parslow was by this time in next year's mode and class teachers were still scrambling to finish up the last units of work and prepare junior classes for their exams, there was one staff member who was neither of those things. At this time of the year, with only a couple of weeks of term to go, Charles Herbert found himself often reflecting, asking himself one very basic question: had he done the right thing in ceasing parish work and becoming the College chaplain?

It should have been easy to answer, yes. In many ways he felt less pressed for time than he had been in the parish. In the school he had found time for the Sunday suppers, time to think through his sermons and the

Wednesday morning talks, time to prepare classes for the groups he taught for scripture. It was not only his time that was freer: Rebecca, he saw to his delight, was immersing herself in the seventeenth century, that strange, tumultuous period in English history that produced the killing of a king – an inept one, like most of the Stuarts, but still – parliamentary prayers that rambled on for hours, the King James Bible, *Paradise Lost*. It was an extraordinary time and he was content to see Rebecca get herself lost in its variety, its swiftly changing colours. She had worked so very hard in the parish, and now this time was hers.

So far, so good! But there was a more urgent question: was he, Charles Herbert, making anything significant out of the chaplain's role? Could it satisfy him? He had begun to doubt that it could. He was happy enough in all his regular duties and he felt confident that he was connecting positively with many of the boys. But he had a nagging worry that it wasn't enough.

He thought back over his various interactions with staff, with the community in which he lived. There had been the talks about forgiveness, but they had met a solid wall of blankness. In the common room he felt at ease with a few, such as Doug Anderson, but it seemed that many were wary of him, as though he might be some kind of converting machine, one to which it was not wise to come too close. In fact, this was the problem: in terms of the adult community, he was finding it hard to establish any pastoral role at all. Given that such pastoral work made up a large proportion of the parish clergyman's life, the change was hard to accept. He remembered a council meeting when he had still been a member of that body and a discussion with Parslow during which he had tried to push for greater pastoral oversight of the staff. Parslow obviously thought that such an issue, if it existed at all, could – and should – be left to take care of itself. He had not seen it as something with which a headmaster should engage. Could it be that Parslow was right, and that the staff might resent any implication that they needed caring for just as much as the students did? If that were really true, then Herbert had put himself in the wrong job.

He sighed deeply at that reflection. And yet, and yet... he saw a desperate need. He was aware of it almost every day. The misery that had enveloped the Frasers, the attempts to undermine Sam Baker, the oddly changeable behaviour of young Flem Harry, the way the Andersons had made it clear to him that they were longing for a year away from the College: time and again he saw things that made him uneasy. There was a large group of people living and working together, but there was no community. If he was to stay and feel a worthwhile part of the College, then he had to make a contribution in that area. You can't just have fun being a football coach, he said to himself with a grin. The reflection only made him think of Peter Gryce, another brick wall. There were so many. Perhaps that was the problem – he was trying to break through a settled way of living, a way of living that resisted intrusion. Perhaps change would come and he had to be patient. He could see something coming, in the form of Felicity Madigan, a person who simply refused to stand still and be content with how things were. He was not like that, he knew. He would have to encourage, not stand aloof but not blast in either. The world had not fallen in when he had walked down the aisle of the chapel to take his seat, greeting boys along the way. And six months was not very long, not if the College had been as it was since Noah's time. At that reflection he could go no further and began to think of a cup of tea instead.

Doug Anderson felt that the end of the year was almost within his grasp, and not a moment too soon. Since the third week of term, his load had been immense. True, he had lost his Year 12 teaching to their exams; but, in place of that, he had extra work with Year 11. The end of the Fraser presence should have signalled rejoicing, pure and simple. In some ways it had, except that, since his and Fraser's Year 11 classes shared an identical timetable, Baker and Madigan, in their wisdom, had simply combined them. This was met with relief by the ex-Frasers, with disgruntlement by his own class, and with a huge amount of marking for the poor sod in charge of forty-two boys. The reward? They had taken him off Saturday sport, so he did not need to supervise for an hour or two at the pool on a Saturday morning. In terms of hours, it was hardly a fair exchange, though he did try to explain the obvious sense in it to Jenny.

"I know you're trying to be a stoic about this, Doug. But to me it feels like a parting shot from the ghastly Fraser."

"Nothing to do with him," Doug responded. "I did wonder whether

Sam might have stepped in himself, but that could not have gone on for the whole term. This arrangement works."

"It certainly makes you work!"

He did not press the point. To have been delivered from the sniping and disparagement of Ben Fraser and from the evil innuendo of Mrs Proudie, as he liked to call her, was too obvious a blessing. After that grotesque unpleasantness of the English department meeting, he did not see either of them again. It was as though they had ceased to exist. He put it like that to Libby once, when she had collected Penny from day care.

"I think we all want to get them out of our system mighty fast," she had said, with unusual vehemence. "I haven't seen Maya look so relaxed in months."

Doug could only wonder how they would get on without Libby, as a dear friend for Jenny, as an extra family member for all of them. She had already had an orientation day with her replacement, an interesting and, she hoped, resilient young man, and a weekend at her next school in Sydney. Things move on, inexorably, thought Doug, as they must, but there would be a huge gap in their lives when Libby's final departure came.

He couldn't complain. After all, he and Jenny, plus Penelope and one more, were making an escape too. Not a permanent escape, though one could never tell. He was greatly looking forward to it. There had now been letters back and forth with both the Chaddlehangar principal and Mr Millane, the exchange partner, so that the whole operation had an air of reality about it now. He had found out more about the area in which the school was set and about his likely load of teaching. He knew what his accommodation would be and the extra duties required of him. To his dismay, he discovered that he would be expected to supervise a rugby team, that silly game of endless scrums and mauls and off-side rules. But then he thought of Millane trying to accustom himself to the beautiful fluidity of Australian football and he felt that after all he might have the easier side of the bargain.

To be out of the College for a whole year: that could only be good for Jenny, too. They could see something of the world, a little bit of it, and Jenny had already started planning holiday destinations. Only the day before she had suggested a round trip of Channel Islands, Paris, Rome (a must for her, she said) and home again. It sounded idyllic, until he reminded her of the needs of two little people.

"Oh, yes," she had said blithely. "They'll fit in, you'll see."

He didn't see – it couldn't be as simple as that. Just like the year about to end, there were bound to be unknowns, loose ends that tended to tangle, just like the seaweed at Mallacoota. It had been a whole year of tangles and they had caused problems much more serious than a choked propeller.

One item gave him confidence, however. Parslow had been in the saddle for a week or two and, apart from a brief comment of thanks for the double class at Year 11, he had had no contact with Doug. That was unsurprising. Daily communication came through Felicity while Parslow handled the big issues, which were no concern of Doug's. But one morning Parslow had waylaid him and had obviously wanted to put forward an idea, which, with Parslow, meant a settled decision. He dragged Doug off to his office.

"I won't hold you long," he said, "as I know you have lots to do. I have made almost all the arrangements for the new house…"

"Yes, Guy Somerville will be great there," interposed Doug and then wished he hadn't.

"… as you say, he will, and, to come straight to the point, I want you to join him there. The change won't hurt you, it will support Guy, and it will be a better fit for Mr Millane. The new man in French will take your place in the House."

Parslow smiled genially, as though offering his employee first prize in some competition or other. Doug gulped.

"And," added Parslow, "I don't think Mr Custance will mind, when I tell him."

Doug was very ready to agree with that. It had flashed through his mind, as Parslow was speaking, that Custance might have engineered this. But that was obviously not the case. To put distance between himself and the current master of the House seemed to him one of the most obvious attractions of the move. Somerville, Matron South, a fresh start – it might almost be worth coming back!

"That seems a fine arrangement to me, Mr Parslow," he said. "Thank you for slotting me in in such an... an agreeable way."

Parslow thought that Anderson must be finally growing up, if he was able to risk even that small degree of irony. 'Slotting'? Yes, he did do that, but it was, after all, his job. Others might be able to exist with loose ends – he couldn't.

"It will work well for all concerned. I won't keep you."

That brisk dismissal made Doug feel more slotted than ever. Yet it might turn out to be an excellent slot, one he could explain to Jenny with confidence. She would think he trusted the good faith of Parslow too readily – but you had to accept good fortune if it fell in your way. The move to the new house could only be seen as a blessing.

A blessing? – Charles Herbert would have put it in those terms, Doug thought. An appallingly difficult year was drawing to a close, a year of much frustration, of constantly feeling harassed, and yet it seemed as though it might end serenely. Not neatly, but with a feeling of greater calm and poise than he had been wont to feel. He didn't know much about Phillip Larkin, some English poet he had been told to prepare for Chaddlehangar, and so he had dipped here and there into a collected edition. He had stumbled on a delightful piece, about weddings on a special weekend, Whitsunday, or something like that, and he remembered a line or two. The poet saw himself, along with the Whitsun married couples, as they neared London on a train, standing 'ready to be loosed with all the power that being changed could give'. Perhaps this Larkin bloke has something to say, he thought. He had seen a powerful change at work in Sam Baker, for instance, and he hoped that change might work productively in him too. It might loose him like an arrow on to something fresh and stimulating. He began, with renewed intensity, to look forward to the year ahead.

'Being changed'? It took Sam Baker a good three weeks of absence from the College before he felt up to much at all. This surprised him. On leaving, he felt that he had come through the half term rather well. Pleasant things had been said at his farewell and he had withdrawn gracefully, not like two years previously. He expected, therefore, to be able to pick up the threads of his life in the hills energetically. But, apart from necessary shopping and some desultory housekeeping, all he wanted to do was to sit, watch the ever-changing bush and reflect.

The bush did change, he knew that. Perhaps it was in minute ways, as the winds shifted or the clouds shadowed different parts; or, more dramatically, as storms altered the entire outlook. So it was that, a week into his second retirement, Sam would have breakfast, make a second strong coffee and sit in his rear sunroom, windows wide open, the still fresh air of a late November morning making him feel very comfortable. The time was his own. That feeling of needing to get half a day's work done before anyone came to disturb him with a fresh crisis was gone. Nobody came, with or without envelopes of resignation; there was no anxiety about the building programme or the level of enrolments. He smiled – that was the least of the College's problems right now. Of more concern was the idiotic Mr Trumble, the very thought of whom made Sam half choke on his coffee. He experienced great relief in finding that he could toss aside all those things and let his thoughts revert to himself. He was very far from being narcissistic in this. Rather, he felt the need to work out how, and maybe why, he was different from the man who had walked away so full of frustration and self-doubt once before.

What had prompted these changed feelings? He knew it had something to do with Doug Anderson, or with the Anderson family. Doug had told him that he had changed – had he gone so far as to say, mellowed? And the mere fact of Jenny Anderson's not rejecting him, allowing him into their little family circle, however briefly, announced that she saw some change in him too. He knew that he had felt, over those five or six weeks at the College, both more at ease with himself and more in need of the company of others. Some others, that is, well-meaning others. And that meant others who were totally unlike the Sam of earlier years. So, yes, there was change, and he spent his first weeks at home coming to grips with it, to full acceptance of it, before he felt any impetus to rejoin the world beyond his garden. Then he managed a daily walk out his back gate and into the bush, on paths overgrown and over the odd fallen branch, keeping a sharp lookout for snakes and perhaps a feral cat. Apart from all this, he needed nothing, until suddenly he thought it would be good to call Ralph Langton.

"I thought I might drop in tomorrow, Ralph. Is that coffee shop of yours still functioning? You haven't frightened all their regular customers away?"

"And it would be nice to see you, too, Sam. I thought you'd forgotten all about me. Did being an Acting turn your head that much, then?"

Such an exchange was normal enough. But Sam was taken aback at Ralph's last words.

"Not in the way you mean." Then, after a pause, "I'd like to chat about it. Is tomorrow OK?"

"It is indeed," responded Ralph, who registered with delight the tone of one who needed to download after his recent experience. He knew he needed communication with the likes of Sam, too – it cut both ways. "I hope you're not in a rush. I've nothing to rush to, as you well know. My next check-up is still a month away. So why don't you stay overnight?"

Relieved at being so readily accepted, Sam relaxed. He should have known Ralph better. It was just that opening up, for him, had never come easily. He was too used to guarding his emotions and generally, it must be said, thereby misrepresenting them. Still, he wanted to open up, just a little. That must be a step towards something, he thought.

They met at Ralph's apartment and Sam quickly discovered that there was to be no settling in.

"We'll walk now, while the day is good. I see clouds building up. There could well be a thunderstorm later on. They come sweeping over the bay, just as they did at the College." Ralph stopped suddenly, feeling that he might have mentioned the College too soon. "Let's go."

It was still a fine afternoon, enough to make Sam doubt his friend's weather forecasting abilities. At least he had not pretended to be as dictatorial on the matter as Lady Catherine. They set off, both content with bland comments about the wind and the half dozen yachts they could see in the bay, until they came to Sands. They took take-away coffees and wonderfully sticky Danishes and sat almost at the water's edge, well screened from the road by tea-tree. For some minutes they enjoyed the stillness.

"Has that acting business tired you, Sam, more than you expected? It was bound to be a tough assignment."

Sam bristled. "But you are the one who told me to have fun. Enjoy myself, you said."

"You always did enjoy the tough assignments, after all."

Ralph was prepared to wait. They polished off the coffee and pastries.

"I was part of it and yet I wasn't part of it," said Sam. "Occasionally I felt I was being used – used to get rid of the chap Fraser." Ralph was all ears – we all can fall prey to some degree of vanity at the possibility that we were not outshone by our successors. "But he had to go. Something was very badly wrong between him and Allan and, I rather think, between him and several other staff too." He paused, like a comedian leading up to his punchline. "I believe he has an unhelpful wife."

They chuckled companionably, both with a shrewd understanding of what could go wrong and neither with any real feeling for what could go very right in a marriage.

"Anyway, I did what I was asked to do and I had time to observe. I saw teachers, quite senior and very junior, committed to helping boys grow and learn. They are not committed to the school, not as we once thought of it, but they are committed to the boys. And the boys respond. I now realise that, if they lose that kind of commitment, they lose everything."

"Anyone in mind?" asked Ralph as casually as he could.

"Custance. But perhaps he never had it. Peter Gryce, which is very sad, because he did have it, once. His PE classes are mostly commando self-torture sessions now."

Sam thought he should cease the naming. There had been so many good things going on.

"And maybe I had lost sight of that devotion to the boys and their learning myself," he said very quietly. "So when I left the first time, I was just an angry man who didn't belong because he had lost that sustaining fellow feeling. There's a chaplain there now who has the human compassion that I had lost. I hope he does well. This time, then, I enjoyed the people, most of them, and in responding warmly to them I felt better about myself. Does that make any sense, old man?"

Ralph could not but be moved. It was a changed Sam indeed. He held out a hand.

"Let's shake on that, you other old man. It took me a while to realise what you have just said. Six months, maybe – but you were always a bit slower than I."

They might have discussed grammar at that point, but Ralph suddenly pointed out to sea.

"Yes, the storm's coming. I wouldn't give us even an hour. Let's move."

They took a longer route back to the apartment, so that Ralph could point out the row of ancient bathing boxes further down the bay, worth, or so he claimed, millions now.

"Out of date, and yet worth a lot," he said, with more than a trace of wistfulness.

"If so, it's for where they are and what they represent," said Sam. "But it would spoil a wonderful day to try to apply that to us."

Then it was time for Ralph to show off his newly acquired skills in Asian cuisine and for Sam to open the wine. The storm did come and Ralph was pleased that it gave him no hint of palpitations, not even when the windows rattled and between the worst gusts there were moments of deceptive calm.

"I'm glad I'm not at the College on a night like this," said Sam.

Ralph nodded and poured more wine. There was no need to comment.

"I don't want to be there. And yet..."

Ralph looked at him in surprise. There was no 'and yet' for him, not now.

"But I wish – it's stupid – I was young Anderson, just for a bit. His life is a wonderful muddle, but my word he is going to make something out of it."

"So did you, Sam. I hope I did too. For now, I'm content with more wine. This is not a bad drop you've brought me. Didn't waste your entire superannuation fund on it, did you?"

"The woman Madigan recommended it." A glass of wine, some good memories, a job tolerably well done. After all, he had convinced Matron South to stay. That was worth something. Perhaps all that was enough. Now the rain came in torrents and Sam hoped his own house was standing up to it. He settled back in comfort, though, and Ralph threw out the observation that Ian Rankin was pretty good, if all you wanted was to get drunk vicariously. Sam laughed at that. They had both had enough of the College, for now.